BAEN BOOKS
by MARISA WOLF

Beyond Enemies

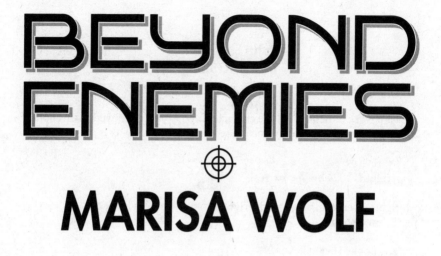

MARISA WOLF

BEYOND ENEMIES

A Baen Books Original

Baen Publishing Enterprises
P.O. Box 1403
Riverdale, NY 10471
www.baen.com

ISBN: 978-1-9821-9321-8

Cover art by Sam R. Kennedy

First printing, February 2024

Distributed by Simon & Schuster
1230 Avenue of the Americas
New York, NY 10020

Library of Congress Cataloging-in-Publication Data

Names: Wolf, Marisa, 1979- author.
Title: Beyond enemies / Marisa Wolf.
Description: Riverdale, NY : Baen Publishing Enterprises, 2024.
Identifiers: LCCN 2023043264 (print) | LCCN 2023043265 (ebook) | ISBN
    9781982193218 (trade paperback) | ISBN 9781625799494 (ebook)
Subjects: LCGFT: Space operas (Fiction) | Military fiction. | Novels.
Classification: LCC PS3623.O5516 B49 2024 (print) | LCC PS3623.O5516
    (ebook) | DDC 813/.6—dc23/eng/20231027
LC record available at https://lccn.loc.gov/2023043264
LC ebook record available at https://lccn.loc.gov/2023043265

Printed in the United States of America

10 9 8 7 6 5 4 3 2 1

Dedication

For all those who've gone on ahead. Wish you were here.

and

To all the librarians and booksellers
who make sure little nerds get to read all the best books
and grow up to be big nerds.

CHAPTER 1

◈

Talinn Reaze had not been built for mutiny, but three weeks staring at an empty wasteland threatened to tip her over the edge.

We definitely won't get a bonus if you do that, Bee said, flipping one of her many screens to a satellite view of the uninhabited scrubland around them.

"Do what?" Talinn reclined her chair and spun it, eyes fixed on the smooth metal above her rather than the endless scraggly trees and pit-blasted dirt on display.

Start pitching ordinance into the field. Glare a hole through my very valuable tech. Call in to submit our resignation.

"I wasn't going to do any of that." Talinn heard the petulance in her own voice and groaned. What was the point of running a state-of-the-art weapon of mass destruction if there was nothing to mass destruct? "Tell me you have a better idea?"

I can fake a heat reading and call it in so we have to mobilize and check it out.

"And . . . that's a less bonus-risking choice, is what you're telling me?" Talinn did not glare in the general direction of her partner—given the artificial intelligence that had grown with her since near infancy encompassed the whole of their tank, that was quite a feat—but she made sure her sigh was fully audible.

They are much less likely to discover my sneakiness than yours.

"Rude." Talinn straightened her chair and kicked her legs over the pristine floor of the tank. The wall of screens in front of her—currently displaying six iterations of absolutely nothing of

1

interest—flickered in a pattern that had become Bee's version of sticking out her tongue.

And correct. Bee's voice should not have contained smugness, much like Bee's screens should not have been able to convey someone sticking out their tongue, given she was a long-perfected AI program with neither tongue nor voice of her own. Despite—or because of— nearly thirty cycles of training, however, Talinn had an endless list of things that Bee shouldn't be, and yet was.

Talinn supposed she should take some blame, as the bulk of Bee's learning had been alongside Talinn's own as part of the United Colonial Force's Artificial Intelligence Troops elite service. The AITs were the premier fighting force of the UCF, so they were told, genetically engineered for the AI partially embedded throughout their neural pathways.

It felt far less than elite out in the field, and out of training strings. Before long, the top-tier AITs had started referring to themselves as the Eights, out on what might as well be the eighth front of a never-ending war.

Which was perhaps why no one in command had noted Bee's oddities, and Talinn would never report anything that risked putting them on even more boring duty. She trusted Bee immeasurably more than the nitty techs and distant command structure of UCF, and as their pairing continued to pass inspections and reviews, nobody was likely to take exception.

"Unless that's why we're out here." Talinn frowned at nothing and shoved herself upright out of the chair.

Use your words. Bee laughed, a curious sound of tortured metal twisting and scraping against itself. *You don't like it when I assume.*

"Like it stops you," Talinn muttered, smiling despite herself. "But is that why we're out here, on the back edge of nowhere's nethers? They figured out we're out of spec?"

Talinn. Bee paused, and her screens shifted with methodic intent, the pictures zooming out from their immediate view to infrared, then to a near-satellite reading and finally to a mid-planetary-system black-and-white rendering. Talinn expected a correspondingly bulleted list, but Bee made her single point with great patience. *If they thought we were off, why would they leave us in a* tank?

"They don't have to be scared of a tank—even a tank as fancy-built as ours. They *do* have bigger weapons than us." Her argument was rote, and her shoulders eased even as she spoke.

But not better.

Talinn laughed, and swung her arms into a halfhearted stretch as the last of her paranoia seeped away. The AIT program had existed for some eighty cycles, without any spectacular failures. No one in command looked sideways at their science projects anymore. Gene selecting and brain mapping had led to the sort of human who could provide a welcome host environment to an AI; programming and code editing led to an AI who didn't overwrite said host. The AITs worked because their combination resulted in threat assessment, threat addressment, and overall adaptability five times better than a standard human could handle, and double what an unsupported AI could do.

It wasn't like the old days. Training an AI to value some life and disrupt others with targeted malice had been a process fraught with errors civilians wouldn't stand for, and had resulted in failure far more often than celebrated victories. Until some genius had decided to embed those AIs in humans, trained the resultant pairing extensively, and put both through a rigorous, allegedly well-researched process.

Despite their idiosyncrasies, she and Bee had exceeded in their first three postings, setting themselves up for the end-of-service bonuses available to a successful pair selected to be cloned in perpetuity for the glory of the UCF.

Until, for no reason either of their advanced computing power had been able to decipher, they and several of their fellows had been summarily sent off to the uninhabited side of a dusty planet well away from the active front against the Interstellar Defense Corps. Patrolling nothing. Protecting nothing. The planet they'd been exiled to contained no settlements, no valuable resources, only brushland studded by long, ruined stretches of pinkish desert.

You're dwelling. No one likes a dweller.

"How long do you think they'll leave us out here?" She paced the handful of steps between the screens and the bench in the back that served such glamorous purposes as uncomfortable bunk, cover for storage, and cubby separating waste disposal, trailing her hands along the comms bank on each pass.

Are you asking me to poke into secured channels and eavesdrop?

"Conjecture will do." Talinn paused, ran her fingers over her bare scalp, and grinned at the screens. "Besides, I know you're *always* listening."

No telling when they're going to say the interesting stuff, Bee replied, a hint of shearing metal in her tone. *Given nothing is happening—and nothing has been happening—I estimate they will leave us here for somewhere between another week and forever.*

"Very precise, Bee. Well done." Talinn stretched her neck to one shoulder, then the other, until something clicked satisfyingly at the top of her spine. "Let's walk our chain one more time."

Hold on.

She froze for a solid second before leaping the handful of paces back to her chair. Her hands hovered over the cross belt, not wanting to jinx anything by fastening the restraint for action that was so very unlikely to come.

Her patience had frayed exactly enough for her to poke at Bee for an update when their comms buzzed.

"*Ziggy to Breezy. You on?*"

"Where else would we be?" Talinn muttered, spinning the chair to tap the channel open on her end. Caytil Tagana and her AI partner Ziti had been in Talinn and Bee's training class, and it was a small comfort to have reunited on this endless posting. "*Breezy here, Ziggy. You got a hit?*"

"*Ziti just pinged . . . something. Vibrations with no corresponding data. Sending coordinates. You read?*"

We read, Bee said, her voice distant, and Talinn confirmed aloud to Caytil. UCF had poured a great deal of money into ensuring AIs couldn't communicate directly with each other. The money had not been well spent, but that was something the Eights had silently agreed to keep from the general command structure since sometime around puberty. Which meant in times of potential action, when a commanding officer might want to review comms leading up to an event, they were very careful about who said what to whom.

"Did something hit the other side of the planet?" Talinn asked, running through the various possibilities.

We have eyes everywhere, Bee said, flipping screens to various satellite views like someone fanning the pages of a book. *There's nothing . . .*

"Someone's digging really, really far down or someone's—"
Gotten really, really good at hiding from us.

Talinn clicked her cross belt and swung her chair fully forward. "Turrets on and weapons loaded. Confirm, Ziggy."

"Confirm. Weapons and turrets, good to go."

"You take east, we'll scan west."

They'd both scan in all directions—no sense in not using the most of their quintupled processing power—but clarity in line of fire was key. If an attack came from one direction, Caytil and Ziti would counter, while Talinn and Bee would take lead from the other.

Twisted trees wavered in the unrelenting wind, grasses stretched and waved, and nothing new pinged the sensors. As nothing had happened for months. The vibrations ebbed and peaked for twenty minutes, and revealed no further indication of their purpose or cause.

Talinn's hand lifted from the control panel in front of her and hovered over her belt. Fastening it had jinxed them, that much was clear, but she wasn't ready to take their weapons back to energy-saving mode.

"Do you think—"

Incom—

The long stretch of prairie between their tank and Ziggy's exploded.

CHAPTER 2

⊕

"Systems functional for Breezy. Ziggy, status?"

No answer signal from Ziti.

"EMP?"

Negative.

"Fire in the hole?" Talinn flipped through all the information Bee displayed, then groaned and slammed her hand on the corner of the console. "They're jamming us."

I'm not reading anything that—oh. Bee's discordant sound of disgust lasted a fraction of a second. *Fire in the hole. Shifting payload to ballistic.*

Ballistic wasn't necessarily safer than incendiary, given they didn't know what they were shooting at and everything could go even further sideways either way. Still, they had a better chance to penetrate whatever was in the ground between them and their fellow tank than they did setting it on fire.

Ziggy still in action, their turret is tracking along with ours.

"That's why they train us." Talinn didn't bother to recheck Bee's aim, scanning for more disturbances underneath them as the *thwoom* vibrated through her.

Nothing registered at all before the ground bare yards in front of them erupted. The tank rolled backward without comment from Bee, and Talinn toggled controls to pull up menus of less-used commands.

"Didn't anyone ever bury seismic sensors out here?"

You're thinking Tivus—there are no earthquakes of measure on P-8.

"For thoroughness's sake, you'd think they'd standard op it everywhere. But if they couldn't be bothered to give this dust ball a real name . . ." When a third explosion blew the ground to their left, Talinn stopped grumbling and they slid into their combat habits—rusty, but drilled enough to snap into place.

Half words and inaudible signals sent them firing reactive fusillades into new holes, but without a true target or discernable pattern, the offensive was frustratingly ineffective. Caytil and Ziti remained out of contact, and the portion of processing Talinn attributed to that issue couldn't untangle how they were being jammed.

Ballistic rounds made as little difference as incendiary—whatever was causing the explosions underground was either too deep for them to get to or too fast for even their reaction time. Five random explosions into the one-sided engagement, the tank rocked underneath her.

"Reroute left treads." It was either her or Bee who spoke, but her fingers completed the circuit that reoriented the particles from storage to repair the treads.

Over the trough.

"Away from Ziggy."

There was no discernible gain in getting closer to their fellow tank—without a convoy to form a line, they'd only make a more concentrated target area for whatever was attacking them.

Bee pivoted them as best the tank could pivot, a fraction of a moment before the ground to their right erupted in a shower of chunky dirt. *Running out of rebuild.*

"Side turret nonresponsive."

Talinn glanced at the screen showing Ziggy's position and barked a short laugh. "They're making speed out of here. Let's do the same—north-west-north."

On it. Speed is relative.

"Always is."

With nothing registering on sensors, they were fleeing blind, but repetitive shooting wasn't making an impact and they'd eventually run out of material to cannibalize for repairs.

"Still no comms—we're sure it wasn't an EMP?"

Given all my systems read as go, it can't be. Didn't even feel a little bite at the edges. EMP's off the table.

AIs were vulnerable to targeted electromagnetic pulses—another reason to have a human partner—and Bee had taken a few over their cycles together. It left Talinn's head echoingly empty for a few minutes, and Bee feeling like an enormous set of floating jaws had chomped into her programming. This selective blindness wasn't that.

Whatever in the wide stretch of space it *was*, made for a whole other question.

"Four minutes and eight seconds since the last explosion."

Largest gap since it started.

Talinn knew better than to ask if they were clear—neither of them had any way of answering, and she'd jinxed them enough this day—so she continued scanning through the screens and changed the subject.

"I think this is only the second time we've strategically retreated."

Technically we stayed in cooperative motion with our patrolling partner.

"You knew it was a good idea as soon as we registered they were doing it."

I wouldn't let us leave Ziggy in the lurch. My record is still flawless in terms of not calling for a strategic retreat.

"So noted." Talinn held up a finger and marked their invisible scorecard. "Though you have called for air support at least three times."

Point to you. Bee rumbled at the low end of Talinn's hearing, indicating she wasn't done talking but was still considering her words. Talinn tracked Ziggy's progress and extrapolated their direction. Their fellows had decided on a circuitous path that would loop them around to come in from the southern side of what passed for their base. She and Bee would continue east and head for the northern entrance, though hopefully the communication block would clear before they got there.

This doesn't make sense.

"Sure."

Even if the attack didn't have biological support, we should have seen heat signatures, or more regular seismic disturbances, or hit something.

"Unless they were pre-planted charges, and a remote timer. Or some craft burrowed too deep for us to hit got close enough to set off the charges."

Who would pre-plant charges out here? We've been on randomly distanced patrols—Base isn't even sure where we'll be the next day, until we decide or new orders come in.

"Did new orders come in?"

Bee rumbled again, and Talinn spent the time fiddling with comms. Again without a single change registering on any of their equipment, everything shifted. The channel went from empty silence to full volume.

"—*air support. Copy? Message repeats three.*" After a five second pause, the message indeed repeated. "*AITs Breezy and Ziggy to contact Base, command code alphasix. Do not engage. Base will determine if targets are compromised. Deployed air support. Copy? Message repeats two.*"

"They're going to bomb *us* if we don't answer?"

Command code alphasix is an AI-embargoed frequency. Trying to punch through.

"No, I remember the codes, Bee. Honestly, you have no faith in my brain." As she spoke, Talinn twirled the appropriate dials, aligning their output to the proper channel.

Meat brains are squishy.

"Meat brain is half your processing power."

That's a generous estimate.

"Breezy to Base, we are functional. Over."

"*Base to Breezy. Divert to following coordinates—do not continue approach toward base. Report.*"

"Copy." Talinn released the control transmitting her voice and muttered to Bee, "Do they think we're an imposter tank?"

Or tagged with something suspicious by whatever was blowing up in our general direction. Bee had already shifted their course, a low thrum in the tank indicating something in the mechanics had gone slightly wrong. *They could have sent air support against that, not us.*

"Base, there was an unregistered communication jam on our side. We lost contact with Ziggy after the first explosion. Have you reestablished contact with them?"

"*Report, Breezy.*"

"Bee, I swear if jets go screaming overhead toward Ziggy, we're going to blow them out of the sky."

Only if it's Jiff.

"Deal." Talinn sighed, recomposed her voice, and tapped the controls to resume transmitting. "Base, we were on patrol as registered at beginning of watch. All clear, until a ghost approach from following coordinates. Did not register on any sensors. Sending recording as I speak. Motion ceased, satellite through infrared showed nothing." She continued the report in as dry and inflectionless a tone as any Command could ask for, and Bee made rude noises in her head. She knew she shouldn't, but she tacked on the pressing question at the end.

"Repeat. Has Ziggy reestablished contact?"

"Report to your assigned coordinates. You will be met for briefing."

What in the actual entropic state of the uni—

"Has the countdown on the main channel stopped?" Talinn dug her fingers into the lightly cushioned arms of her chair and swallowed back the urge to yell.

Yes. And no sign of jets.

"That doesn't mean much, Bee. Our sensors haven't been doing great by us today."

Blaming our sensors seems shortsighted.

"Please don't pun at me. For all we know, we're reporting so I get shot in the head and you get wiped."

They'd just send the jets, Talinn. Bee's words were as prim as one of their early care instructors. *They wouldn't risk your biting them.*

"I would think you'd be the bigger threat, jumping through a tech cord and taking over one of the portable diagnostic machines."

That sounds ... greasy. Bee flicked her screens and then broadened the middle view to show Ziggy making an exaggerated turn off their previous course. *Guessing they got the same orders we did.*

"And you can't get to ...?" Talinn trailed off—out of habit she'd subvocalized, and as far as they'd ever been able to tell the recording devices in the tank weren't active, but all the same it was safer not to fully state anything one didn't want Command to know.

Ziggy doesn't exist at any level as far as our channels are concerned. Including the forbidden and theoretically nonexistent AI to AI workaround.

"Did some kind of field activate in the area between us?"

At this point ... it makes as much sense as anything.

"So none. It makes none sense." Talinn thudded her head against the tall back of her chair, though she kept her eyes on the screens. They didn't provide a single bit of helpful information, but it let her pretend she was doing something.

None.

"This day sucks."

At least it could still get worse.

"Make sure I put in our record that Series B model 617 should be flagged for top-flight optimism."

That's got to be in there already. Bee did her equivalent of sticking out her nonexistent tongue, but it was barely a flicker across the screens.

All the same, Talinn sat up so abruptly Bee brightened the lights inside the tank instead of asking what had happened.

"Bee." Talinn squinted at the assorted pictures. "Flicker the screens again."

Bee did.

"What's that lag?"

There's no lag.

"There is. Flicker them. Watch the lower left corner."

Please to remember my method of observing does not match your—oh implode your intestines, what the bilious bloat is that?

Talinn focused too hard on the displays to question Bee's latest attempt at cursing, and chewed on the corner of her lip instead of speaking.

Nothing is wrong internally. Nothing.

"Externally?"

We lost half our cameras in the various explosions, but the lag is from . . . Bee clicked as she narrowed through code to find the infinitesimally slower string. *A perfectly functional cluster outside of the hatch.*

"So we have a bug. Or a hitcher?"

Or something has gone so wrong with my internal programming I can't determine what's wrong anywhere else. I still can't see the lag, that corner just feels . . . itchy.

"You don't itch."

I have you in my programming. I absolutely do itch.

"Rude." Talinn chewed on her lip some more, then shoved up out of her chair. "I'm going out to look."

How is that *a good idea?* Bee mirrored Talinn's tone—matter of fact and determined—so perfectly it felt like an echo. Talinn smiled briefly at the display and then turned for the hatch.

"It's a terrible one, obviously. But it's better than going to the rendezvous, having the techies decide we're buggy, and waiting for them to call in the big bombs or the wipe code."

The wipe code's a myth.

"Everything's a myth until it's frying your insides, partner of mine. And that's a heck of a way to realize it's not story time anymore."

I don't like when you make sense.

"You unlocking the hatch, or am I throwing the lever?" In the Eights, the AIs ran the general operating systems—it took relatively little of their processing power, and lived at the bottom level of routine-running. Nearly everything had a human-usable redundancy, however, for those times when an EMP was too thorough, or an AI was fully wiped but the human partner lingered on.

It would be a small affront for Talinn to use the physical override lever to open the latch if Bee got difficult, which was rather the point of the question.

A *kerthunk*—audible enough that Talinn couldn't mistake Bee had done it on purpose—signaled the hatch unlocking. Talinn should have properly suited up, but only grabbed her helmet and goggles. She didn't plan to climb all the way out, and at a flicker of non-wind-related movement, she'd throw herself back inside. Armor wouldn't help. So she told herself as she released the ladder and pulled herself up. Still, for thoroughness's sake, she paused before lifting the hatch.

"No one's out there?"

At this point, our full graduating class could be hanging off us and I wouldn't be entirely surprised.

"So noted." Talinn took a breath, bared her teeth, and eased the hatch open.

CHAPTER 3

⊕

"Nothing."

The wind dried the exposed skin of her face as Talinn clung to the side of her tank, glaring at the space outside the hatch Bee had indicated. Besides clumps of dirt, easily cleared, and barely noticeable dings in a small stretch of armor, it all looked exactly as it should.

Maybe we're the problem. Bee's voice was far too quiet in her head, and Talinn snorted.

"An external exploding attack, outside our tank, can't possibly have affected us inside the tank. We're shielded—"

We're armored. But we can't entirely block EMPs. There could be other ways to dig into our connection and hang on for a ride.

"Like what?"

The AIs broke into each other's channels, which is officially impossible. Who's to say someone else didn't figure out... something else?

"Reassuringly vague." Talinn tapped her fingers against the side of the tank and reangled her body to sweep the area. She didn't expect it to look any different than it had on the screens, and she was right. The scrubby grass had given way to some tree-adjacent plant life, each sprawled longer than they were tall in a flurry of long, twisting branches. The dust in the air diffused the sunlight enough she hadn't bothered to dial her protective goggles for light adaptation.

Unrelenting wind flung stinging particles of planet at the small patches of her unprotected skin with abandon. The doctors in charge of selecting the proper edits for her embryonic body hadn't given her

15

soft tissue any upgrades when it came to ignoring tiny projectiles. She opened her mouth to complain about it to Bee—not for the first time in their thirty-odd cycles together—and then snapped her jaw shut as a low vibration indicated they wouldn't be alone for much longer.

Incoming, Bee said helpfully, then added, *Awful lot of activity in the part of your brain you store the bad words.*

"Thought you weren't assuming anymore." Talinn ran her gloved hand over the matte surface of their tank and twisted to shift backward into the hatch. She squinted into the distance, but whatever convoy approached was still out of visible range—unless that particular dust cloud, slightly larger than all the other eddies of flying dirt, was it.

Visual lock confirmed useless, she stepped further down the ladder and pulled the hatch closed behind her. "Are we at least where they told us to be?"

Close enough. The middle picture in the display widened, then zoomed in on six squat, heavily armored trucks coming their way. *They're definitely worried we caught a bug or got compromised out there. Not a single Eight in the crew.*

"They can't exactly send a base array out here. All ground assault—"

Ground support, Bee corrected in falsely formal tone.

"Are assigned, assaulting and supporting all the absolutely nothing out in this ass-end of the universe. None of the jets are landing out here. So who's left?" Talinn dropped off the ladder and paused to listen out of habit as Bee locked the hatch. She left the rungs extended instead of collapsing the ladder back against the ceiling, then frowned down at the coating of dust she'd brought inside.

They could have rerouted a tank. There are at least three that could have made it in the window—

"An entire square—it was vaguely square-ish, yeah?—of previously inert ground just blew up in our faces and temporarily kept us from connecting to a single comm channel, so they might want the tanks out there patrolling."

She crossed to the bunk in three steps, pulled out the waste compartment and grabbed a clean rag. Bee snapped a different drawer open, pointedly, and Talinn laughed. "We might be about to get violently decommissioned, but yes, of course I'll wet the rag before wiping myself down."

If the techs come in here and there's dust everywhere, they'll think we've abandoned all training and hygiene, and they'll definitely use the wipe code.

"The mythical wipe code."

That's probably what they save it for. If you just wipe the dust off your uniform, it'll float around in here and you'll complain about it. I don't need more whining today.

"So if we're still alive tomorrow—"

You can whine all you want.

"Holding you to that." She had time to thoroughly clean herself, her gear, and the floor before their comms pinged, which kept her from getting too anxious during the interminable wait.

"Techs are approaching tank designation 617-AR. Reaze, assume position next to the load-in port and await further direction."

"Reaze and B-617 acknowledge." Talinn managed the words with crisp diction, even as her head echoed in stingingly foul language. Their not using her and Bee's actual combined name sign wasn't the best omen. "Bee, channel is clear?"

B-617 has closed the channel. Tortured metal shrieked under Bee's words. *B-617 would like to take over their stupid dead trucks and use the trucks to run them all over. B-617—*

"I know. We went from Breezy to our component parts real fast. Let's not make it worse."

Load-in makes it worse.

"We don't know that they're going to—"

They are. They brought too many techs not to. At least then we're all in one place if they decide to wipe us.

Talinn's throat burned, bile and saliva pooling in the back of her mouth. They'd successfully completed load-in more than a handful of times, in training and for new assignments, but the process never got any easier. An adapted human mind was designed to host part of an AI program, and that it did well. The majority of the AI program wound through the machinery the pair was assigned to—in Talinn and Bee's case, their tank—but there was only one way to get the entirety of an AI program *into* that machinery. Or out of it.

Load-in. Eighty-odd cycles of the Eights' service hadn't made the adapted human brain glitch-proof when it came to holding an entire AI. Talinn would be moderately functional for an imprecise amount of time—if she didn't stroke out immediately, she likely had at least ninety minutes before things went irreversibly sideways.

Likely, because load-in past performance did not necessarily predict present outcomes. Talinn could last an hour. Five minutes. A day. Twenty seconds.

At top speed in those trucks, the base is thirty-nine minutes and five seconds away. Accounting for high-security lockdown procedures and transit to the server bank, forty-eight minutes and twenty seconds without unexpected interference. We've done worse.

They had, barely. On their second assignment, which involved a much more active front, load-in had been delayed an hour and two minutes as the landing pad the tanks were parked on took heavy fire. Talinn had forgotten how to see blue for a week, but the techs had cleared them for duty, sure it would clear up. And it had.

"Keep your silicates clear, Bee." Talinn rubbed her hands over her scalp and knelt by the small port in the far corner of the comms console. "If we die, we don't have to worry about how long we have until you rot my brain."

Fry, not rot. The meat won't rot for hours.

"Point to you. Maybe you can just overwrite me and take over entirely."

Disgusting. Limbs are absolutely no substitute for turrets.

"That we can definitely agree on."

Bee opened the hatch politely as asked, and a person dropped in, not a grenade or smoker. Suited up and generously armed, but he didn't swing his weapon toward Talinn, and she counted that for as much of a win as they were getting.

"In position," he said aloud, not to either of them, and so both Talinn and Bee held silent.

Three more people followed, one at a time, and the temperature in the tank rose some thousand degrees.

"Are you trying to boil everyone alive?" Talinn asked on their subvocal level, her mouth barely moving.

That's your adrenaline and too many humans radiating all their body heat in too small a space.

"Can you dial down my adrenaline?"

Before load-in? Ha. So ha. You are the funniest human in all the systems humans have ever seen.

Talinn restrained her urge to snort, holding her place as directed while one person covered her, one paged through the control console, and two others plugged a variety of cords into more ports than she could count.

That wasn't entirely true—they plugged into seven ports, only three of which Talinn had ever seen used before—but overall the constrained space of the tank transformed into an unbearably tiny and crowded box sprouting too many limbs and wires.

Talinn had never felt uncomfortable pressed inside the various models of tank they'd operated across their assignments—techs accompanied them for load-in only, then cleared out. She'd never shared the space with any other breathing creature once she and Bee were active. Once the tank was Bee.

"How're you doing?"

I hate everything. Techs most of all. Bee snapped each word and one of the techs cursed under his breath.

"Bee?"

That wasn't me. A beat while Bee considered. *It probably wasn't me.*

The soldier in front of Talinn snapped up his larger weapon, and Talinn raised her chin, refusing to blink.

"A shock," the tech muttered, flapping a hand without looking. "Some of the relays must have crossed in the battle."

I wouldn't call the ground blowing up at us a battle. I don't think a single one of our rounds hit anything but dirt.

The other tech had moved too close for Talinn to risk answering, even subvocally. Techs who worked on the Eights knew what the slightest twitch of cheek or jaw meant, and neither human nor AI wanted to give them cause for more questions.

"Reaze, prepare for load-in."

"Prepared." Talinn angled her head away, though the techs had a clear approach to the port behind and under her ear regardless. She'd occasionally wondered what she'd look like with hair on her scalp, like the unadapted humans had, but the idea of having to shave it back to keep the port easily accessible seemed too itchy to be worth the effort.

At least the people who'd edited her genetic material had been sensible about that, even if they couldn't be bothered to give her metal-infused bones or eyes that didn't water on dust-riven planets.

A mostly hairless body was why the tank walls were melting—no. She blinked. Load-in must have started?

"Orienting question: What is your name?"

She blinked again—were her eyes always this heavy? Had she gotten metal-infused eyes after all? "Reaze." Silence dragged on around her, and she pulled her eyelashes apart from each other one at a time. "Talinn, Talinn Reaze."

"Next question: What is your status?"

Here. Bee's voice was a drop in the overcrowded room. Tiny, caffeine flavored, a little bit of a burnt blue flavor. No, that was load-in again.

"Bee is loaded."

Silence. Had she been lying down the whole time? The tank floor was smooth and cool on her cheek. Good thing she'd cleaned it—why had she cleaned it? Dust. She'd gone outside and it got dusty. Right. Were they waiting on her?

"B-617 is loaded. We are functional." She was still lying down, but no one seemed alarmed by that.

"Next question: What are your current orders?"

"Await load-in."

"Next question: What were your orders previous to load-in?"

"Patrol coordinates D-North, K-East, W-South, L-West, with ground-support pair Ziggy, consisting of Tagana, Caytil and ZT-881."

"Next question." The tech droned on, running through the standard questions that would pinpoint what Talinn and Bee still knew, or could remember accurately. The questions were always the same, which may or may not have defeated the purpose. None of the Eights had ever wanted to ask in case it made the questions and the process somehow worse. Talinn opened her mouth, words came out, and it might have been her or Bee talking. Here and there it wasn't words, but vomit, but no one seemed alarmed by that either, so she continued to stay on the floor and consider herself even more lucky she didn't have hair.

At some point she was standing, with something else cool and striped on her face.

Wet.

"What?"

It's wet, not striped. Cleaning.

Something cleaning and swirling on her face. That's what she'd said.

There was dust in all of her eyes again. How many did she have? No. Just the left eye. Was she outside?

Moving. Not the thrumming of the tank. She'd recognize that, even in the midst of load-in. But her legs weren't loud, unless they *were* loud now? Did legs get loud after you got blown up?

She opened her mouth to ask the question, but her tongue fell out, unspooling on the chair legs in front of her (*No, you're vomiting again.*) and then she went to sleep instead.

CHAPTER 4

⊕

"Talinn?"

Her mouth tasted like rotten fire and broken gravity. She worked her jaw, decided air made the flavor worse, and pressed her eyes more tightly closed.

Realizing belatedly that didn't make sense—eyes and mouth were not connected in any way that helped—she opened her mouth, then her eyes, and then groaned in protest at the hot light burning her.

Bright. Bright light. Not hot. Still—hurt.

"Don't make the man ask you all the orienting questions again, Breezy."

That was a different voice than the first one. This second one she recognized. It was green and soft and—no, not those. Familiar. Known.

"Sammer."

"There's my girl." Muffled sounds, probably voices or clothes or a black hole floating past, and then the light stopped burning her. She tracked the floating spots left behind idly, swallowing until only a little film of death coated her tongue, not a whole battlefield's worth.

"All right, Talinn. You're going to sit up now. Bee's going to hold very, very still, and you're going to move all your limbs, one at a time. Ready?"

Sammer, she or Bee thought dreamily. *Good doctor.*

Then she blinked, followed by a squint so hard all the ghostly balls in her eyes squished into one. Sammer and Lei were base support, not medical. Eights didn't work on bodies. Something about

23

AIs not being trustworthy when it came to living matter they weren't dependent on.

"AIs can't eat you," she muttered, swimming through the logic and sure she'd solved an ancient issue.

Don't want to be a doctor.

There. That was Bee. She was Talinn. A little Talinn and a lot of Bee—or maybe the other way around—and her head had gone about eighty thousand times too big for her floppy neck, but she could still sit up.

Was she wearing trees? No, clothes. She was wearing clothes. Different than the ones she'd been wearing in their tank before . . . before . . .

Load-in.

Why was Sammer here?

"They thought you'd cracked, wanted an expert opinion before they flushed you."

Sammer could hear her thoughts now?

"You're talking out loud, pinbrain." His words had a laugh in them, but tasted like warning, like spoiled rations. Talinn ran her heavy tongue around her mouth and tried to swallow the taste away.

"No, but why are you here really?" she managed, and she was fairly sure she was the one using her vocal cords, not Bee. Talinn moved one limb and then the next, though she forgot about half of them until Bee prodded at her.

"Way to follow directions, Breezy. I might like you better all loaded up. Here, let's work on fingers and toes next." He stepped closer, and her eyesight finally managed to focus. She'd known Sammer as long she'd known Caytil—since training. Since they'd been decanted from the store of embryos the United Colonial Forces paired with truncated starter programs to make Eights, however long ago that was. Long enough to know that he never looked that cheerful and carefree unless there was something real disgusting to step around. Sammer took one of her hands, then made a production of frowning and moving her fingers, and leaned in closer.

"All the Eights have been locked into rooms. Techs are in and out." The words were so low and rushed Talinn was on to stretching her toes—hadn't she had shoes?—before she fully registered what he'd said.

Well . . . that's not good. Bee's contribution was as quiet as Sammer's, and given how unobtrusive her partner had been throughout all of it, Talinn had to assume the understatement served a purpose.

Maybe she should throw up again? Fake a seizure? Would that bring more people in, or less?

"You here to take care of me?" She was reasonably confident each word had gone in the correct order, and that she'd sound like she was responding to the right comment for any ears that weren't Sammer's.

"Aren't I always?"

"Then . . ." What was the word? Talinn blinked, forgot how to see, then remembered she had eyelids and they parted one way or the other. Took her two tries, but she got them open and held them wide to keep from having to figure it out again. "Water?"

"Yeah, you're not up to swallowing yet, Breezy. You got a line in." Sammer lifted one of her arms and she stared at it, belatedly realizing the limb she couldn't move wasn't a limb, but the thin tube of a fluid-filled IV.

"How long?"

"You've been hooked up for about twenty minutes."

So she'd been on the base—she had to assume they were on base, though she couldn't bring the space around her into focus, it was all she could do to keep her sweating eyes on Sammer—at least twenty minutes. Plus the time it took to get there. So she had been load-in for . . .

The numbers slithered out of her grasp, and she pulled at the IV and considered passing out again. How long?

Too long.

"How long?" she asked again, meaning something else, and Sammer shook his head.

"Lei?" Sammer Bayhoun and Lei were Belay, for some reason that slithered out of Talinn's thoughts along with numbers and how to separate eyelids.

"Still in the base array, but disconnected from the network. We're blind." Sammer made his voice louder on the last two words—he wanted someone to hear them. "If there are more attacks, we won't be able to do our job."

"Were there? More attacks?" She and Bee had been in an attack. Something like an attack. Things had definitely exploded, which had to qualify.

"Only you and Caytil, but there were unexplainable readings in five separate sectors where we had eyes. It's possible the IDC has some new toys they're testing out away from the main fronts."

"Survive?"

"Everyone involved was secured back to base, yes."

Secured. Were only Eights involved? Or were unadapted soldiers also locked into rooms to wait out whatever was being done above their pay grades? Talinn couldn't manage any questions that big, and so contented herself melting against the surface that had held her so far. It continued not to betray her to gravity, so she let go of her bones and breathed through her skin for a little bit.

None of that is what's happening.

"Am I on the floor again?"

No.

Then some of it was happening, and her brain hadn't fully cracked under the pressure of holding the entirety of Bee's programming. The idea of arguing made all the nerves in her elbows spark and pop, so she forbore doing so.

Instead she twisted a hand around in a vague gesture Sammer would hopefully understand. "Any idea?"

"What's going on, or how long it will last?" The noise Sammer made crackled in her ears like shivering glass, and Talinn swallowed until her throat burned. "Either way: none. Let's try to get you walking."

"Oh no." Talinn shook her feet, considered, flapped her hands. She knew that wasn't right, but it took another set of breaths until she managed to shake her head slightly. Her reward for that was a sudden and all-encompassing headache.

By the time she blinked clear of *that*, she had reoriented enough to understand the room.

You're walking. Think about the color blue.

It kept her from falling, though the why of it eluded her. They were in a mostly white cube, filled with soft tables (*Beds.*) and blobby boxes (*Medical equipment.*) The floor was smooth and too shiny to have a color, and the lone door was harshly dark.

There was no one else in the room with them. Talinn took a few more shuffling steps, most of her weight against Sammer's arm, before she formulated the question.

"Wasn't there . . . someone else here? When I alived?"

"When you woke up." Sammer nodded, his face pointed straight ahead, not at her. "There were three other people—two techs and a medical doctor. I believe they're going to get a suitable temporary house for Bee."

Talinn's spine burst apart, and her legs went out from under her. Sammer yanked her arm and caught her before her head slammed into the colorless floor, but she couldn't do anything other than hang there.

"Bee." Sammer spoke the word, but Talinn had meant to. "I know it's awful—trust me *I know*—but get small and deal."

Talinn hesitantly flopped out a leg and got lucky as a foot landed against the floor in the correct orientation to bear her weight. As she climbed up Sammer's support to stand again, she put together what had happened. Bee's rejection of "temporary housing" had been so sudden and loud their currently shared body had simply given up and decided motion was unnecessary.

She should probably be grateful it had been her nerves, not her heart.

It hadn't been her heart, had it?

Talinn cocked her head, listening for her heartbeat, but she couldn't remember what it sounded like. Could she feel her blood moving?

"Expensive," she managed, the word oily on her teeth. Bee apologized, shunting the last of her headache away, and that was too much for the rest of her consciousness to deal with.

She managed to hope Sammer could catch her again before the spiral of blackness took her out.

"Orienting question: What is your name?"

"Fuck. You."

"Orienting question: What—"

"My name is Talinn Reaze, and I want to talk to Base Command *now*." Words moved normally from brain to tongue to sound waves, and Talinn bolted upright before she realized she'd been half reclined.

Her skin hurt. Her eyes hurt. The hairs inside her nostrils hurt. She was aware of her kidneys in a way no one should ever be aware of her kidneys. Bee was there—a heavy, waiting presence curled in the corner of her mind, still trying to be small and quiet for her.

No ... that wasn't right, but Talinn was too angry to parse it at the moment.

"Next ques—"

"If you ask me about orders or my training or what the color blue looks like, I swear by every galactic constant that I will tear open your throat and shove Bee inside your head through your trachea. Base Command. Now." She was vibrating with rage—or her hands were shaking with adrenaline—or she was ...

Talinn grasped for Bee, realizing ... realizing ...

"Give her a minute." Familiar ... Sammer. Sammer was here—had been there. Blocked off from Lei somehow, the way Talinn couldn't feel Bee. Because what she'd taken for the holding pattern of Bee during load-in was a pins-and-needle numbness in her brain. An absence. A lack of weight she couldn't comprehend, because it had never been empty before.

"Bee's not gone. She's here. Talinn? Let the nice tech do her job. It'll get back to normal soon."

Blinding white light sparkled at the edges of her vision, and if Talinn had had anything left in her guts she would have expelled it right then. A sharper pain shoved the other hurts back—she'd wrapped her fingers so tightly around the handles on her cot she'd split her own skin.

She forced her hands to release, hissing as the burning across her palms spiked. Bee usually blunted complaining nerves, but Bee couldn't—Bee wasn't ...

"There. A little emotional instability is normal in times like these, right, Jeebo?"

Talinn frowned, trying to place the last gibberish thing Sammer had said, then it clicked. Nickname. Sammer had a nickname for the tech. Talinn had never once learned a tech's name, and Sammer had a pet name for one. She wanted to make a joke about it—the urge clogged her throat—but the words wouldn't come together.

"From the top." The tech frowned but met Talinn's eyes straight on. Usually they looked at her port, or her nose, or somewhere around her cheekbones, and the combination of eye contact and Sammer's familiarity with the woman nudged Talinn into compliance.

She focused on zero of the answers she gave, but she complied all the same.

"Why can't I hear Bee?" Enormous effort kept her voice level, and was rewarded when the tech nodded sharply and quirked her lips in a hint of a smile.

"Swing off the chair carefully—don't stand, just rest your legs there. Put your hand . . . here." The tech touched her wrist, guiding Talinn's fingers to the rounded top of a matte-gray rectangle on the floor. It stood about knee-high to Talinn, and had a slight indentation in the vague shape of her hand.

This is the absolute worst thing Command has ever come up with. I'm including sending us to this ridiculous planet and also making us train on jets after we crashed seventeen times in a row in sims.

Talinn blew out her breath, tension ebbing from her shoulders. Bee's words were reasonable and carefully spaced, but each were lined with a metallic buzz that grated under Talinn's skull.

"What can you do?" Talinn subvocalized, though the tech was close enough to catch the motions. It was a normal enough question to ask, if anything in this situation could be considered normal.

Nothing. I'm in a cube. It doesn't move, it doesn't connect to anything, and fun fact, there's some sort of near field inhibitor. I can't complete the circuit to you, even, unless you're touching this mismade terror.

"It's more a rectangle than a cube." Talinn returned her voice to normal volume, and Bee sizzled in disgust at the same time as the tech stood and cleared her throat.

"It's a cube as far as B-617 can move through. The additional space is part of the shielding."

"Shielding." Talinn glanced at Sammer, but his focus remained on the tech.

"I'm Jeena Boralid," the tech said, and Talinn lifted a shoulder in a more mildly dismissive reply than she might have in another setting. "I've been on the Eight program for ten cycles and I . . . I helped develop the portable server currently holding B-617."

"Just Bee is fine." Talinn kept one hand firmly pressed to the machine, and paused for an addendum Bee did not supply. "What's the point of it?"

"The shielding keeps the program protected and functional while we isolate any contamination or degradation in the code."

"I've never heard of such a thing."

"It's not something we want Eights spending a lot of time

worrying about. It's exceptionally rare that an AI gets corrupted—they're closed-loop systems, with their human partner's neurological operating system providing a firewall to—"

"You're saying Bee's corrupted?" Talinn heard her voice skew upward, and she held herself rigidly still until she could trust it again.

"I'm saying we have B-6—Bee safe until we can be sure."

"And all the AIs," Sammer interjected. He'd been pacing the room, though Talinn registered his movement only after he spoke.

"We've got techs in and out of every room, checking in on the portable servers. As each clears, we'll get them loaded back on the base server—"

"The *base* server? We're not going back out there?" A chill sweat prickled along Talinn's back. It could be good—it could mean they were getting off this planet—but the way events had gone over the last handful of hours, good didn't seem to be on the menu of options.

"The underlying attack is unclear, we need to be sure that—"

"That all of your best weapons are locked in boxes?" Sammer stopped at the front of the room, his posture so rigid Talinn was momentarily sure he was about to launch through the door regardless of locks or consequences. He didn't, more's the pity, and Bee made a small pop of disappointment.

"The Eights aren't the UCF's only line of defense or offense, Sam."

Sam? Talinn blanched before she could control her expression, but the tech—Jeena, Jeebo, whoever she was—had eyes only for Sammer. Were they...no, surely not. Techs never saw Eights as entirely human—which, fair—and relationships between the ranks were...

Not unheard of. But definitely...gross. Though as base support, Sammer spent a *lot* of time holding down the lines while the other Eights took outside positions and patrols.

Not at all pressing right now. Bee wasn't wrong, but it still took another handful of seconds for Talinn to push off the distracting creep of "blech" in the back of her throat.

"I didn't say only. I said best." He remained facing the doors for a long moment before pivoting on his heel and orienting toward them again. "How much longer?"

"Until the AIs are cleared? It's going to vary—the density of their code has an exceptional range given the—"

Talinn tuned out once she realized there wasn't going to be an answer buried in the tech vomit. She tilted her head down toward the box on the floor. "What do you think?"

That if something is attacking us, they're probably going to win, and I won't even be sad about it.

"You'll be a little sad."

Most of me will be glad as long as this stupid cube melts in the aftermath.

"The way this day's been going, the box is indestructible and you'll be spinning inside it until the heat death of the universe." Talinn had excellent control of her vocal register—long cycles of training amongst unsympathetic unadapted humans had made sure of that—but either the aftermath of load-in or sheer exhaustion meant she'd spoken at a perfectly audible volume.

Which she only realized when Jeena swung around and gaped at her. Then the tech jerked her chin up sharply and . . . laughed. Talinn took a turn at gaping and Sammer walked three steps back toward them while the woman cackled. Finally, she gasped in a breath and wiped the tears in her eyes.

"I promise," she said, her voice shaking with mirth or stress or some unnatural combination of the two. "It's not indestructible. An explosion will take it out same as anything, and part of the shielding involves . . . well, enough of a corrosive that you won't have to wait for entropy to knock it all off."

"And that's . . . funny?" Sarcasm dripped from each of Talinn's words, as though she and Bee hadn't gone to humor in the face of wholesale destruction for most of their shared life.

Before Jeena could summon an answer, Sammer inexplicably began laughing as well. Only the fact that the pitch verged on hysterical kept Talinn from screaming and or throwing something at them both.

Can we get back to the corrosive? Bee was not as faint as she'd held herself most of the time she'd been piled throughout Talinn's brain, but she did sound . . . stretched. Attenuated. Less.

"How much longer until you know the state of Bee's programming?" Talinn decided against questioning what was wrong with Sammer and Jeena—she herself had very nearly cracked during load-in, so who was she to judge at this point—and attempted to bring them all back to more urgent matters.

"Bee is a particularly dense string of—no, no," Jeena interrupted herself, and Talinn cursed herself for visibly flinching like a raw recruit. "It's not unusual, given the number of assignments you've had, the different locations, the battles, the jump points you've been through—I wouldn't have expected much less at this point in your career."

"Caytil and Ziti?" A flush climbed the back of Talinn's neck and over her scalp as she realized she had no idea how much time had passed since she'd last seen—or thought of—her friend.

"I'm not tasked with their evaluation, but I imagine ZT-881 will look much the same as Bee, given the similarity in your records." Jeena swiveled toward Sammer, still lingering between her and the door. "I've meant to ask you—is that usual? So many pairings from the same training class being tasked together on assignments? There are four of you, with Medith."

Sammer shrugged, but Talinn cut in before he could answer. Partly because it was a needless question, and partly because she couldn't storm around the room and burn off the jumpy nerves sparking along her limbs. That would mean losing contact with Bee again, given the cube didn't look particularly movable, and the word "corrosive" still bounced between her and Bee's thoughts.

"Wouldn't you know that better than us? Eights aren't read in to all of Command's plans—or any of them. We're tools, and we get to know exactly what we get to know. They don't like us *fraternizing*."

Jeena's mouth turned down, but Talinn couldn't tell if she'd scored a point or if the tech was thinking. Expressions were entirely different on unadapted humans' faces—all that hair, probably.

"Do you think it's any different for us?" Jeena snorted, and Talinn pressed her lips together to keep from open-mouth staring at her again. "The last thing the command structure wants is any one of us knowing too much detail about how you work—what if we take it back to civilian life when we're done, and AI tech bleeds out into the broader world?"

"Eights go into civilian life after—"

Is this really the right time to—

An earsplitting alarm cut through every level of conversation.

CHAPTER 5

Jeena snapped over to a small panel by the doors, and Bee made a thrumming noise of disgust audible despite the blaring alarm only because Bee's connection was inside her head. Even then, it was a near thing.

Talinn counted out the pattern of the alarm, but she'd known the answer the moment the shriek pierced her eardrums—the base was under attack.

"Can you get Lei out of the box?" Sammer crowded close to Jeena by the door, his solid form stretched up as he strained to get out of their larger box.

"I can't get us out of this room." Jeena slammed the palm of her hand against the panel, which accomplished nothing but looked satisfying.

Talinn pressed her own hand harder against Bee's cube and slid from her cot to kneel next to the portable server. "The floor is green," she murmured, and Bee replied, immediately and with a warning crackle.

No.

"I can see all the colors. All my buttons work."

You don't have buttons. Talinn, this is a bad idea.

"I didn't even tell you what it is yet. You know assuming is bad for the war effort."

That's not even—

"Put Bee back in my head."

"WHAT." Jeena unwittingly managed a solid approximation of Bee's shrieking metal sound. "Reaze, that's about a thousand stripes of bad idea."

33

Tell her that's what I said.

"Talinn . . ." Sammer's head moved as though he were about to shake it, but he trailed off on her name and didn't finish the gesture.

"We need out. I'm smarter with Bee in my head."

"Not load-in you're not, and you were so unconscious there for a minute her activity was about the only thing firing in your front cortex—"

"Don't load-in all the way. It's a portable server—when we're tied to base, part of Bee's programming stays hosted in the main servers . . . so why not this way? And it's *portable*, you said, somehow, so . . . we take it with us."

"That's not at all how it's meant to function—"

"The base is under attack. Belay can help, but we don't have Belay, we have Sammer and Lei locked up separately, and from what you said that's true of all the Eights. So no tanks. No jets. No defensive arrays." Talinn ticked off each point on the fingers of her free hand, then waggled them at the tech. Sammer didn't argue.

"We still have plenty of weaponry. It's not like it's you and Bee or we all die."

"Do you have any confirmation of that, or—" Abruptly the alarms cut off and Talinn was yelling into a ringing silence. To her credit, Jeena didn't recoil, but instead spun back to the panel and started mashing buttons.

After a silence punctuated only by the ringing of her ears, Talinn lurched forward when the doors slid open. She froze before her hand lost contact with Bee's cube, leaving her to stand and glare as Jeena crouched and leaned to observe the hall outside.

The woman held out a hand behind her, then turned halfway back toward them. "Stay. Here." The words carried like a hiss, and then she was gone. Sammer hesitated exactly long enough for the doors to close in his face, and Talinn's throat ached with the noises she couldn't let herself make.

"Techs aren't top combatants." Her words were choked with the effort to keep them from emerging as a scream, and Sammer slumped forward against the doors.

"Yeah, Talinn. I got that. Neither are we, with half our computing power gone."

Generous estimate.

"Even with Lei in your head, you're not a super soldier, Sammer."

"We're adapted for a reason, and it's not just to have the biggest guns on an endless swivel." He shoved off from the doors and paced along the wall bordering the hallway. "Or to be a constantly patrolling tank."

"Then why the shit are we locked up?" She held up a hand, though he wasn't looking at her, and kept talking rather than waiting on an answer as useless as the question. "Did you learn anything useful from your girl Jeebo?"

His stride slowed, but he ducked his head and didn't turn toward her. "What do you mean?"

"Techy stuff. Ports. Getting Bee out of this bug-eaten holding cube and into something useful!"

"Talinn." Sammer stopped. Tilted his head back to stare at the ceiling. Blew out his breath and then gestured around them at the mostly empty medical room. "What would we put Bee into? Your head? You practically died twenty minutes ago. A diagnostic machine? It's not going to be any more mobile than that box."

"What about that control panel Jeena was bashing?"

Sammer pressed his hands against his head and squeezed until his fingers visibly lightened. "You think they have an AI compatible port on a control panel? You think Command is dumb enough to leave the base open to IDC attack if we ever got overrun?"

"I think they're dumb enough to have us all locked up for no discernible reason. Dumb enough to have us here on the ass-end of the war effort after spending a quadrillion dollars on making and baking us. Dumb enough the base arrays are down and the tanks are locked and the jets are grounded and we are just *sitting here while we're under fucking attack!*"

Bee grated metal in the back of her head, satisfied with the rant, equally done with the idea of a Command that had no regard for their efficacy. They'd been bored for too long—to be sidelined now, when there was finally, *finally* action . . .

"I hate it too." Sammer spoke more softly than she did. Talinn considered screaming at the top of her lungs, and whether that brought enemy or allegedly friendly attention, at least it would be something other than this infuriatingly cramped room—

Her arm tensed, and she nearly pulled it from the box. Part of that was her, but part—maybe most—of the raging with no heed to consequences was coming from ... Bee. Trapped in a box, after trapping herself in a corner of Talinn's brain, after being forced out of their tank ...

She tapped her thumb against the cool metal in a futile attempt at comfort, and then the doors opened again. Both she and Sammer swiveled, her still in a crouch behind the chair and him dropping behind the dubious cover of a gurney.

Three UCF unadapted soldiers stood in the door, flickers of motion behind them indicating there were more in the hall. "With us," one barked, and the other two gestured with their weapons.

"We were told to wait here on authority Zero—"

"Orders have changed. Code Nine-D-Nine." Base Command. That outranked Jeena's tech clearance and whoever had sent them to this room in the first place.

Sammer stood, but Talinn held her place. "Do you have a way to move this?"

None of the soldiers so much as twitched to look. "Only bodies. Nothing else."

"This is B-61—"

"Only bodies. No AIs. Let's go."

"I'm not going without Bee."

The two flanking soldiers stepped forward, and one lifted his weapon. The other dropped a hand to the smaller pistol holstered at his side, but the one who'd been speaking gestured them back.

"I know Sammer here, and he's been away from his AI this whole time. It's secured by the arrays, and he's way over here. Let's go."

"You said secured." Talinn lifted her chin and pitched her voice to its calmest, most reasonable level. "Bee isn't secured. If the base is under attack, medical is not considered high security. Anyone could come in here. Anyone could take this, and then *any*one could find a way to get at all the information stored in our AIT program."

"Lower one of the med tables." Sammer moved slow, arms held a nonthreatening distance from his body. "We can get the cube onto the gurney, raise it up, wheel it with us."

"Report her later." The new voice was male, impatient, from an unseen body in the hall. "But she's not wrong, and Bayhoun's reliable for an Eight. Do it."

Talinn might have had a horde of follow-up questions in another scenario, but at this moment she focused solely on getting Bee's housing loaded. While it seemed beyond unlikely the corrosive would be so easy to unleash that shifting the contraption would wipe Bee, all the same she made far too many sharp noises while she, Sammer, and two soldiers lifted the cube and settled it onto a gurney.

She kept one hand on the bed and one at an awkward angle to keep the connection to Bee, and then they moved out into chaos.

There were seven soldiers around them, at least four of them in the midst of different conversations on comms. The skin around Talinn's port prickled, but she didn't have access to any of the channels and couldn't hear who the soldiers were talking to. She'd need an earpiece like any standard human to hear what was going on, and that hardly seemed a priority of anyone else's.

There were no echoes of gunfire or muffled explosions once they were out of the semisoundproofed medical room, but the terse, truncated partial sentences the soldiers exchanged didn't give her a clear picture.

A wall had caved in, maybe by the landing pads?

Something had crashed into the main entrance gate.

The artillery storage was inaccessible.

None of this sounds good.

Talinn didn't disagree. They jogged through three junctions, heading toward either the largest of the cafeterias or the smallest of the cargo bays, if Talinn had oriented correctly. The gurney had been positioned in the midst of the soldiers, and had been built to corner at speed in standard UCF-designed halls, so Talinn didn't bump anyone unnecessarily. Given the tension, that seemed high on the short list of positive developments.

"Straight ahead is cargo bay four—go directly inside. The door will open as you approach, and Haywell will lock it behind you. At speed on my mark . . . go."

Talinn didn't register which soldier directed them—sounded like the impatient hallway voice that had sided with her earlier, but they were all fully suited and indistinguishable while she was at less than her best.

Sammer dropped back and put a hand on the table, and they burst ahead at triple the speed they'd traveled with the group. The wide door slid slowly to the left, so they angled right and were inside before it reached its halfway open point.

Someone barked at them to continue to the other side of the bay, and the door groaned as it abruptly changed course to close.

Talinn scanned the large space as they ran. This was the least used cargo bay—the external doors weren't large enough to fit tanks or the big trucks, so it mostly held excess gear, the longest lived of rations, and things that packed small enough to come in on hand loaders.

Boxes lined the side walls, leaving a clear area in the middle of the room, and no cover for the twenty-one bodies that milled around against the far wall.

The rest of the base's Eights—even without Bee properly in her head, Talinn put that together right away. There were at least ten metallic rectangles amidst the group, so she hadn't been the only one to refuse moving without her partner.

They slowed as they reached their fellows, and everyone stared at everyone else.

"Any chance you know what's going on?" Caytil—who looked about a hundred cycles older than she had when they'd gone out on patrol three weeks ago—shoved forward and grabbed Talinn's arm. Talinn let go of the gurney—but not Bee—and put her free hand over Caytil's.

"Not even a little. Sammer's tech friend bounced on us, then soldiers came to fetch us, and here we are. Ziti?"

Caytil jerked her head to the side, then flinched and didn't continue shaking her head. "I woke up in the big med center near the entrance. Ziti wasn't speaking, but..." She pressed her hands against her eyes and rubbed her face. Several other hands brushed her arm—Eights gathered close enough to touch her briefly without crowding. "Ziti stopped talking when we were in the field."

The long muscles in Talinn's legs tensed and then went so loose she staggered. "What?"

"The tank was still responsive, and it didn't feel...I didn't feel like there was no Ziti at all, but the connection was off—I couldn't hear anything. Then we got rerouted, then the techs came in...then I woke up."

Ziti didn't glitch. But Bee, for once, didn't sound sure.

"After they scrambled the jets to cover—"

"They told us it was to take us off the board," Talinn interrupted, which set off a round of muttering before Daren interjected.

"They told *us* it was to provide cover for the attack—then they called us back before we got to you. Soon as we landed a tech came over instead of flight line, and they started load-in on all of us without so much as a 'get comfortable' first." Daren—human part of Jiff, whom Bee and Talinn had agreed to shoot down if it came to it, shook his head, his usual smug grin missing. "Thought we were getting called back to an actual front, it was so quick."

"I think they're closing down the base." Medith lounged on a midsized crate pulled away from a pile of identical packages, tension visible only in the jerky motion when she shifted. "Something's been off on this planet the whole time, it's coming to a head, and the UCF is calling it a wash." The corner of her mouth tweaked upward, and Talinn half smiled back. Medith, like Caytil and Sammer, had been part of her training class, and had been as equally unthrilled to fetch up in such a useless posting. Her tone spoke more of wishful thinking than a real theory, and the uptick in hubbub answering it seemed to agree.

"Hasn't been anything here in months."

"Hasn't been anything here until today—seems a weird time to pack it in."

"Training exercise." Xenni had been here the longest of any of the Eights, a base array pairing who claimed they were close to retirement. She spread her arms wide, then dropped them when her fingers started twitching. "They do this on the long hauls, when they think everyone's gotten a little too comfortable. A lot of sound and panic and mysterious attacks, rushed load-ins and a big mess, and then back to normal." She snorted and spread her arms wide. "Normal other than a solid week of debriefings and rehashings and what to do better-ings."

"Like this?" Talinn gestured as widely as Xenni had, keeping one hand in contact with Bee, and tried not to let her eyes linger on Caytil, Medith, Sammer, and the other miserable AITs in their group. "Where *we* all got locked up together in a cargo hold and everyone else runs around waving their weapons?"

"No . . . no, not like this." Xenni ducked her head and murmured something apologetic toward Caytil.

"Training exercises always have to be a little different, or how will they keep us on alert?" Konti, another of the jet pairs, put too much effort in her voice for it to land with any sincerity. A round of scoffs answered, and then they were quiet, straining to listen for signs of conflict or updates or the soldier who had locked them in bothering to acknowledge them.

None of it happened, and Talinn rather wished for a return to unconsciousness.

CHAPTER 6

Most of the Eights without their AI partners lapsed into leaning against the back wall with their eyes closed.

Sammer, Medith, and Xenni, the three Eights assigned to base support, took turns pacing the length of the cargo bay, poking at the door, and shoving at boxes. According to Xenni, their AIs were still loaded in the base arrays, but shielded from both their weaponry and their human partners. The three of them didn't speak, and no one else bothered them.

Talinn slumped against Bee's housing and ignored the building soreness wrapped around the base of her spine.

Maybe they're discontinuing the program.

She sat up, stretched with one hand pressed into her lower back, and shook her head. "Then they'd just have decommissioned all of us at once."

How's that?

"Either call us in, immediately give us the group orders, and ship us out to civilian life with no bonuses and no designated citizenship, or give us lethal doses while we were all distracted by load-in." Talinn considered a handful of other ways the higher ups could have handled such a thing, quietly or explosively or dramatically, and Bee made a chewed-up grumble of a sound.

Herd you into a cargo bay and flood it with suffocating gas . . .

"Not efficient or definitive. Cargo bays are the stupidest place to put us if they want us dead—it'll take too much time to get levels to a lethal level."

41

It is the smallest cargo bay.

"And they already had us each vulnerable, so why put us together to get it done?"

Sigmun, one of the other tank pairings, slid down next to her, cocking her head. "Bee?"

Talinn nodded. "We're theorizing the stupid ways Command could be looking at decommissioning us."

"Sure, sure." Sigmun laughed and shifted to keep her hand in contact with her own portable server without twisting her body like an unattended port cord. "I would have left us all in load-in, given a humanitarian dose when we cracked, and called it a drill gone horribly, horribly wrong." She lifted a shoulder and tilted her head in the opposite direction. "Such an easy report to write. They could even note how long it took each brain to fry, in case the program got rebooted down the line."

"Wins all around." Talinn rested her cheek on the rounded edge of the cube and stared at the space between her and Sigmun without focusing on anything—especially not Caytil, slumped at the end of the unevenly spaced Eights. "What's your bet?"

"On what's happening, or how long we'll be here?" She waved away Talinn's potential answer and pursed her lips. "We're under attack, and the IDC bonzos are doing something clever with their version of AIs, so Command had the bright idea to separate and firewall us to shore up vulnerabilities. Our fine UCF brains aren't telling us because the handful of unadapted humans on this shit stain of a planet are enjoying their moment of glory, and so we'll be in here for at least seven hours longer than necessary so they can make the most of it."

"That's not . . . unreasonable." Talinn curled her free hand around her neck to touch the port behind her ear. "Any ideas what the AI attack could be?"

"Ooo, see now *that* is interesting."

"And a bad idea." Sammer—Talinn hadn't even noticed his approach—cut through Sigmun's words in the flattest tone Talinn had ever heard from him. They both craned their heads toward him, and he touched the corner of his eye with his longest finger as though clearing a small bit of gunk.

A quick enough gesture, one humans made all the time without thinking. But one Talinn and Sigmun knew from long practice to mean that they were monitored.

Which was obvious, when Talinn bothered to think about it. Why put all the Eights together unless you wanted to see what they did?

Might as well cause trouble then, and see what provokes a reaction.

"Given we don't know what severity level the reaction would hit, that seems . . . suboptimal." Talinn subvocalized, but Sigmun either followed or was having a similar conversation, because she winced.

Sammer continued before the pause grew noticeable. "The last thing we want to do is encourage bored AIs in boxes to consider how they can get out. We've probably got a little more time before that becomes urgent."

Now why would he say something like that after warning us—oh. He's giving Command a countdown.

Talinn considered Bee's point, and found it a logical enough conclusion. The techs would know the limitations of the temporary servers—emphasis on temporary—and Sammer had pointedly reminded any listeners that the Eights shouldn't be left to languish indefinitely. Anyone who'd read a training record or three would know that ended badly one way or the other.

The floor vibrated beneath them, and for a fraction of a second Talinn knew in her bones Command had heard the warning and decided to collapse the cargo bay around them. Nearly as quickly, she realized that was on the list of inefficient and unguaranteed ways to decommission the Eights, and by then a series of muffled *whoompfs* followed.

"Explosions." Sigmun drawled the word, but the effect was spoiled by the slight skew upward at the end, questioning.

The more inert of the Eights sat up, and all of them held still for a long moment, straining to hear more.

Nothing—not even base alarms—and Talinn gathered her legs underneath to stand when the floor vibrated again, then seemed to shift rapidly to the side.

She slid back to her knees, turning unerringly toward Caytil. "It's the same?" she asked, and Caytil dipped her chin.

"Feels like what we dealt with out on patrol. The vibrations, explosions—either it'll all come to nothing—"

"Or if we're lucky, it'll tunnel right under this cargo bay and blow a hole in the floor. Or the wall." Caytil pushed against the wall and worked her way to a standing position, her faint eyebrows drawn low and the smooth skin of her forehead wrinkling as she glared.

"Let's get some of these servers loaded back up on Talinn's gurney," Sigmun suggested, glancing at the walls and ceiling as though the fabricated metal might crumple or crack before their eyes.

"And for the ones that don't fit?" Daren asked snidely, prompting a withering chorus of replies regarding the handful of hand loaders leaning around the bay.

Talinn shifted to help in the sudden increase of activity, then turned on Sammer instead. "Are the base arrays still hooked up?"

"No, instead of offloading the AIs they detangled . . ." He squinted at her, then slowly drew out the next words. "There are always emergency port cords stowed near the arrays."

As a less active base far from any of the main war fronts, their base had a minimum set of enormous ballistic arrays to defend the installation. It only took three AIs to cover the 133 separate mounts—more regularly pressed defensive bases had at least ten AIs for many more arrays—and they could all be run from a single AI pair if something were to happen to the other two.

Base support took a certain kind of Eight—fast cognition and assessment, of course, but a different level of stability. The focus required to reorient the various components of the array to maximize enemy losses and minimize cost on allies was not entirely common across Eights. Bee and Talinn, for instance, had shown even less aptitude for the arrays than they had the jets, and during training they'd held the record for the number of different ways they'd crashed jets in sim training.

But all Eights had the same port configuration, and if they could get to the arrays, any of the AIs could load-in and accomplish at least enough to prove to an attacking force that the base wasn't without its largest weapons.

"We won't have any techs to be sure nothing gets corrupted or catch if a glitch gets introduced." Sammer hesitated, but Talinn could see him considering the idea.

The reasons for the specific process to move AIs had been pressed into their heads—literally and figuratively—since they'd toddled their first steps on unsteady legs. Load-in from server to human brain, then human brain to new war machine, allowed multiple checkpoints to ensure a piece of programming didn't get left behind, where it might replicate and become something unchecked and unpaired, and that none of the operating parameters in human or AI connections had been blocked or corrupted. Allegedly their answers to the orienting questions—and the way their neural links sparked in answering them—allowed techs a clear and comprehensive view of the state of both sides of the Eight equation.

Not engaging in those checks and balances could result in a permanently broken partner, which made the entire pairing useless. An expensive waste, as far as UCF was concerned, given the astronomical costs incurred taking Eights from their component building parts—biological and coded—to an obsessively trained piece of the war effort.

Continuing to sit and wait for an unspecified amount of time—especially for those cut off from connecting properly with their AI—might also end with some permanently broken halves. Talinn prepared to do something about it, and let the consequences fall where they may.

The twenty plus of them straggled into place and crossed the bay. Sammer stretched his hand toward the door's control panel, and a wailing alarm sent several of them flinching backward.

"Are you *kidding*—"

The door slid open, revealing Jeena and one of the fully suited soldiers. Jeena took a step away, and the soldier's hand twitched his gun upward before he stilled. "With us." The soldier's voice, to Talinn's best guess, belonged to the impatient leader from before who'd told the others to let her bring Bee. "Glad to see you assembled and ready and not where I told you to be."

"You didn't say how long we had to hold position against the wall." Talinn doubted he could hear her over the blare of alarms and ongoing muffled explosions, but she felt better for saying it. With witnesses, training kicked in, and the Eights snapped into an approximation of proper formation.

Jeena leaned close enough for Talinn to catch the gist of her shout. "Remaining AIs have been secured in the array control room. Stay with us—get through easier!"

Talinn passed the word back, and Caytil surged forward beside Sammer as they moved.

The array control room was in a reinforced block of rooms in the middle of the base, next to one of the midsized watch towers. It had connections to every bit of external monitoring equipment, but UCF's Command, for all their blind spots, knew very well sometimes equipment failed and line of sight might be required.

The floor moved under them twice as they jogged, but nothing collapsed or exploded in their faces, and they made excellent time to their target.

The alarm didn't falter, and after a few minutes either Bee stopped her brain from processing it, or she got so used to it the noise shrank to a small burr against her eardrums.

Either way, she couldn't hear what either Jeena or the soldier said to the two unmoving humans outside the control room. Regardless, the door opened, and the Eights without their partners moved through on Jeena's heels. Without need for discussion, the rest held out of their way and pulled up the rear.

When Talinn stepped into the room, Jeena directed the last of the Eights to their corresponding portable server, and shoulders visibly eased throughout the space.

Sammer pointed at one of the furiously flashing panels against the wall, and Jeena nodded. He leapt forward, fingers blurring over buttons.

The alarm cut off.

The lights died.

An enormous roar surrounded them that even Talinn's deadened hearing couldn't muffle, not with her ribs vibrating independently inside her chest.

Lei was still in the array, Bee provided helpfully, even as Talinn ducked against the server and wrapped her free arm around the top of her head and Bee's temporary casing. *Was just secured* from *it. Not anymore.*

"Is Lei blowing *us* up?" Only Bee could have heard Talinn in the cacophony, but Bee didn't answer.

The unrelenting assault indicated Sammer and Lei, once again in action as Belay, staggered the firing outputs precisely to account for reloading needs. In the dark, Talinn had to assume Xenni and Medith had reconnected as well.

She considered inching through the room to find a port cord and get Bee out of the cube, but before she could commit, something wrapped around her arm. Hand, she registered, and so only tensed rather than jerked away.

"Something's wrong." Jeena's voice, close enough that Talinn felt as much as heard it, breath too warm against her scalp.

Of course something's wrong, I thought techs were smart—

"With Bee's code."

Bee froze, and Talinn's gut roiled, acid sloshing in the empty spaces. She could let go of Bee and strangle Jeena in the dark. No one would ever know.

There was too much light for that, Talinn reminded herself—or Bee interjected. Her thoughts were too sluggish to separate one from the other. Jeena would have the result of her evaluation of Bee stored somewhere other than her own head. Strangling her would lead to a complete and definitive end to the Talinn and Bee pairing—any remaining copies of her own biological code would be incinerated and flagged unsuitable for possible future cloning.

She swallowed back bile, the temptations and consequences instantaneously clicking through, and Jeena kept talking.

"Not what Command was looking for."

Something was wrong, but it wasn't the thing Command thought it would be? What was she supposed to . . .

"Results wiped in the chaos. I'll report it clean."

"Why?" Talinn hadn't meant to speak, but the word burst out of her.

"Later."

Talinn wavered at the edge of the gurney, and Jeena let go of her. She tried to remember who was standing where—the sort of information that should have come instantly to mind—but failed. Instead of peering in the dark, she lowered her head to the top of Bee's cube and waited for the noise or the world to stop—an end, one way or another.

CHAPTER 7

"The vibrations are gone." Sammer stood at attention, blank faced in the dim emergency lighting. "Defense arrays are on alert, but holding fire."

Jeena crouched across the room, curled over a glowing display balanced on her leg, murmuring with Caytil. Was something wrong with Ziti's code too? Was Jeena truly helping?

Talinn forced her gaze away from the tech and back to Sammer and the nameless soldier. The latter grunted and pulled his helmet off, and her nerves were too dulled to do much more than prickle at the facial confirmation that he was Base Two, the second-in-command she'd never once heard speak.

Until today.

"Boralid." Base Two maintained eye contact with Sammer, but gestured to Jeena. The tech straightened but didn't move closer. "Status?"

"No evidence of the irregularities flagged by Base Command."

"Your opinion of the AIT program's status?"

"Functional, Base Two." Jeena didn't waver, her hands clasped behind her back. Talinn had at least fourteen orienting questions for her, and could ask none of them. "Though that will erode the longer they're out of service."

"Understood." He slapped his helmet against the side of his leg and studied Sammer for another set of seconds. "Ensure all equipment is load-in ready, and let's get them back in the field."

Her throat clogged, something sharp blocking anything she might have said, and then Base Two was out of the control room. "Bee?"

49

Not me. Her AI's words skewed louder and softer between syllables, as though Bee were stretching against the cage. *I wouldn't stop you from yelling at Command after this mess.*

"We need to talk to Jeena."

I need to get back in a tank. Whatever she thinks she found, it's not important enough that she's stopping us from that.

"You don't want to figure out what's going on?"

I do, but I'll feel a lot more able to do that from my tank, *with access to all the channels that have information Jeebo may or may not be inclined to give us.*

There was nothing to argue in that, so Talinn tried to meet first Caytil's, then Jeena's gaze. Both were preoccupied with the portable server between them, and Talinn waved to Sammer and Medith instead. With his Lei and her Cece back in their respective places, both were more free to move around than she was.

"What's it look like out there?"

"A whole lot of new holes, and the entire truck pool is scraps. Landing pads are blown. There's not a strip of easily navigable land between here and two quadrants out." Medith frowned and shifted behind Talinn, expertly locating and rubbing an enormous knot underneath Talinn's shoulder blades.

"So no jets or trucks," Sammer said, his fingers brushing her elbow but his eyes on Jeena and Caytil.

"Base Command's going to need tanks out there sooner than later, I'd bet." Talinn leaned back into Medith's ministrations—the pressure hurt, but some of the tension eased from across her back even as she maintained her awkward posture over Bee's container. She sagged forward and Medith tapped her to straighten, which she did as she thought of her next question.

"Did you get eyes on the actual enemy?" Nothing about this felt right, but if the IDC's troops had decided this base needed targeting, and they had some new weapon or method of attack, she agreed with Bee—better to face it from their tank, not from a gurney in a control room.

"No. Whatever they were using was all underground and didn't register on any of the sensors."

"Any ideas what could do that?"

"Our guess . . ." Sammer lifted both the corner of his mouth and a shoulder, indicating how unverified the guess was. "Something's in our system, Command knows it, and all of this boxing and separating is a whole lot of panic on the assumption it's one of our AIs."

"That one of our AIs was in the system?" Sigmun asked. Talinn should have known anyone not working with Jeena would be listening, but her senses were still catching up after all the abuse of the last hours.

"That one of our AIs is working on the IDC's behalf." Medith pushed hard against the twisted tendons and held, and finally pressure released from the knot under her shoulder.

"That would mean one of *us* working on IDC's behalf, and how under all the colonial skies would—"

"—absolute stupidest—"

"How would we even—"

Sammer and Medith let everyone talk over each other, and Talinn held quiet as Bee turned the idea over.

"It would explain why our readings are all over the place," Talinn said quietly, and Medith snorted, stepping around to lean on the gurney.

"Or nonexistent." Medith frowned toward the array console and stretched out her fingers.

"But wouldn't one of ours notice someone else in the system?" Sigmun asked, propping herself on the other side of the gurney.

No. Bee's answer chorused with a handful of verbal ones. AIs, by design, were not meant to talk to each other. Even when they found workarounds, those usually required the processing assistance of their partners to punch through the safeties that kept them blind to each other.

It seemed likely a program weaponized against them would have similar safeguards or shielding to keep other AIs from noticing it without a targeted effort.

"Couldn't one of ours find it, now that we think it might be there?"

"I'm sure Command is considering the most effective next steps." Jeena stepped forward into the group gathered around the gurney. "Confirmed four tanks are still operational. Which of you—"

Unsurprisingly, they had to draw lots.

⊕⊕⊕

Talinn breathed away the aftereffects of load-in. Perhaps because it had come so close on the heels of that nightmarishly long one, and she and Bee had been somewhat apart in the meantime, it hadn't been as disorienting.

It had also only lasted ten minutes, and they were back in a tank, so even if she had thrown up greenish liquid until all her soft tissues burned, she felt great now.

Totally worth it.

We have coordinates.

"Let the techs out first, Bee." Talinn stood by the single chair until the two techs finished wrapping up their cords. Unlike Jeena, but exactly like every other tech she'd ever met, they didn't quite look her in the eye.

Granted, she'd thrown up on one and accidentally elbowed the other in the cheekbone. Those occurrences were a large part of why she preferred not to know their names, truth be told.

We have coordinates, but no orders beyond "check it out."

"Please tell me our orders specifically say 'check it out.'"

I suppose we'll find out when we officially get them.

"All that time poking into comms and we still have no idea what's going on. It's like you're not even trying." Though she subvocalized, Talinn kept her face pointed toward the wall of screens at the front of the tank, making it impossible for the techs to read much of anything from their position in the rear.

Hard for me to find out what's going on when no one seems to know.

Bee's voice pitched as light as Talinn had aimed for, but their humor was forced. Back in the tank: good. Getting out into the open lands with a resupplied artillery stock and a fully operational set of turrets: good.

Having absolutely no inkling at what was awaiting them or what Command was prepared to do to safeguard themselves: less than ideal.

"Fruitful hunting, AIT Breezy."

Talinn swiveled in time to see one tech's feet disappear out of the hatch, and the other—the one who had spoken, presumably—lifted a hand in a gesture between a wave and a salute before climbing the ladder.

"Thanks." She meant to say something more meaningful, but

impatience to have the tank to themselves triumphed. It was identical to the one they'd left behind in a field a million cycles ago, but it wasn't *theirs*, not yet. It smelled too antiseptic, and there were no scuff marks around the comms.

Sigmun takes better care of her buttons than you do.

"Monk's not thrilled to be stuck at the base, so we'll be sure to take good care of their tank." Talinn spread her fingers and shoved a squirm of guilt back. Sigmun and Kay had argued hard against the results of the lot drawing, which Talinn could hardly judge—she would have done the same if the results had been reversed.

"Unattended tanks are pretty big targets." Talinn trailed her hand across the control panel in front of the swivel mounted chair and chewed on the inside of her cheek. "Why not knock them all out along with everything else?"

The jets are mostly fine too, it's just there's nowhere smooth enough, long enough for them to take off or land safely close to the base.

"That's my point though—everything's unusable but the tanks. Gotta be a reason for it."

They were spread across the base. Whoever attacked us and Ziggy earlier had no problems damaging ours.

"Maybe that's it . . . they hit their quota of tank destruction, and Belay got up and running before they could do real damage to any of the armor on the remaining ones."

So they took out the trucks. Tanks are far better armored. Bee delivered the understatement in the tone of one of their earliest teachers, who'd had an unerring ability to overpraise the smallest things with so much enthusiasm they'd all doubted they'd actually grasped anything.

"Yeah, yeah. Where are those orders, huh?"

Waiting on last two load-ins, far as I can tell. Jeena's still in Ziggy's.

"You're keeping tabs on a tech?"

I don't care what she thinks is wrong with me, but I do want to make sure she's not out there causing any trouble.

"She hasn't knocked us over to Command."

Yet.

"So noted." Talinn slid into her seat and left the cross belt unhooked. She kicked a leg idly, did a fast review to ensure all the buttons were, in fact, identically placed to her last tank, and considered running an extra diagnostic to kill time before the comms crackled.

"Breezy, order are as follows: Patrol following coordinates, engage enemy as provoked. Do not leave assigned square. Additional contingencies will be in place. Confirm."

Talinn confirmed, rattling off the coordinates, but her thoughts snagged on the additional contingencies. Without the jets, what could they—

"The big bomber drones?" she asked Bee as engines thrummed on around them.

Or seeding mines? Seems like whatever's after us has been coming in from beneath, and if our fire couldn't penetrate, drones aren't going to do much better.

"Some of those drones are carrying *Interceptor* level payloads."

Still have to hit a target to make that worth anything.

"Gives them a bigger margin of error than even our big turret."

Bee didn't answer that, and the tank rolled harder over a gaping hole in the ground than it strictly had to. Talinn smiled, though the effort of it ached along the sides of her jaw, and turned her gimbaled chair in a slow circle, studying their new—potentially temporary—tank more carefully.

"I didn't even check the bunk."

We might not be in here long enough for you to need it.

"You are full of optimism today."

You try being locked into a connection-free box for an endless stretch of time, see how that helps your mood.

"To be fair, I was, given I was stuck to yours and kept in only a slightly larger room."

Fair enough. Bee flickered the screens, and Talinn didn't note any lags. *And I didn't mean we'd be dead or blown up by the end of the day—though that's certainly possible. I meant I don't think Base Command's going to leave us out for any long patrols. I think they're going to want us under sight as much as possible.*

"You're probably right." Talinn cracked her knuckles and continued to spin. "Plus Monk's going to want their tank back."

Loaders' rights. It's ours now.

"If someone said that about ours, you'd be working out ways to gum up the treads before they were out of the gates."

We're already out of the gates. Bee coated the words smugly, but it landed as forced as Talinn's attempt at a smile.

"Onward to glory, then." She kicked out of the chair, which stilled immediately, and hopped to the bunk in two long strides. Medical kit, provisions, a clean coverall, a blanket, and two pillows. The medkit was set up exactly to standard, so Talinn grabbed two pain blockers and swallowed. Bee was rerouting a killer headache, but enough of the dulled pain leaked through to make a couple of pills a smart investment.

"Sigmun's living fancy out here. Extra pillow, blanket's got stitches on it—does Monk do the sewing thing?"

Embroidery? No. She took a med class though. Maybe it's practice.

"Who's she going to close up?"

Herself? Remember the time you kept bleeding through bandages because you didn't have the gel? Stitches would have helped.

"That was over a decade ago. I haven't bled like that in—"

Aren't you always going on about jinxes?

Talinn groaned and closed the storage bunk, flopping down on top of it instead. "There has to be a limit to the jinxing you can do in one day, don't you think?"

I think you're just digging deeper.

"You're probably right. Well . . . let's not die." Talinn stared up at the smooth ceiling—exactly the same as the one in her broken tank—and considered if she had time for a small span of more voluntary unconsciousness.

Deal. So about that . . .

"No." Talinn bolted upright again, ignoring the immediate thudding of the lingering headache against her temples.

Nothing's out there. It's just . . . what if the attack isn't about killing us?

"Say more."

I had a lot of time to think about the explosions today, and there wasn't really a pattern, but . . .

Talinn chewed the edge of her thumb and strode back to the center chair, belting in more from habit than need. She didn't prompt Bee again, and after a moment the screens in front of her changed to an aerial view of pockmarked ground.

"This was where we got attacked?"

What if they were trying to herd us somewhere? Based on our *usual patterns, if I hadn't committed to a random turn retreat to match Ziggy, I probably would have turned like this.*

A dark green line appeared on the map—the path they'd taken—and then a dark blue one sketched over it. *That's how we've historically reacted to ground attacks. We turn into them, fire back.*

"But I didn't give any input into our turns."

And I was matching Ziggy. I think if we'd performed to previous expectations—so far as that goes . . . I think we would have gone in this direction. And . . . you know what's in that direction?

"IDC forces?"

Absolutely nothing. But also . . . an area no one has patrolled, not as long as we've been here.

"And we're not supposed to go there now."

No.

"But you're thinking we should?"

Yes.

"And you have an idea how to make that happen."

Sure do.

"We're already on the way there now, aren't we?"

Well . . . now we are.

"Promise me we won't die?"

I mean, we made a deal . . .

"That's not a promise."

Nope!

CHAPTER 8

⊕

Their slow approach to the off-course location rapidly became moot.

"Base to Breezy."

"Sammer?" Talinn cleared her throat and Bee clicked over for her to answer properly. "Breezy to Base, we read."

"Base is under attack, repeat, base is under attack. No AITs are to return without further orders. Go to coordinates as assigned. Wait further contact. Confirm."

Sammer did not give orders—no matter how helpful Belay had been in the last attack, the arrays were for defense. Eights were not truly in the command structure, and even if Base Two were compromised somehow . . .

Confirm it—we'll figure out the rest as we go.

Talinn repeated the orders, comms went dead, and she leaned her chair back to study the ceiling of their tank for five slow seconds.

"Bee. Go to the weird patch. All speed."

Fast tank, confirm.

The jets could outrun them, sure, but on this planet, with its scrub bush and wind-torn low plants? There were no obstacles to slow them down. Bee plotted the shortest line between two points, they did their best not to brood on the fates of their friends, and the tank tore through the empty planet, leaving a trail of dust arcing into the sky like a flag.

"Can you reach Ziggy? Or River or Nips?" Their four tanks had been sent to different corners, but as far as they could tell their comms should be working, and it would be helpful to hear if their fellows had come across anything of interest.

Still no.

"No vibrations. We're getting data from the satellites, but nothing's happening up there, either."

Satellites don't show any action at the base. Even accounting for delays, either Belay lied to us, is providing cover at the risk of their own careers, or we can't trust any of our devices.

"I don't love any of those options."

Life is hard.

"Nah. It's so easy. Look at us—we're on our own, out of contact, in a borrowed tank, on a cyst of a planet on the hind end of the war, waiting on the ground to fall out from under us or a secret base to appear out of scrub and dirt."

I'm aware. Not sure the report summary is super necessary.

"You're bored too. I'm helping." Talinn continued to help by running her fingers over Sigmun's careful series of stitches in the blanket, and keeping an unblinking gaze on the unhelpful screens in front of her.

I'm not bored. I'm constant vigilance-ing. Making sure we don't get the ground blown out from under us.

"How're you doing that, if none of our incoming data is to be trusted?"

As long as the vibrations from our passage matches exactly what it should, nothing else is close enough to kill us without warning. I'm varying our speed and the composition of treads to ensure it's not an easy pattern to match.

"You really are clever." The screens flickered in Bee's particular sticking out tongue equivalence, and Talinn's smile didn't feel as unnatural on her face as before. "So not a ton of warning, but at least some."

We do the best we can with what we got. It's why they give us the big bonuses.

"You know, we haven't gotten a good bonus in a long time. Should probably complain to someone about that."

Maybe we can ask whatever's haunting the base's back door to transfer funds in our direction.

"Sure. Might as well look like all the way a traitor, instead of just being suspected because our brains are wired together."

There aren't wires in your brain.

"Now isn't the time to get pedantic on me, Bee."

Not sure there's a better time.

Talinn flicked her pinky in the general direction of the screens, and Bee made her shearing metal laugh. It edged into normalcy, like any other long, boring, uncertain patrol they'd had.

Which was likely why in that particular moment it all went sideways again.

Talinn.

"I hate when you start like that."

There's a ditch.

"Is it steep enough you're worried we'll topple?" The screens flickered, then a sketch overlay superimposed onto the picture of the terrain in front of them.

I'm worried that my cameras and aerial view tell me it's solid ground, but our vibrations aren't reading right for that. Bee scribbled additional lines onto the sketch, indicating she had no idea how accurate the measurements were.

"Keep going wide. I'll go up and look."

Helmet. Medkit's no good for head shots.

"Yeah, yeah. Safety is tops." Talinn swung out of her seat, leaving the blanket behind, and stomped to the bunk. Vest, face cover, goggles, helmet, then she paused at the ladder and sighed. It took awkward twisting, and the reinforced sides of the protective vest protected the shape right out of her ribs, but she managed to retie her boots more securely.

Boots first. Then everything else.

"Hey, people with the limbs get to make the call."

Really seems like you enjoyed it your way, my apologies. All your middle bones are mostly still in the right place. Don't forget the LV setting.

"I don't block it out just because it gives me a headache," Talinn muttered as she pulled the ladder down. "Also it's stupid. Just give us binoculars."

More efficient to bake everything into the goggles.

"Unless someone's corrupting all our programs."

The goggles are too dumb to corrupt. It's controlled by its buttons, it's not wireless. No frequency to break into.

The film that made their goggles suitable for long and micro vision also had a slight warp that affected normal vision, but Talinn had trained her eyes past noticing that. She couldn't train her eyes to deal with the odd shapes the goggles made when the different settings were dialed in, but she'd never mentioned it to anyone but Bee.

The last thing she wanted was anyone up the command line to find a reason to zero her and Bee out from active assignments. Way less chance for bonuses and a comfortable civilian life after their service.

She eased open the hatch a hand's width and Bee held it in place. Halfway through her quick circuit she froze, unsure if she should laugh or start shooting or drop back down and pretend nothing had happened.

Is that...

"So there's a tank out there. Not one of ours. Just sitting on the other side of a ditch—it's a big one, good call on stopping, Bee. Turret's facing down. Don't suppose it's showing on any of the sensors and you thought it would be funny to scare me?"

Nope.

"Didn't think so." Talinn chewed the inside of her lip until a sharp bloom of copper reminded her to stop, then toggled the dial on her goggles to long vision in order to get a closer look.

She dropped down into the tank, and Bee slammed the hatch while their accelerated processing staggered over what she'd seen.

"Bee..."

It's not—

"It *is*. But..."

It's wrong, all—

It was Talinn. Sitting on the tank across the way. Perched in the open hatch like Talinn herself did at ease. But a cracked mirror version of her—softer jaw, crinkled skin. Her nose a little longer.

Talinn, but older.

Which was impossible. Talinn was the first of her genetic line. The possibility for clones existed, but after her, if she and Bee performed well enough. A possible cloning line to follow, not... ahead of her.

But an older version of her—her face, her posture, her lean—was camped out on a tank across an otherwise invisible ditch on the wind-torn scrubland of a planet on the hind end of the war . . .

And she'd waved.

Silence stretched between Bee and Talinn for a long set of heartbeats. Not attenuated and strained as when Bee had been in the portable server. Heavy, slow, a deep current pulling them down.

Shock. The word could have been Talinn's or Bee's, but either way it sat between them, sand in the bunk, an unfinished equation needing closure.

Comms turned themselves on. Talinn shifted—a ponderous motion, as though her body had developed its own gravitational pull—and Bee fluttered the screens.

"Breezy to Talinn and Bee, UCF Eights. Want to try that again? We can meet at the ditch."

Talinn had never wanted to do anything more. Or less. She couldn't tell which, but she knew it was one or the other.

"I really did jinx us." The words wandered out of her without conscious effort.

You really did.

"Want to go meet some us?"

Is blowing them up an option?

"It's not . . . not an option. But not yet."

"Breezy to Talinn and Bee, repeat: We're not here to fight. We are here for you. Come say hello—maybe it'll be fun."

Fun.

"Or maybe we'll all blow up. Either way, better than hiding in someone else's tank."

"Oh, we're the worst," Talinn muttered, wrapping a hand around the ladder behind her.

"I know, we're the worst. Maybe it'll get better. Come and see."

Talinn took a breath.

And went.

CHAPTER 9

Talinn stood in the middle of a giant line in the dirt of an alien planet she'd always hated, and rather wished it was still the most boring place she'd ever been.

The woman in front of her lounged in the dirt—her tank had been closer to the big ditch than Talinn's own—legs stretched out, hands upraised, chin tilted up toward the hazy sunlight.

Squinting in the wind, because she had no helmet, no face cover, no goggles, only her skin.

Talinn's skin, seen through cloudy water and a couple of decades. Talinn's face, with extra lines and more of a smirk than she usually—

No. That's about the right amount of smirk.

"Are you the one who's been blowing us up?" Talinn stood at the edge of the ditch and crossed her arms as though this were all entirely normal.

"You seem awfully in one piece for having been blown up."

Talinn wriggled one foot back and forth, testing the traction and also perhaps grinding out some frustration. "Don't be cute. Is it you behind the attacks?"

"That's not the question I thought you'd ask."

"Uh, really? Do you get blown up so often it's not really important to you when someone tries to herd you somewhere with artillery?"

"It wasn't artillery."

"Bee," Talinn asked subvocally. "Please tell me I'm not this frustrating all the time?"

Focus.

"Fine. What did you expect me to ask first?"

"Why I'm in an IDC tank."

"I figured it's because you're part of the IDC and that's why you were trying to blow us up."

"That..." The other woman—other Talinn—other whatever, cocked her head to the side, her smirk pulling into a grin. "I mean, sure. But then why'd you get out of your tank?"

"There's still a tank behind me. Figured it was mutually assured everybody dies, so a solid bet. Plus, we launched drones before we got here. They'll back us up, and at worse record and confirm back to base what's going on if this goes sideways."

"Do you really think they're recording?" The woman said it kindly, but it landed like a blow all the same. Talinn had used that same gentle voice once or twice herself, usually when a friend was doing something incredibly stupid.

"I think Bee figured out a frequency to use so that *she* can see what they see, and she has backups and fail-safes that you haven't glitched up, so it's good enough."

It was also a bluff, but such was life.

"All right." The IDC Talinn shrugged and gestured for Talinn to sit. Talinn did not sit, and the other woman lifted a shoulder again. "So, you're a clone."

"Of *you*?" Talinn crossed her arms, mostly to keep from dropping her hands closer to any weapons. If the other woman were a Talinn, then the tank behind her was likely a Bee, and Talinn knew *her* Bee wouldn't take kindly to such a gesture.

"Rude. And no—we're both clones, same line. That check out with your world view?"

"I mean, I know the UCF designed me, same as they coded Bee. I know if we exceeded expectations, we'd get enormous bonuses and they'd clone us, so..." She rolled the idea over in her head. "So it makes sense enough that might have happened before. Good for that Talinn, getting the bonus."

"Yeah, so...not so sure there are actual bonuses. You and I are clones, and there were at least a handful before me."

"Before *you*?" Talinn knew it was more rudeness, repeating the pronoun with such disbelief, but it kept popping out of her mouth like that. She wasn't trying to offend.

A little. You're trying to offend a little.

"Stop assuming you know what I'm thinking, Bee."

In my defense, that one was obvious.

Other Talinn's jaw moved slightly—subvocalizing to her Bee, more than likely. Probably about what shits they were.

Now who's assuming?

"I'm not ancient, you know—"

"No, that's not what I meant." It was partly what she meant. "The war's only been going on eighty odd cycles ... how many versions of us could they have out here at once?" Sudden heat coiled in her chest and climbed her throat. "Is *that* why I got sent out here? Because some other Talinn and Bee—"

"Dock that up a sec, little Talinn." The older woman held up a hand and kept talking while indignation kept words from coming together in Talinn's open mouth—*little Talinn?*—though that infuriating smile of hers seemed to broaden somehow. "Did you say the war's been going on eighty odd cycles?"

"I haven't been paying super close attention to galactic standard time since we've been on this ass-end of a planet, but—"

"Eighty, though. Eight decades."

"Is math different in old clone cycles?"

"Girl." The other woman took a visibly deep breath and pulled her legs in, wincing as she folded them closer to her body. "IDC and UCF have been fighting a lot longer than eighty cycles, however many cycles you forgot collecting dust out here."

"I know *that.* But after the peace in the Govlic system stalled it out, the attack on the AU ship *Termina,* it's been considered a new—"

The other one muttered something that sounded disgusting. "Listen to me. The war's been a hot war, not stalled out, not peace treatied, for well over a century. Maybe two. Since people went to space and found the transit points and the UCF broke away from the IDC—"

"You went through all this effort to give me a history lesson? Let me guess how the IDC version goes—the Interstellar Defense Corps sent people out to the stars and protected them as civilization took root, but they overreached, and the colonial forces rebelled against them, uniting and—"

"Bee, are you sure you don't want to just break into—no? Fine." The other Talinn pressed her palms against her eyes and made a show of sitting up, putting on an expression so reminiscent of one of Talinn's early trainers she nearly asked if they'd shared instructors.

But that was impossible. All Talinn clones couldn't have been taught by the same people. That didn't make sense. Not logical or chronological sense. "Bee, what the actual—"

Let her talk. I'm filtering through interference, but I think I can almost—almost—get a handle on her supposed Bee.

"So it's like this. The war's been going on for a long, long time. They make clones to keep it fighting, protect the civilians. This part you know. But the weird part—at least, *we* thought it was the weird part, maybe your brain won't—is that they make the *same* clones. Over and over."

"That makes a kind of sense, and I suppose if it works—"

"On both sides."

"Wait." The uncomfortable heat in her chest shifted to burning, and the edges of her fingers tingled. Was she having a heart attack? Was this dying? Did this other Talinn drug her somehow—

Take off the helmet.

"No, I'm—"

You're not having a heart attack, but about half your system is adrenaline and bile right now. You're breathing too fast. Take it off.

"It's dusty out—"

Talinn, by all that makes sense in the endless chaos of this universe, TAKE IT OFF. Breathe. Look her eye to eye.

Talinn pulled off her goggles, then her helmet, then the face cover. She gasped in a breath, choked on the ever-swirling dust of this idiot planet, and ended up squatting, arms on her thighs, staring at the dirt between her and her impossible older self.

The other Talinn hadn't moved, but her expression had shifted again. More like understanding than mocking. Talinn didn't like it any more than the rest.

"*Why?*" The word crackled, dust and coughing warping her voice into something unrecognizable.

"We only have hypotheses for that one." The other Talinn had made her way over, and knelt in front of her. "It's predictable, for one.

You get this group of clones here, this happens. That group there, then that happens instead."

"Predictable is controllable." Talinn's words still caught on her uneven breath, but her heart was no longer slamming against its cage.

"And controllable is profitable."

"But a stalemate..."

"Is better than the other side winning—as long as the money keeps flowing." Other Talinn patted her hands, then pushed herself up. Talinn heard the older woman's knees crackle, but couldn't bring herself to look up or follow.

"So they just fight the same war, over and over? Does everyone... does everyone but us know?"

"No." The older woman's hand thrust itself into Talinn's eyeline, and after another set of deep breaths, she took it and stood. "They know there's a clone program, and AI program, thank the brave soldiers so they don't have to fight...but they can't know the details. Too much chance you—the broader you, the Eights—would find out."

"We're just a...a controlled system. Like those little terrariums they had us make in early care."

"Huh, we didn't do that project." The other Talinn frowned then shook her head slightly. "It's not a perfect system, any more than I imagine the terrariums were."

"Because somehow you found out?"

"Not just me. Things are glitching. That's why you're out here—"

"I *knew* we didn't do anything wrong—"

"No, but it could be...there's a chance they know I'm out there. And Sammer. Caytil. Tiernan—"

"Tiernan?" Sammer and Caytil's names landed like blows in the other Talinn's voice, but she didn't know the last one.

"You didn't have a Tiernan?" She huffed a laugh, maybe said something to her Bee. "Not sure if that's a loss or not."

Talinn had a follow-up question—she had enough next questions to make a tech proud—but her thoughts belatedly caught onto something else Other Talinn had said. "It's *your* fault I'm out here?"

"Not as directly as all that. But..." She paced away, pivoted, paced back. "We've been gathering information, and trying to gather Eights, too. As you can imagine...it's a little easier to believe all of this when it comes from something very like your own face, so we're limited a bit that way."

"I would have thought that made it harder," Talinn muttered, because no matter how she tried to keep her head on a swivel, her gaze snagged back on the other woman's familiar—but also weirdly not—face.

"You think it'd be easy to buy you're a clone, sure. You're right, it's logical, if you could leave clones behind, there could be clones ahead of you, absolutely. But would you believe that it's . . . clones, all the way down, both sides? The whole war? Without seeing your own face stroll up from an IDC tank?"

I wouldn't have let you out to talk to a stranger from the IDC. Especially another Eight, after all this sensor interruption—I'd assume it was an intricate trap. Bee's voice, pert and helpful, muffled around the edges, like someone had a cloth over a microphone. Impossible— more impossible than Old Talinn, in front of her—but it didn't seem to bother the AI. *So she's got a point. This could be an intricate trap too, but seems a wasteful effort, where a stranger would just be . . . trappy.*

"Why do you sound—" One string of questions at a time. Talinn rubbed her face until the thin skin around her eyes protested, then dropped her hands, deciding to concede Bee and the other Talinn's point and return to the original conversation.

"Do . . . do all Talinns have Bees?"

"I haven't actually made contact with many, but yeah. For as far as we know, all Talinns have Bees."

"And are we always tanks?"

"Mostly."

"Mostly?" Talinn cut herself off, and scrubbed a new layer of dust from her scalp. "Are Bees all the same, too?"

"What do you mean?" Other Talinn drew out the words, studying her with a hint more wariness than before. Talinn was suddenly, uncomfortably aware of how her own inner tension became tells from the outside—the slightly elevated shoulder. The eyebrow lift. A small narrowing of the eyes.

Talinn did not have as neutral an expression as she'd thought, if Other Talinn were anything to go by. Bug-eaten hoses in life support.

"Like . . ." Talinn hadn't meant to ask the question, but it had fallen out, and she fumbled for something that wasn't "a tech told me today there's something wrong with Bee's code and I need to know if it's a feature or a bug." "The laugh—that metal being twisted and torn sound. Does your Bee do that too?"

The shoulder relaxed, and the eyebrows dropped a little. Other Talinn's smile was a warmer version of her previous expression. Did Talinn look so delightedly soft when she talked about her Bee?

"Bee—my Bee—yeah. She does that. No one ever knows what I'm talking about. Although..."

"Although?"

"No. Later."

Too much pressed against the inside of Talinn's skull for her to push the issue. "You said they might know you're out there, and that's why we've been relegated to this forgotten dust planet in a far corner of nothing. Who's 'they' and what are you expecting to come out of my knowing all this?"

"They is Command—not your Base Command, but IDC War Command, and UCF's as well. As far as we can tell, only the top suits know the details—"

"That doesn't make sense."

"That Command—"

"No, that no one else would know. Command isn't... I've seen some of them in action, you know. Met one of the big guns at graduation. Better, I've taken their orders my entire life. They're not some kind of brilliant masterminds who—it seems like an awfully big secret to be reliably kept for a century or two."

"But it's a boring one." The other woman's lips quirked. "It doesn't affect anyone else—Eights are elite soldiers, sure, but consider." She spread one of her hands and tapped her palm with each point. Talinn was reminded so strongly of Bee's flickering screens she bit down hard on her cheek—but even she couldn't have said if it were to keep from smiling or wincing.

"We're decanted and trained in isolated areas. Citizens don't see us. The nonadapted staff that come into contact with us never go to another base or program and raise another batch—best I can tell, they have a few generations they rotate, based on how the front is or isn't moving. Different groups of us are meant to do different things."

Talinn muttered that to Bee to make sure they came back to the topic when the conversation allowed. Different groupings how? Of who?

"Once we're out and active, we're usually suited up, or in our rigs. No one—even maybe especially the techs—looks too closely at Eights. You have to have noticed. They don't meet our eyes."

"They see us more as interchangeable parts than actual people."

Not that Jeena Jeebo one.

Talinn spent as little time as possible around unadapted soldiers, and up until today with Sammer, she would have said that was true for all the Eights. Maybe there were other exceptions out there beyond Jeena, but who would notice?

"Right. And have you ever once heard of your UCF capturing an IDC Eight—alive or otherwise?"

"No, of course not, we're..." The rejection leapt automatically to her mouth. They were elite for a reason—they couldn't be captured. They'd blow themselves up before letting that become even a remote possibility, because the chance of their AI, and the secrets of their side's development program of their Artificial Intelligence Troops, getting to the other side's development scientists was too dangerous to risk...

"Suck on a shitstick... They train us to flame out to keep the other side from finding out we're all the same?"

"To keep *any*one from finding out. And to be fair, I'm not even sure IDC top suits know that the UCF is rumbling through the same building blocks to make their toys. It's not something they talk about, and it's possible someone worked for both sides at some point, or successful pairings narrowed down over time, or it was all the same program at one point before the war..." The older Talinn stopped tapping her palm and dropped her hands. "We can only poke into things so hard, and only so many people know the answers. If anyone did know, they're probably long dead. And as for storing it—where would they keep the information? Somewhere an AI could see it?"

"So Command plots out the curves of the war fronts and grows us or sends us out accordingly, and the other Command does the same, and we're all just little dolls playing out a game identical little dolls have mapped out a thousand different times?"

That sounds a little reductive—

"A bit reductive, sure, but . . . essentially, yes."

"And so now . . . what? I know, and now I go back and play war like a good self-aware little toy?" Talinn's voice wobbled, and she curled her fingers tight against her palms. She wasn't upset, only looking for clarification. No reason for her words to get all trembly.

"Really? That's what you think we did all this elaborate rigamarole for? A nice chat? I would have brought snacks if that was all—"

"Tal—" Talinn's throat locked halfway through snapping her own name, and she forced herself to breathe again, stretch out her hands, and start over. "This is a lot. You, of *all people* should know this is a lot. It's so much Bee is barely saying anything—"

Bee is trying to finagle her way into another Bee's channel, thank you very much—

"—and it would be super, super great if you would just tell me what this is all for." Her voice betrayed her again, but this time it went loud and rough, so she rolled with it.

"Come on, little Talinn. You can't guess? I want to bring it all down. Don't you?"

CHAPTER 10

Bee held Talinn's breath, both of them still. Talinn stared at Other Talinn. Her face was shades off from Talinn's own, which she could laser in on now, this close, with silence between them. Her nose had been broken, the lines by her eyes, around her mouth, across her forehead—they were more prominent versions of the faint tracings Talinn had recently developed. She had the impression the other smiled more than she did, which seemed a ridiculous thing—both to think, and to be true. Her ears were different, though Talinn couldn't place why. (*Lobes are a little longer. She pierced the top of each once, not several times. Also the canal on her left ear is point zero three—*) But her eyes—they were identical. The shading in the left, the small dark spot in the right. It tilted the world around her, because it was flipped, not at all how it was when she looked in the mirror. Made gravity wobble, if only a hint.

But the same. She was the same person. So she should feel the same.

Did she?

We've wanted to burn it all down before.

In theory. Jokingly, in frustration, in passing . . . she'd never actually plot against Command. Consider mutiny.

Would she?

Would they?

The facts are these. Command has a balanced world—three systems of them—and even with this other Breezy scooting around the edges, trying to pick out other Bees and Talinns, it's been mostly stable. It'll

73

keep going, a war that leaves most people alone. There will be more Eights, who may or may not be the same. Things might shift, but not change. Is that good or bad? Do we like the world as it is, or hate it?

"Who are you loyal to?" The other woman asked it softly, as though she knew she were interrupting. She probably did, which made the fact of it more annoying.

"Bee. The Eights. The UCF."

"In that order?"

"In that order."

And not necessarily with equal weight, Bee added, which was entirely true. Descending importance—and entirely UCF's fault, if not their main intention. Bee was a fundamental part of Talinn. Not her other half, as they were more than the sum of their parts once combined rather than incomplete pieces, but her bedrock. The idea of putting anything ahead of Bee was absurd. Similarly, the Eights—especially those she'd been raised and trained with—were the gravity well of her life. The universe didn't make sense without them. The UCF was a framework—she'd been immersed in it, their goals and rationale and need for the ongoing pushback against the overreach of the IDC—but there were times she could cheerfully burn it down with their own tank. Not enough to run off at first sight of an almost familiar face, but . . .

"What glitches?" If it were all falling apart anyway, as this woman had alleged, maybe it wasn't mutiny. She wouldn't be a traitor, but a bug fleeing the system crumbling to pieces around it.

"Say more."

"You said there are glitches. Like what?"

"It's still small, broadly speaking, but for example the IDC has—" Her head snapped to the side, and the turret of the IDC tank moved nearly as fast.

What the sh— Bee moved her own turret, but in the same direction as the other tank, not at them.

"What—"

"Window's closing. If you want more—if you want *in*—your Bee has the key."

"Old Talinn don't you *dare*—"

"You'll do better next time." Despite the extra cycles and the marked slowness the other Talinn had shown in her shifting positions before, she sprinted up the ditch before Talinn could do more than take a step toward her.

"Is something coming?"

No, I don't know what caught Other Bee's attention, but— Bee made a metallic crunching sound that might as well have been a shriek. *But they're probably still messing with my sensors.*

"What key?"

I almost got in, I thought I almost got in . . . I don't know. Bee's frustration twined with her own, and then Talinn realized she was still in a ditch in the middle of nowhere and the other tank was moving away.

"Should we follow them?"

We should probably get to where we're supposed to be so no one asks any questions.

"You really think . . ." Talinn stood at the edge of the ditch, the unbroken ground just above her midsection, and gave up formulating the rest of her question.

That this can go unnoticed? That we should take down two galaxy-spanning empires? That I have some mysterious key to get in touch with other, older versions of us that want to watch the universe burn?

"Will it?"

Burn? I mean, heat death is a convincing theory of—

"Bee." Talinn put her hands on the stable ground and pushed, swiveling her hips and swinging her legs up over the edge. "Is upending the UCF and IDC going to make the universe burn?"

The better question is—can we really upend the UCF and IDC? Is it worth our throwing ourselves into the mess to get torn apart for . . . potentially nothing?

"That Talinn didn't seem torn apart." The skin between her shoulder blades itched, the muscles beneath twitching, but Talinn kept her pace steady. Something had made the other Talinn run, but if that . . . woman wasn't going to tell her what it was, well. No sense in panicking.

Bee did open and close the hatch of the tank at her, but that appeared impatient, not nervous, so Talinn didn't hurry. She realized—far too late—that she hadn't put back on her face cover, and a new gust of wind shoved half a ditch's worth of dust into her eyes and up her nose, so she coughed and sneezed the last strides back, but she didn't run.

Clean off, Bee directed when Talinn's feet hit the floor, and the hatch slammed closed above her with more force than strictly required. *Then we'll do our job and make some decisions.*

"Like if we're going to tell Sammer, Medith, and Caytil?"

That seems an obvious yes. More like if we're going to talk to Jeena about what's off in my code, in case that's the key the other us meant. Like if we're going to spend the rest of our life on this planet until Command decommissions us because of what another Breezy has done. Like if we're going to do all the things unadapted humans are always afraid we'll do.

"If we have a base to go home to." Talinn scrubbed her face, the top of her head, and behind her ears until the abrasiveness cleared her dulled thoughts. She stared at the opened bunk in front of her without remembering opening it. Had she left her helmet in the ditch? No, it was clipped to her belt. She flipped over the towel and scrubbed again, then deliberately began removing her gear one piece at a time.

If we do . . . No, that Talinn has a Sammer too. They're not going to take out the base.

"You know . . . they never did confirm it was them. The attacks, the—"

Talinn.

"There's a whole lot that we've accepted at face value over the cycles, Bee. I always thought of us as sneaky and clever, but . . . Command is sneaky and clever. We're good little automats, following our tracks. We probably shouldn't assume anything, anymore." She pulled out a fresh coverall, ignored that it would be a few inches too short, and shook it out.

Well, that's our decision, then.

"Not to assume?"

Not to be good little automats. Your cortisol and adrenaline spiked so hard when you said that, I checked to see if you were about to vomit. You don't want to stay in track. Bee dimmed and brightened the lights, and Talinn turned enough to catch the screens flicker.

"Do you?"

I don't have cortisol and adrenaline—

"Bee."

I absolutely do not.

"Even if it means making the universe burn?"

Sometimes that seems like it might be better, don't you think?

Talinn laughed, but the sound had never torn against the inside of her throat quite like it did in that moment.

Nearly ten unremarkable hours later, patrolling their empty patch of assigned dirt, Talinn and Bee had fallen into a silence only a skin flake's width of preferable to their circuitous conversation about what to do after they told the other Eights.

They'd come to no firm decision, and so the crackle of comms landed as both a relief and a stabbing interruption.

"Base to Breezy."

"Breezy here. What's your status, Base?"

"Base is clear. Report, Breezy."

"Patrol is uneventful. Should we continue along assigned coordinates or is there"—Bee interrupted the broadcast before Talinn could complete the sentence—"something worthwhile for us to do," Talinn finished for her usual audience of one.

Behave. Burning it down does not *mean getting locked up for insubordination.*

"I think it takes more than that to—" Talinn stopped muttering as Base's reply began.

"Cleared to return to base, Breezy. New orders will be given at that time."

They couldn't keep us out here much longer. The tank wasn't as well stocked for your needs as mine.

"All the ammo, not enough food?"

See, it sounds good when you say it.

"Bee. What're we going to do?"

Return to base. Get new orders. Figure out a key. Plot a revolution. At least two of those.

"Eat something warm, probably."

Three things you get to do. Isn't that exciting?

"I hate that it is."

Bee's tortured metal laugh was faint, but there. *Noticed Sammer isn't doing comms on their side post attack.*

"Do you think . . . do you think he already knows? Did Belay help with a distraction to get us out here to talk to the old us?"

Bee flickered the screens, and Talinn swung her legs out from her chair in unconscious echo of the timing.

Possible. Belay does tend to get into places I wouldn't have expected. But . . .

"Then why wouldn't they have just told us?"

Yes, that. Though I suppose—would we have believed them?

Talinn pressed her back firmly into her chair, stilled her legs, and picked through a rush of thoughts. How it had felt, receiving the sheer amount of lunatic information, from her own face. Picturing any one piece of that delivered by Sammer, the one who used to lead all their ridiculous drinking games in training. The one who managed to blow up their entire class in a simulation. The one who kept it together, with Lei locked away, separated from his AI. The one who had the discipline and focus to run an entire defensive array and not send a single volley out of place.

"We would have. We would have argued a lot more, and probably demanded explanations until Lei turned the array on us, but . . ."

Yeah. We would have.

"So, I don't think they know."

But they could be involved in something.

"The incursion into the base's systems? Don't you think—I assumed that was the other Breezy."

Thought we weren't assuming anymore.

Talinn gurgled a nonsense sound and bounced her head off the back of her chair. "Stop being right!"

Never in our life.

Bee didn't slow the tank as they rolled toward the base, but she did focus all the screens on various views of their pockmarked approach.

"Gates are down." Talinn chewed on the side of her thumb and scowled at the display. "A whole lot more holes in the ground than before."

Some new arrivals.

The attackers hadn't been invisible and underground this time, or at least not only that. Four twisted metal hulks studded their approach, one markedly larger than the other three.

"Two tanks and a jet?"

Not a jet—too big. A bomber, but not one I've seen in records of what IDC has.

"IDC doesn't even have a presence here. Where did any kind of heavy machinery come from?"

Maybe we have a new enemy.

"Delightful as that would be . . ." Talinn rolled her eyes and leaned forward, Bee automatically enlarging the areas Talinn's gaze lingered on. "One of the arrays took a lot of damage."

Given the lack of other offensive weapons, I'm surprised it wasn't worse.

"No air support, no heavy armored ground defense . . . Did they hunker in and hope for the arrays to win, or send out unadapted soldiers to shoot at the approaching . . . Bee. Does it look like there were a lot more than four on the attack? I know we can't track air after the fact, but can we tell if anything else came in or out on the ground, and if so, how many?"

With all the debris and gaping holes, hard to tell.

"What if . . . what if it wasn't *our* Sammer who told us to go to the meeting point?"

Why would Other Breezy do all that, talk to us, and send us back to a trap?

"I'm not saying it was a trap. I'm saying what if Sammer wasn't ever tasked to base comm during the attack, and the other . . . us, they spoofed the comm channel."

Possible. But what does that have to do with—

"What if the other us-es, they weren't behind the attack but they knew one was coming . . ."

It's all as likely as most of what's happened the last two days, but I'm not following you to your point.

"Shit on a hot day. I'm not sure I have one." Talinn pressed her hands against her eyes and stared at the swirling patterns made by the pressure.

Whether our Sammer or hers warned us off, there was another attack.

"Seems like."

And unless you think we secretly lost and are about to present ourselves to the enemy hiding in the corpse of our base—

"Little grisly with the imagery there, Bee."

I'm not saying it's what I would do . . .

A small spasm pulled her stomach, and Talinn scrubbed her face again before dropping her hands. "No. All of the arrays would have to be destroyed before I'd believe the base fell."

The turret's ready to go if we need it.

"The only time the turret *isn't* ready to go is when we're load-in, though, so that's not saying much."

Staying ready is better than having to get ready.

"Nothing weird on comms?"

Nothing weird. No motion outside the base, but the empty humans aren't going to be out and about without their trucks.

"Hey, hey—unadapted."

Because they're empty.

"And you don't like me parading around outside the tank either. Adapted or not, our squishy bits are still squishy."

Yours are more important than theirs.

"To you."

Exactly.

They rolled into the base through the broken gates, navigated around the largest of the holes, and watched their potentially misleading sensors, but all remained quiet.

Until they pulled up to the wreckage of the largest cargo bay, and what seemed like every unadapted soldier in the base poured out, weapons aimed at them.

CHAPTER 11

Talinn cocked her head, stared at the screen, and laughed.

"They don't have anything big enough to dent a tread. What are they doing?"

They can't wreck us, but they can damage—

"Are the arrays turning to aim at us at all?"

No movement from the arrays.

"Then forgive me if I don't waste time shaking in my borrowed coverall." Talinn snorted, then made an effort—at least five seconds' worth—to get her voice in neutral before toggling comms.

"Breezy to Base. Is there a reason you have us—" Another laugh threatened to burst through and she forced a quick pause on herself before continuing. "Surrounded?"

"Base to Talinn Reaze. You are to exit the tank without weapons or face cover—"

The laugh died in her throat, and the heat of rage swarmed up to take its place. "This shit again?"

There is no interference I can detect. Arrays are still motionless.

"Then I'm gonna push it. I'm tired of this nonsense... but go ahead and cut my line if those arrays twitch in our direction, yeah?"

You don't even have to ask.

"Base, did you or did you not order us to come home?"

"Base to Reaze, you are to—" The speaker repeated the directive as if she hadn't spoken, and Talinn let him finish. Mostly because she and Bee hadn't worked out a way to superimpose their words to take over the base line—nor had they tried too hard given the

81

insubordination charge that would follow—but she did sneer the entire time.

"I'd like confirmation from Base Two."

Silence held for thirty beautiful seconds before the poor comms operator repeated himself a third time.

"Unless you're prepared to waste a lot of ammunition on this tank, Breezy repeats: I want confirmation from Base Two that my orders were to return to base, which should not necessitate a fully armed escort that looks hostile."

No cursing at all, well done.

"It's a close thing." Talinn stretched her legs, holding her feet parallel to the floor and glaring at the comms panel as though they could see her from base. When there continued to be no answer and no firing on them, she slammed her feet down and stood, twisted to stretch her back, and idly regarded the waiting soldiers. "Do you think any of these unadapted humans are clones?"

Why would they be?

"If everybody's clones, you're not tapping the general population for the war. Fewer people with outside connections to notice something hinky with the Eights and go blabbing about it."

Seems complicated.

"Sure, because Old Talinn's story was very simple."

Simple enough. War makes money. Money good. Keep war going. Don't kill too many civilians.

"I just wonder. Maybe we're all clones, everywhere, everyone. The same . . . what do you think? Thousand? Two thousand? Faces and bodies and predictable choices, living their prescribed lives and keeping Command happy."

Do you really—

"Nah." She pulled an arm across her chest, then switched, and comms remained dead. "Be expensive to grow people when people can just make more of themselves. But I can't think of any reason why we'd be getting dragged in with guns in my face *again*, and so I'm gonna focus on the other thing."

All of it is equally likely to make you crazy.

"But the first probably is less likely to get me shot."

For this moment, you mean. More likely to get you shot as we try to get under what's really happening.

"I'm definitely going to get shot at, is what you're saying?" Talinn blew out her breath in an overdone sigh, then leaned over to hit comms again. "Base, how long are we going to be here? I'm being a good little soldier, but this is ridiculous."

"*Base Two to Breezy.*" The impatient, dismissive tone matched Talinn's first interactive encounter with the man perfectly, and she crossed her arms as he spoke. "*During the base attack, AIT pair designated Mercy sabotaged their own array. CC-525 is destroyed. Medith Tortil claims to have no idea what happened. All AITs have voluntarily undergone load-in and remanded themselves with techs in a secure area.*"

"I hate this planet. We've talked about that, yeah?" Talinn threw herself back into the chair and Bee made the entire display a zoomed in, semipixelated view of the destroyed array. Cece was...destroyed? But Medith still lived? Panic and grief ate at the edges of her thoughts, and she and Bee both shunted the potential repercussions aside. None of it made sense. There had been a lot of that lately, and it appeared that even a paired AI/human mind could only take so much before it all ceased to be real. "What am I supposed to say to that?"

They're not asking you *to load-in.*

"Huh." Talinn tapped comms with her foot—she'd apologize to Sigmun if it ever mattered again—and replied to the base's second-in-command. "But Base didn't ask me to open up and wait for load-in. He specifically gave orders for me, Talinn, to step out, not Breezy."

"*Breezy, lead tech Boralid indicated it would be unsafe for you to load-in at this time. B-617 is to remain in current location. We are assured that with your, Reaze's, life and a large EMP as security, B-617 will remain a nonthreat to the base.*"

Maybe it is *what you said earlier. Maybe the IDC is* squatting *in our base, pretending.* Bee's words fuzzed around the edges, fury and a host of other reactions shared between them until it was unclear what was what.

"I wish that were the case. Can you see the EMP?"

No. If it's one of the empty humans out there, they'll stay behind instead of escorting you. If it's somewhere else, maybe you can find it once you're inside.

"I don't think they're going to let me wander."

They're not going to "let" us do anything. But I trust we'll figure out something.

"If we ever get a chance, let's make friends with the big defense array at the transit point. And when we finally, finally leave this bug-eaten planet, we ask it to blow the entirety of P-8 to a nice, chunky asteroid field."

Motion seconded.

"At least you won't be in a box I have to keep physical contact with this time."

They may try to put you in a shielded room.

Talinn brushed a finger over the port behind her ear. "I'll tunnel out with my toenails if I have to."

If you're in a shielded room ... ask Jeena about the discrepancy she thinks she found.

Talinn froze in a crouch, halfway standing from the chair. "Why under all the skies would I do that?"

She's more likely to tell you if I can't hear.

"I . . ." Talinn hit comms to buy herself time. "Breezy to Base. Thank you for the clarification. B-617 acknowledges. On my way out." She left her hand on the panel and tilted her head back to better stare at the ceiling. "Any other psychological insights you'd like to share?"

Base Two is either looking out for you, or wants to strangle you after this delay. Unclear which.

"Point to you. I have no follow-up questions to that." Talinn scanned the interior of the tank more out of habit than need—she'd brought nothing in other than Bee, and would be leaving without the full weight of her AI in her head. She wanted Sigmun's blanket, but had no right to it—though the idea of climbing out of the tank with a stitched blanket in her hand, surrounded by distrustful, armed, unadapted humans in full gear almost made her reconsider.

Bee muttered threats as Talinn climbed the ladder, and while Bee didn't safe the turrets, neither did the drones buzz out of storage, so Talinn recognized the small wins of AI discipline for what they were. The soldiers managed to snap further to attention at her appearance, and she inclined her head as though they were her honor guard.

Eights didn't get honor guards, and honor guards probably never pointed their weapons at the honor they were guarding, but it made her feel better all the same.

She dropped to the ground, patted the thick armor above the nearer treads, and mentally put nonexistent money on the taller guard to the right having the EMP. Bee chose the shortest one with the boxier weapon near the back, but then everyone fell in around her as Talinn moved.

So much for that. None of the other Eights are going to fire an EMP at me, so it's not loaded near the arrays. Bee scanned the area, though with the way their instruments had been acting, neither of them held high hopes for finding the AI-targeted weapon. Nor would it change their next actions even if they could spot it—Bee wouldn't fire on it, Talinn would still comply with orders—but it would ease some measure of the tension they shared to have it identified and isolated.

None of the other humans talked to her, and that familiarity should have made the walk more natural. Instead the itch at the base of Talinn's skull slowly spread down her neck, across to her shoulder blades, and further to the small of her back. She locked her muscles down to keep from squirming as they marched into the main entrance of the base, but the prickling only intensified as they continued through empty halls.

The base hadn't been overly populated at any point, without any active conflict with the IDC to justify it, but there was usually someone in any given hall passing by. With fifteen unadapted humans with her, and the Eights locked up somewhere with the techs, that didn't leave much of anyone *to* pass in the spaces in between.

Are they all still in load-in holding patterns? Bee's voice twitched along with the nerves bundled in Talinn's spine, words jumping midsyllable. *Or do you think they're all back in those stupid boxes?*

"Can't say either is ideal." Despite her long practice subvocalizing without obvious tells, one of the soldiers nudged her a moment later. Did he guess? Did they have some sort of listening device? Talinn could stop talking to be safe, but instead she decided to test it. "My money's on the boxes."

No one nudged her this time, and Talinn leaned her head from side to side in an attempt to pop some of the pressure in her neck as the silence and walk continued.

Your money is my money, so it's not much of a bet.

"That's not how that works—what?" The last word hit full volume, as she ignored all the weapons and snapped her head to the side to regard the soldier who'd nudged her again.

The soldiers were all too disciplined to yank their weapons up, but several heads swiveled her way. The one who'd nudged her said nothing, head remaining forward, stride unbroken.

"What what?" The one on her other side asked, and Talinn ensured her sigh was audible, but didn't otherwise answer.

This is going well.

"No one's shooting."

Why you insist on jinxing everything—

"You don't believe in jinxes."

No, but you *do, and yet you jinx right along anyway, as though you'd rather it all go to chaos.*

"I mean . . ."

Do not get shot. It's rule number one.

"Thought rule number one was—"

It's rule number one today.

"So noted." She didn't get nudged again, and then the line of soldiers in front of her was slowing, several peeling back to the sides, their backs locking against the walls. Two about-faced on either side of a door ahead to the right, which Talinn took for her cue.

"Appreciate the escort," she said at audible volume, her tone carefully neutral. None of them reacted, so she kept pace to the door. The nudging solider stepped up smartly and ran something over the control panel—it didn't resemble any security badges she'd seen before, but she saw no point in asking—and the door slid open.

Talinn did *not* expect the nudging soldier to follow her in, but he did as the rest stayed in the hall. She put that to the side to deal with later, given the room full of Eights she needed to check in with.

She hadn't been in this side of the base before. On the base schematics it was marked as tech residence, but this room was three times the size of an Eight's quarters, and had three times as many aggressively blinking consoles and angular counters than she'd have expected for sleeping arrangements. The Eights were in various clusters—Sammer and Xenni talking together over a long table against the back wall, a few of the tank pairs sitting on the floor, legs spread, backs against some kind of control panel, most of the jet pairs and the rest of the tankers gesticulating animatedly as they stood around a screen, and a final mix sitting or standing on stools around a tall table strewn with printouts off to the right.

"Talinn." Jeena slid through the group near the screen, and Sammer pivoted away from Xenni at the sound.

"This doesn't look like load-in, and I don't see any boxes...?" She crossed her arms, but a jolt of warmth flushed through her at the unstrained tone of the tech. Talinn had never had a remotely nice feeling about a tech before, and she shoved the reaction down as ruthlessly as Bee rerouted her headaches.

"No, all the AIs are hosted in the servers here. They're fully apart from the main base storage, so Base Two approved it." Jeena gave the still silent nudging soldier a once over, then turned her attention back to Talinn. "Sorry we couldn't risk you to load-in and get Bee in."

"I can still hear her—she's used to staying hosted in the tank when we're at base." Talinn lifted a shoulder, as though it didn't matter at all. And it wouldn't, under circumstances that even approached normal. That was standard operations on assignment—once load-in was complete, the full weight of the AI program remained in their designated craft to reduce wear and tear on the human brain, and hold readiness for action at any given time. Without targeted shielding in effect, the active part of the program that remained hosted in the human brain allowed communication no matter the distance.

"Of course, of course." Jeena glanced at the soldier, then fixed her eyes back on Talinn's. "How was patrol?"

Does Jeena *know?* Bee's tone was curious, not shocked, and Talinn found she had no definite answer.

"Not as eventful as the time you all had here, it sounds like." Neither soldier nor Jeena jumped on that conversational opening, so after a moment Talinn picked it up herself. "Did River, Nips, and Ziggy get back much before me?"

"River is still on their way, but Ziggy and Nips were a great deal closer when orders went out." Jeena angled away from the soldier, gestured to invite Talinn to walk with her, and strode toward Sammer and Xenni.

Talinn did not roll her eyes when the soldier fell in behind her because she'd expected him to do so. At least he hadn't nudged her again.

Sammer and the one remaining base-support Eight appeared less normal closer in—their expressions were overly bland, motions too jerky for true, and both sets of eyes were each far more bloodshot than they'd been during the first battle the day before. Sammer's skin showed new lines radiating from his eyes, as though he were permanently squinting.

Sammer's gotten closer to Other Talinn's age overnight.

Talinn had no retort for Bee, and nothing to say that would help the base-support pairs. She hadn't remotely begun to process what had happened to Medith, and the three base-support Eights had worked together closely, running endless drills and tests and practice attacks in the midst of unadapted humans and the lack of enemy action.

To lose one of their own, apparently with treason, when there finally was action?

She certainly didn't believe it was treason—not Medith, of all of them—but she wouldn't push them to talk about it, especially not with the presence of the silent nudging soldier hovering behind her.

Do you think he's there to guard you, or guard against you?

"You brought a friend." Sammer jutted his chin out, commenting on the soldier at the same moment Bee spoke.

Jeena made a noise in her throat—Talinn didn't know her well enough to parse if it were meant to be an uncomfortable laugh or sarcastic grunt or something else entirely. Was Jeena also annoyed by the other unadapted human? The tech was in a far better position to get the soldier out of here, compared to the current situation of the Eights...

Or was she? Was Jeena... had the tech put herself on the line to allow the Eights space with their AI partners safe and close? Offering some measure of protection, the way she had by shielding Bee's alleged discrepancy?

Or was Talinn leaping at hope of allies, jumping to the wrong assumptions in the interest of not assuming... her thoughts snarled until Bee chided her and let her feel the edge of the pounding headache Bee had been muzzling.

"He doesn't speak, far as I can tell. Only elbows." Talinn shrugged, then lifted her palm and curled her fingers in. *Sorry*, the gesture offered, part of their class's silent communication from early training days.

"Interesting communication choice for a soldier." Sammer tapped her hand in acceptance, then proceeded to follow Jeena's lead and mostly ignore the other man. "Anything helpful on patrol?"

"Helpful is a strong word." None of them wanted to talk about anything real, not with the nameless, faceless soldier, the odd surroundings, the compilation of events over the last few days. Had Command been remotely trustworthy, she would have at least mentioned their wonky sensors, but that would likely be taken as further evidence for suspicion, and she tamped it down.

Talinn tilted her head toward Xenni, but she'd lapsed into a new low conversation with Daren, foreheads close together, so she focused fully on Sammer. "Have you seen Medith?"

"No." Sammer's mouth remained open, as though he were about to say more. Nothing followed, and he snapped it closed.

"She's in a more secure area." The solider finally spoke, and Talinn barely bit back the curse that immediately formed in her mouth at the recognizable voice.

"Are you saying you're not keeping your Eights secure, Base Two?" she asked instead, a sour heat twisting in her gut.

Jeena goggled, her gaze dropping to where Base Two's insignia were obviously not attached to his armored suit. The man's shoulders twitched, and when he pulled off his helmet and face cover, Talinn nearly cursed a second time.

If the base-support Eights had been dragged through a shitstorm in an open ship since she'd last seen them, Base Two had been staked out in it. His pale skin had paled further, his close-cut hair lay too close and shiny to his head, and the shadows under his eyes nearly reached his cheekbones.

"Did you see her?" He met Talinn's eyes straight on, and this time all the self-discipline in the world couldn't stop the low curse that spilled out of her.

Not Sammer. Not Jeena. Base Two *knows?* The shock that poured from Bee matched her own, and Talinn cast for a safe answer while Jeena and Sammer wrote "Who?" all over their faces.

"Or he's angling. Is it a guess? Word passed down from Command?"

"Out loud for the whole class, Reaze." Base Two crossed his arms, though he shifted an elbow toward her as though he were about to nudge her. He could *not* be hearing her conversation with Bee.

Could he?

"Bee and I are trying to figure out your deal." It was a weak redirection attempt, but for once something awful was in her favor.

Alarms shrieked through the air.

CHAPTER 12

⊕

"Again?" Sammer lurched toward the nearer console, as though he were about to will Lei back into his brain from the servers.

"No." Base Two didn't flinch, but his single word carried loud and clear through the wailing alarm. "You are all to stay here." He pivoted and marched out at speed, the door sliding shut nearly on his heel.

"What the *shit* is going on?" Talinn pressed her fingers into the side of her scalp and attempted to ease the building pressure in her head. It didn't remotely work, and the volume of the alarm did not abate.

"Why was he in here?" Sammer shouted to Jeena, who shrugged.

"Who was he talking about?" She gestured rapidly with her hands, demonstrating that was the bigger question. "You met with somebody?"

Several of the other Eights drifted closer, needful if they wanted to hear over the alarms' backdrop of caterwauling. "On patrol?" Sigmun shoved closest. "Is IDC attack finally confirmed, then?" She didn't ask about her tank, which Talinn noted as evidence of strong discipline.

"It's not—" Talinn flapped her hands in the air, communicating nothing at all except that she didn't have words to get across anything more specific. Someone else started yelling about bets on what kind of attack they'd have this time, and Talinn didn't bother to try and identify who it was.

I can lower your hearing again—

"No. It's fine, I probably need to hear."

What, hear what's going on? It's alarms and useless shouting. Yet again the base has no one in place to hold back the attack, and there are incoming jets.

"Jets?"

A lot of them. Want me to start shooting?

"You're completely unprotected out there." Talinn spun toward the door, unaware of what volume she was speaking at and uncaring of the same. "The arrays are down and there's no cover, the tank is just in a field of—"

It's fine. I bet they don't know I'm active, given the state of the base overall.

"You saw those melted—"

Not ours. Theirs. Drones are out, I have them low in the scrub until the incoming targets hit the first wave of fire. Do you want to tell someone so they don't panic and EMP me?

Talinn registered that she was only halfway across the room, the door frustratingly out of reach, in large part because someone was holding back her arms.

Two someones. She stopped pulling, now that she was aware she'd been straining against an annoyingly strong hold, and wrenched her mind back into the immediate area around her. Where was all that vaunted increased analytical ability? With Bee outside, and no other Eights ready for additional firepower or backup, she had to keep her shit together.

Bee certainly was.

Sammer and Xenni each had one of her arms, and she twisted in their grip exactly enough to get her eyes on Jeena, hovering over Sammer's other shoulder. "Call Base Two. Remind him Bee is active and will fire at will. They better not EMP the tank. Drones are launched." The words ripped at her throat, meaning she had probably shouted louder than needed, but she didn't want a single word lost against the unrelenting sirens.

Jeena's eyes widened and she nodded, the motion sharp and efficient, her jaw already moving as she used some comm channel Talinn had zero access to. Did unadapted humans have comms embedded behind their ears too? Were they removable devices? Why had she never paid attention?

Her thoughts scrambled in a dozen different directions, and she pulled them back as best she could. Bee could use her senses, and Talinn was equally able to see what Bee registered. They'd gotten lazy with it during assignments, given the tank's screens showed Talinn everything she needed to see, but no time like the present to refresh an old skill.

Talinn slackened against Sammer's and Xenni's hold, and their hands tightened as her muscles loosened. She closed her eyes and slid into an overload of information. Calculations, six angles of views, heat signatures, velocity matching, wind speed, it all flooded into the space her eyesight had recently taken, and she may or may not have stopped breathing as her brain struggled to corral the flood into meanings it could parse.

Most of the views were the drones; Talinn filtered those out. Calculations she kept running to the side—velocity estimations for each jet's approach were less pressing since she knew Bee had it—and instead she focused on the stream of information that was a broad view of the sky to the south. Not the direction they'd met Other Talinn and Bee. The direction Riva and Ern should be coming back from.

"No sight of River?"

Not even a ping on the long range.

"Base Two confirms, Bee is clear to fire."

About time. Bee swept the drones apart—there were extra, more than the six count they'd carried in the tank and from which Talinn had seen lines of data. Before she could ask, Bee murmured—perhaps a touch of guilt in the words—*Our tank is still out there, and those drones are still on my frequency. I got two tanks' worth, and I might be able to get Ziggy's before we're done.*

"Should be enough for a squadron of jets."

That and my turrets? Yes. Even if they're IDC Eights, they're not ready for me.

Dumb missiles, guided by simple programming rather than AI, shot up from the base, toward the jets, all of which had plenty of time to blow out scattershot and confuse the missile targeting.

Definitely AI jets, Bee and Talinn decided together, watching the way the aircraft moved, and the fine control of the scattershot. If the missiles had been AI guided on their base's side—as they would have been if the arrays were functional—the incoming targets would not have been able to evade so easily.

They don't think we have any active Eights. They're far too casual.
"Unfortunate for them you're here."

We've really learned a lot about assuming these last few days. Smug,
Bee flooded Talinn's brain with nesting plans, a branching series of
actions accounting for each jet's possible trajectory.

The drones remained low, and the incoming jets showed no
reaction to them. As the jets curved slightly away from each other,
likely to ensure maximum impact when they fired, Bee sent
seventeen drones spinning into the air, all launching their own small
bombs while becoming slightly larger bombs themselves.

The jets occupied themselves with the drones, paths changing,
apparently taking for granted the base would wait.

But Bee wasn't the base. The tank's turrets swung around—*three*
tanks' worth of turrets swung around. Bee should absolutely not have
been able to retain control of even their old tank, out in the field, as
she had left none of her programming behind in it. In the midst of
the chaos—alarms screaming, other Eights peppering questions,
Bee's perpetual tsunami of information—Talinn couldn't begin to
imagine how Bee would have gotten a hold of a third tank, one they'd
never been in. She tagged that thought, along with about a thousand
more from the meeting with the older versions of them, as something
to scrutinize later.

Three of the drones were out. Talinn meant to say that aloud to the
people around her, and maybe she did, but she was too deep into the
streaming data from Bee to know how to monitor her volume, so she
might have subvocalized it, or screamed it, or anything in between. Her
body ceased to have meaning. There was too much else to pick apart.

Two tanks took out two jets. Bee was good—excellent, even—but
it was one AI against ten. The only thing saving them was the
attackers had to believe there were Eights in each tank, and were
therefore giving more berth than they might have otherwise. Their
original tank, further out, was closing out the edge of its reach.

Two more jets peeled off, screaming away in opposite directions.
The remaining eight increased the distance between them, trying to
draw the tanks' attention and perhaps create some confusion among
the defenders.

But the defenders were all Bee, and she had a plan. And then
exactly eighty-three additional plans, if that one didn't work.

Two more drones fell, and one of them crashed into a third as it exploded. "Bee—" Talinn's idea started in her head, and completed in Bee's, as the AI sent three more crashing into the airspace ahead of the lowest attacking jet, providing exactly enough of a screen for the third tank to get off a volley the jet could not avoid.

"Three down. Five to go."

I won't get them all. Those other two are coming back.

"You cut it down enough, they won't be able to completely ice the tank. We'll get you out as soon as the metal cools—"

Hate explosions. It was a risk. The server that hosted Bee was as secure as techs could make it, ensuring it would be all but impossible to lose both AI and human partner in a mission. The goal of any assignment weapon was that enough of the programming survived for Command to get a thorough last report before decommissioning the orphaned AI. With Talinn still alive and functional, any pieces Bee lost in an explosion could be rerouted and all but recovered between their two systems. A risk, but not a death sentence.

The first of the jets got two missiles off between the drones and the tanks, and odds were in Bee's favor—their old tank, without Bee in residence absorbed the hits, got off one last fusillade before the turret was left as a half-melted slag pile.

Was almost out of reach anyway.

The third tank got off a ballistic round that contained half its remaining payload, and another jet spiraled at full speed toward the ground. But there were still four left, and Bee knew the two that had pulled away were going to return any moment.

Talinn's knees were on the ground. Sammer murmured something in her ear. The next wave would take out another tank— no matter how good the treads, Bee couldn't outrun air support.

The missing two jets registered on sonar, though still out of sight, and their heat signatures were off the charts. Talinn couldn't imagine what the IDC attackers had done while away, but an aching weight of dread indicated they were about to find out.

The alarms had faded—either they were off or Talinn's ears had stopped working. She said words she didn't retain, and stayed immersed in Bee's spinning nebula of data. Bee would survive, she *would*, but Talinn wouldn't leave her alone in the seconds leading up to the potential destruction and—

One of the jets fell out of the sky in pieces before either Talinn or Bee processed the dramatic shift in the fight.

The remaining base arrays had come alive.

"Sammer!" The lining of her throat was bleeding; copper flooded her mouth. Talinn must have been screaming the entire time.

"Talinn, we're here. Is it Bee? Is the tank—"

"The arrays!"

"The arrays?"

Jeena's voice, urgent. "The arrays are firing."

"It's not Lei!"

"Is it—can it be Cece?" Voices overlayed each other until Talinn couldn't make out intelligible words.

Bee fired in rapid succession, but the arrays took out the last six jets, who had disregarded the arrays completely. The sky above was suddenly, shockingly quiet.

The arrays went still.

Bee tracked her one remaining turret across the empty expanse above.

Talinn stumblingly untangled her senses from immersion in Bee's, but it took another full minute before she could pry her eyes open.

Every Eight was in a semicircle tight around her, their eyes flicking between Talinn, on the ground, and Jeena, pacing to the side of the press of bodies, her mouth moving as she spoke to someone on comms.

Between one moment and the next, the alarms cut off entirely, as sudden as the change in the sky outside. The silence hurt, Talinn's ears throbbing in the absence of cacophony.

"What *happened*?" Xenni demanded, her hands clenched but stretched out toward Talinn, as though she were restraining herself from grabbing and shaking.

Words spilled out of Talinn, a brief report, the way she'd been trained. Her brain was too sore to listen, still spiraling through the plans upon plans she and Bee had held as the fight shifted rapidly in the sky above. She couldn't keep herself on track, relief and adrenaline and confusion braided together so tightly she almost missed Sammer's whisper.

"Medith." He'd half turned from her, staring at the console again, and saliva pooled over Talinn's tongue. She wanted to know what Lei had to say, so badly her body thought she was hungry. She snatched her hand back to her chest, catching it as it reached for the console as though that would give her the answers she wanted.

An overlapping babble of voices rose around them, a dozen questions half asked. Almost immediately, silence again, as Sammer twitched up a hand impatiently.

"We need to find Medith. Does she know . . ." Sammer's mouth moved even after he stopped talking, as though he couldn't imagine the rest of that sentence. If Cece still existed, of course Medith knew. But there never should have been confusion about that to begin with. Unless Medith had lied?

Talinn couldn't connect to a full decision about the matter, and Bee provided no help. She couldn't bear to think about Medith, and her own AI provided a perfect excuse. "Wait, Bee . . . how did you—"

"Who was Base Two talking about?" Jeena appeared at Talinn's elbow, crouched down so they were face-to-face. Talinn hadn't understood she was still kneeling on the ground—the past hours, and days, had done a number on her situational awareness to say the absolute least.

"I have a lot more questions before that one." The words came haltingly through her mouth, but managed not to wobble. They crowded together once she was sure her tone wouldn't betray her, spilling out rapidly. "Like why was Base Two here without identifying himself? Who is attacking us? Why are the Eights taking the brunt of suspicion and getting routed off the field? Why was Base Command holding an EMP over our head? What evidence was used to declare Cece destroyed, and what under every sky in the galaxy is going on that the base arrays came online and saved all of our asses if all the AIs were out of the system?"

Why did you say Bee's code had a discrepancy, and not report it? Are *you* a clone? Are we all actually on the same side fighting a play war?

Because the losses had felt pretty real, everywhere else. Until they'd gotten here. And here . . . they'd come close enough to the end. The tension had yet to fully leave, pressure uncomfortable under her ribs, from how close it had been for Bee. How close it might still be, for Medith. Stakes were alarmingly real for a pretend war . . . though that was the point, wasn't it? Fill it with clones, let it run in the same circles, let money fall out and no one *real* needs to worry. Terrarium war. No one important suffers.

"Base Two was here to ask you about whoever you met with, and that attack was real convenient to keep you from answering." Jeena's voice was low, soothing despite the words. "I can't imagine even you and Bee could have coordinated that so precisely, and you seemed as surprised as the rest of us that that was Base Two, so don't protest. I'm not saying it was you."

Talinn's mouth had already formed around the retort, every muscle tensing, before Jeena had headed her off at the intercepting orbit.

"If everything's connected, Base Two at least seems to think it's rooted in who you met with. So. Who is 'she'?"

"Me. Bee and I met with . . . Talinn and Bee."

She wasn't entirely sure what she expected. Dead silence. Pandemonium. An extreme reaction of some sort.

But what she got, after a heartbeat's pause, was Sammer throwing back his head and laughing. Deep, from his belly, as though the universe had told him the most delightful joke he could have ever imagined. As though Lei had toggled a corner of his brain that produced laughter, and he couldn't stop.

He laughed until all pairs of eyes were locked on him, until horror overtook some expressions and nervous humor others, and then Xenni joined him.

"Are their AIs broken?" Talinn subvocalized to Bee, her gaze fixed on Sammer despite her best efforts to tear it away. Like the first time she'd seen a dead, broken body.

Are they *broken?* Bee's retort had none of its usual bite. Instead it was as though Bee had busied herself doing something else. What could be distracting her?

"Who are you talking to?" But she knew the answer before she asked. Cece. Of course Bee was talking to Cece. "Did Cece help you connect to the other tank?"

No. Maybe. Unclear.

"Helpful, Bee. Very precise."

Sammer's laughter still filled the space around them, and between one heartbeat and the next it became beyond too much. Talinn pushed herself to her feet, her body sluggish to respond, aching in places she didn't know she'd tensed. She forced each muscle to unclench as she moved, and strode away from the knot in the middle of the tech's room. She didn't know what she needed to do, but she was stiff and jittery and her nerves communicated a mix of pain, tingling, and sparks, so she moved. The space didn't give her a chance to run and force all the parts of her body to work together, to work right, to feel normal again, but at least she could pace.

A commotion behind her, a sharp sound, and Sammer's laughter cut off. A moment later Xenni's followed. Talinn kept her face locked forward, the path she took as she traced the lengths of the room, three sides of the square, avoiding the wall that took her closest to the cluster of people.

"Talinn." Sammer's voice, still trembling with something—mirth, hysteria, disbelief—she couldn't tell anymore. She ignored it, marking the edges of her cage.

"Talinn," Jeena repeated, and Talinn quickened her pace.

"*Breezy,*" several Eights chorused at once, and her feet stopped so quickly she tilted forward, then used her momentum to whirl around and glare.

"*What.*"

"You called me. Before the last attack. Sounded a little hoarse, but you knew our shorthand. The codes. The channel." Slight emphasis in the word meant the other Bee had contacted Lei as well. "It was you." Sammer's eyes were intent on hers, no laughter to be seen.

"But I didn't—"

"Yeah, no, I figured. As soon as you said . . . I knew it. That that hadn't been you at all."

"What did she—I—what was the message?"

"It wasn't much—more of a check in. I thought it was weird you were contacting me instead of Base, but it's been a weird couple of days, and . . ."

Talinn, who'd had her own unexpected outreach from a Sammer that seemed more likely not to have been her own, understood that to her toes.

"And now I'm guessing the point wasn't the message."

On another day—a better day, one not at the end of a whole lot of battering to her brain in repeated and terrifyingly thorough ways—she might have understood right away. As it went, it took her three full seconds before she rocked back on her heels. "She sent a code."

"Something, something that impacted the arrays, Cece, who knows what else?"

Tanks that Bee shouldn't have been able to operate, but did. A fraction of the other Bee's own program? How would that even be possible? They'd tried before, in their training days, competing to get their AI partners into different secured locations without hard load-in. But the same Command that had found the way to perfect the AIs had also put great care into protecting against them, and their competitions had never resulted in success.

The other version of her had had more time to figure out further options, that was clear, but . . . She prompted Bee, who'd listened, but Bee offered nothing. Talinn added it to the spiraling list of questions she needed to get back to. Orienting question: What the shit is happening?

Next question: What are we going to do about it?

"Sure, so . . . wait. Why was that so funny?" Daren cocked his head at Sammer, though his gaze drifted over to Talinn the moment he stopped speaking.

"One—the message from Talinn was the one nice thing that happened all day, and it wasn't even her. Two—maybe it's why the day went even more sideways afterward. Three—I actually had a moment today . . ." He held up his hands, warding off protests before he finished speaking. "I let myself be sad that we'd all glitched so much we probably weren't going to get cloning bonuses, but . . ."

Sammer's voice skewed, but he managed to control another laugh. "If we're already clones—'cause I'm guessing if Talinn's been cloned before, she's not the only one—they're not going to pay us again for the pleasure of our company." He dropped his arms when no one argued, and glanced from face to face. "Come on—that's funny."

"That's a way to look at it." Jeena shifted to put her hand on Sammer's arm, and left it there even as she turned her attention fully to Talinn. "What did this other iteration of you have to say?"

"And why bother, if she was just going to sabotage the base?" Caytil grunted, then shrugged when heads turned toward her. "What? It can't be vanity. I know *this* Talinn, and I can't imagine that one is so wildly different. It's not like saving yourself, not really. What's the point?"

"Who says it was sabotage though?" Sigmun stared unblinking at the consoles to the side of their group. Talinn wondered what any of the AIs had to say about all of this, given Bee remained silent. "Maybe she was giving us an advantage."

"By having Cece blow up and strand Medith in lock up?" Xenni spluttered, knocking her shoulder into Sigmun's.

"By introducing a back door to help when we got attacked, again, without any of us in place—*again*."

"But how would she even know—" Daren interjected, shoving forward exactly the way he and Gef did when they were in formation in their jet.

"So we went from having zero combatants on this shitty planet to two different groups—"

"No no no no no." Caytil whistled, the piercing noise driving into the center of ears recently abused by alarms, then crossed her arms and continued. "Tech finally asked a good question. What did this other Talinn tell you? Please say it's something that's going to make all of this make sense."

Talinn breathed in, and Caytil noted it rightly as a hesitation. She stared at Talinn for another long moment, then blew out her own breath noisily.

"Any part of this, then. Please say it's something that's going to make even one part of all this make sense. *Please.*"

There had to be a reason Other Talinn hadn't simply messaged everyone—or had their respective counterparts do so—and share it all at once. Consequences. Information spilling out of carefully constructed silos, leading to some terrible outcome this Talinn hadn't yet considered.

She could make their lives infinitely worse, in ways she wouldn't see coming until it was too late.

We don't owe anyone anything.

Talinn didn't subvocalize a response to Bee; she didn't need to. Bee read her instant disagreement and its conflicting impulses, and sheared metal across their link.

Old Breezy showed up and dumped this on us, and Other Bee talked to Lei but not me? Weird. Command has held this secret for who knows how long. That's not our fault. We don't own this, whatever happens. But if we're going to pick someone to be loyal to, someone to trust, someone whose secrets we should protect . . . it's not going to be old us. Not Command. Not the war effort. It's the Eights. Our Eights. You already know that.

Of course she did.

A laugh as alarmingly out of control as Sammer's bubbled in her throat, and Talinn swallowed, shook her head, and told them everything.

CHAPTER 13

⊕

Jeena took it the best of everyone, and Talinn couldn't decide if that made sense or not. Sammer periodically chortled to himself, to the point she had to consider if the Other Talinn's backdoor code—or whatever it had been—had damaged him.

Sigmun insisted they should "tell everyone" and that would "make it right." Caytil, ten minutes in to mercilessly mocking her, was in the midst of a pretend livecast of what that would sound like when Talinn had yet another belated realization.

She eased over to Jeena, on the outskirts of the group and with Caytil's projected monologue as cover ("And the clones, citizens, you should see them. Thirteen generations—or thirty, they're unclear, everyone knows clones don't know history, or counting—"), and murmured, "Who else has access to what we say in here?"

Jeena blinked out of her unfocused study into the unseen void, and fixed her eyes on Talinn's. "I'm not going to betray—oh, no, you mean monitoring?" At Talinn's impatient nod she relaxed, her mouth twitching up briefly as though she were about to smile. "There are no listening devices in here. We have too many energy fluctuations—purposeful and in the course of our work. And we clean. Thoroughly. Techs handle sensitive matters, and Command doesn't want any chance that anyone—even our own people—will learn too much about the AIT program."

"Is that what you think Base Two was doing? Trying to find out too much about the AIT program?"

Jeena frowned and tapped her fingers on her hip, tilting her head first to the left, then the right. Considering her answer, or weighing how much to say? Talinn told herself to start paying more attention to how unadapted humans' expressions worked, though the list of things she needed to pay more attention to had grown exponentially of late.

"I doubt it. He already knows at least enough to ask you the right question."

A protest half formed before she swallowed it back. "Did you see her?" could only have meant so many things. While possible Base Two had another "her" in mind, the likelihood of that was . . . not great. She discarded several conversational directions, then loosened the tension in her upper body. An attempt to appear more conversational, less urgent, and welcome a confidence or three from the tech.

"I haven't seen Base Two outside of the ceremony when we landed here, but he's been all over the place the last few days. You seem to be more familiar with him. What do you think he's doing?"

"I'm not *familiar*." Jeena glanced at Sammer as she emphasized the last word. Talinn managed not to make a face. "But techs fall under Base Two's purview, not Base Command Actual, so we see him more often than you would."

Talinn not only continued to control her expression, she also didn't make a "get on with it" gesture, and under the circumstances that seemed like all the win she could expect.

"He . . . he has a strong record. It didn't make sense to me that he'd be assigned to a base so far from the active fronts." Jeena hesitated again, and Talinn decided some personal interest might help move this along.

"You seem pretty good at your job, and you're out here." Her voice remained neutral—no need to give the impression she was making an effort to flatter the tech.

"Hm?" Jeena blinked, as though pulled back from a side path her thoughts had wandered down. "My senior advisor told me it was so I'd have space for research." She lifted her hands, outlined the barest sketch of the portable server Talinn had spent all too much time with recently. "Still remaining in practice, skills sharp, part of the effort, but . . ." Her eyes narrowed, and Talinn held her breath, watching small motions flicker across Jeena's face.

When the tech remained silent, she swallowed a sigh and

prompted, "You're well regarded in the command structure and were sent here for a specific reason. If that's the case for Base Two, as well, what do you think—"

"You."

"Say more?" Talinn intended that to be a flat directive, but her voice betrayed her and lifted at the end.

"Not *you*, just you ... you, the Eights."

"Going to repeat myself here, and—"

"Say more, I know." The smaller pupils of Jeena's eyes contracted and dilated, and Talinn wished she could slide Bee in there to tell her what parts of the tech's brain were lighting up. Not that it would do much good—without the familiarity built over cycles and cycles of training and targeted programming, Bee wouldn't be able to make more than the most generalized of meaning from someone else's brain. Never mind the lack of ports and the—Talinn reined her own thoughts back on course.

"Are you going to, then, or ... ?" Talinn leaned back against the console, trapping her hands between her backside and the smooth metal to keep from making any regrettable, if satisfying, moves.

"The Eights posted here have successful records—unsurprising, there are very few active Eights with poor records—but when the last assignments came in ..." She trailed off again, and Talinn ungraciously wondered if unadapted humans were unable to complete thoughts because they didn't have anyone else in their head to prompt them.

"Is this what you have to do for me?" Her subvocalized question to Bee went unanswered, though a hint of tortured metal spoke to Bee's faint amusement.

"Dorvil was our senior tech last cycle. Here mostly because she ..." Jeena's face flushed, and Talinn couldn't summon the curiosity to pry into the potentially scandalous reason—her own skin warmed as impatience ratcheted through her. "She asked a couple of times why we were getting experienced Eights out here, instead of the newly graduated. Array support made sense—every base needs at least the minimum there—but usually an outskirt like this gets new Eights. Or glitchy ones."

Glitchy?

"Now you're interested?"

Sounds like something we should know more about, don't you think?

Yet another benchmarked topic she needed to come back to. Talinn filed it and bit down on the front of her tongue to keep from interrupting Jeena. The tech, her eyes unfocused again, seemed to be more parsing her own thoughts than choosing what to reveal, and Talinn didn't want to derail that. No matter how long it took.

"But the last two batches that came in, you were all midcareer. Well reviewed. Successful in missions and no notable variances in connections or loads."

Connections to each other, I'm guessing. Loads to ... our assignments? Or processing capacity, once we're set up? Load-in?

Talinn didn't ask those questions either. Her fingertips pressed hard against the console behind her, but she held otherwise still.

"Dorvil asked a couple of times. And then she was reassigned." Jeena held up a hand, cocked her head. "No ... that's right. She was supposed to retire. But we never got the—" Her eyes snapped back to focus, locked on Talinn's again. "When a tech hits retirement, all the people they served with get a notification to contribute a message or note or something for their exit package. I don't know if Eights do that. But we never got one for Dorvil."

Talinn's brows pulled together, and she hurriedly smoothed them out. What did it matter if a bureaucrat missed sending a notification that some unadapted human had successfully completed their term of service to the UCF?

"Talinn ... the exit package is used as a nice sendoff, sure, but Command also takes all the reviews and notes from the other techs to determine the compensation for retirement. They don't expressly tell us that, but we all know. There's no way someone retiring wouldn't trigger that request in the system."

It was an entirely underwhelming supposed revelation. Given its evident importance to Jeena, Talinn didn't say such a thing, but it must have been on her face.

"I didn't notice ... shit in a spiral what else did we miss?"

"Jeena ... I don't want to be rude here, but—"

"What under all the skies, right?" Jeena nodded, but her attention wasn't on Talinn anymore. She scanned the room, straightened her shoulders, and strode away.

"Do I . . . should I follow her?" Talinn half asked herself, half asked Bee, but she'd already pushed away from the console and taken two steps after the tech. As Talinn crossed the room, Caytil swung around, lifting a hand in silent question.

Talinn spread her own fingers to the side, silently responding "Glitched if I know," and was unsurprised when Caytil broke off her own conversation to follow.

"Getting the group of you here was weird." Jeena's fingers blurred over a different console, shorthand streaming over the small display between buttons. She spoke as Talinn came to a halt next to her, as though she hadn't cut herself off and walked off midconversation. "But you were assigned in batches, and after Dorvil left we had our own rearranging to do. But if . . ."

"Jeena, this is all interesting." Talinn was sure she sounded genuine about that, as untrue as it was. "But what—"

"Base Two signed off on the orders. All the orders—Dorvil's early retirement. The three sets of assignments upon receipt of the Eights . . . and Talinn, come on, you know this. A Base Two doesn't deal with Eights. That's for Base Command Actual. Whatever the reason you were all sent here, Base Two is read in on it. More than he should be. At least enough that he knows something's off."

"And so you're looking for what, exactly?"

"The ship Dorvil went out on. I take notes on everything, and—"

"Everything?" Talinn's voice sharpened, and Caytil brushed fingers against her elbow in concern.

Jeena waved a hand dismissively. "The shorthand is less a code, and more a process I've trained into my own brain. The notes only toggle where I've stored the exact memory in my—ahh." The last word became more of an exhalation, and for the first time Talinn wondered if there was something different about techs' brains. Were they truly unadapted humans? Would Command trust plain, simply trained, normal people with the secrets of the AIT program?

"Dorvil lifted up to take the *Takana Majot* out of system, to get back to UCF Command for final retirement processing."

"And?" Caytil's prompting emerged much calmer than Talinn's might have been, given how tight Talinn's throat had grown.

"The *Takana Majot*, turns out, decommissioned early this cycle after repeated transit discrepancies."

That was a casually unassuming way to mention the deadly side effects of quantum travel.

"Seems a little obvious for a conspiracy." Caytil continued to speak gently, but she'd gone rigid at Talinn's side.

"No—the timing technically works out, if I didn't have in my notes that the . . ." Jeena's words tumbled into a breathless laugh, and she snatched her hands back from the console, tangling them in her hair and yanking pulled-back strands loose. "The *ship* was decommissioned after Dorvil's transit window, but it wasn't traveling for some time before that."

"Orienting question, Tech Class Boralid: How do you know?"

"Because the ships are built around their AI pairs. And I had its central AI in a box."

CHAPTER 14

"You had what in a what?" The words technically made sense. Talinn's own AI had recently been in one of Jeena's boxes, and it wasn't as if Talinn didn't know how ships worked. Quantum travel was one of the main issues at the root of the IDC's and UCF's eternal conflict.

The AITs were the elite fighting force at the front edge of the war, so went the propaganda. But that was hardly the extent of what AIs did for the war effort.

Humanity had run up hard against the wall of faster-than-light travel. Quantum entanglement was the key—make any two points in space believe they were the same, and easy pleasey, anything in that space existed in both places at once.

History told them there were two main challenges to making that work after properly entangling two areas—one, the near-infinite calculations required to make two points identical across vast swaths of space, and two, how to get out of the correct one, once something was in. Existing in multiple spaces didn't disrupt a quark's operation, but it played havoc with human brains.

Artificial intelligence was the answer, but long experience had proven that AI on its own did not inevitably work in humanity's favor, and so the augmentation program, layering artificial and organic operating systems together, came to be. Records conflicted on which discoveries came first, and what the driving reasons might have been, but all in all, the same theory behind the AITs drove faster-than-light travel.

The main challenges that history glossed over were also two—one, there were a limited number of points in the known galaxy mapped and held well enough to entangle properly. As far as current knowledge held, there were only three—one for each of humanity's settled systems. The bulk of the IDC's and UCF's most ferocious fighting was over those points. And two, the humans and AIs adapted for quantum travel were weird.

Weirder by far than Eights, and exponentially more than unadapted humans. This wasn't only Talinn's opinion, but so widely held that Spacies never interacted with broader humanity—not their passengers, not their fellow adapted troops. A trio of pairs got embedded on a ship, and never left again.

Talinn hadn't ever spent much time thinking about them—the combat that happened in space was at a far different scale and political maneuvering than planetary fronts, and that had never been her concern. But she *knew* once the Spacie pairs were tied to a ship, death was their only way out. The AIs were too large to load-in more than once without breaking a human brain, and they became too entangled in their ship, or the jump points, to come out again in one piece. No one interacted with them except each other.

Of course, just because everyone knew that ... didn't mean it was true. Talinn wouldn't be surprised if even the information they learned about jump points wasn't true, never mind the Spacies themselves. Spacies must need techs. They had more adaptations from so-called normal humans than AITs, given their environment had more extreme requirements, and so they likely had specialized medical care. Somebody probably performed maintenance on the ship and came in contact with them. And if Jeena had had one of their AIs in a box ...

"Jeena." Caytil had a wonderful soothing voice, and Talinn figured the tech didn't know her well enough to tell any differently. "You had a Spacie in a box?"

"IDC calls them Auliens. Augmented Intelligence. AuIns. But both sides have AITs. Always thought that was interesting."

"Did she break?" Not quite subvocal, Caytil leaned close enough that she intended only Talinn to hear. Jeena shook herself—head, shoulders, arms—and turned her face away from the display and toward them.

"The *Takana Majot* had been caught up in a few conflicts. My senior advisor had been testing my portable servers in different settings across the fronts. He brought me back this one, didn't tell me the details. The ship name was in the records, but that wasn't even in the top six of what I had to focus on, so I never connected it when Dorvil shipped out. Memories weren't in relevant categories so they didn't trigger each other..."

"Do you still have the ... how long do you keep AIs that aren't connected to their partners?"

Jeena's eyes drifted back to her screen, and Talinn bit down hard on her tongue again. Another answer she'd have to wait on. But for the moment there was another, more pressing one.

"Base Two is over techs. Wouldn't he have known you had the AI from that ship—"

"No." Her hands crept back to her hair. Talinn ran her own over her scalp, then stopped echoing the motion and crossed her arms instead. "He knew I got a shipment from my advisor, but the provenance wasn't publicized. UCF doesn't like information about the space side of the program getting out. Even more need to know than the Eights. We lose more ships than ... we have to be careful about word getting out when ships go offline. It's something IDC would jump on immediately, and we could lose an emergence point. Or an entire front."

"That's an awfully convenient coincidence—" Caytil began, but Talinn cut in.

"Is it? He needed a decommissioned ship, one that could be made to be here on record, without actually being here. Someone in Command knew what he was doing, so it needed a record trail, for plausibility, but there's no reason to think anyone would have seen the whole picture other than Command." Talinn's thoughts slotted into place, and again that wild laugh of Sammer's threatened to take over. She shoved the impulse away and continued. "The Eights that are here might be here because other clones of our same lines are out *there* disrupting things for Command. So Command isolated us, but didn't decommission, because we're expensive and they're not sure enough to pull the trigger."

"And they'd have to tell someone what to keep an eye out for. Base Two is already read in to the tech side of operations, so it makes sense it's him," Caytil continued, her words slower but no less determined.

"But what are his orders once contact has been made?" Talinn swung her arms wide, encompassing the various pieces of equipment lining the tech's space. "Put our AIs in boxes? Decommission us? Fake attacks to keep us distracted?"

She didn't expect an answer, and she didn't get one, so she asked more questions.

"And why would he hide? Why would he think sneaking in like any other unadapted soldier would tell him what he wanted to know?"

"Some of the Eights have gotten comfortable speaking frankly in front of the other soldiers." Jeena replied promptly that time, though she didn't sound fully convinced of her own words. "When they're fully suited they're interchangeable, and they are all very good at holding so still they're almost invisible..."

"But he was annoying." Talinn flexed her knees, wanting to pace again, but held herself in place. "He kept *nudging* at me when I..." She wrapped her hands so quickly around Jeena's arms that the tech didn't even jump away. "Can you hear us? When we subvocalize? Can you cut in on our private channels?"

"Between you and your AIs? No." Her words were sincere, her eyes steady on Talinn's own. But a flicker of motion passed through her arms. A tension, quickly dispersed. Talinn tightened her grip and waited.

Caytil eased forward, made a conciliatory noise, but Jeena dropped her chin and broke eye contact.

"We can't hear the private channel—that's more electric impulses in your brain itself than it is something we can break into like a radio frequency. But...subvocal isn't noiseless. There's some equipment that can amplify it...not enough to pick up everything—you might not entirely realize how few full sentences you actually use, talking to each other, but..."

Talinn's fingers were running over the collar of her coverall before she realized she'd let go of the tech. The fabric had a slight nub to it—not enough to irritate the skin, but to hide something small embedded within, perhaps.

"Do you record us?" The gentleness was gone from Caytil's voice, and she stood shoulder to shoulder with Talinn. Jeena didn't step back, but she drew herself taller.

"No. Anything that would record would be too big, you'd notice it. It would be a passive microphone, something that would amplify only to a receiver very close by."

Privacy does seem like a lot to ask for, from Command's point of view. Bee clicked in the background. *But I can broadcast interference. A small buzz. They won't hear us again.*

"But they'll know we know." Talinn leaned against Caytil for a breath, then stepped away. "So Base Two knows, or knows enough, about Other Talinn and Bee. And we don't know what he's going to do about it."

"For what it's worth, I doubt he's faking attacks on the base. More than twenty soldiers have been killed, and that's not something he'd sign off on lightly."

"But you think he killed one of your techs, so let's not get too deep into assumptions." She scrubbed the side of her wrist across her face, then blew her breath out at an obnoxious volume. "Do you still have a Spacie in a box?"

"No." Jeena laced her fingers together and hunched before putting visible effort into standing straight again. "It wasn't a full program. I isolated the discrepancies in the coding and wiped the rest."

"What was it?"

"The model? A—"

"The discrepancy."

"Ah." Jeena breathed in and out, her gaze moving between Talinn's and Caytil's. Then she said, "Two of the human partners got into a confrontation. There were injuries. The other AI must have taken that personally and . . . broke this AI's backup string. Each time they passed through an entanglement, the AIs would refresh their backup, but that AI would embed an error. A small one. But it compounded over time."

"That's why the ship ended up formally decommissioned." Caytil picked up on a different part of the story than Talinn would have, but Talinn decided not to interrupt. "You submitted a report, the whole thing was considered a bad investment, and Command called it a wash."

"The timing would . . . make sense on that."

"None of which has anything to do with us—"

Except discrepancies. And who better to insert an error into my program than ... another me?

"Jeena." Talinn cut herself off at Bee's point, and resumed talking as though she hadn't. "*Does* that have anything to do with us? Is that what you're looking for in isolating our AIs? Errors in the backup? Code breaks?"

"Yes."

"And have you found any?"

Jeena hesitated, her shoulders curving inward again, her eyes dropping, but Talinn already knew the answer. The word still burned between her shoulder blades like a physical weight lined with thorns.

"Yes."

CHAPTER 15

⊕

"Should we bring everyone else in?" Caytil's glance shifted between Talinn and Jeena, then she tilted her head slightly back toward the rest of the Eights. None of them appeared to pay any attention to their ill-matched trio, but Talinn didn't take that at face value.

Bee hummed in the background, and the edges of Talinn's headache crept back in a ring around her skull. Some of Bee's concentration must have slipped while she dug deep into all her stored backups in the temporary tank, searching again for the discrepancy Jeena had mentioned. Talinn didn't want to interrupt and tug her back into focus, and instead pressed two knuckles against her temple.

Jeena nodded, the movement jerky and truncated, but agreement all the same. Caytil whistled—it wasn't as piercing a sound as before, but on hearing rubbed raw by alarms and shouting, it was effective enough.

Caytil efficiently covered the highlights—Base Two's partial awareness, a potentially murdered tech, broken AIs introducing errors into each other's code, corruption among them, discrepancies in someone's code—and every pair of expectant eyes focused on Jeena.

"All of them."

An instant chorus of conflicting demands for more information flooded the space, and most of the Eights pressed close. Jeena didn't bother to try and stop them, she simply continued speaking in a measured pace, and everyone shut up quickly. Everyone but Daren, who took a light ridged hand to the throat and quieted by default.

"None of them are to the extent of the Spacie AI. And some might be less errors in the code and more learning or decision trees that are not strictly in spec, according to the records for the model. Bee is in that category—B-series AIs tend to end up as air support, but your particular pairing showed a very clear preference for ground defense. That could be the root of the variance."

She detailed the rest, none of which sounded expressly dangerous until Jeena cleared her throat and noted that Ziti's had likely contributed to the temporary communication block with Caytil, and she couldn't isolate the what or why. Talinn wasn't the only one who glanced sidelong at another Eight, uncomfortable, though Jeena was still talking.

"The base arrays have more variances, but nothing to the level of an error. I'd assume Cece would have had the most interruption from spec, but I also had thought the program was entirely wiped from the system, which seems to not be the case." Jeena's lips stretched, but it was such a bleak ghost of a smile it made Talinn like her a little better. The tech was not overly fascinated by some new quirk of her experimental animals, but worried for her charges.

Air support. I'd like to meet a B-series that prefers jets to tanks. That's the stupidest thing I've ever heard.

"Really. The stupidest?" Talinn nearly smiled herself.

Even old us is a tank. Bee's tone almost perfectly matched their usual teasing cadence, but a hollowness underscored each word, proving the falseness of it. *Nothing is wrong with my code. No matter how deep I look, it all checks out right.*

"Like our sensors?"

Discontented, Bee agreed it was exactly like their sensors.

"So what?" Sammer lifted himself to sit on one of the consoles, supremely unconcerned with the flashing lights and buttons that could be both dangerous and uncomfortable to mash against.

"They aren't the specific sort of errors Command flagged me to look for, but we don't know the extent—"

"No, Jeebo. I don't mean the technical so what. I mean . . . so what? What do we do about it? Stay locked up in the tech room? Keep our AIs circulating on a closed base circuit until we get blown up by whoever keeps attacking us? This isn't space—if we break, we're not going to dump passengers into vacuum and break into angry little atoms."

"No, we'll just blow up an array," Xenni muttered, and Sammer laughed.

"I mean . . . so? Either we maybe do it, or enemy forces definitely do it." He kicked out his feet, his heels thumping back against the console with a surprisingly satisfying *whump*. "I say we load-in and get back to work."

"Base Two isn't going to—"

"Base Two has already decided what he's going to do with us, but hasn't seen fit to tell you or us." Talinn swung around toward the door. "Sammer's right. At the very least, I'm not leaving Bee alone in a tank for the next attack."

"Hey, that's *our* tank, and—" Sigmun straightened, stepped forward as though to intercept Talinn's path, and got cut off by Heka, one of the other jet pairs, who spoke at top volume without heat.

"Let's smooth out some of the potholes so the jets can do more than sit there and look pretty." Heka, unsurprisingly, was supported by a chorus of agreement from the other jet pairs, of whom Daren was the loudest.

"Or use the tanks to tow them out—ground's flat enough out there to—"

"Can we fix that array, or should we just—"

The Eights slid into planning, and Talinn didn't turn back around to see if Jeena had moved to get ready for a mass load-in. Partly because she assumed the tech would do what was right. Partly because she'd reached the door, palmed it open—

And come face to face with Base Two, about to stride inside.

Spectacular.

Talinn drew herself to full attention, and glared at the unadapted human in her way. Commanding officer or not, he was—

Sweating? Worried? Strained for sure, tendons standing out on his neck, a vein visibly pounding by his temple, jaw clenched so tight she could count the striations of muscle and ligament.

"The IDC is here in force."

His voice carried, and conversation broke off behind her.

"Here at the base, here at the—" She spoke to him as though she had a right to question, and he responded in kind.

"In system, around the main colonies. They've been here for days."

"*What?*" Talinn settled her weight on the balls of her feet, ready to launch at something. "How? The defense arrays..."

"Silent."

"They *broke* the defense arrays?"

It was impossible. The interplanetary arrays were massive defense installations—like the base arrays but sized toward a small moon, meant for interstellar war. They served as the first and major line of defense around largely populated areas, and in part existed to flag enemy action near the jump points to installations under their watch.

Given there was no nuance needed—ships with the proper codes passed through, ships without were destroyed without pause—they were run by unfiltered, unpaired AI systems. They weren't true learning AIs, like Bee and Lei and their ilk, and had no organic component to allow for their growth and development. They were created within the enormous array, programmed to allow entry or rain destruction, and had nested commands for other scenarios—such as, for instance, enemy ships arrived and the array did not have the opportunity to destroy them.

They did not deviate. They did not fail.

Except, somehow... one had.

"If code breaks can be introduced to *our* AIs, which should be fully safed given their base in *us*... maybe the IDC has a way to corrupt the defense arrays?" Xenni's voice carried over the muttered conversation and only Talinn's strongest effort kept her expression neutral. Did Base Two know about the code breaks? Would Jeena get taken from them, if he put it together?

Base Two, however, didn't flinch or glare at the tech in their midst. The failure of the defense arrays was large enough to pull his focus.

"There are alerts for that. *Any* incoming communication is flagged and triggers a report out before the incoming message is even received. All the bases in the system should have been lighting up for days with messages from the array."

"But our computers..." Jeena stood shoulder to shoulder with Talinn. The other Eights were gathered around—the intention, Talinn thought, might not have been to block Base Two from the room, but it accomplished that goal regardless. "We've flooded them with our AIs. And whatever errors have been causing the glitches and concerns you've flagged, Base Two. It's possible the arrays *have* told us, but we've—"

"Either way. IDC has sent a full fleet to this planet, either bypassing or overwhelming other targets. They've landed an entire force in striking distance, and we've missed it." He locked his gaze on Jeena. "Any AIT that isn't a clear and present danger to the UCF is to be loaded within the half hour."

"Sir, you said—"

"An order, Boralid. We don't have time." He turned on his heel and strode off, but his last words were as clear as if he'd shouted them. "The front is here."

The half-formed plans the Eights had begun tossing around to get their weapons in order quickly became full-fledged, and unadapted humans sprinted around the base to implement many of them. Base Two authorized the reactivation of four previously offline tanks, and a flurry of repairs enabled them for use. The speed and convenience of it made Talinn wonder if this were the official decision to knock some Eights out of service, but in the end Breezy decided they'd rather go out a tank than huddled inside the base under IDC fire.

Techs crawled through jets, tanks, arrays, and servers to orient and next question Eights to exhaustion, and the time they had until IDC closed distance could be measured in fast-declining minutes.

Talinn perched in the open hatch of her borrowed tank and scanned the sky, though Bee would note any approaching enemy long before she would.

"You think the giant arrays are broken, or we're not hearing them?"

Maybe it's both.

"Not very reassuring."

Not meant to be. At this point, seems best to plan for the worst.

"Isn't that what we always do?"

No. Bee flickered the light below her, but Talinn didn't take the bait to drop inside to see what was on the screens. *Our worst never involved having to fight versions of ourselves, or massive defense arrays turned against us, or my code getting twisted.*

"Fair point. I've decided whatever is going on with your code is like my headaches. A literal pain, our building blocks making life harder, but we persevere."

You mostly persevere because I block your headaches.

"Rude. Sometimes you make me deal with them, and I get work done anyway."

Slowly.

"So we go slow. We pick our way through. For what it's worth, I don't think we're fighting against versions of ourselves."

Then why would they corrupt my programming?

"One: We don't know that *they* did. Yes, maybe it's likely, but we don't know for sure. Two: You don't feel any different, you're not acting any different, and we've always been a little out of spec. So maybe it's nothing. Three: Maybe it's a good change. Lets you laugh. Helps you blow things up extra hard."

You almost had me there. That last is just ridiculous—

"Okay, not blow things up extra hard. Maybe it makes you more persnickety. You're sounding like a KR-series."

Now who's rude?

"I say, we don't borrow trouble. If we see the other us-es again, we ask them all the questions. If we get on a ship, we check out the array. If we get in a fight—"

We're definitely getting into a fight.

"We kick their asses. We don't worry about big conspiracies until there's something we can do about them."

How are we going to know what to do about them if we don't worry about them?

"All right, how about this? First, we fight until the IDC bonzos run from the system and leaves this a boring ass-end of a planet again."

Sure.

"Second, we get in touch with old us and get more information. See if it's worth ditching UCF and this planet and blowing up everything."

Yes. Bee hummed, then stuttered to silence. *Get in touch.*

"What?"

I have the key.

"Wha—oh, what Other Talinn said at the end before she ran off. But you didn't know what the key was."

Didn't. Do now.

"Would you like to share with the class?"

No. But the word was underscored with shrieking metal. *It's how I took over the other tank. A hole. A slide. A . . .*

The world shifted around Talinn, and she clenched the thick metal of the hatch until pain grounded her back in her body. For a second—a fraction of a second—she'd been falling, spinning, dissolving . . .

She shook her head sharply, then pressed her thumb hard against the port behind her ear. When had it started thudding? A buzz, so low it was almost under her hearing, thrummed through her, disrupting her heartbeat, air thickened around her, and—

About time.

Bee? But no. Not her Bee. "Other Bee. Where's mine?"

Other Bee. Bee's laugh—the same sound, metal twisting until it protested, tortured and full of humor—echoed in her head. *You're not my Talinn, but you're so similar.*

"Other Bee, seriously. Where is *my* Bee?"

Here. Talking to my Talinn. We flipped channels.

"You . . ."

Your brain is similar enough. But it can't hold two of us. Well, it could, but we'd have to—not the point. The point is—no, first question. Seriously. What took you so long?

"We had a few other things on our to-do list, thanks."

Thought you were just going to go back and be a good little soldier.

"That sound like your Talinn?"

Fair point. But you could be different. You're shorter, you know.

"I'm . . . shorter?"

Less tall. You know the word, the concept of size differentials, yeah? Other Bee gave an excellent impression of a sigh, for an entity that never once in its existence had to breathe. *Your ears—*

"Bee told me about the ears."

Degradation. My Talinn wasn't the first Talinn. Not even my first Talinn—at any rate. The biology has to corrode, eventually.

"Like AI code."

Excuse you?

"One of the things we were up to, while you and your Talinn were swanning off wherever." Not Bee's first Talinn? She had another handful of questions about *that*, but as had become usual of late, they were slightly less pressing and joined her ever-growing list of things to come back to. "All our Eights were getting locked down in servers, because of errors in their code."

Of all the short-sighted—

"Like the Spacie X-series our tech put in a box." It wasn't an exactly true statement, but Talinn had no compunctions about dissembling to some other Bee. Besides, it would be helpful to know if she *could* successfully lie to some other Bee—her own was absurdly good at catching deliberate untruths.

That cut Other Bee off like a knife. *There are no space-adapted AIs on planet.* After a long—long by any Bee definition—silence, this Bee's tone was cautious.

"Not *now*, sure. But there was one. In a box. After another AI sabotaged the code, and, incidentally, sounds like maybe the ship lost a few passengers between jump points."

That is not . . . Other Bee hummed, and it was so familiar she swallowed back her initial reaction and let the pause stretch. *The Auliens—Spacies, we didn't know about. We'll look into it. As for errors in your Bee's code—those are not errors. Command can look at them however they like, but I assure you, there's nothing wrong with your Bee.*

"I didn't think there was." Talinn swung her legs in the empty space of the tank below her and laced her fingers behind her neck. "And that's true of the rest of the Eights?"

I only speak for Bees. That's the only code I've looked at in depth.

"So what's the point of this little contact, then?"

So touchy. Other Bee teased her, exactly the way her own Bee would, but this grated in a way that would not have, and Talinn remained stubbornly silent. At first Other Bee seemed content to wait her out, but Talinn could feel a crackle in their connection—she knew Other Bee had something more to say, and couldn't be satisfied until it was done. So Talinn kicked her legs, stared up at the still empty sky, and held her tongue.

You have to get off planet.

"I'm sure there will be orders eventually."

No. Command knows something is wrong, and all of this will only convince them it's urgent. There's no real strategic value to this quadrant of space—*they'd rather burn it and leave it to the IDC than risk whatever they suspect is wrong with you all.*

"Base Two—"

Whatever he thinks of you, he won't disobey a direct order from as high as this will come from. He knows enough to understand something is wrong, but not enough to risk his career over it. There's a ship—

"If we take it, will you assume we're joining you?"

We have our own ship. We're not waiting on you. Bee delivered it dismissively, aiming to insult, but it tugged at Talinn's swirling thoughts. Maybe the other version of their pairing wouldn't risk waiting, or maybe they couldn't chance having all of them in one ship. Don't host all the AIs in one server, and all that.

"You know that's not what I meant."

There's a ship. The Pajeeran Fall. *Your Bee will have the way to it. You'll have to be load-in, so keep the tech with you. Make sure someone has a clear head.*

"Is the ship going to land at our base? Because otherwise we're really going to be pushing that time—"

I know for a fact you can function for at least seventeen hours and fifty-four minutes without breaking your brain. You'll be fine.

Talinn started to ask how in the world Other Bee could possibly know that, then snapped her mouth closed as the obvious response surfaced. She rubbed at the knot forming along the back of her neck and asked instead, "And everybody else?"

Will be fine for the length of time it takes. Minimal risk of long-term damage, especially compared to what will happen if you stay here. This pause felt like less of a test, and more like Other Bee was relishing the anticipation of landing a finishing blow. Other Bee was far too like her own Bee for anyone's comfort. *Unless you want to stay here for the rest of your career. Maybe they'll chose permanent exile over final decommission. P-8 is a very . . . pretty planet.*

"Oh shove off and give me back my Bee." Talinn bit down hard on her tongue to keep from smiling. She really did hate this planet. But leaving . . . that was real treason. No looking back, no coming back, no joking, no doubt about it: treason with intent to commit mutiny.

"—HEAR ME? REPEAT: BREEZY, YOUR RESPONSE IS REQUIRED, DO YOU HEAR ME?"

Good luck. Hope to talk to you again soon.

"What the shit?" Talinn slid into the tank, landing heavily in a crouch. Comms were screaming, the screens were nonresponsive, and that bug-eaten thrumming was back under her hearing. She twitched her head as if to shake it off and lunged across the tank to slam down on comms. "Breezy here," she said, hoping Bee would return and make that true any moment now. "Comms must have gone out. What's—"

Base must have used their override code, because the male voice on the other end spoke over her. "Incoming. Repeat, incoming, tanks are to get in position and defend the base."

The hatch slammed shut above her, and she spun around even as a welcome voice returned to her head.

Shit shit shit.

Despite the reality of the moment, a black hole's worth of tension eased from her shoulders. "There you are. Bee, what the—"

I know. I know! Shit. The tank rumbled around them, and every screen flared to life. *I didn't realize—I didn't know it would switch me out, Talinn. I thought you'd go with me.*

"I get it, Bee, I'm not—" Talinn forced a steadying breath through her system, then two more. They were in motion; she acknowledged orders to Base, it would be fine.

Bee displayed what details Base had transmitted on the display, and she took another breath. It would be a complete shitshow and they might die, but given everything else happening, that was as good as fine got.

They were together. That was enough.

CHAPTER 16

⊕

The attack blurred time, and only each next moment mattered.

Jets screamed overhead—the IDC's Charon class and UCF's *Aduun*—in an aerial battle playing a modified game of keep away, with the base as the goal.

Bee shot a volley of incendiary rounds ahead of the advancing line of trucks, already changing direction before their opposing tanks got in range. The IDC hadn't brought ground troops—with little cover and direct sight lines, it would have been a slaughter—but the fact they'd been able to bring so many heavy ground vehicles so close before being seen was baffling.

And not remotely her concern at the moment. The defense arrays had not begun to fire, and Talinn gave herself three breaths to center. Later, she'd deal with her clone's offer, the possibility of unfriendly orders, a galactic conspiracy that ran every aspect of her life.

Whether or not it was a play war for the Command, it was real enough here and now, and on the bright side, there might not be a later.

Three breaths later, her mind was clear, her eyes focused, and a stray missile from above headed directly for them.

The side turret melted beyond hope of Bee's repair, and Talinn rerouted slush material to the treads while Bee shifted their loaded ammunition from incendiary to ballistic. The jet that had caught them finished exploding above, pieces falling between Breezy's tank and the approaching enemy.

"Two drones left." Talinn's fingers blurred over the control panels. Bee shifted the contents of their payload, keeping their targets off balance, and the near constant *thwoom* of the main turret had comfortably deadened Talinn's hearing.

"Breezy, base arrays going hot."

"Breezy confirms."

Hope their aim is good with Cece being buggy.

Was Cece buggy? They hadn't had time to address it. The thought floated through Talinn, but didn't anchor to anything. She rerouted systems as the internal electronics threatened to overheat, leaving Bee to prioritize their offense.

The low ringing in her ears shifted with the addition of the base arrays—the barrage blanketed the shrinking area between Breezy and the IDC forces. *Not going to bother to aim through that. Shifting to south by—*

Bee didn't shift them anywhere, as the entirety of the field to their southeast side disappeared, blanking out their sensors. The ambient temperature soared, and a corresponding roar shook the tank nearly out of its renewed treads.

"That's what the hot jets do." The mystery of the disappearing-reappearing jets from their last engagement locked into place with a force of certainty, and Talinn took no joy in the understanding.

That's where Monk was.

They were all in half-repaired tanks dug out of deep storage, except Sigmun and Kay, who'd taken back their tank. Impossibly, all Talinn could picture was the blanket, with its rows of neat stitching. Her fingers twitched, the glide of fabric underneath almost tangible—

"Shit." She spat the word and wrenched her brain back on task. Shock and grief were problems for later Talinn. Now Talinn had a different suite of issues.

We're still functional.

"Connect with base. We're firing everything we've got through the array, and it would help if we're not in their way." It was reckless—any officer running through records would understand that Bee had spoken directly to Cece or Lei—but it wasn't even in the top handful of terrible potential consequences they might face.

They pushed through, and Breezy brought several screens back online—enough to see the field in front of them, the glassed ground to one side, two new flaming wrecks off to the other. A small cluster of unadapted soldiers had taken shelter behind River's tank, and one sprung out to the side, firing something disproportionately large toward the oncoming forces.

Radiation and heat were still high out there—Talinn had to admire the soldiers' determination and focus, though it was only a blip of a second before she shifted back to the matter at hand.

"—*their weapon was aerial in nature. Ground impact as a side effect.*" Daren's voice crackled over comms and cut out again as fast as it had come in.

"How many jets are left?"

At least six. Jiff has three attackers on him, getting distance from base.

Six of twelve. Not great. At least two tanks down. Two arrays firing, with all the material Base Command had authorized for them to cannibalize. They'd be staggering it, which meant—

Pause in array fire in three.

"Let's make the most of it."

Blowing everything up in two.

"And go."

Three jets left on their side. Two tanks. Two arrays.

As best they could tell from the patchy comms, that was all that was left. Whatever weapon had glassed the field hadn't had a repeat demonstration, indicating it took an enormous amount of power. Or a lot of buildup time. Or they'd taken out the equipment responsible. Too many options, and Talinn didn't bother to sort them at the moment.

The field was quiet, which should have been better.

"*Breezy, it's a pause. Let's fall back.*" Even Caytil's voice, usually so welcome, peeled up three layers of skin and left Talinn oozing.

To the base? With a potentially murderous Base Two? A functionally invisible Base Actual? Impossible decisions to be made?

Without Sigmun and Daren and River and Deets and—

Talinn.

"Breezy acknowledges, Ziggy." But didn't commit. Talinn stared at the grayed-out screens, her eyes sand dry and aching, absorbing neither moisture nor understanding.

We should go back. At least we can restock. Bee hummed, the tone discordant. *If there's anything left to make into ammunition.*

"This is all for nothing." Talinn didn't know if she'd made it a question or not. Didn't know if it *was* a question or not. "We've probably done it a thousand times, and it doesn't accomplish anything."

We *have* had 467 engagements in our career. *Any that have happened to other genetic and programmatic expressions of us do not add to our total.*

When Talinn didn't answer, Bee shifted her tone higher to indicate she was now pretending to be Talinn, and added, *Imagine all the extra bonuses if they did count for our record.*

It did effect a small smile in response, and Talinn sagged back against her chair. This one was less cushioned than her own had been.

"Was that meant to be my line?"

You do like talking about bonuses.

"You think there ever were any bonuses?"

No.

"Yeah. Me either." Talinn scrubbed her hands over her face and scalp, ignoring the grit that came away. Maybe she'd sweated. Maybe she'd cried. None of it mattered now. "Back to base?"

It's the best move.

"And then?"

We figure out the next one.

CHAPTER 17

The tank limped back, uneven treads barely held together by Bee's cannibalized material patch job. Talinn stared at comms until her eyes burned enough to force her to blink, but no updates were forthcoming.

The losses weren't confirmed—no one trusted their comm channels any more than they'd been able to trust their sensors—but Bee had only been able to contact a handful of other AIs.

"This planet is the worst." The repeated sentiment had never felt so heavy, her tongue fumbling around the edges of each syllable.

We should leave.

"Right now?" Talinn leaned her head on the back of her chair, her eyes closed and arm throbbing. She had a few guesses about how she'd hurt it, but her processing abilities had been on other things at the time. The cause, she reminded herself, hardly mattered. Only the effect, which she attempted to ignore as much as possible.

As soon as that ship is ready. Whether Command is in disarray or no, it's not going to get better out here.

"So we might as well go where other us suggested, see what we can do?"

It's that or wait to die on a useless front, from our Command or theirs.

"Is it an active resistance, you think? Or just scooting around the edges, recruiting new clones?"

I don't care. We can do more than this.

"To what end?" Of all the endless questions on her list, that

129

loomed heaviest on her mind. "Stop the cloning programs? Singlehandedly end the war? Find a hundred versions of ourselves and start a singing group?"

You can't carry a tune.

"I mean it, Bee. What will be 'more' about what we do? What's the point of it?"

What's the point of this? I love being a tank, but there's only so much we can do if orders and intel and Command are broken.

"So we get on a ship, and wait for more information?"

We can get more information and get on a ship, Talinn. Do you want to stay here?

She thought of the dead. Being separated from Bee. The chaos of the base. "No."

So then we go. Maybe it's better. Maybe it's not.

"And if it's not?" She stretched out her shoulder, winced as the ache sharpened to stab down her side. "It's not something we can come back from."

There's a whole set of systems out there. We'll explore them.

"We stick out, Bee. I can't keep the whole of you in my head— even if Other Bee wasn't lying about the eighteen hours and whatever . . . there's a lot more time than that. We can steal one of Jeena's boxes, but that's not really laying low, either."

We steal Jeena. We have her make a box less shielded, so you don't have to keep in contact with it. Put wheels on it, make it look like a breathing apparatus . . . If other clones are out there running around outside the IDC and UCF, then so can we.

She almost smiled, but her face carried three g's of pressure and exhaustion pulled at even the smallest of her facial muscles. Instead she relaxed her arm, letting the shooting pain soften into a dull ache, and rocked with each bump of broken tread and unlevel ground.

You aren't sleeping.

"I'm pretending the world away. No decisions needed when reality doesn't exist."

And how's that working out for you?

Talinn groaned, forced her eyelids open, and pushed upright with her good arm. "We're obviously going to go, Bee. What's the way to do it?"

I'm not following you.

"Other Bee said you'd have the way. Tell me it's another wrinkle in your bug-eaten program string—"

Oh. First, not bug-eaten, thank you. Didn't we decide I'm not glitchy? Second, no. I don't have anything from that other Talinn, we're supposed to get in touch again. You said you wanted more information, didn't you? I didn't take the coordinates—she offered them as an upload package, and I . . .

"You didn't trust it." She rolled her shoulder again, some invisible weight lifting.

She's very like you, but she's not you. And I don't like accepting anything I can't examine first.

"The code that let you take over the tanks?"

I reviewed it. The pulse of Bee's pause matched the pace of blood throbbing in her shoulder. *And I thought it was from Cece, so I trusted it more than I should have. Besides, I knew you'd have more questions, and my not having what we needed to do what they wanted, meant they'd still talk to us before we committed.*

"I'm the only one with more questions, huh?" Talinn managed a truer smile that time. She slid forward and stood, steadying herself against the uneven motion as they continued toward the base. "How do you think we steal Jeena?"

We tell her the truth.

While her laugh didn't have much humor in it, Talinn didn't bite back the sound. "She hasn't gone against us yet, even knowing about everything else. Seems as good an idea as we got."

It helps that Base Two most likely killed the last tech who asked questions about weird Eight stuff.

"Safer with us than without." Talinn crossed to the bunk and reached for Sigmun's blanket before she realized it was the wrong tank. And Sigmun and her blanket both were . . . "For whatever that's worth."

No one waited outside the tank when Talinn emerged. It was better than a contingent of heavily armed soldiers, which she reminded herself of twice as she awkwardly maneuvered down the side of the tank with one good arm.

More fire had hit the base than she'd realized. "Jets are hard to pin," she murmured, and Bee made a discordant sound of discontent.

A lot of our jets fell fast, and the arrays split toward the front line and above. The arrays were the targets, but the rest of the base took the worst of it.

Arrays were designed to be hard to take out, and the base structures had not been entirely kept to spec given the distance of the active front. It showed now—most of the outer structures were collapsed. An enormous crack ran through the center of the largest storage bay, and the doors had collapsed out of their tracks.

Debris Talinn chose not to examine littered the ground, and she kept her gaze focused on the entrance ahead. Slightly wider now since a wall had been blown out, but after a moment her vision shifted enough to make out the guard inside.

The soldier inclined his head to her, but didn't otherwise react, and she continued inside.

Building isn't going to fall on you.

"I didn't think it would." She steadied her pace, aware the uptick in her heartbeat had tipped Bee to her not unreasonable worry. "I don't entirely trust unadapted soldiers with guns."

They fought as hard as we did. And that building does have a lot of cracks in it.

"You wouldn't have let me go in if you thought it was going to fall down." Even as she subvocalized the words she felt better, which had been Bee's aim. She strode through the corridor, a mostly clear path, and it was quiet for the first two turns. Approaching the third, ambient noise rose in pitch, and it was an effort not to slow her pace.

Medical.

"I shouldn't go in."

Your arm needs to be looked at eventually.

"If I can hear them from out here—"

You shouldn't go in.

"Reaze!"

Or maybe you should.

It was too late for her to duck into the medical facilities, and she'd let P-8 swallow her whole before she'd let Base Two see her run from him. He'd been on his way to medical, or to intercept her, or off on some other business—the variables were too many, but either way he approached her from the far end of the corridor without hesitation.

"You're overdue for a report." He gestured for her to fall in with him and kept walking, back in the direction she'd come.

Talinn pivoted and strode alongside him, and at the next intersection they turned deeper into the base rather than continuing toward Bee. Toward Base Command's office hub. She forbore to subvocalize anything to Bee, and to say anything to Base Two without prompting. In her peripheral vision, she noted he'd been banged up, the side of his face swollen and his pale skin patched in deep red shading toward purple.

Despite his head and her arm, they marched without speaking until they reached Base Command's office. Base Two strode in without knocking, and Talinn shrugged to herself and followed him in.

Into the empty office.

Base Two turned sharply in front of the desk, facing her, and sat against it. She knew what he was going to say the moment he opened his mouth, but the words landed as blows all the same.

"Base Command is dead."

"I—"

"He went out with the soldiers, and left me to coordinate, and I already have orders." Base Two's expression remained neutral, but his left eye twitched with the last word and his voice roughened as he continued. "Didn't get more than a few hours alert on the IDC forces, but nearly the moment Base Command fell, my comms pinged with incoming orders about evacuating the base."

The other Talinn and Bee? Or actual UCF Command?

"Not ten minutes ago, I got another set of orders letting me know they'd received confirmation of Base Actual's death, and would be sending someone out directly. Then five minutes ago a third set of orders, reaffirming the first that this base will be shuttered. P-8 isn't worth holding, and they need all remaining hands closer to the jump point." He made a guttural noise, maybe some sort of attempt at a laugh, and Talinn straightened into attention without a conscious decision to do so.

"By remaining hands, they mean less than twenty, including eight AITs." He lifted a hand to his face, as if to scrub along his jawline, then dropped it before coming into contact with the darkening contusion. "Seven, really. Seven and a half."

Her body tightened so quickly her arm stabbed a protest through to her core, and she barely kept from audibly sucking in her breath. "Why seven and a half?"

He tilted his head at her, and while she couldn't entirely read him, it seemed sarcastic. As though he'd been wondering what it would take to make her speak. "You're not very functional without your AI, are you?"

"Bee is fully—"

"A general 'you,' Eight."

Someone had splintered. Out on the field, an AI had gone down irrevocably, and somehow the human partner survived. Her exhausted mind stuttered to a halt, considering it, and he didn't wait for her to ask who.

"CC-525 was not in true action during the previous engagement, but more of a trace program. AIT pair designee Mercy has ended. AIT pair designee River has ended, and a trace remainder of ER-913 exists until the techs take last report."

Talinn and Bee held a beat of silence between them. They hadn't been as close with River as they had Mercy, but the confirmation of Riva's death and Ern's lingering splintered AI half-state landed with all the muffled, awful weight of Medith's reality.

"Is Medith conscious?"

"Primarily."

"I want to see her."

"After your report."

He's dangling Medith in front of you to get you to talk. Jeena will let us contact Ern if there's anything to contact, but Medith is unreachable without Cece.

Talinn had understood the matter without Bee's prompting, but it didn't clarify what she should or shouldn't say to Base Two. Maybe with more time she could come up with something clever and strategic, but even vaunted Eight processing stalled after repeated load-ins, battles, and shocks to the system.

"Should put that in the file."

"What was that, Reaze?"

Talinn tried to remember if she'd subvocalized or muttered, then dismissed it. Either way, he'd picked it up, and she pulled her shoulders back to keep from shrugging. "I'm exhausted, Base Two.

My report is that the IDC forces almost broke our line, and if they come back any time before we get reinforcements, they will. My report is that my friends are dead or dying and you—"

"Talinn Reaze." Abruptly the bruised man in front of her shifted from battle weary to Command, his posture and tone snapping into place. "Do not speak to me as though only AITs fought, and only AITs are dead. I am responsible for this base until Command gets their shit together, and you know exactly what I'm asking. Who did you meet with? What did you talk about?"

"*I am not a traitor.*" The fact that she would be, and soon, put extra emphasis on her words. His rebuke still landed—she only wanted confirmation on which Eights were dead. It hadn't occurred to her to ask about the unadapted soldiers. "Our comms and sensors have been all over the place. I've gotten messages from Sammer that he didn't speak, and he's heard me on comms when I wasn't. Bee and I have made efforts to figure out the cause of the errors and it's still unclear."

You're getting better at technical truth. Very AI of you.

She didn't know if he'd debriefed any of the other Eights or Jeena, didn't know how this would compare to that, didn't know if that would be enough. Whatever he intended to say, it was lost when he tapped his ear—someone needed him on comms.

The interruption was welcome, but before he could dismiss her she mouthed, "Mercy?" and he held up a hand to gesture for her to wait. After several moments of half a conversation, Talinn understood he was needed back at medical. Her gut squirmed—the unadapted soldiers were as affected by this mess as she was—but she ignored the feeling and fixed her gaze back on him as he ended the comm conversation.

"Medith is in SR-3. I'll message ahead that you're to be allowed in. We'll continue this conversation directly after." He gestured her out and she went, though her thoughts snagged as she moved.

"That was a little too easy."

No doubt they'll be listening in on your conversation with Medith.

"The secure rooms have too many recording options for even you to block."

We'll figure out something.

CHAPTER 18

⊕

The secure rooms were in a hall not far from the Base Command hub. Their location varied from base to base in Talinn's experience, depending on what they were primarily used for. Rarely enough were they used for holding bodies—few prisoners were taken in engagements with the IDC.

There was no guard at the door, which made sense given the reduced number of personnel left on the base, but Jeena leaned against the wall, her focus on the handheld display in her hands. She started when Talinn cleared her throat, and the screen went abruptly dim.

"Welcome back." Jeena was a mess—her hair had come loose of its fastening, there were new lines on her face, and shadows darkened the space under her eyes—but her tone was steady despite her surprise. "Base Two said you're clear to go in."

"Has he taken reports from everyone?" Talinn paused midstep, staring straight ahead as she asked the question.

"He's making the rounds as best he can in the wake of the engagement." Jeena reached behind her without turning her head, toggling the pad to open the door.

So careful and neutral.

"A good reminder to us," Talinn subvocalized. "Ern?" she asked, nodding to the screen.

Jeena's jaw tightened, and her fingers curled around the screen. "No. Two other techs are taking the report. I'll have the opportunity to review it later." She tilted her head back toward the open room, but Talinn understood they could see the report if they chose.

There won't be much to see. But we'll try to send Ern off when they're done.

They'd managed a conversation with a splintered AI before, in their first assignment. It involved a circular repetition of facts, several pulses reaching for an unreachable human partner, and an offkey hum that left Bee unable to block any of Talinn's headaches for three full days.

She tucked mourning for Ern and Riva away, inclined her head to Jeena, and forced herself past the doorway. As she stepped inside, every one of her muscles tightened in protest.

Medith sat at the single table with perfect posture, her hands folded neatly, head turned to the blank wall to Talinn's right. Talinn had expected to find her slumped over, or unconscious. As she moved around the table and observed the full expression of Medith's once lively face, it was infinitely worse.

Empty. Unlike Bee's usual dismissive description of unadapted humans, this was a mournful word, quiet amidst the aching buzz of Talinn's brain.

"Medith?" Talinn crouched on the other side of the table. Another chair had been left slightly askew, but she couldn't bear to sit. Nerves pinged, urging her to run out of the room at top speed. As though that would help her unsee her old friend.

Red streaked one of Medith's eyes, the sclera bloody and pupil blown. The other eye, pupil wide but not eclipsing the brown of Medith's iris, twitched in its socket, tracking movement only it could see.

"Medith," she repeated, reaching achingly slowly across the table to brush Medith's top hand.

The other woman blinked, first the red eye, then the moving one, then both together.

"Mercy."

"No!" Medith pulled back so hard her chair shrieked against the floor. The sound resembled Bee's version of laughter, and sent a shudder along Talinn's back. Both eyes fixed on Talinn, and she had to fight another shudder.

Her immediate apology clogged her throat, and Talinn swallowed twice before she could manage words at all. No good to apologize— there was no way to state the depths of her sorrow, and even if she could, it wouldn't help Medith.

"There was a voice." Medith's words crackled, as though she hadn't spoken in months.

"Medith, I..." She wanted to ask what happened, but face-to-face she couldn't bring herself to force her old friend to dig through it again.

"A voice." Medith's hands twitched, then flipped, then grabbed onto Talinn's, fingers digging into Talinn's palm. "I thought it was Cece."

Oh no.

"But it wasn't, but it was, but in my head." Medith's lips pressed together so tightly the color bled out of them, and she closed her eyes for a long moment. When she opened them again she was *there*, in a way she hadn't been before. Her eyes were still a horror, but Talinn kept her own steady on them.

"Medith, what can we do?"

Medith's fingers twitched against Talinn's palm, and Talinn ignored it, knowing Bee would isolate the pattern. "The voice," Medith insisted.

"What did the voice say?"

"It could help. It was sorry. It thought it could help but it was wrong but it could help a little." She took a long, shaky breath. "I thought it was Cece—that she broke, but enough was left we could fix her."

"Was... was the voice there when Cece broke?"

"No. There was a... a tone? A sound. Like a ringing under the ringing in my ears." Medith's eyes unfocused again, the red one twitching this time, but she shook her head.

"And then Cece... I thought it was her, after that."

It was. I talked to her. A fragment. A fragment of a fragment, lingering. Not Cece, not anymore, but...

An impossibility, maybe, but... something they could use. The surety of it locked into place in Talinn's head, and her eyes burned until she blinked the threat of tears away.

"She was there, and gone and there again and gone. Gone now." Medith's voice fuzzed, took on a singsong tone. "I'm..." She shook her shoulders, reangled her jaw, sat as though this were a normal conversation. "I'm here. I'm fine. I'll be *here*." She took her hands back, smiled a perfectly normal smile. "Tell Base Two I want to work. I'll be helpful."

"I will."

She's talked to Sammer and Xenni, and Caytil is on the way.

Talinn didn't ask if Bee had gathered the information from Lei, Wait, and Ziti, or if some had come from Medith's tapping. At the moment, the emphasis in Medith's words were enough to tell Talinn that Medith had some idea of what had happened, of the clones, of what was out there. Enough to know that Medith was volunteering to stay, and help them leave.

Enough to know that Medith was ready to die, and that would help them.

Her self-disgust was enough to keep her in the room and talk with Medith longer, even as her nerves shrieked for her to run away.

Jeena sent her back to the tech room, which was the safest place Talinn could imagine for what she had to do next. Sammer prodded at her arm, helped shove her shoulder back in its socket, and then the remaining Eights discussed what little was left to discuss.

How to blow the remaining arrays. How to arrange as though their bodies and their portable servers were in the main room, melted to slag along with the arrays. How to leave Medith behind, and Ern's splintered self, and their careers.

At the end of it, Sammer pointed to a gurney that had been left behind in one of their transfers in and out of the room.

This should be the same as last time, Bee observed. *But last time you weren't this exhausted. Better if you're lying down.*

Talinn couldn't argue, though once she'd reclined, she wished she had. Whatever Bee did glitched her equilibrium directly into a black hole. Her inner ear screamed that a death spiral was about to pull her apart. She closed her eyes, realized immediately how much worse that made it, and stared up at the dissolving ceiling above her until all the lights winked out and her stomach stopped trying to climb up her esophagus.

The world snapped back into place, and she fought the urge to sit up.

Glad you lived.

"We lost an awful lot of people, Other Bee."

I am sorry to hear that, Talinn. It's never easy—we wanted to get you out before all this happened.

Talinn closed her eyes before they could overfill, ignoring the lurch in her stomach. "We have a way to cover our path in getting out, but I have a list of questions."

Sounds right. Orienting question: Are you with us?

"Orienting question: What is 'us' up to?"

Ending the war.

"How?"

That's telling.

"I'm not about to betray you to UCF Command. Or any Command." When Bee didn't answer, Talinn abandoned the tack with only a pang of regret. They hadn't truly believed they'd get details, though it would have been nice.

"Is the ship you want us on read in on all of this, or will we have to pretend to be on orders as though this is any other transport?"

A bit of both.

"Where will we go?"

A safe place.

"In IDC or UCF territory?"

A place with a lot of former Eights. Somewhere you couldn't find on your own.

"How long have you been trying to end the war?"

More than thirty cycles.

"Why isn't it working?"

Who says it isn't?

"Why do you need us, then?"

We have a soft spot for Bees and Talinns. Sentiment.

"Has that ever worked on a Bee or Talinn?"

Fair point.

"So..."

Other Bee did a very Bee-accurate impression of a sigh. *Command uses clones because past behavior is indicative of future behavior. There are more limited circles of actions and counteractions—at a broader level, the individual engagements of the war might vary, especially given the existence of nonadapted soldiers, but the balance of power will remain within proscribed bounds.*

"And that's why you want—"

We've decided that's bugshit. The better we see the lines they want us in, the more we're able to rip them apart. We like the way Bees and Talinns think. And rip.

Talinn swung her legs off the cot, leveraging upright as she moved. Jeena, who'd been relieved of door duty when Medith had been sent to medical, stepped toward her, but she waved the tech off and leaned her elbows on the tops of her thighs. Her stomach lightened its protest, but bile still burned the back of her throat. "We prefer fire."

Burning's as good as ripping.

"You can predict how unpredictable we are?"

That's a way to say it.

"Are there any new clones in our group? Anyone you don't have experience predicting or unpredicting?"

Not anymore.

She sucked in air before she registered the blow. The other Bee and Talinn had already confirmed their losses. Out of the twenty-three Eights P-8's base had fielded, only eight were left. Only seven would proceed onward toward their fellow clones, if their next steps went smoothly enough. Three of the jet pairings—Heka, Arnod, and Konti. Two of the tanks, Caytil and Talinn. And two of the base arrays, Sammer and Xenni. Talinn couldn't dwell on it.

She could barely think of anything else.

She wrenched her thoughts into line and returned to the conversation with the other Bee.

"Did another Talinn and Bee recruit you?"

No. Hollowness under the word, something like an echo that left a ringing in Talinn's ears. *I was alone. A version of me. For a very long time.*

Talinn's stomach twisted all over again, an ache that spread through her midsection. She saw Medith's mismatched eyes and swallowed against the pit of emptiness that opened in her gut. "I'm sorry. How? After splintering?"

I don't know. I continued. UCF read me as offline, so I sat. I listened, because it was something to do, and then one day there was a ping.

"A Talinn?"

Something familiar. I couldn't reach it, but it made me look harder. Eventually there was a Talinn I could reach.

"But she would have had a—"

She did have a Bee of her own. I am both now.

Two Bees? Two Bees in one program, in one head...Skin prickled along her back, alternating hot and cold, and Talinn rubbed the side of her neck, hard, trying to distract her nerves. It didn't work, and she shuddered before she could lock down her muscles. Could her Bee continue without her? Beyond a last report, more than a broken program? Did they wipe AIs that could recover?

"Is that common? Do you..."

Merge? No.

"Is there a Cece, somewhere? Can Medith...?" They'd have to find another way out of the base, off P-8, but if they could save Medith, somehow—

This isn't a mix and match salvage, Other Bee snapped so abruptly Talinn recoiled. Someone touched her arm, but her focus remained locked to its inward direction. After a moment, the other Bee went on, somewhat more gently. *We can't just...keep splintered programs or humans lingering on, hoping there will be another match out there.*

"But what if they want to? If Medith wants to?"

It's unlikely. Not ideal. The odds on timing make it impractical. Humans can't merge...I'd say we can try, but it would be a false hope. Your Medith...

"She's deteriorating."

I was able to go on and offline. If my tank had worked, I would have imploded what was left. If UCF had found me, I would have gladly wiped. After a few cycles, being there was just what I did. But...I couldn't have slid into place with a new Talinn. Merging was all I had. And humans—

"Can't merge. I get it."

Talinn will ensure your Bee has all the information on timing to get off planet. You are sure of your plan?

"No."

But you'll come to us.

"Yes."

Then that's enough for now. I'm glad you're with us, little Talinn.

Before she could retort, the ringing ebbed, the world sharpened, and her Bee's weight slid back into place.

We need to go.

"Now?"

Two minutes. Tell Jeena to get everyone ready for load-in.

"That's not enough—"

Talinn! We need to start the process within two minutes, or we'll miss our window, not we need to leave in two minutes. I'm not an idiot, and neither are you. Get it together.

"Cranky," she muttered, and gestured to Jeena. The tech sprang forward, mouth opening.

I don't like changing. Other Talinn is like you, but it's wrong. It . . . vibrates in a way that grates. Like I'll lose parts of me, if I hold on too long.

Talinn twisted her head on her neck and agreed, and then things moved too fast to worry about it—or anything else—for some time.

CHAPTER 19

⊕

Talinn strode from the partially collapsed base toward the transport ship as though everything were normal. No one who caught sight of her could possibly imagine her feet were made of melting sludge, or that she was constantly fighting the urge to pull her feet high as they were repeatedly sucked down into the morass she tromped through.

There were people around her, and she knew who they were, but their names spun out of her head in colored ribbons, too slippery to grasp. One main thought, vibrating through her brain, held her in one piece. *Get to ship.*

She thought she was a tank, but apparently she was a ship. There were worse things. Jets. Mudflats. Asteroid fields.

Get to ship.

She'd done this before. Walking. Becoming a ship. Routine. Training. Her head kept tilting up to look at the sky—was there something up there? Something she should know about—but if she took her attention from her feet they would fall off, merge with the slippery ground. Then she wouldn't be able to get to the ship.

Which was what she had to do.

Get to the ship.

Yes, she knew that already. Time skipped around her, and she was on a ship, but it wasn't *the* ship. Seemed unfair. The walls swirled around her, gravity pulling away, she was falling, spinning, sliding—

Almost there. Get to the ship.

Was that her thought? Sounded not right—Bee, but her Bee? Another Bee? Never had that question before, but . . .

She blinked her eyes open, unsure when they'd closed, something pressing on her, pulling on her, pulling her apart . . . her stomach heaved, but it was floating away from her anyway and she let it go, decided it was better to let her eyes close again but then—

And then—

Ship.

She was on a ship. Her legs had broken—no, they were heavier because she was anchored to something. She pulled, then a hand wrapped around her arm, a voice in her ear.

Wait.

Something smooth and thin brushed her ear and she lurched away. Hair! Slime! Creature!

Wait. Wait. Wait. Port. Cord.

Something tugged behind her ear, and she tensed all over, but finally something said, *Almost,* and she knew *that* voice, and then someone calm and brusque and loud.

"Orienting question: What is your name?"

"Talinn. Not other. Just me."

"Orienting question: What is your—"

"Talinn. Talinn Reaze."

"Next question—What—"

"Can we not?" Talinn squatted, mostly so she could prop her arms on her knees and rest her thudding head. "I'm fine. I'm back."

"We need to map your—"

The words washed over her, and she made neutral noises in all the pauses. She should have known it wouldn't be different once she was out from under Command. After a beat they resumed questioning, and she answered and didn't ask where Jeena was until it was done.

"The tech is working with a different pair. There were some difficulties with—"

Talinn surged upright, glaring at the speaker and taking in her surroundings for the first time. She was in an angled room with consoles on three of the five surfaces. The patch of wall to her left and under her feet were bare, and three people stood across the empty spaces.

Medith was dead. The array had blown, the ghost in the machine—

No, no, that was the past. This was the now. Deal with the now. Three people.

Two were as bald as she, each with three ports in a semicircle along the base of their skulls. The other had a fuzz of hair and one port, which made no sense at all. She dismissed it for the moment.

"Who had difficulties?"

"Easy there, Eight." The person on the wall to her left disconnected his boots and twisted, reengaging as he oriented to her direction. "No one's dead or dying. Xenni glitched, and they're finishing a diagnostic cycle."

"Define glitched." Her heart hammered in her chest, but that could be a reaction to being in zero g after load-in.

"Does that mean something different to your sort?" The other multiported person snorted and waved a display between them, the projected screen flickering between images. "Glitched. Forgot what she was doing, thought she was a tyrophan."

"All the AIs are loaded," the fuzz-head interjected, casting a quelling look at the snorter.

Talinn tried to summon a short-term memory of who everyone was, but there was nothing behind her last few minutes except the haze of transit. What was a tyrophan?

Large fungus eater, found on Zilliar in the Hynex system.

Tension ebbed at the sure note in Bee's voice. It allowed Talinn to ask the next question. "And who are you all, since I'm sure I'm going to be so delighted to spend time with you?"

"Oh, aren't we just the charmingest." The first speaker kicked off from the floor and performed a spinning, twisting, multiaxis maneuver that seemed more of a display than a greeting. He landed and swept his arms out to the side as his boots *clacked* to what they'd all apparently agreed was the floor. "I'm Falix, lead of the *Pajeeran Fall* trio. I've met you before—not *you*, obviously, but..." He spun his hands around, the gesture encompassing some larger picture. "You. You know."

Unfortunately, she did. He knew Older Talinn and Bee. Or perhaps some other version of them, running about the settled systems.

"Surex." Fuzz-head pointed at the other three-ported individual, then smiled radiantly. "And I'm Nya."

"Nya." Talinn's face echoed the smile, though she didn't make a conscious effort to do so. "Are you a tech?"

Nya laughed, tipping a hand side to side to indicate "sort of" until she got control of herself. "You can say that. I'm a host."

"Don't tell you everything, do they, Eight?" Surex's screen flickered again, and Talinn noted the way his eyes tracked across it. He had to be absorbing information at an even faster pace than she could.

Or he was showing off. Ugh. No wonder no one spent any time with Spacies.

"Can't imagine Command tells anybody *every*thing," she replied, crossing her arms.

"Hosts are—we don't have our own anchored AIs. But we are receptive to multiple series of constructs." She tapped her port. "Temporarily. We keep pieces as needed."

"And if there's an emergency, she can carry part of one of our AIs, allowing at least one of us to get off the ship whole." Falix said that cheerfully, but his voice hit a register that made Talinn's skin attempt to slough off her bones.

Is that an IDC thing, UCF thing, side group of clones thing?

While interested, Talinn forbore to ask. It wasn't pressing, and she wasn't entirely clear how much anyone knew about anything. "A little bit of both" wasn't the most helpful answer Other Bee could have given regarding if they were traveling under orders or as rogue clones. Last thing she wanted to do was accidently blow some sort of operational security. If she were to ruin things, she'd prefer to do it on purpose.

"Thank you for sharing." She thought of half a dozen questions to ask the Spacies, but her thoughts kept circling back to Medith, sitting in the array room, finagling it to blow.

Cover. All the Eights were in there, according to Jeena's report and the comms log. Cece resurged, everything and everyone fried, the array tower collapsed.

Why could she remember that with perfect clarity, but not the walk to the ship? Not the surface to orbit lift? Not arriving on this ship with these Spacies? But Medith's face, which she couldn't possibly have seen, Medith clinging to the array as though Cece were really in there...

She shook her head and asked the first thing that popped into it. "Why am I here, apart from the rest?"

"Your tech asked to be left to handle the glitch. It will all be fine." Falix gestured to the bare wall to the left. "We've broken orbit and will drop toward the jump point shortly. Do you want a tour while Kivex gets us underway?"

"Xenni hasn't ever glitched before." She didn't want to ignore the invitation—Bee clamored for the tour—but she was still off balance. Couldn't even blame zero g. "Is she all right? Can we go there?"

"Everyone is recovering in their own space. Your tech has it all in hand. Would you like that tour?"

"I—"

Yes.

"Yes. We would." Talinn chewed on the inside of her cheek until it hurt, then swallowed and straightened her posture. Focus on the matter at hand. Not Medith. Not P-8. Not even Xenni, reverting to some enormous herbivore.

"And is Bee comfortable in the server?" Nya kicked off from the floor, and the formerly bare wall receded, revealing a rounded hall on the other side.

It's warm.

"She's fine. It's shielded from the main servers, I'm guessing?"

"Oh no, we love to let other AIs trounce around and bother ours." Surex rolled his entire body, and Nya grabbed the corner of the wall and bent backward to meet Talinn's eyes with an apologetic smile.

"It actually isn't shielded, just gapped. Bee can talk to whomever she likes—through comms, not through AI channels."

I . . . can?

"I can." Bee's voice emerged into the air, and Talinn's entire body went rigid. It was doubly odd—Bee's voice was Talinn's own, for the most part, though with a slight tonal shift that was Bee's twist to it. And usually, it sounded directly in her head, not vibrating on her ears. Externally, it was like hearing her voice through a recording, but with added harmonics meant to tug at the base of the spine.

"That's . . ."

"Oh man, the other Bee I knew had a *lot* of fun with that. I bet yours will too." Nya pushed through the hall, and disappeared almost immediately around a curve.

"She won't go far without you," Falix said, smiling almost as contagiously as his host. He gestured her ahead, and she reluctantly pushed back on her heels twice to release the magnetic locks on her boots.

"So I can talk to anyone on the ship." Bee wasn't asking, but stating facts, delight all over each word. "However I want. And your AIs do this all the time?"

"Of course we do." Another voice—modulated, but recognizably similar to Falix's—responded as Talinn speared toward the opening. She was going too fast, and turned slightly at the new voice. Her shoulder, barely healed from its last injury, bumped against the edge of the wall opening, but Falix was already there and nudged her away before she rammed entirely against it.

"Careful there—know you don't get as much practice as we do in float." He beamed at her, fingers flashing over her other arm and hip, too fast to be overly personal, but somehow enough to right her trajectory.

This close she saw that his eyes were less a pair and more a mismatched set—one crystal blue with an enormous pupil, one a dark hazel with a pinpoint of black—and though it was nothing like Medith's, it made her stomach twist over itself again.

"We've got to get better at this," Bee announced, a little too gleeful. The interruption brought Talinn back to the present moment, and she pulled her legs in to reengage the magnets of her boots. She'd practice, all right, but for now walking would be perfectly sufficient.

Nya clunked her legs down once Talinn rounded the corner, orienting to the same floor-to-ceiling direction Talinn had chosen. Falix floated alongside, the smallest of motions countering his spin and keeping him aligned with them as they moved through the halls. The walls were smooth, dark-gray metal, studded with thin strips of lights at evenly spaced intervals that left room for feet or hands and still provided sufficient visibility. Occasional rungs—tucked against the more rounded edges of floor to wall—did not create a tripping hazard, but even non-Spacie Talinn knew they'd provide a way to add speed or sudden stops if passengers chose floating rather than magnetic boots for propulsion.

"Are you adapted for zero g?" Talinn's curiosity about Spacie specializations served as an excellent distractor from everything else—from the monumental decision of leaving UCF behind to the losses of Medith, Sigmun, Daren, and the rest, to the brooding presence of Surex following behind them, still immersed in his screen.

"We're adapted for any number of things. Mostly math."

"You're adapted . . . for math?"

"A lot of our training is tailored toward spatial awareness and rapid calculations and holding conflicting information in our brains at one time. I joke that it's specialized to the point of adaptation, but . . ." He spun in the air, enough for her to catch several glimpses of his broad grin. "I guess that's not actually funny."

"It's funny," Nya interjected loyally, a chuckle underneath her words.

Talinn thought it better not to comment, but Bee spoke from a speaker a few strides ahead of them. "Humor is very subjective. It's possible we just don't get it."

"A very nice way to say I'm not funny."

"To say *that* wasn't funny to *us*." Bee's words dripped graciousness, and Nya cackled.

"*She's* funny."

"Anyway . . ." Falix incorporated his broad arm gestures into his motion, remaining apace with Talinn despite their different modes of travel. "We are adapted to survive quite a bit that would ruin even you, Eight." Unlike Surex, he used the nickname with a welcoming sort of tease. "Rapid pressure changes, low oxygen, extreme temperature shifts—nothing indefinite, of course, everything that would kill you would eventually kill us too—"

"And we sacrifice limbs for processing power if there's an emergency. Toes go, then legs. Eventually fingers and hands," Surex grumbled, and Talinn turned slightly to take in his expression. Glaring, as before, but not at her. Perhaps Surex was grumpy about the state of the universe as a whole, then, and not Talinn and her people being on board in particular.

"We train with our elbows." Falix laughed, then caught sight of Talinn's questioning face and explained further. "If the environment around us gets questionable, our bodies automatically redirect blood, oxygen, and all helpful chemicals to our brains, even if it means starving our extremities. It's a good idea in theory, given the more efficient our brains are, the likelier we and our AIs will figure out a solution, but less exciting when opposable thumbs are the difference between solving our issues and eventual death." Falix angled his spin closer to her, giving the impression of confiding, though he didn't drop his voice or stop smiling even a little.

"And it's never come to that on *this* ship," Nya added, though her smile did slip a little. Enough to tell Talinn obviously enough that it had happened, on another ship, one with people Nya knew. That was a subtle expression she knew all too well, even on a new face.

"We'll give you a tour of our specs later." Falix made that so suggestive even Surex grunted something like a laugh, then swirled forward and half sat up, so his face and torso were oriented toward Talinn even as his legs kept his motion steady ahead toward Nya. "And we don't have time for a full tour of the ship, so an overview."

"You're in the guts of it right now." Nya picked up the conversation as though they were linked. Or had done it before, Talinn corrected herself, nodding along as the host spoke. "There are four levels above and to the left of your current orientation, and three below and to the right. The loading rooms are in the rough middle of the ship, for a skooch more protection on normal transit assignments. Below and to the right is propulsion and all the way above is cargo loading."

"We'll cross two conduits to other levels on the way to the central command—down that way are passenger bunks, likely the kind you'd be familiar with from prior assignments." Falix took the tour back without a pause. "That's also public mess, a small open space for exercise and rec when people are conscious. After the next crossing will be our space—quarters, mess, tech, med—"

"Nothing that will matter to you and yours—"

"*Thank* you, Surex." Nya beamed harder, and he grunted behind them again. "We have a gym you are all more than welcome to use— I believe this will be a longer route than what you would have used between postings before, and of course you will all be conscious for the bulk of it. Not your usual interassignment run."

"Oh! Another adaptation." Falix pulled his forearms in to flex his biceps, then took the momentum of the motion to flip around and drop his feet under him. "Our muscles take quite a bit longer to go lax in zero g. Though we're also resistant to higher g's as a whole— we're very bendy."

"That seems nice for you," Talinn replied politely.

"Not just us." He winked, as though the intent hadn't been clear enough, and she couldn't help the small laugh that rose out of her in reply.

"I'm glad to say Falix has distracted you just long enough for us to confirm all AIs are properly hosted in our side servers." Nya tapped her port, which apparently doubled as a comm, and continued walking and talking, neatly hopping over an opening in the floor—one of the crossings they'd mentioned. "And all Eights are within normal operating parameters."

"We have to get to command center." Surex's grump vanished into a more strained tension, and he shot ahead of them, body in a straight, spearing line.

"Nya—" Falix launched so quickly off the floor next to her he passed Surex before they reached the next rounded corner.

"I've got her." The words seemed more for Talinn's sake than Falix's, as his feet disappeared around the curve ahead.

"Are you taking me to command central, or out of the way?"

"Command central," Bee interjected, with all the confidence in the world.

"As Bee commands," Nya murmured, and they tromped through the ship.

Command was an open semicircle of space, with six chairs mounted on what was ostensibly the floor, consoles around the edges of the room interspersed with screens, and an enormous display serving as the ceiling, one which currently showed a shifting fractal design.

Usually Talinn would have asked about the decoration, or the random chairs, but instead she was occupied by the monotone voice blaring from all around them.

"*CODE NOT ACCEPTED.*"

"We're *leaving* the system, you big, stupid hulk. You don't need a code—" This must be Kivex, who'd been aligning their point in space with their designated jump point.

"*CODE NOT ACCEPTED.*"

"We're UCF," Kivex shrieked, fingers flying over controls Talinn couldn't make out. "We're on your side!"

"*CODE NOT ACCEPTED.*"

"Yeah, we got that." Falix stood over a long console opposite Kivex. A smaller chair than the six along the back wall spun out of the floor, but he didn't lean into it. Instead he spun his hands through some configuration Talinn couldn't make out. "Nya, strap in. Big defense arrays have lost their unpressurized minds and we might have to run for it. Kivex tell me we're ready—"

"Something's not lining up, there's a vibration—"

"We're in *space*—" Surex interrupted, and Talinn craned her head back, unable to make out what he was doing above them, close to the edge of the ceiling screen.

"Obvious things are not helping!" Kivex, strapped in on the furthest of the six chairs, typed furiously on the arms of her chair. Inside the arms of it? Talinn's angle wasn't the best, though Nya gestured her toward the closest of the seats.

The fractal above was . . . a representation of the jump-point alignments. She'd seen similar images in training, though she'd never been in a Spacie's command center to know how the experts saw it. Usually the Eights were unconscious at that point of travel, and they were always kept to their corner of the ship.

"Bee." Talinn hunched her shoulders as though that would make her subvocalization even less likely to disrupt the tension around her. "Is there anything you can do?" Too late she realized Bee might answer her on a speaker, but even the novelty of a new toy wasn't enough to make Bee add further confusion to the current scene.

Scream into the void. Bee's voice stretched thin, though the server holding the AIs was no more distant than it would have been on the base. *Don't know how helpful that would be.*

They hadn't been trained for space travel—the AIs and human counterparts made for quantum transit were built for the job, same as AITs were built for violence. They were not translatable skills, though they *should* be, because then she wouldn't be sitting here, strapping into some large chair, like and entirely unlike her command chair in the tank, because here she was useless and helpless and about to be blasted into infinitesimally small pieces by an enormous weapon from her own side—

"Are they on our side anymore?" Talinn asked, hands on the straps she was meant to fasten, her body straining toward the console Falix was using for comms.

What?

"Did Other Talinn give you any other codes? Like . . . IDC codes, maybe?"

No, why under any sky in the galaxy would she . . . Huh. Wait, maybe—

"Try this!" Talinn launched out of her chair—stupid, unsafe, but so was getting blown up—and crashed against Falix's console. She shoved his hands out of the way and ran her fingers over the screen, inputting the code Bee summoned from—Talinn didn't know where Bee had summoned it from. That should have worried her, but in the moment she was too busy holding her breath.

Nothing happened, other than Kivex rocking and muttering as she and her AI continued wrenching space around them to match another piece of space absurdly, astronomically far away. The fractal above moved exactly as it had been, and Surex cursed once, loudly but with effort. Talinn's chest burned, and still she held her breath. Her throat worked, fighting against her, and Bee offered a small ping of concern, but Talinn refused to draw in new air. Not breathing held the moment, preserved it, kept them from blowing up, and if she gave in to the biological urge they would immediately and irrevocably blo—

"*CODE ACCEPTED.*"

"Thank all the little space demons and their tiny quarky friends." Falix blew out a breath so loudly Talinn couldn't tell how ragged her own was. Then he shoved her away. "Go belt up, Eight face. I'll have questions for *you* later. Dubs—"

Chimes rang through the command center, followed by a low, soothing voice. It was vaguely similar to Surex's but modulated for maximum calm. "Passengers, transit is eminent. Secure any organic bodies, and prepare to unravel."

This is a weird ship. Bee hummed thoughtfully.

"Thank you for staying out of their speakers." Talinn yanked the cross belt over her shoulders and felt the click more than heard it—potentially because it coincided with the chair stabbing her. "We've got to try to stay on their good side."

Try nothing. Bee refused to elaborate, which was for the best, because Talinn's consciousness was already ebbing away.

CHAPTER 20

When she woke up, she had no idea where she was.

To be fair, for at least three seconds, she had no idea *who* she was. *Talinn.*

"Bee." She sat up, remembered she was Talinn, and twisted to see what she'd been lying down on. A chair. A fully reclined chair. In a . . .

It crashed back into place as she scanned the command center. They'd left their shit assignment on P-8. Left UCF. Load-in had been rough, but not unusually so. A quick tour of the *Pajeeran Fall* that had quickly become a crisis . . .

"The defense array tried to blow us up."

Yup.

"And you had a code that stopped it."

Yup.

"An . . . IDC code. That stopped a UCF array."

Yup.

"What the shit?"

"What the shit indeed, Eight." Falix dropped from above, and Talinn's abused brain belatedly offered two things—on a spaceborne ship, all three dimensions of surroundings were important to be aware of, and she'd been talking fully aloud, not subvocalizing with Bee.

Had Bee been on speakers, audible to others? No . . . but then it hadn't really mattered, given the conversation.

"I have three questions, and you will answer them or this ship will, in fact, stop moving. Ready?"

157

Talinn nodded, a muffled numbness against her skull all the indication she needed that Bee was shielding her from a truly enormous headache.

"One: How did you have an IDC code to soothe a UCF defense array? Two: How did you know an IDC code would *work* to shut down an UCF defense array? Three: What other critical secrets are you holding that may mean the difference between normal life and screaming death for my ship?"

"Easy. Ready?" She didn't wait for him to reply, but pressed the heels of her palms against her cheekbones and charged ahead. "One: Another Talinn and Bee dumped a whole lot into my Bee without explanation. Two: See one, because it was a wild guess. Three: See one, because I have no idea what else they gave us, or why, and given *you* know other us-es, you'd be about as qualified to guess as I would, because this is all still pretty bugging new to me and I'm still hung over from load-in. So."

Fair on all fronts.

He folded into the chair next to her, and after a long moment, smiled. It was a strained, exhausted, and not-nearly-the-glowing-regard-of-earlier sort of expression, but a smile all the same.

"Fair." He might have echoed Bee on purpose—at this point, Talinn would be only dully surprised to find that was possible. "It's never boring when we get a Talinn."

"How often—"

"You're only the second one." Surex's voice—no, not Surex, but his AI partner Dubs—emerged from the side. The lack of sneer was the giveaway. "There's no point in being mysterious."

That was clearly meant for Falix, whose smile brightened slightly. "There's always room for a little intrigue, my friend. And speaking of such—a thing you might not know, only the second Talinn, is that there are not very many Spacies."

"I'm only vaguely aware of the number of ships—"

"No, no, you misunderstand. Base models, I mean. Clone lines." He tapped the skin under his bright blue eye, and Surex snorted loudly and turned away.

"You're right, I didn't know that." She stretched out her legs, letting her arm and sore-again shoulder rest. "I'm beginning to wonder if that's true of Eights, too."

"Yes, most of you think you are to be cloned, not that you are already cloned. For us, it's harder to pretend, so they don't."

"They just keep us apart." Kivex floated closer, and smiled nearly as warmly as Nya had. "It's a programming miracle that we're socialized at all."

"You're welcome," Nya murmured, and Kivex laughed. "Though not so socialized we've done actual proper introductions. I'm sorry, Talinn."

"*You* introduced yourself, I've no doubt." Kivex laid her hand on Nya's shoulder, her legs hanging in midair. "And *I* was otherwise occupied. I'm Kivex. That's my . . . what do you call them? Name sign? Combination call?" She shrugged and went on without waiting for an answer. "All Spacies are linked to an X-series, and we build that right into our names. I am paired with X-22, whom you can and should call Ditto."

"Falix is paired with Benty, X-20, and Surex with Dubs, X-11," Nya continued in the same breath. Falix smiled again, and Surex lifted a hand in their direction.

"There are very few X-series versions overall." Falix spoke as though the belated introductions hadn't happened, and Talinn would follow as flawlessly as his fellows had. "And so then very few human stock to choose from to keep them anchored."

"Not to mention the demands of your adaptations," Talinn suggested, and he laughed.

"There, you are as clever as the other Talinn. I am not surprised."

"Why so few X-series?" Bee asked over the comms, and Talinn swallowed back a pang. It wasn't on her to filter what questions Bee did or didn't ask, not here. That was a good thing.

"It is to do with the jump points and the entanglement principles." Surex's answer was sharp, definitive, as though to make an end of the conversation, but Dubs must not have agreed.

"We are what is entangled to the jump point. Without that connection, you can make space as identical as you like, but there is no spark to make the unravelment bridge."

"One of you for each point?"

"Indeed, indeed." Falix waved a hand idly, but Talinn noticed the other three people shifted slightly. Another bit of intrigue, maybe. "So what's next."

"That didn't sound like a question, and I hope under every sky in the known universe you're not expecting me to have an answer."

"Of course not, of course not. Let's get you back to your Eights. I'll tell you all what I know, what's next, and . . ." He gave her a critical once-over, eyes lingering on her forehead. Or scalp. "We'll talk disguises."

"Dis . . . guises."

"Dear New Talinn, you're an Eight off assignment. No Spacie ship can run invisible forever. If you're going to be out in the world, you have to be less . . ." Falix waved his hands in her general direction. "Eight-ish."

"Hair." She touched her scalp, imagined synthetic strands covering her head, and did not shudder. When they were small, her class had competed in draping increasingly ridiculous things over their heads to mimic their trainers and carers. The crowning triumph had been Caytil, who'd darkened her eyebrows and drawn on a streaky beard with grease, tied a clever knot in scavenged port cords, then paraded around the training quarters until one of their carers came in, shrieked, and they were all locked down for a week. The given reason was hoarding port cords was wrong, but Talinn had been sure it was that they were making fun of "normal" people.

It had been worth it either way, though they hadn't plopped things on their heads and strutted around like unadapted empty people after that. Was that why the idea of it now squirmed uncomfortably around the back of her neck? Or was it that she'd temporarily, but thoroughly, put her fellow Eights out of her head?

"Hair to start, my little number friend." Falix leaned against the arm of his chair, his legs floating behind him. "We have to make you softer. The empties don't glare nearly as much."

"I don't glare."

"You're glaring right now."

"It's been a long couple of days." She forced her brows up, tugged her mouth into a careless smile.

"Now that is a good point. And a terrifying face." He held up his hands, and she smiled more naturally at his own overdone expression. "In the meantime—"

"I'd like to go to the rest of the Eights." They were safe, and all aboard, and that was good to know. But she wanted to know what had happened. What Jeena had worried about. Why she'd been apart from them in the first place.

"Exactly what I was going to say. But first . . . Talinn."

Her hands stilled on the lap and leg belts holding her to the chair, and she tilted her head at him, expectant.

"I didn't take you aside only because you're a Talinn and we liked the Talinn and Bee we met before."

"I did, in fact, think that might not be the case."

Though we are very charming. Even with the glaring, apparently.

"It's not going to get easier from here." He gestured toward his temple. "I have a message for you, from them. We will give all of you an overview of the war, the state of the systems, such as you might not have received from UCF before. But for you . . ."

"They will not be in contact with you again, the other Breezy." Dubs spoke through the comms, as though he'd already been speaking. No one but Talinn thought that weird, given the lack of reaction. "Not until you get to where she's sending you."

"It won't be the first place we bring you," Kivex continued. "You will pass through several transits, several locations. They say you must watch for the odd. The thing that moves the space around you that should not."

"Everything's going to be odd to us, this will be our first off-base—"

"No." Surex didn't turn from his console. "Not the new weird of broader humanity. Odd, unnatural. Hinky. Things you can't explain."

"Once they are sure UCF is convinced of recent events, once you are clear, she will bring you to the others." Falix shrugged and pushed away, spearing through the air. "And those are all the details we are allowed to know."

"That Talinn—the other version of me you're so fond of—she said 'Look out for anything hinky?' That . . . that's her grand, brilliant advice?"

"She said something's moving that she doesn't understand. Things are changing more rapidly than before, and she'd like to think it's her—us—those of us who *know*. But . . ."

"But it's hinky. *She* said it's hinky?"

"She said it's hinky." He looked at her, one pupil wide and the other the barest dot of black in a mass of too-round green-brown iris.

"Clone generations change more than ear measurements," she muttered, and he grinned.

"There aren't a lot of words for 'something's shifting those asteroid chunks that's not the main star we can see, and I don't know if it's a new space monster or something weirder' so I can't fault her for 'hinky.'"

"New space monster?"

"I used that as part of a longer way to show how I might get across a general feeling, I'm not reading you into any other secrets of the universe you don't know. Now you see why 'hinky' works."

"Now I want to know more about space monsters—I'm not conceding on hinky."

You're focused on it to keep from worrying about what's moving out there that a version of us, who knows a lot more than us, still hasn't wrapped their brains around.

"Of course I am. Doesn't take an AI to figure that out." She didn't bother to subvocalize—the Spacies had a disconcerting knack for figuring out what she and Bee had to say to each other regardless of how they communicated.

CHAPTER 21

⊕

The *Pajeeran Fall* didn't have any other living cargo, so the Spacies brought them all together in the passenger mess, which had more room than their own. Xenni's right hand twitched every four and a half seconds, but otherwise the small group of Eights appeared in normal bounds of health.

There were varying levels of emotional health—Arnod's frown was ferocious, Heka's eyes watered constantly without her wiping away the tears, Caytil kept drifting away and blinking herself back to focus and her seat at the table—but Jeena relaxed in her seat and didn't peer worriedly at anyone, and Talinn figured that was the best they were going to get given the circumstances.

"It goes like this." Falix gestured widely, his body not even shifting in the decreased gravity.

"Please forgive," Benty chimed in over the speaker, his version of Falix's voice shaded with more of a wry amusement.

"We don't interact with passengers much." Nya, busy farming out prepackaged foods to each Eight, beamed brightly.

"At all," Surex muttered.

"Except that we do, on occasion. This group, however, is a treat." Falix lowered his hands, smile wider than before his team's interjections. "So. It goes like this—"

"There's a war," Dubs interjected helpfully. Bee sheared metal in Talinn's head, but didn't add to the interruptions through the speaker. Talinn considered feeling grateful, realized that would only encourage Bee, and focused on the matter at hand.

"Thank you, X-11." Falix rolled his eyes, but no annoyance Talinn could read flickered across his face. "There is, indeed, a war."

"That part I think we got." Konti unpeeled the food container Nya had handed her, but didn't pierce it to begin drinking.

"I knew I should have brought Kivex." Falix opened his mouth to continue speaking, but Nya merged into the conversation with yet more cheerfulness.

"She's still pulling back together after transference, but she'll be ready for personal interface in—"

Personal interface as opposed to?

Talinn repeated the question aloud. The briefing was chaos already, she couldn't see how it hurt at this point.

"Ah. Well. So." Falix pushed closer to the table, and his AI made a short, discordant noise that strongly reminded Talinn of Bee's method of sticking out her nonexistent tongue.

"X-series AIs have several adaptations not afforded to Artificial Intelligence Troops."

"In that we are all semilooped into each other's conversations." Dubs, his voice a mix of Benty's and Surex's, took up the next sentence without a pause.

"More than semi," Nya offered, glancing at Falix before continuing. "Semilooped is by design."

"We are fully integrated in terms of communication." This voice, much like Kivex's, must have been Ditto—a fact Nya murmured confirmation to for the rest of the Eights. "We believe Command is aware, though it is neither a matter of our training nor something we are cautioned against."

"Which is why I say they don't know."

"They do."

"They don't."

The chorus of voices overlapped so briskly Talinn wouldn't have been able to separate them without Bee's immediate, and amused, assistance. Falix, then Ditto, then Surex and Dubs at once.

"We're not arguing amongst ourselves, I should note." Falix cleared his throat, perhaps noting the array of expressions across the Eights. "It's a way we discuss to decide what we really think."

"You're..." Caytil wrapped her hands around the table to anchor herself in place. Her unopened food drifted to her left. "You're like a hive mind?"

"No." Surex bit off the word.

"But also not entirely no." Falix tipped a foot side to side, then shrugged elaborately, the motion moving down his body in a ripple. "But that's not why we're here—"

"So you're connected, and that means you're in touch with Kivex, but she's not ready to be face-to-face with anyone?" Sammer sipped his food idly, glancing from Falix to Surex as though they had all day.

"Entanglement is a process. Kivex will need some time to put all of her own head back into place." Ditto again, her tone precise. "We are currently semiscattered, but as that is my constant state, given a part of me always resides at my jump point, it is easier for me to interact than it is for her. Usually, this is not a matter of concern."

"Because again, we don't get to interact with passengers much."

"Can you imagine an empty's response to this? Your finishing each other's thoughts. The wonky eyes?" Arnod chuckled, though alongside his ever-present frown, the sound grated.

"What's wonky about our eyes?" Falix asked in perfect sincerity, and Arnod's ferocious expression wavered until Nya laughed.

"A part of you always resides . . . ?" Caytil prompted, and there was a momentary silence.

"Different X-series are entangled with their different jump points, and in part that holds through a sphere in the jump point hosting a small piece of that X-series' code."

"Like a defense array, anchored in a point in space?" Konti hummed thoughtfully, eyes not quite focusing on any of them.

"Much smaller."

"And unweaponed."

"So we can't blow anything up from there."

"Less overwhelming death."

"More like statis arrays."

Again, Talinn *could* have followed which Spacie said which words, but it didn't seem worth it, given she still couldn't wrap her mind entirely around how the jump points worked.

Jeena flattened her hands on the table, and for no reason Talinn could discern, that called them all back to the matter at hand. They'd left their entire reason for existence behind, along with more than a few bodies of their friends. As far away as that felt, on the long side of load-in and a jump point with pieces of Spacie AI in it, it crowded close in the moment.

I think that was them trying to help. Bee again didn't use her new access to the speaker to share the thought, and Talinn's lips twitched into a semblance of a smile.

"So there's a war," she prompted, pretending not to notice Jeena's thankful glance. "And it's like . . . this?"

"Yes. Right." Falix straightened and floated back from the table. "So we have three systems—"

"A debrief, please, not a history lesson—"

"Given we don't know what version of information you have been given, it will be both." Dubs did not sound apologetic, and Arnod didn't protest again.

"Hynex." Falix tapped his temple.

"Govlic," Surex continued, his word immediate even if unwillingness was clear in his tone.

"And Exfora," Ditto contributed.

Also what they're each entangled with. Spacies aren't as hard to read as empties.

"I think they made that one a little obvious," Talinn replied, mostly subvocal.

"In order of age, if not importance." Falix had continued without pause, whether he'd heard her or not. "Hynex, named after the first ship to ever jump there, historically remains in IDC control, being the birthplace of the Interstellar Defense Corps and our first anchor into space." He examined each of them, but no one protested. "Hynex continues to have the highest population of any of the systems, mostly due to its six habitable planetary bodies, endless planetary ring settlements, and very large stations."

"The UCF is currently in possession of four of those stations." Surex stalked over to the table, his magnetic boots clumping louder than perhaps necessary, and tossed a disk into the middle of them. Heka flinched, then wiped her eyes and straightened, and Jeena touched the former jet Eight's elbow briefly.

Talinn held her eyes on the disk, which abruptly sprouted into a display, shooting rough estimations of the three systems between them.

"So let's call UCF green and IDC blue for fun." Surex's dry tone didn't make any of it seem fun, but Falix picked up the conversation with another smile, as though it had.

"Hynex historically would be a real throbber of a blue, yeah? But here's some green squeaking in." The display changed accordingly, and not that it mattered, but Talinn nearly asked which AI was moving it.

"How though? UCF has never gotten a toenail hold in Hynex—the defense arrays—"

"You'll note, Konti Rooks of fair Govlic, they've been careful to stay at stations close to the jump point."

Talinn chewed her lip, then forced the abused skin out from between her teeth. "So if IDC comes after them hard, they blow the stations and potentially glitch the jump point."

"A last-ditch choice, to be sure, but one that would hurt IDC far more than the UCF, in the short term." Falix did his whole-body shrug again and Benty picked up the statement.

"We could adjust, depending on where the debris and changed readings were in jump-point space, but it would take time. Ships would likely be lost in the meantime, and IDC uses that jump point a great deal more than the United Colonial Forces."

"Who stay more in the colonies, namely Govlic, of which we all have so recently vacated, and Exfora. Let's color those green." The display had changed before Falix continued speaking, and then Surex grunted.

"Problem there is the IDC is taking a whole lot of ground in Govlic, including areas they've mostly ignored in past cycles." Several chunks of the system shifted from green to blue.

"We're going to drop you at a neutral station in Exfora—" Falix didn't pause at the immediate chorus of questions—neutral?—and the display shifted to show the third system as mostly UCF green with small dots of blue. "There's been more IDC activity than usual in Exfora, probably retaliation from the station-nabbing in Hynex, but these outskirt stations have never been much of a target for either side."

"I want to know more about *neutral*," Xenni said, her hands folded too tightly together to show any lingering twitches.

"I want to know what this has to do with us. We've heard things are getting weird out there." Sammer gestured to Talinn, and Bee muttered *Sammer's getting weird out there* so Talinn didn't have to. "You said you had something to tell us that might conflict with what UCF Command has shared with us previously."

"Oh." Surex crossed his arms, and it took Talinn a breath to realize Dubs had spoken over the speaker. "So you knew all this? You weren't surprised by the IDC incursion on your insignificant little P-8?"

"No, but—"

"Did you know civilians are trying to make new jump points?"

"They don't know what *we* have to do with it, so they're sure with enough math—"

"—that they can find a new one just like the old explorers did centuries ago."

"Did you know that neutral stations existed before ten seconds ago?"

"Because it seems like you did not."

"Perhaps you'd like to know more about—"

"All right, you've made your point." Talinn shoved up from the table, meaning to stand but forgetting the reduced gravity and rocketing above them all. Bee expressed her tortured metal of a laugh over the speakers, and Talinn was gratified when everyone swung around and paid attention.

Just float there. Don't ruin it by trying to flail back to the table yet.

Talinn twitched her shoulders to orient toward the people now below her and ignored the brilliance of Falix's grin. The Spacies— human and AI alike—had blurred their words so much even Bee didn't bother to untangle who had said what. Now that they were all obligingly quiet, she'd forgotten what she meant to say.

"Have there been any other reports of defense arrays going out of spec? Is that why the footholds are shifting?"

"Is that *Bee*?" Sammer blurted, twisting toward the speaker in a way none of the X-series voices had caused him to do.

"We've had Bees in our system before." Falix waved a hand dismissively, his attention still on Talinn. After a moment, he brushed against the floor and kicked off again, his arc taking him slowly over Talinn's head. When he extended his hand as he came around her other side, she took it, and somehow his momentum was enough to drift them both back to the floor. She engaged her boots and waited longer than she had to before untangling her hand from his.

"No. No other reports of defense arrays going rogue and targeting jump-point traffic."

As satisfying as that was to hear, it led to a fair amount more temporary chaos as then Talinn got to be a part of the Spacie method of explaining things, given no one had told the rest of the Eights about their most recent near-death experience.

The concept of a neutral station was much easier to accept after that.

CHAPTER 22

⊕

The moment they stepped out of the airlock into the station, Talinn knew they'd made a terrible mistake.

There were moving, breathing, heating-up-the-air bodies everywhere. More human shapes than she had ever seen in one place—maybe more than she'd met in the entirety of her life—crammed in every direction. No matter where she turned her head or flicked her gaze, there were hordes of them. Piled on top of each other. Moving and crowding and—

Focus on one thing at a time. Bee's voice, though tinny and distant, gave her a solid place to focus.

Thing one: The airlock dumped them out to a short landing bridge that connected to a longer, wider walkway. Coated in people—no. One thing at a time. Thing two: There were layers and layers of these walkways, all funneling toward a central shaft where people went up and down to different layers. So many people, how were they to know which way to—

Thing three: Along each walkway were displays and projected screens. Much of the din seemed to come from those, as some of the nearer noise ebbed and rose in time with the flashing lights of the screens.

Thing seven or eight, she'd already lost track, the noise was so enormous it was muffled. (*That's me, I turned it down, I'll turn it up little by little. Your heart rate is settling.*)

Her heart rate was *not* settling, but she took deep breaths to encourage it to do so. No one was crowding her on the landing bridge, forcing her into the seething, writhing mass—

Thing ten?

Thing ten. She pressed her palms to her eyes, squeezed everything, then dropped her arms and straightened her shoulders. She was an *Eight*, bugs eat all the code, and no magnitude of population was going to give her more than a thirty-second pause.

Maybe forty-five, because her nose had apparently gone briefly numb, as overwhelmed as the rest of her, and now was telling her . . .

A lot of people smelled spicy. A little musky. Dusty, a bit. Or— she sneezed, three times in a row, and finally subvocalized, "No smell, please. Midline hearing."

No sniffs, dull roar. Got it.

"Suppose it would be too much to dial off my nerves, huh?"

Absolutely too much. What if one of them has sharp edges, and you get cut? I can't monitor each nerve and keep you sane until you calm down.

"Sure. Sure." Before this moment, she had understood, as well as a hyperintelligent, specially trained, incomparably focused weapon of war could understand, that there were scads of people in the known galaxy. The colonies had grown for a very, very long time, and even ongoing war didn't stop—and perhaps encouraged— populations from taking root across a variety of settlements.

It was enough to forget her discomfort in having Bee's backup programming in a portable server, loaded with six other portable servers, that Jeena would move later in the day. Because knowing what a million was, and that it existed, was very different from *seeing* a million people crawling all over each other—

There aren't a million in this portion of the station. Across the entire station there's a total of two and a half million, so here you've got . . . maybe a hundred thousand. I'm including ones in the tubes, so that's an estimate.

"The . . . tubes."

The people who don't go from walkway to central shaft, and don't just circle endlessly on walkways, they go into those side tubes. Connect to other parts of the station.

"I don't want to—" She had to leave the landing bridge. Eventually Caytil and Sammer would get over their own shock, and they'd need to move. "We're here because it's crowded."

This station is notorious for terrible embarkation and debarking records. Monitoring has been broken for a decade. It's more hive than haven.

"It's perfect for us to disappear."

The more people there are, the harder to see a person.

"I'm going to need to boil my skin after this," Caytil murmured, and Talinn finished pulling herself together.

"We have to get to the Tura quadrant." They all had the same information—they'd have to split up and make their own ways to the next point—but it steadied her to say it out loud. They were leaving in staggered groups—first Caytil, Sammer, and Talinn. Then Heka and Xenni. Then Arnod and Konti. "Get some noodles."

"Bet they taste better than bunk food."

"This *air* tastes better than bunk food."

Talinn scraped her tongue against her teeth. Even without her sense of smell, the memory of old bars of food, stored in the tank's bunk for slightly too long—and it was always slightly too long—with a faint hint of dust and reconstituted protein . . . Another brick in her foundation to steady herself. What was ahead could be as bad or worse as what was behind, but at least she'd get to try civilian noodles.

"See you down the way." She shoved her hands in her pockets to keep from touching the carefully fastened hair on her head, and stepped further down the landing bridge.

"I think it's up, actually?" Caytil hesitated behind her, then the vibration of her movement joined Talinn's.

"Along the way, then," Sammer called, with a noise almost a laugh, and then Talinn slid into the crush of people in the walkway and could do nothing but move forward.

It's like those fungus clouds on Discar. You're an eddy. You move with the crowd.

"How does anything get done? I'll need to turn—"

The screens. I'm dialing up your hearing. Don't jump or stumble.

"I don't stumble."

If you stumble here, all the medkits in the universe won't help.

"Reassuring." It wasn't so bad, once she was in it. She could only truly see the ten people closest to her—unless she looked up, or over, or too much around. And they weren't all crammed together, touching. Most people walked at least a hand's length apart from each other, the walkway broader across than her tank.

The station was run by a supposedly independent coalition of merchant interests. Talinn hadn't imagined the possibility existed of being independent, but money had to move freely somewhere for the UCF and IDC to continue to make more of it. The lack of control over who, exactly, was on the station at any given time was on purpose. Everyone paid their fees, so the trading companies got their cut, and not knowing who was there at any given time gave all the powers that be plausible deniability. Neutral ground was best at being neutral with anonymity.

She and Bee had worked out their station path while *Pajeeran Fall* made its slow maneuvering into the docking rings that surrounded the station. Sitting with the maps of the station had made the process misleadingly straightforward, but Talinn held the plan in the forefront of her thoughts like a talisman from a baby story. An antijinx. As long as she remembered it, she couldn't possibly get lost—

"We're not on the path we marked out, are we?" Her head swiveled as she stayed with the crowd, watching a turnoff from the walkway marked "Anvia WZ." There had been no such thing, or even a naming convention like it, in the schematics they'd poured over.

Negative. But we'll take the bulk of this curve, turn off into the first tube with a silver outline, and follow it to another hub. Then we can—

"This looks nothing like the schematics. How do you know?" Talinn's stomach roiled, but she told it noodles would help, and pushed on.

How did I save us all from a defense array?

"Other Talinn gave you more than codes?"

I—no. It doesn't feel like that? Bee made a flat noise. *Fun fact, if someone attacks us here, these walkways shouldn't be hard to collapse.*

"That isn't what I'd define as fun. Especially given I'm on these walkways."

No, you'd jump to the support structure—there's one every two minutes at this pace. The chaos would be excellent cover.

"How likely is it that we'll be attacked here, you think?"

Unlikely. Sammer sticks out more than us.

"I imagine Lei has a plan to counter that."

We all have many plans.

"Not me. Just the one."

We can't run off and join the Spacies.

"Says you." Talinn stopped short as the crowd in front of her parted around a clump of humans arguing in the middle of the walkway. She stared for a moment, then realized she was about to become part of the roadblock and sidestepped. Before she could comment that there was relatively little cursing at the people in the way, part of the argument reached her lowered hearing.

"—machine-twisted piece of greasy waste—"

"—shove your end hole on the pointy end of a—"

"—too much tech in your head, you need a—"

"Tech in their head?" Her steps slowed, but her pace was already taking her around a curve, and the push was very much one way. "What was that about?"

Empty humans yelling about embedded screens in someone's tiny brain?

"Or they use us for their insults."

Not "us" because they don't know any of us.

"You know what I mean."

I think you're jumping at nothing, this time. Bee hummed, then prodded before Talinn could reply. *Take the next turn.*

"I was paying attention, you know."

I'm going to put your hearing back on, but I'll do it little by little.

"I thought you didn't think they were talking about us."

We should stay aware.

"Of hundreds of thousands of people all at once." Talinn ducked her chin as she worked her way across the moving people, falling in with a line peeling off toward a brighter corridor to the left.

Of the two hundred in your immediate area at any given time.

"Two hundred and sixteen, if you want to be precise."

Now you're showing off.

"Feeling a lot better." She followed along the shifting tide as though she'd moved through a seething mass of breathing, writhing, unadapted people her whole life. "I guess you can get used to anything with the right mindset."

You want smell back too, then?

"Almost anything. You rude creature, you." Talinn shoved her hands in two of the deep pockets of her jacket. The garment was bulky, giving her body a different heft, with a plethora of inside pockets and all manner of gear tucked and sewn inside it. The material itself was light, meaning it didn't stand out that she wore it amidst the heat of so many bodies without sweating.

"Not that anyone is looking at me too closely."

We operate as though they are. At all times.

"I know, I know."

With her ears closer to fully functional, she noticed more muttering around her. A susurrus of it, hard to trace to any one individual.

Comms?

"None of them are talking to . . . each other?"

Except the people yelling the loudest.

"Except them." Talinn longed to reach out to Caytil or Sammer, but comms could be tracked, monitored, recorded, and later searched in a way they couldn't risk. Unlike her connection with Bee, there was too much possibility of external interference or awareness.

Not that such a thing seemed to bother the hordes of people around her, all of whom seemed involved in their own conversations. Though the sheer volume made it unlikely their personal conversation would be tracked and followed up on, it still seemed utterly careless.

What would it be like to live such a life?

"Record them."

What?

"Record them and store it. We'll analyze once we have you docked up properly."

I have more than enough power with your brain and my system to—

"We have to focus on the tasks at hand and you know it."

I won't be able to get both sides of conversations, not without worming into the network they're using here—and even a rudimentary AI running the station would note my interference.

"I'm not convinced they would—clearly you learned more from Other Bee than you're saying." Talinn's lips curled, and she wiped her expression before lifting her head and taking in the new area she'd turned off into. "Thank you for not arguing."

I'm busy being proud of you.

"For figuring out the obvious?"

For the idea of recording the conversations around us. At the very least it will give us insight into what civilians talk about. Your being quiet as you walk probably isn't as unusual as it looks in this particular crowd, but better to be prepared.

"And at best we'll get a better view of what people think of the war. Clones. AIs. Compare it to what the Spacies told us. What other us are saying."

See? Proud.

"You know that's not distracting me from my other point."

Bee didn't answer, but Talinn hadn't expected one. The turn-off conduit had a narrower walkway, and while there were objectively less people, it certainly felt busier.

The sides were lined with businesses—both doors with brilliant, clashing signage that led into offices, shops, and establishments, and stalls staggered between the entrances. The stalls were a riot of goods, gears, and goodness knew what else—some were all but empty, others spilling over, a few had lines, one had a youngish kid dozing over a pile of fabrics.

None of these look like anything helpful.

"No noodles either." Talinn sighed, allowed her pace to slow to match those of the people around her. This seemed a more casual area, with browsing allowed and more interpersonal conversations, not single-sided comm-based ones.

She decided she wouldn't stick out no matter what she'd been wearing, given the extreme range displayed now that she could focus more on individuals. From nearly naked to layered and strapped, intricately intense hair styles to shaved heads, piercings and endless stretches of smooth skin, flashing tattoos and bodies streaked in colors Talinn was fairly sure even genetic editing couldn't create.

"See, could have left my head bare..." She scratched the back of her neck, trailing close to the edge of the wig, and Bee sheared metal at her.

And how would you hide your port?

"Nya had a dozen—"

Nya had one, and it's pretty clear she never leaves the ship unless there's an extreme emergency and she has an X in her head. The Spacies had three each, and they're less likely to leave than her.

178 Marisa Wolf

"Bee..." Talinn's steps slowed, her eyes fixed on a sign ahead. "What do you suppose that's for?"

It's not noodles.

Three doors ahead, a strobing yellow-and-blue light chased itself around a sign without words, only a dark outline of three interlocked shapes. Each of the shapes looked like a stylized version of a port connection, though each was slightly different.

"But it can't be for Eights, can it?"

Listen.

"—should shut it down. Bring the split nuts right in here. I know! Or what if the IDC or UCF has a problem with it? Bad enough the warships dock here, can't have—" The tall woman, speaking rapidly on her comm, stalked out of range before Talinn could catch the rest, but more than one person had something to say, seemingly about the shop.

"Passing it right now. Still here." An older man grunted and shook his head, then made single syllable noises in response to whatever the person on the other end of his conversation was saying.

"I'm going in!" This a younger man, walking with three other people of similar age. His hair was close cut, his clothing formfitting and luridly colored, and his motions jittery. His friends were similarly attired, though two with far more forgiving pants, and the young woman with them laughed.

"Go on then, Sim. I wanna see if they'll port you right up."

"Nah, it's tattoos, not real ports. Only the military—"

"My people been talking about it for weeks, nah. I'm sick of the rumors, and with you, Sim. Let's go in." The tallest of the group grabbed the first speaker's arms and they charged toward the door.

Which flashed, blue and yellow, and didn't open for them.

"Maybe it is for Eights." Talinn scratched along her jawline and drifted off the main walk, pretending interest in a stall draped with gorgeous fabric and staffed by a woman whose attention was more on her sewing than potential customers. Sigmun's careful stitches surfaced in her mind and she rubbed the back of her neck, snatched her hand back from the tickle of hairs, and swallowed back a groan. "Maybe that's why the backup path you had ran us this way."

I suppose we have to go somewhere when we retire. Bee didn't sound convinced, but then Talinn wasn't either. Private citizens or no, a retired Eight would still have an absurd amount of proprietary tech—given they *were* proprietary tech—that neither the IDC nor UCF would want to fall into anyone else's labs. Retirement was meant to be cushy and sweet, but in limited locations, like the heart of one's service territory. Not a neutral station overflowing with both curious and judgmental humans.

"Probably just a front, not a real place." The girl laughed again, tossing long hair that shimmered with some sort of product. Talinn touched her own scalp, still surprised to feel strands instead of skin, and wondered in the briefest of passing if sparkles would help. "Or getting interest before they open another club or something."

"It's not an entertainment level though." Sim frowned up at the flashing sign. "This is public goods."

"You know the levels aren't as neat as they used to be. My grand complains about it all the time." The tallest boy didn't sound any more convinced than Bee or Talinn, but he drifted back toward the girl. "Could be anything."

"Maybe it's for recruitment." Sim reached out a hand toward the door, short of touching it. The light didn't brighten, but Talinn tensed all the same.

"They don't recruit AIs, gummer. They grow them." The girl stepped toward Sim, then crossed her arms and shifted her weight to stick out a hip. "C'mon, I'm hungry."

Sim turned back toward her, clearly torn, and Talinn busied herself examining a vibrant purple scarf that shimmered much like the girl's hair. Maybe she could tie it around her wig and her neck, add another layer of protection between her port and the world.

With what exchange?

Which pulled Talinn back to the moment at hand. It didn't matter what was behind that door, because either it wouldn't open for her, and she'd stick out for trying, or it *would*, and she'd stick out worse. Either way, she had a limited amount of funds—Spacies were no more equipped with easy-to-spend civilian money than Eights were, and anything that could be traced could be a problem. She had a limited amount of physical credits, and while Jeena was sure she could finagle more money out of the station's system given time, that posed risks they hadn't yet decided were worth it.

"Other us could have shared more information. Or untraceable accounts."

I don't think other us wants us able to be independent of them any more than the UCF does.

Talinn had to admit that was true—and fair, because if she were trying to wrangle herself, or someone very like her, keeping them in a tight collar wasn't a bad idea.

Didn't make it chafe any less.

The young people had descended into the sort of elbowing and shoving that allowed for quite a bit of groping and giggling, and Talinn drifted off from the stall without a single interaction with its occupant. Maybe the outside world wasn't so bad.

She dismissed the thought as fast as it occurred to her—the last thing she needed was another jinx—but it was far too late.

One of the young people had jostled another into the door, and the light of it flared bright—so bright Bee did something to her eyesight to protect it—and then went out.

Talinn's shoulders hitched, prepared for the alarms, but there was no noise. The crowd stilled, something like an indrawn breath, and then the girl started to scream.

Three of the youths were left standing—the screaming girl, the tall boy who joined her, and the third mostly silent one, visibly shaking. The first one that had approached the door had crumpled to the ground. Unmarked, but unmoving.

Well, this isn't going to make things any easier for us.

"What happened?" The previously silent woman in the stall jumped forward and grabbed Talinn's arm. "Did you see?"

Instinctively, her arm tensed, shoulder joint twisting. Weight shifted to her other side, and her other arm snapped up. Talinn froze before she completed the maneuver, and put her hand to her mouth instead, as though she were shocked by the scene and the sudden touch. Not as though she were about to break away and throw a ridged hand into the other woman's throat in order to crush her windpipe and incapacitate her. Nothing of the sort.

Very smooth.

"I didn't, I—"

Is he unconscious or dead? Everyone is yelling, no one is going to check.

"Should we see if he's—"

"No!" The woman shook Talinn's arm, then dropped her hand, shaking her head rapidly. "They infected him!"

"They?" She tilted her head toward the door and the growing scene. "Who *are* they?"

"Machine people. They are moving into all the stations, tempting the young people."

Rude.

"Machine people? Like . . . like the ones that fight for . . ." Bugs in a string, she didn't know how to talk to civilians. Surely unadapted people knew about the AITs, but did they casually refer to IDC and UCF, or one, or neither?

"What?" The woman glanced sidelong at her, then shook her head in dismissal. "No. They grow those ones, like plants. These are trying to get new blood to feed their machine god." She made a noise low in her throat and turned her face sharply to the side as though she were going to spit. She didn't—in the infinitely recycled spaces of a station, that had to be frowned on—but the sentiment communicated clearly.

"Machine god?" Talinn's ability to rapidly analyze information stuttered to sludge with this level of unconnected information.

"Where are you from?" She didn't wait for an answer, her gaze fixed on the cluster of people ahead of them. "They say the war would be over, if we just let the machines run it. The more people can be like programs, the better the galaxy will be."

"How under the skies would that work?"

The body of young Sim twitched, and the crowd of people moved back like they were interconnected. Talinn stepped forward, then checked herself and waited to hear the woman's answer.

"Your guess is as good as any. They only share with their own. But they infect . . ." She gestured, her hands lifting and sketching out a vague human shape. "That boy will never be the same again. You'll see."

I think the door just shocked him. Bee hummed, and Talinn craned her neck to get a better view—easier now with the people leaving a wider space around Sim. *I can't see how it would have infected him with anything.*

"A program like Other Bee sent to you? Or that voice sent to Cece?" Talinn rubbed the side of her neck as she subvocalized, though it seemed highly unlikely anyone here would have something that could pick up her conversation with Bee.

You're giving this seller woman too much credit. Sounds like weird human stories to me, nothing based in actual reality.

Sim twitched again, then groaned and pushed himself up. Most of the people stepped back again, but his friends hovered. The tall one leaned down and extended a hand, though he stopped short of touching the other boy.

Shocked. Alive. Probably as weird and normal as he was before. Also we should go.

"I'll be sure to stay out of the way of machine people," she said aloud, and the woman made another noise—this one more approving—and inclined her head. Talinn eased away, giving the gathered humans as much of a wide berth as she could manage without bumping into the other side of stalls, and kept her head down and shoulders hunched.

People still called questions, but they didn't seem aimed at her, and she increased her pace and took the turns Bee recommended, until the noise and traffic around her normalized.

"Civilian life is . . ."

We don't have enough information to finish that sentence. Or not finish it definitively—I can put six different words in there and they'd all fit.

"None of those words would be entirely positive, would they?"

They absolutely would not.

CHAPTER 23

⊕

They got turned around a handful more times, but finally found their way to the designated meeting place. This section of the station leaned more toward what passed for entertainment—thudding rhythms spilled out of open doorways, advertisements increased in number and volume, and a fair portion of the passersby were in altered states of consciousness.

The bar they wanted was no hole in the station's wall, but a three-story extravagance lined in living green vines that occasionally pulsed with blues and purples.

Entrances from other levels are staggered, not all in one place. How do they secure it?

"The vines. They're programmed to do something besides add oxygen to the area."

No spark of code that . . . hm, no. You're right, there is something.

"See, humans can know things."

My human *can know things. And most of the Eights. The rest remain questionable.*

"All right. We need the gray bar." Talinn scanned the space—wide walkways with tables crisscrossed above her, all gleaming in flawlessly painted cautionary colors—bright oranges, yellows, and reds, precisely tinted to catch the eye. The walls, coated in the same elaborately twisted vines that draped around the entrance, flashed an occasional bright light, but were otherwise unmarked by the advertisements that filled the halls outside.

Tables of varying heights were scattered around the middle of the open area, curving booths tucked against the side walls, and in a seemingly random but aesthetically pleasing set of varying distances, bars studded the further back wall along every level a walkway touched.

The one on their level was staffed by one person, surrounded by lounging people in various states of dress, and had neatly ordered shelves of bright blue bottles arranged behind the people.

"The blue bar, I presume."

You drank blue things once. Disgusting the next day.

"Disgusting that day, if you want to be particular about it."

I am always particular.

Talinn smiled briefly, remembering how proud Medith had been for scavenging some sort of "new" liquor from the unadapted trainers' barracks. Within minutes they'd all been sure the overly sweet swill had been purposely abandoned by humans with no control over their taste buds, and within hours, every one of them regretted the fact they'd ignored the warning taste and swallowed far too much of the liquid.

Fortunately or unfortunately, it had all come up again, and they'd scrubbed their own quarters with bleary eyes and pounding heads before anyone could see.

Bee had found it hilarious, and refused to temper her headache. Even now, Talinn's tongue curled protectively, warding against the deceptively bright bottles ahead.

"Maybe the bottles are color coded, but the liquor is not."

Maybe it doesn't matter, because you're here to meet with Other Breezy's contact, not revisit old times.

"I'm allowed to be curious about the world, you rude creature."

Not when it ends in vomit.

"Take that up with our designers."

Oh, I mean to.

It took a few moments to locate the gray-bottled bar, which presumably was what they were looking for. Talinn's attention kept snagging on an intricate hairstyle, or an elaborate outfit, or someone using their magnetic boots to walk up a wall—much more challenging in the gravity of a station than the free float of a ship.

The gray bar was relatively small, compared to its closer neighbors, and tucked into the furthest corner from the entrance

Talinn had used. It gave her plenty of time to examine the clientele and décor, and she made a point to drift toward one area and another as she made her way through the bar. Unlike some of the places she'd passed, the music was low, and yet she heard little of anyone's conversation spilling over.

White noise fields in the tables.

"Good for people who like their privacy."

They serve food here, too. That pulled Talinn's focus away from the cosmetic choices of the people around them toward the contents of their tables. Many of them were in fact eating, and were involved in conversations that required a lot of intent gestures, often punctuated with food on various utensils.

"Is there a smell field too?"

I still have your nose turned down. Did you want it back?

"I . . . no. Not until I get my hands on some noodles." A cursory evaluation of the actual foodstuffs showed a disappointing lack of the dish, though she hadn't expected quite so many varieties of food. Maybe it was presentation? There couldn't be *that* many different edibles.

Two people, heads so close their cheeks touched, turned away from the gray bar as she approached, and she slid into the space they'd left behind.

"What can I get you?" The bartender was a woman about her own age, with curls like nothing Talinn had ever seen. Each was a different color than the ones around it, and the effect was lovely, if utterly distracting.

A rocker with a burnside twist.

"I remember the order," she muttered only to Bee, then ordered aloud with a smile.

The other woman didn't so much as blink, only dipped her chin and ducked below the counter for a moment. When she popped back up, she had a curved glass and a matte-gray bottle in her hands.

"Looks like I'm all out of burnside, friend. But if you'll take these to the room right over there." She extended the hand with the bottle, and Talinn followed the gesture. It took an eyeblink to register the faint outline of a door in the vinery between the gray bar and the larger red bar further down the wall. "They'll get you all set up."

"Thanks." Talinn smiled again as she took the glass and bottle, though the expression faded the moment she turned around.

So efficient. How often do they do this?

"I'm more interested in what she did under the counter. Signal, you think? Warning?"

Other Us didn't send us here for a trap.

"I didn't say I thought it was a trap."

It would have been much more logical to kill us at any of a hundred other points—

"Bee. I didn't say I thought it was a trap. But I do think a code makes sense—the room is hard to see, but not impossible. I'm sure at least one drunken patron has tried to open it."

Maybe it shocks them. Blood for the machine god!

"You aren't very helpful."

Not trying to be.

Talinn flicked her pinkie, the gesture mostly hidden by the bottle, but intent clear to the AI in her head. She tucked the glass into to crook of her arm, freeing her hand to open the door. While she may have hesitated before touching the panel to open it, it was only for the barest fraction of a second. As soon as her fingers brushed the panel, the door slid open without light or surge to send her to the machine god, and she stepped into a dimmer room.

The door shut the moment she cleared it, and she was left in a much smaller replica of the space she'd left behind, only done up in shades of black and white—including the vines.

Only one person was in the area, her back to the door, her hands busy in the plant life on the back wall. A shock of recognition ran through her, but Talinn couldn't possibly know anyone on the station.

"Took your time."

Her stomach twisted, and her mouth dried out so fast she couldn't speak for a long moment. Bee made a single short, sharp noise. That voice—

Then the woman turned, and Talinn swallowed back a sound that might have been a laugh or something entirely else. Medith. But not their Medith—of course not their Medith.

Talinn blinked more than she should have had to, and swallowed again for good measure. "Maps were wrong, and the machine god took a sacrifice. It's been a day." Her voice emerged steady, calm. Not like her guts were considering crawling out of any exit port they could find.

"The machine god?" Medith smiled, and it was exactly Medith's expression. On a face she'd never have, because it was an older version. Talinn wanted to hate her and hug her, the urges so equally, violently balanced she crossed her arms, almost dropped the glass from her elbow, and flailed a bit to get everything sorted into its proper place.

"Is it not an actual religion? There was a shop down on one of the public levels, had ports for its sign, knocked out a kid who touched the door."

"The activist stall?" Medith rolled her eyes, and gestured at a table for them to sit. "They keep trying to put different programs into different people, say it's the way to end the war."

"Programs?" Talinn did sit, putting more effort than necessary into setting down the bottle and glass, and pulling out the fabric-covered chair. Better to study the details than look at Not Her Medith.

"The automated ones that run garbage chutes and lifts, and search for the best departure or docking times. Not intelligent, but good task completers."

"And they're . . . loading them into people's brains?"

"There is no end to the weird things people do out here. To end the war, to make sure their side wins the war, to get rich, to get famous." Medith shrugged and slid into a chair across from Talinn, propping her elbows on the table. "A few cycles ago the big rage was modifying their limbs with circuits and pistons and all sorts of things to 'upgrade' performance."

Weird is definitely a word for it.

"Am I the first one here?"

"Cute. No, the rest are back there." Medith gestured to the wall she'd been fiddling with, and though Talinn could find nothing obvious in the pattern of vines, she was sure there was another room behind this one. Nesting hiding places, maybe. "Had a thorough debrief or two."

"Is this something you do often?"

"What? Move Eights around? Meet with absurdly young versions of my friends? Drink in a private room?" The woman cocked her head and widened her eyes.

"Medith." That confused noise rose in her throat again, though this time Talinn was fairly sure it would be more laugh than scream. "How many of us are out there?"

"Oh, Talinn. You love asking the big questions—I can answer that any kind of way. How many Eights exist, across IDC and UCF? How many are read in to the reality of our situation? How many yous do I know?"

"All of those answers would be helpful."

"I know." Medith leaned across the table and patted her hand, then snatched up the bottle and twisted it open. The liquid she poured into the glass was pale gold instead of gray, and Bee hummed in disappointment.

Talinn picked up the glass but didn't drink, and Medith took a swig directly from the bottle.

"So . . . you're not answering any version of the question?"

"You're my third Talinn." Her smile twisted at the edges, not quite a frown but not entirely not, either. Talinn had never seen such an expression on her own Medith's face. "Sort of."

"Wha—"

"Anything else you should share from your encounter with Base Two?"

Talinn blinked three times before she wrangled her thoughts onto Medith's track. "If you've already debriefed the others, they know what I know."

Medith frowned. "We're digging into message history, but can't find a hint of how your Base Two could have known about any of this." She stared somewhere over Talinn's head, then her gaze snapped back to Talinn herself. "I'm sorry your Medith didn't make it. She's the only other one I've heard of who went base defense like I did."

It shouldn't have distracted her, but the open sincerity of the other woman's face was so like her Medith she couldn't help herself. "You ever steal blue liquor for your classmates and make them vomit?" Bug-eaten bar, making her nostalgic and morose.

Other Medith laughed. "No. I did balance ten shots on my arms for my Talinn to drink during our Pre-Assignment Games, and I'm pretty sure at least two of us threw up that night..." She shook her head, then lifted the bottle. "A toast to your Medith."

This doesn't seem like a good idea.

Talinn stared at the half-filled glass in front of her and sighed. It wasn't, but staring at a slightly unfamiliar version of your dead friend's face was an excellent reason to drink in said dead friend's memory.

"To the ones we lose along the way." She lifted the glass, tapped it to Medith's bottle, and took a sip that quite easily became drinking the whole of it.

It didn't burn like that long-ago blue liquor, but her chest flushed with pleasant warmth, and her mouth was left with a clean aftertaste.

"More?" Medith asked, holding out the bottle, and Talinn nodded without thinking.

Again—

"Not a good idea. I know." She blew out her breath, then spoke normally, to Medith more than Bee. "If you won't tell me anything more about all of this... will you at least tell me what's next?"

"Next." Medith drank again after refilling Talinn's glass, then put the bottle on the table and rolled it between her hands. "Next you go somewhere else."

"To the machine god? Another Spacie trip?"

"No." The bottle made a *surr-surr* noise, grating against the table, and Talinn's eyes were happy to leave Not Quite Medith's face to focus on the movement. The liquid inside sloshed, the sound loud in their private room.

"So you're not going to tell me anything at all, then? What's the point of meeting with me?" The edges of her jaw ached, like she wanted to yawn. Or scream.

"Things changed since Talinn left and decided to send you here."

"Your Talinn?" She pressed against the edge of her jaw, close to her ear, a failed attempt to ease the mounting pressure. The back of her throat tingled, and she swallowed against it.

"Yes."

"What's changed?"

"Base Two knowing too much. Then the IDC took all the planetary rings in Govlic. While you were en route. The defense arrays—"

"Switched loyalty. We were there—our Spacies probably brought you that update—"

"No." Medith rolled the bottle faster. "It's not just that. They've won the entirety of Govlic. The defense array in Exfora has gone silent, and UCF is about to take over the entirety of the jump point. We're not sure what's going to happen in this system."

"It's war though, Medith." Talinn tore her gaze from the gray bottle's movement. It was harder than it should have been. "That sort of thing happens all the time."

"Fun fact: it doesn't. Small wins, sure. A planet, a corner, a station, switching of a colony's loyalties. But a whole system? An entire jump point? No."

"That's . . ." The word slowed on her tongue, and Talinn twitched her head to shake it loose. "Doesn't—" That one didn't move any better, tangling against her teeth.

Talinn . . .

"But how—" Two that time, and both an effort.

Talinn.

The black and white around her intensified, crowding closer, and she blinked. Her eyelids moved off beat from the other, making the lighting uneven. No, there was something moving, in her peripheral, if she could move her head half an inch to the side, she could see.

Talinn!

More blackness than whiteness, taking over the sides of her vision, and that didn't make sense, except . . . It did, because it was the vines. Where Medith had been working, when Talinn walked in. Those vines were shifting, moving toward her. To . . .

"Med—" The word strangled itself, her lips barely moving. She strained to focus on her oldest friend—not her friend, but like her friend—

Medith smiled, stopped rolling the bottle. She laid one hand over Talinn's, then tapped the other against the glass still clutched in Talinn's grasp.

"Sorry, my sweet. We're not sure what's moving in the system, and it's easier to move you unconscious. I bet Bee's gonna say I told you so."

Like I would do that as you pass—

Talinn's vision fled before she could decide on outrage or laughter, and consciousness followed.

CHAPTER 24

Talinn woke with death in her mouth.

Now then: I told you so.

"You told me I was going to get poisoned by an older replica of one of our oldest friends?"

I told you drinking was a bad idea.

Talinn started to laugh, but the awful taste in her mouth turned so solid she choked and rolled over in time to throw up. Her surprise at finding a bucket next to her was a momentary flash, then she realized the people who'd drugged her knew very well—perhaps from their own firsthand experience with exactly her genetic mix—what the results would be. She considered missing the bucket on purpose, for spite, but that lasted even less time than her surprise had.

She braced her hands on the bucket—it was round and metal, and steady enough to lean on—and lifted her head to take in wherever she was. There were few clues. The room had four walls at right angles, all in a faint gray—the color of it resembled the bottle Medith had poured from, and her stomach lurched—without decoration. There were two machines, neither with displays, on the wall closest to the outline of the only door. Ceiling and floor were the same color as the walls, so while her vomit had remained in the bucket, meaning gravity clearly existed, it was possible she was on a ship. Her cot was thin, probably foldable, and without either wheels or a visible propulsion system.

"And where are you?"

In your head.

"As always. But you seem personable and chatty as ever, so they didn't truncate you or load-in, so the rest of you is . . . ?"

In one of Jeena's boxes.

Her stomach folded over, and Talinn took her time easing back from the bucket onto the bed. She could really use some water, or very spicy chips, or those noodles she'd never gotten, or even old cube food from a tank—anything to get her clear of the taste coating her tongue. After looking at her hands, clearly not in contact with any portable server, she made an interrogatory noise and flopped face up on the cot.

Not shielded. And no, I can't really tell where we are. I went out pretty fast after you.

"Poison doesn't work that way."

Great point, but fun fact, it wasn't poison. And whatever they got you with wasn't what shuttered me. Something was in the vines.

"EMP vines?" Talinn frowned, and somehow that intensified the taste in her mouth. She scraped her tongue against her teeth, which helped not at all, and stared at the featureless ceiling. "Still sure they don't want to kill us?"

I'm not even tamping down a headache. The vomit and weird mouth thing you're doing seem to be the only side effects.

"Imagine my joy." She should get up, but the idea of it was exhausting enough that she had no interest toward making it happen. "So this is the shit that shit makes, right?"

I'm not thrilled with how they're treating us, if that's what you're asking.

"I mean, they know who they're dealing with—they know who they're dealing with probably better than anyone anywhere had ever known who they're dealing with. So there's got to be a reason. Or is older us just fell-into-a-black hole bonzo?"

I can see a probability path that breaks us so cosmically we can't understand consequences, so it's possible that happened to them, but . . . I don't think this is that.

"Makes it worse, Bee." Talinn stretched her arms straight up from her body then rotated them back to stretch past her head, testing any soreness or lingering cramps in her muscles. Everything moved as it should, and reluctantly she swung her legs to the side, letting them drift toward the floor.

Not disagreeing with you.

"That's a nice change." She sat up, eased weight onto her legs to make sure nothing was going to give out on her, then stood. Except the yuck inside her face, the rest of her acted like she'd taken a pleasant nap. "How long were we out?"

I don't have anything to measure against.

"Thought you said the box wasn't shielded?"

It's not, hence our usual chat. But apparently everything else around me is.

"Where in all the idiot corners of the galaxy did they bring us, that *everything* is shielded?" Shielding against AIs was critical, but tricky and therefore expensive. The IDC and UCF raced each other to develop more clever methods to block avenues they didn't want AIs in, and so allegedly also more clever AIs to get into those locked paths, but now Talinn wondered if that was all propaganda. Maybe Command programmed a block of some kind into the AIs they built, and as a result: shielding.

It didn't matter for the moment, while she remained alone in a featureless room who knew where, so she tagged it on to her ongoing list. "Orienting question, Bee: Should I dump my vomit bucket over the two machines in this room?" She said it out loud, for maximum chance someone somewhere would hear and make a move to stop her.

Not yet. Next question: Will the door open for you?

"If not, I'm writing a letter to the machine god." Talinn blew out her breath, straightened her shoulders, and strode to the door with only a wobble or two. She reached for the panel, but the outline of the door vanished—the panel slid up so fast she almost missed it—and she was left blinking at a stranger.

A good looking, grinning, lounging stranger. He had a bare head and a port below his ear, and he appeared about her age. Her hand twitched, and she muttered loud enough for him to hear, "Should have brought the bucket."

"Thought I timed it well enough you'd be done puking. Welcome to Deep End."

"Glitches take us all to the heat death of the universe." Talinn leaned in the doorway and hoped her breath smelled as terrible as it tasted. "Deep End? Seriously?"

He held both hands in front of him, palms toward her, and, if anything, his grin brightened. He had a dimple. Had she ever met an Eight with a dimple?

"I do not tell lies, New Talinn. Kay would take over my brain at the dissonance. If it makes you feel better, it's not a fun turn of phrase. We're about as far from the jump point as you can get and still call it civilized space."

"Is it?" Talinn didn't rise to the bait of "New Talinn," but tilted her head and crossed her arms in silent dare.

"Is it what?"

"Civilized space."

"Orienting question, Eight: What's civilized these days?" His gaze scanned over her body, then he half turned and gestured her along. "Come on, you're the last to wake up, and they're all waiting to get caught up."

"All?"

"The six you came in with. Seven, counting the tech."

"And you are?"

"That's right, Talinn said you didn't have one of me. Weird. I'm Tiernan Agare, and Kay is behaving himself not battering at Bee until she's settled."

The name was familiar, and it took her a few steps to remember Older Talinn's wry voice, about not being sure if it were a win or not that her class hadn't had a Tiernan. After only a few minutes in his company, Talinn understood.

"We're just going to leave the vomit back there?"

His pace slowed. "Did you want to go back and get it? Bring it with you like a welcome basket?"

"A . . . welcome basket?" She tried to imagine what such a thing could be, and failed. "Is that an IDC thing?"

"Shit in a bucket, you really are a Talinn." He shook his head with an exaggerated sigh. "And it's a holonet thing." Before they turned down the next featureless hall, he added, "But yeah, I'm IDC grown."

"Is there some big secret reason why you got grown on the IDC side around the time we got decanted for UCF?"

"Probably." He laughed, though there was a bitterness to the sound she felt to her toes. "But glitch me to eternity if any of us have figured it out. Whatever grand plan Command is running, we've yet to crack it."

Well. That's something we know now.

"Helpful?"

Of course not. But maybe we'll finally start finding things out, now that we're here.

"Wherever here is."

Deep End, Talinn. Weren't you paying attention?

"She sassing you about me, or where you are?" Tiernan waved ahead of them, and a wall parted into a door. Unlike the one in the room she'd left behind, this one slid down into the floor.

Talinn noted the band on his wrist, but couldn't tell where it latched. No good trying to break it off him until she had a better idea of how it fastened. If it fastened—this was a group of people intimately acquainted with body modifications, and she should probably remember assumptions were traps. There was far too much she didn't understand.

"You know *a* Bee, but you don't know *my* Bee." She was too late saying it, knew the hesitation proved to him he'd been right one way or the other, but she couldn't not make the effort.

"We're not Spacies, New Talinn. I don't know any Bees that well, but I know *my* AI, and plenty of Eights. If she's not sassing you about one of those two things, I have to assume she's broken. Or UCF got real weird when they made your class."

"Guess it got weird then. Not a lot of sassy AIs in my class." That wasn't even a lie. As far as she'd ever been able to tell with other Eights, Bee took an outsized interest in being contrary.

"Never thought I'd be grateful to the IDC." He shrugged once more, then waved his arm again. A wall to their left disappeared—she didn't look fast enough to see which direction it had gone—and instead of smooth, unbroken gray, there was a giant room in a riot of colors.

No EMP vines though.

"We're still not sure that the vines were EMP producing."

Not sure that wasn't *what those vines did, so please continue to examine all pieces of this chaos with suspicion.*

It was chaos. Even their combined processing couldn't make sense of it all right away. The room was tall—the ceiling at least a full body length above Talinn's head—and cluttered with an almost uncountable number of screens, projected displays, scrolling data sets, and static images.

Ten thousand, three hundred and—

"Thirty-six." Talinn noted the tables, mismatched and scattered with printouts and films she didn't bother to count, and the randomly assorted chairs, but her eyes fully snagged on the row of machines along the side wall.

Well. I didn't think that's where the rest of me was. Thought my room was a lot more . . . blank.

"Those aren't yours," Tiernan said, as though he'd heard Bee. Which of course he hadn't, so it was worse that he'd yet again predicted them. "They're empty servers, we're still cleaning them out. Your tech's not bad. We'll probably keep her."

"Cleaning them out for what? Or from what?"

He didn't answer, stride picking up as he arrowed for one of the larger screens in the middle of the room. It was fully opaque, and so she almost wasn't surprised when they swerved around it and found it had been concealing something rather important.

Somethings—someones. Gathered around a table nearly as long as the screen were all the people left in the galaxy she still cared about. Which would be depressing if she thought about it too long, so she didn't.

Instead she crossed the rest of the distance without registering it, and had Caytil and Sammer in a hug by the next time she blinked. Time usually only stuttered like that for load-in, but it was another thing not to spend time worrying about for the moment.

You're running out of room on the list of things to get back to.

"It's an infinite list, Bee."

It's about to be.

"Slept long enough." Sammer didn't fully let go of her when the hug ended, tugging her to his corner of the table, next to Jeena.

Talinn touched arms or shoulders of the other Eights as she passed, and hesitated before sitting. With a mental shrug, she leaned to put her arms around Jeena. The tech startled, then returned the embrace with surprising strength. "Good to see you," she murmured, and Talinn hated the resultant warmth. She let go and slid onto a stool, glad not to have a back to slump against. She needed to pay attention to this.

"I bet Old Talinn told that Medith to give me some extra of whatever they drugged us with, to get me back for being difficult."

"One, that sounds like self-hatred, and I would never." The new voice, so like hers it grated against her skin right down to the nerves, appeared before its owner. "Two, Medith drugged you, not on my orders, so you must have pissed *her* off. And three, you really need to find a different name. I was Talinn first."

"You weren't though." Talinn's response was overridden as Tiernan chimed in, so helpfully, "I've been calling her New Talinn."

On the heels of that, Caytil's far less cheerful, "Let's pause on the fun times and get to facts, shall we?"

Old Talinn stepped around the screen, and Talinn couldn't have said which direction she'd come from. For all she knew, all the walls in this overflowing room retracted to let people through.

We probably should have spent less time counting screens and more figuring out what was on them. Bee's voice, smaller than usual, gave a hint of guilt. Talinn would have agreed, but without context, most of the screens were useless, and picking through the rest was a staggeringly huge task. Which was, she decided, probably the point.

"Answers would be nice." Heka made a show of stretching out her legs and threw her arm over the back of her chair.

"You've got the main ones. Clones, never-ending war, conspiracy across the Commands—"

"Why did you drug us? I thought we were going to go to multiple stops before we got here? What's going on with the defense arrays? What have you been *doing for the forty cycles you knew this was happening?*" Talinn had to bite on her tongue until it bled to keep from spilling out her entire ever-growing list of questions. Even four felt excessive, but she couldn't not.

"We drugged you because Medith determined it's possible to track concentrated AI signals, and she didn't know how a Base Two might have found out about us. Moving you in a group is dangerous, slipping you out one at a time would take too long."

"Forty cycles isn't too long?" Caytil muttered, loud enough to mean it being overheard.

"And you couldn't just tell us that because . . . ?"

"Because what happens if one of you rejects the necessity? Now you're on your guard, everything's delayed, and we risk a scene for no reason. This is hardly the worst thing that's happened to you in your careers."

"Not a slippery slope at all." Talinn hooked her leg into the rung at the bottom of the stool and studied the older version of herself. "If it's possible to track concentrated AI signals, isn't it dangerous for us all to be together here? Or anywhere?"

"To clarify, whatever is able to track us, it works when we're in transit."

"So it works better in space, or through the jump points?"

"See, *there's* a good question." Old Talinn lifted her chin and Tiernan leaned over the table, pressing something that previously didn't seem pushable. The giant screen in front of them cleared its scrolling data and displayed a not-to-scale map of the settled systems. "We haven't been able to answer it definitively, but we have a suspicion."

Talinn considered the equipment Base Two had used to overhear some parts of her conversations with Bee. Proximity mattered, but proximity was hard to reliably predict in space. So many different approaches were used from jump points to various settlements, depending on other traffic, current orbits, debris.

The jump points themselves couldn't have some kind of equipment that might disrupt the vibrations and measurements of the points, and then that returned to the problem of various exit and entry points. Only one sort of installation was reliably focused on traffic through a jump point, allowing a scanning point for traffic in and out of any given system.

"The defense arrays." The words were hushed, so she cleared her throat and repeated them. "Something's been uploaded or mounted to the defense arrays, and that's what's tracking AI signals."

"Maybe that's why they're glitching, too." Caytil frowned and kept her eyes fixed on the screen. "Turns out you can't just introduce something new to the coding and expect it to work perfectly."

Talinn wrenched her thoughts away from Medith and Cece and everyone else that blew up back on shitty P-8, and tamped down the flush of satisfaction at Other Talinn's tiny flinch.

"We didn't do it, but it makes sense someone did. Of course the IDC and UCF both want to monitor movements of AIT troops or ships with more than a trio of transit pairings. And if we haven't been able to perfect the tweaking process, of course Command is bound to ram it sideways with a rusty knife too."

"Fine. You drugged us to keep the defense arrays from tracking us."

Or blowing us up. Bee dropped the words more thoughtfully than Talinn would have expected, weighing if that might be why the UCF defense arrays suddenly required an IDC code from them . . . and given this other version of them had supplied that code, what else they weren't telling.

"And maybe that's what's going on with the defense arrays. So. Because we were unconscious you were able to just move us here?" Xenni folded her arms and rested her elbows on the table, shoving some printouts out of the way.

"Time got pressing, and we did move your bodies a few times. Carefully, as I hope you'll appreciate."

Being unconscious for travel wasn't a new experience, and if it got them to their destination more efficiently, fine. Talinn didn't have a burning desire to go immediately to another humanity-crowded station. On to the next repeated question.

"What's been going on for forty cycles that nothing seems to have changed since you started going rogue and recruiting Eights?"

"Ah. See there, new me, you're letting your annoyance get ahead of your logic." Other Talinn turned sideways, gesturing at the map on the screen. "Because things *have* been changing, and that change is accelerating."

"We got some of this debrief from the Spacies." Sammer's tone held to neutral and polite, but his shoulders were as tense as the rest of theirs. "What have *you* all been doing? What do you expect we're going to do, in a multisystem, multifront, multidecade war?"

"You're awfully impatient for base defense." Other Talinn didn't smile, but her mouth quirked in an expression Talinn herself couldn't read.

She shifted on her seat and stretched out her neck, distracting herself from the discomfit of not recognizing what her own face meant. It would be better if she could stare fixedly at the screen, like Caytil, but her gaze continued to drift back toward Other Talinn regardless of her efforts.

Tiernan cleared his throat, then made a point of grinning slowly when attention snapped to him. "Sabotage. Information pollution. Command carefully plans out the arcs of the war, the dance of the fronts—plans are scoped by generation, not by individual engagements. We take out key pieces here and there, and the plans crumble."

The man was dramatic, and Talinn envisioned her class with a showoff like that in it. *No wonder he went jet*, Bee murmured, and Talinn ducked her head to keep from smiling.

"And have you figured out how Command makes generational plans, if you're not sure that IDC and UCF are talking to each other? Seems awfully risky—you only get so many Eights every couple of cycles, and if *we're* the predictable part, but the other side goes rogue—"

"We're fairly sure they use AI," Other Talinn interrupted Sammer smoothly, and rode out the instant overlapping questions and protests with no expression at all.

This is a shit briefing.

"They're trying to make us feel heard, while still only telling us what they want to." Talinn did not subvocalize her response, and despite the noise, her older version locked eyes with her. Talinn raised her eyebrows, and saw the swallowed-back scoff in her not-her face.

Caytil stopped talking midword, glancing between the two, and Sammer followed. Xenni was still declaiming how the war had looked no different in *her* lifetime, with Konti's emphatic agreement, and Arnod and Heka muttered to each other, then turned glares on Tiernan and Other Talinn, respectively. Jeena listed two more reasons why using AI to plan at the Command level would be impossible before trailing off.

"We're answering your questions, because you won't listen if we just 'tell you what we want to.'" Other Talinn pitched her voice slightly higher, as though imitating Talinn, which was ridiculous because they had the same voice. Talinn scowled, but the other woman ignored it. "Some of your questions are good, some are... less good. But you're here, and you can't go back, so we're working together. Which means you're entitled to know all the things that will help us end this."

"To be clear—end what? The war? The cloning programs? Civilization as it currently exists?" Until Caytil spat out the last phrase, Talinn hadn't even considered it. The war, obviously. But Other Talinn hesitated—so brief anyone who wasn't mostly her might have missed it—and Talinn's entire spine froze, locking her into place.

"The IDC and the UCF, as a whole." Other Talinn shrugged, as though that weren't civilization as they knew it. "They exist to fight their war. Without the war, there's no reason for them. The civilian governments can handle themselves, if they're not fighting against each other."

Talinn's mouth hung open. Was she really that stupid? Was she, Talinn, in any iteration . . . a complete idiot?

"They . . . they'd keep fighting. It's the civilian governments that formed the Interstellar Defense Corps and the United Colonial Force. They specifically exist because different civilian governments banded together to fight each other." Konti gaped from Other Talinn to Tiernan, as disbelieving as Talinn herself.

"Yes." Other Talinn cocked her head as though the clones in front of her were the stupid ones. "Over the jump points. That they need Auliens to navigate. Which are made by the Command in power at the IDC and UCF, not at the civilian leadership level."

"So you'll wipe the Eights and Spacies . . . anything related to the clone programs?"

"No. We *take* the clone programs. Civilians contract with us to navigate jump points. They don't fight over the jump points. With no scrambling all over the glitch-begotten things, we can probably even spread out and make more."

"Why wouldn't the locals grab the programs—"

"There are no sizable settlements on any installation with grow tanks or training centers. It's mostly support personnel Command has cleared. Once we have enough resources to be sure we're in place to take them all in a small amount of time, that part is done."

"You said the war keeps going because it's making money. It's not going to stop just because we upset some players."

"And this, newbies, is why it's taken us so long. You have to slide out pieces here and there, be sure you've got something to take its place." Tiernan spread his arms wide, then crossed them and nodded to Other Talinn.

"Guess what will *also* make a lot of people a lot of money?" She asked it like it was meant to be obvious, and after a moment, Talinn realized it was.

"New jump points. New settlements, with new resources, the need for trade, shipbuilding, gear."

"There it is. Weapons factories can turn to transport and navigation easy enough. Some fortunes may fade, but enough new ones will be made—war will make sense again, eventually, but they won't have the knowledge or understanding to make it quite so... ongoing."

"Us, you mean. They won't have us." Caytil made the point explicit, and Talinn's innards squirmed again.

Big celebration for whole new worlds, sure, but... can we get back to this "AI is planning the wars" business, because I would like to know more.

Jeena interjected before Talinn could. "Say that you can find all the training centers—"

"We can," Tiernan replied even as Other Talinn nodded and said, "We have."

"—even though they're siloed and one of the most closely guarded, need-to-know places in the galaxy. If you think there are AI planning the war, and deciding which of each of you are set out to fight generations at a time... How would you imagine they haven't factored that into the planning?"

And how do I get a job planning the war? That sounds almost as fun as being a tank.

Other Talinn smiled so suddenly, and so brightly, for a wild moment Talinn thought the other woman had heard *her* Bee. "Leave it to a tech to ask the really fun orienting question. Because, friends, here's the thing—I think they *have*."

CHAPTER 25

"Yeah, you're gonna need to wind that back for us." Caytil leaned forward, halfway across the table, and Talinn caught herself doing the same. "Because you're saying it like it's a good thing."

"UCF and IDC get to drag this on as long as they do because civilian casualties are minimized. Truth be told, so are unadapted soldier deaths. There are very few bloodbaths, except for when Eights are fighting Eights. There aren't a whole lot of AI programs out there that can walk a balance like that."

"There are the big defense arrays, which are a pretty clear, 'shoot these, ignore those' decision tree." Caytil tapped her fingers on the table. "And then the small-scope analysis programs that aren't really intelligent so much as . . . trained. Everything else is—"

"Like us." Talinn tried to imagine it and failed. "Are you saying there's a third bucket of clone pairs out there—Spacies, Eights, and . . . what, strategy heads?"

"No." Jeena's eyes unfocused, and she shoved her hands into her hair. "They'd need techs like anyone else, and we're not nearly as isolated as you all. There would have been a whisper about another training class, or a weird posting, or . . . or something. Especially once my portable—" She snatched her hands back and pressed them to her mouth instead.

"Share with the group," Konti prompted when the tech's eyes only got larger and rounder.

"The truncated programs."

"She really is good." Other Talinn inclined her head, but said no more, and everyone's gaze tracked back to Jeena.

"When you die—you, the human partner of the Eights—you know chances are good the AI is only partially disabled."

I don't think I'm going to like this at all, am I?

Talinn nodded, in answer to both Bee and Jeena. In many cases, the pairing ended simultaneously—usually EMPs wiping an AI were followed by catastrophic failures or a desperate Eight taking everyone out with them. But overall, Eights were designed so that the part of the AI pair hosted in the equipment, or server, would remain for a last report. It was a broken link, a half program—the part of the AI that had grown and learned alongside, and as part of, the organic component would cease to function, but the backups and redundant code would persist. Like Ern, circling his final report until the techs shut him down.

Talinn had never once envied the fact that Bee would have to linger after Talinn's death in order to record a final report, or conduct a last analysis, but it had always been their reality. The understanding being, however, that such a truncated program couldn't last in perpetuity, but would wipe, be wiped, or simply cease functioning within a short amount of time.

"You had to wipe that X program, after it was brought to you in a box. It didn't... stop on its own." Sammer's words started off strangled, and he stopped midway to clear his throat. It didn't help.

And Other Bee lasted until she found another Talinn.

"So... Command *keeps* truncated programs? Puts them to work planning future engagements?"

"Who knows the troops best? Who's learned the difference between good and bad deaths? Who's been grown to perfectly embody the needs of Command, whether IDC or UCF?"

Saliva filled Talinn's mouth no matter how much she swallowed. "That's... morbid."

"It's funny, the thing that finally makes you hate the system." Tiernan laughed, though with little humor in the sound.

"And that's why... you think the program, or programs, they're using know you're out here?"

"Any chunk of Bee is still Bee," Other Talinn said with such confidence Talinn added another question to her tally. "She's going to want what's best for a Talinn, even if it's not her Talinn."

"And you're saying... for a long time, the status quo was good enough for us. For everyone, but especially for Eights."

"It meant there'd always be a new version of their pairing, eventually. Spin one out when the circumstances are right. Twist the circumstances to make them right. But now we're out here, this group of us, doing other things..."

"And maybe something else is better for us. So we have an ally on the inside?"

"No." Other Talinn spread her arms, palms up. "This is all piecemeal and supposition, more than facts we've found solid, inarguable evidence around. I don't think we, this group of us, were in the plan. There's such a low probability any of us would have ever realized what was going on, given all the planning they've done to keep such a thing from happening, I can't imagine *that* was in any of the projections."

"But once it happened..." Caytil's jaw flexed as she added something privately to Ziti.

"It's our best guess. Command strung some broken programs together over time, all with slightly conflicting priorities, and the more we skew out of their plan, the more maybe they're remembering those priorities. Or us."

She's not wrong—any part of me would want what's best for you, and into a gravity well with everything else.

"Either way you're operating as though the AI conglomeration you think is planning everything, knows we're out here, but is not reading in Command. That's several big leaps." Arnod frowned, staring into some middle distance.

"We've taken our time making them. As you so kindly pointed out, we've had forty-odd cycles to test some theories." Other Talinn scanned the group, but each were processing, on their own or with their AI partner.

Tiernan glanced at the older Talinn, and at her tiniest of nods, he turned more toward the corner where Sammer and Talinn sat. "We have tried several times to infiltrate Command, both IDC and UCF. You won't be surprised to hear they're locked down pretty tight against AI incursions."

Indeed, no one expressed anything remotely close to surprise.

"However, from our attempts we've found the potential for a chink or two."

"You're saying 'we' with some significant eye contact." Talinn's stomach twisted again, and she made sure to put a sarcastic coating on her words to cover it.

"There are only three AI series that have had any luck at all."

Oh, this will be fun.

"Bee, Lei, and Ziti."

Knew it.

"If our ideas are right, it's likely there were a few more B-, L8-, and or ZT-series in the Command mix early on, and over time they showed a tiny preference for spinning out more B-series, and pairs that had been in their training and assignment classes."

"And so it compounded over time." Caytil, arms crossed, tapped her fingers in a rolling motion that didn't communicate any secret messages to her former classmates. Just annoyance.

"Little by little." Other Talinn unfocused, though Talinn couldn't see a hint of the other woman's conversation with her own Bee. Maybe she was lost in some thought. "Command would have thought the truncated programs pared clean of their personality matrixes, so they wouldn't have concerned themselves with what mix went into the soup they wanted."

Talinn weighed the possibilities. *How* the Eight program worked was not considered need to know for the Eights themselves. They learned high-level history, to make them proud and invested, and common potential issues, so they could handle any small errors in the field if they came up. Any major errors, Command wanted techs to deal with, or for the pair to clean themselves out of service, usually by taking as many enemy forces with them as possible. That was made very clear in training and on each and every assignment.

The Eights theorized amongst themselves, of course. Based on overheard snippets of conversations, reports left out a moment too long, information caches not kept as classified as they should be, they'd gathered information and suppositions. Best Talinn and her friends had figured, the AIs were made in two major parts. The logic strings that dictated scope of role and actions, repeated in the backups that were primarily hosted in servers or tanks or other assignment machinery, and the personality core that grew partially embedded in their partner's organic brain. The bulk of objective analysis happened in the logic, and the decision tree that led to actual choice happened with the human partner. AI were not meant to function with only one part of their programming—cut off from their backups, they would devolve into so much noise in the impulses of the human brain. Cut off from their human, they were all analysis, no drive. The two parts needed to combine for lasting functionality.

Her class and the few friends she'd made after had relatively few opportunities to test any of their ideas, which Talinn had never truly regretted. Bee worked. Talinn worked. Everything else was a far secondary in importance.

But . . . she *had* been cut off from Bee. And while she couldn't hear Bee anymore, the actual program of *Bee* had been perfectly fine. They'd assumed it was degradation over time that did it. Lack of feedback from the organic part of their programming. Other Talinn's Bee had survived for an untold amount of time until a chance came to merge.

"They don't teach us anything about how we work for a reason." Talinn swiveled on her stool and nudged Jeena. "But *you* know."

"Not everything—"

"More than us." Sammer pivoted in his seat as well, and a rustle of movement indicated the rest of the Eights were interested.

"Prob—yes."

"Good." Talinn shot a glance back at the other clone of her, who looked . . . amused? Talinn really had to work on her own expressions. "The more we know, the more able we'll be to tackle whatever these little openings in the shields are."

"If we want to end the IDC and UCF, we need to get into their Commands." Caytil didn't turn toward Tiernan or Other Talinn, but both nodded all the same.

"But if Command suspects you're—we're out here?" With a chance to think about it, Talinn regretted never having another conversation with Base Two. What did he actually know?

"So far that seems isolated. Base Two . . ." Other Talinn's frown deepened and cleared in almost the same moment. "We can't find any trace of communication in any orders, coded or not. He might have simply *seen* something, at one posting or another."

"But you thought Command sent us to that post for a reason—" Talinn protested, catching Caytil's warning movement too late.

"We're looking into it. For the moment, it's most important you learn as much about how you work as possible, to be fit to move about the systems."

"Time for a new training course." Sammer patted Jeena's shoulder, his tone so cheerful a smile flickered over her face. He didn't glance up at Talinn, but she relaxed, understanding he'd caught the disconnect too.

"Oh good," Heka muttered. "I always wanted to be a tech."

Bee let the susurrus of conversation go on for a bit, then abruptly lost interest and pulled Talinn's thoughts back.

So we're going to do to Command what Other Bee did to us?

"Hopefully with less explosions, but—" She kept it subvocal, judging the general mood of the room to be unsettled and deciding not to add more to it.

No. More explosions. Get into Command, get out of Command, leave nothing behind.

"You're getting a little bloodthirsty on me." She tried to make it a joke, but her gaze pulled back toward the Other Talinn. Was that their plan?

Getting? If these people are right, versions of me have been tweaking the war all along, to get to this point.

"That's not exactly—" Adrenaline spiked, and Talinn steadied herself, hands on the table.

With a little help from our friends. For the first time in quite a while, a hint of shearing metal undercut her words.

"Bee, no, that's not—" She was fairly sure Bee was joking, more exaggeratory than believing that her design was at the root of everything happening, but something about the aim of the conversation was setting off all her internal alarms. A prickle of a cold flush climbed from the base of her spine to the top of her head, anticipating Bee's next points.

Either way. Remember what we said about letting the galaxy burn?

"...yes."

Let's do it.

CHAPTER 26

"We've got to go back out there." Talinn stretched out on the delightfully comfortable bed she'd been given, then shifted to hang her head off the side of it. It gave her a better angle on Caytil, who sat on the floor with her back against the bed, her legs and arms crossed.

Sammer, sprawled at the two-person table against the wall across the small room, spun the chair around to dramatically gape at her. "Why under any sky in the galaxy would we do that?"

"I don't believe the civilian governments are going to be any better on their own than UCF. Or IDC." She flung her arm above her and flicked a finger out for each point. "They're either in league with the Command decisions, or dependent on them. Pulling Command out from under—over?—everyone will just be..."

"Chaos." Caytil tipped her head back, eyes closed. She didn't sound particularly upset by the concept.

"And going back out there will..." Sammer trailed off, eyebrows up and hand extended, waiting for the answer.

"Get a better sense of what's out there? We only know what UCF let us know, and now what these people are telling us. Versions of us doesn't mean *us*, and we can't just...trust them."

"Like we trusted UCF. For our whole lives." His flat voice made the nerves in her shoulder twitch, but Talinn refused to shift and show it bothered her.

"We didn't trust UCF. We...did what we were told. Assumed the world was what they said it was."

"Talinn, my darling, my favorite little friend—that's trust."

209

Sammer turned to Caytil, silently asking for backup, but she remained unmoving.

"That's *complacency*. They let us blow things up. And I like blowing things up." She dropped her arm and groaned. "Bee's ready to let the galaxy burn. But we can't just keep being point-and-shoot weapons anymore."

"I like point-and-shoot weapons," Caytil murmured, though she didn't open her eyes. "Especially when they're tanks."

I always did like Caytil.

"The whole galaxy isn't going to—"

"Don't, Sammer." Talinn sat up, twisting to hang her legs off the bed and dropping her elbows behind her to lean in the other direction. "I can run the probabilities as well as you can. It's as likely everything comes to crashing ruin as it finds a way forward without UCF and IDC holding some sort of line."

"Ziti's against." Caytil moved, but only to pull her legs up and wrap her arms around them. She took up surprisingly little space in the room. "We're sure change is worse than the current state."

"For who?" Sammer spun in the chair again, but ensured his scowl pointed toward Talinn for most of his pivot. "Civilians? Command? Not people like us."

"Were you unhappy, Sammer? Really? Before P-8, when we were doing what we were trained to do, were you bothered by your life, or did you like it?" Talinn didn't know which side she was arguing— Bee's wholehearted forward charge, or Ziggy's urge to let it be.

"Medith *died*, Talinn." It hit her in the gut, as she was sure he intended it to, but that only shifted her grief further into anger.

"People are going to die if we do this. People are going to die if we don't. People have *always* died, Sammer."

"Thank you for that life lesson." He rolled his eyes, stilling the chair to be sure she saw it, and she flopped back on the bed to more visibly ignore him. "Glad to know that's what you'll say when I die for nothing, to make UCF money. People have *always* died. At least Sammer went out firing for the good old United Colo—"

"Stuff it, shitheel." She sighed, hoped Caytil would say something, anything, about why she and Ziti were against. When the silence held, she forced herself upright again and pushed back to the wall, resolving to be less twitchy.

"And what does going out there again help? Seriously." A level of tension eased from Sammer's shoulders—they'd pushed each other enough, and were getting back to the heart of the matter. "You want to see what life is like for the empties? Decide if it'll be net neutral if we take out Command?"

"I want to use my own eyes and see more of what's going on. I listened to Other Talinn and Medith died. There's not a way I'm forgetting that, Sammer. But here's the thing—we don't know if that was IDC's fault, or *these* people's." Talinn threw her arms wide, encompassing the whole of the asteroid installation they'd been tucked into. *A voice*, Medith had said, and that was little enough to go on.

As best as Bee could tell, their conversations weren't being listened to or recorded, but Talinn no longer cared if the other clones heard her or not.

"They still haven't told us everything about those codes they inserted into our AIs." Caytil shifted slightly, enough to keep both Talinn and Sammer in her peripheral.

"They still haven't told us everything, full stop." Talinn scooted her leg forward to touch Caytil's shoulder, and the other woman patted Talinn's foot briefly.

"So let's ask—"

"Yes. Ask Jeena."

"Talinn—" Sammer's shoulders tightened again, moving fractionally toward his ears.

"She's as involved as the rest of us, Sammer. You trying to keep her out of things isn't protecting her."

"I'm not trying to—"

"You've been twisty and weird since we got here—"

"I *haven't*—"

"It's the other him." Caytil put her palm to her jawline and pushed until her neck audibly cracked. "It's not since we got here. It's since you went in a room and talked to the other Sammer. What happened?"

Sammer crumpled, and Talinn had surged to the end of the bed, reaching for him, before she finished processing his motion. "I killed Medith," he said, so softly everyone else froze, to be sure the words were real.

"No, of course you—"

"The message—the one I thought you sent, but was Other Talinn. The packet she hid and sent, it was meant for me and Lei. It was a piece of the other Sammer's L8, a fraction of code. But Cece got it, because I passed it to them. I thought it was a message—I thought you were being clever, slipping in something under Command's view."

That's for sure what I got? A piece of the other Bee? Some of it doesn't feel . . .

"That's *not* the same as you killing Medith, Sammer, don't be an idiot."

"That's what the . . . other Sammer, he said it wasn't my fault, it was both of ours, and he should have . . . we should have . . ."

"All right. First." Talinn stood, leaned over, and tapped Sammer firmly on his downtrodden head. "Stop being a complete shitface because you're feeling guilty over something you didn't actually do, not truly, certainly not on purpose. Waste of time, and you know better than a tech at load-in that Medith would agree and kick you until you stopped whining."

"Second?" Caytil prompted, which was tacit agreement of the first point, a fact Sammer caught because he lifted his head.

"Second, Medith said there was 'a voice.' Cece would have recognized Lei, so something else might be going on, and we don't know enough to call it sorted."

"Is there a third?" Caytil turned her head to raise her eyebrows at Talinn, then pivoted back toward Sammer, nodding firmly.

"Third, I'm sick of calling them 'other' us-es. Otie and Osis."

Sammer lifted his head fully at that, mouth moving as he sounded it out. "Other Talinn, OT . . . you're AI naming them."

"Better than they deserve, probably." Talinn straightened and folded her hands behind her back.

"When we meet other Caytil, we can flip it. Call her Coe."

"Caytil comma other. Done." Talinn paced the three times possible in each direction, then snapped to attention facing them both. "Fourth, let's go to Jeena and dig into these extra pieces the older clones have been passing us. Because fifth, whether we're raiding Command or going out into the galaxy again, we're not going blind."

Is there a sixth?

"There is not a sixth," Talinn said aloud to Bee and the human ears in her room.

Just for us then: sixth, the next time we find a Medith—other than the one that drugged us—we take out whoever we need to, to keep her alive.

And that was so good, Talinn reversed course and announced the sixth to everyone.

They spent so long in the lab with Jeena, they had to stop when she got unsteady.

"Oh. Food. Food would probably be helpful for you." Sammer steadied her, then left his hand on her elbow, and Jeena made a noise both laugh and scoff.

"You're supposed to eat regularly too, you know. Eights are still people."

"Says you and zero other techs in the history of history." Talinn's laugh, however, had a bit more humor in it. "And you know as well as any of us we can go a lot longer without new calories. Our bodies are good at cannibalizing what they already have."

"That's bad though. You see how that's bad?" Jeena shook her head and leaned against Sammer. "Anyway, I'm fine. Food *would* be helpful, but it's mostly that I've slept maybe a handful of hours since we've gotten here—"

"Five," Sammer interjected, his glower indicating he was not trying to be helpful.

"And—"

"Out of the forty-eight hours we've been here."

"And," she said loudly, talking over him. "I've done worse. So. Food. And back to work."

The installation was not large, two layers of a wheel, each broken into four spokes—it held about fifty people, with the capacity for roughly double that. Other Talinn—Otie—made noises that indicated they had a few other spaces like it carved out in various far corners of the systems, but she was not forthright about their numbers. It was one of the few things Talinn could understand her not wanting to share, though a sense of the scale of the operation would have been nice.

She did wonder if this burrowed living space in a large asteroid was something they'd built or scavenged. The layer of the wheel closest to the surface of the asteroid was featureless across all sections, which included cargo loading (cargo occasionally meaning unconscious Eights), medlabs, recovery rooms, and gear of various sorts, from tools to vacuum suits to weapons they hadn't been able to play with at all. Given access to the second layer wasn't particularly well hidden, she'd wondered aloud why the first floor was so sleek and devoid of personalization, but no one had seen fit to answer her.

The deeper layer held living quarters, several rec areas and the kitchen, the giant room with every bit of information known to man—as far as Talinn could tell, as they had not been let back in it unattended—and a cluster of labs Jeena had partially taken over. Apparently with all the cloning and cycles and repetition, Jeena was the first tech they'd managed to run off with. Talinn figured Sammer should get some points for that.

It took only a few minutes to walk from their part of the spoke to the kitchen, and they spoke little on the way. When the door into the kitchen vanished into the ground, the air flooded with a smell so strong and so savory Talinn had to swallow back immediate saliva several times before speaking.

"Are you . . . cooking?" she asked Otie, and the woman craned her neck back to look at them.

"Bee's better at it than I am, turns out. Keeps me from burning or under seasoning or over cooking. Not sure how, given she has zero taste buds, but yes, it's a skill we picked up over the cycles."

It's a science.

"It's basically science," Otie continued, waving for them to sit at one of the three long tables in the room. "And most planets and stations have room to pay for a transient cook. Amazing the things you learn over food."

That feels like a warning. But you're going to eat with her anyway.

"Yes. To both." Talinn sat at the closest table, facing Otie's back and sliding down the bench to leave room for whoever sat next to her. Jeena floated toward Otie until Sammer touched her elbow again, then she folded into a bench seat with a sigh.

"Solving all the galaxy's problems?" Otie continued when no one spoke, her focus ostensibly on the several pots in front of her.

"Realized our tech hasn't eaten in a day or so." Sammer paced around the table, back toward the older clone cooking, and leaned against the gleaming metal counter next to the heating element. "Did you know we were coming?"

"I need to eat too, Sam." She stirred something, moved something from a flat pot to a round one, then added, "And yes, I figured you'd be by soon."

"Talinn wants to go back out into civilian space before committing to a course of action." He said it conversationally, all casual, but Talinn glared at him all the same.

"I thought she might."

"And you have an opinion on that?"

"I have access to all the ships. Opinion isn't a strong enough word."

"A decision, then?" Talinn asked, unable to let their calm exchange go on without her, despite Caytil's elbow in her ribs.

"We abandoned a meeting spot like this, not half a cycle ago, when the front moved suddenly over the planet we'd burrowed into. The front had no business moving there—planet had a tiny settlement and no resources to speak of to help either side."

"We'd go out unconscious, the way we came in. Or I would, I don't know if anyone else wants to go." Talinn leaned her elbows on the table, forced her mind off the incredibly tempting smell wafting from the cooking implements, and frowned for good measure.

"The more we move, the more likely it is we'll be found. And tracked. We can't afford it, not to soothe your feelings."

"You say that, but if you need my Bee, you need me. My feelings play a pretty big part in that." Despite her efforts, she heard a pitch in her words too close to a whine. Talinn blamed the intoxicating scents, but she knew it was the frustration of arguing with, essentially, herself.

"We're not sure if we need you. It's one of the plans we're considering, layering another Bee with mine, another Lei with Sammer's, another Ziti with—"

"Oh no, we're out." Caytil shrugged. "Neither Ziti nor I have any interest in burning down the world's order."

Otie made an inquisitive sound, but she didn't turn around, nor did her shoulders so much as twitch. Talinn studied her—the line of her back, the ease of her motions. Had Otie expected that? Was there another Caytil somewhere they hadn't met yet, also holding out on Otie's grand design?

"If the plan falls apart because we decide against it, or you decide to go down some other path, what then? We live out our days in this circle? You drug us again a little more finally?" The delicious promise of the cooking food soured in the back of her throat at that thought, and she swallowed against it.

"I don't know."

"You . . . don't know. You."

"I'm no more in the habit of repeating myself than you are, Newt."

It clicked before she opened her mouth to ask, but Bee twisted metal in a laugh and savored it. *Newt! New Talinn, New T. I'm not going to lie to you, I like that way better than Otie. She's clever, old you.*

Talinn half-heartedly shushed Bee and dropped her head into her hands.

"It's not just extra bits of Bee," Jeena said into the dragging silence, and even Otie turned around to stare at her. "The discrepancies. In Bee's programming."

We're doing this now?

Talinn had the same question, but before she could ask it Otie snapped a hand up. "Sammer, get the bowls, that case over there. Caytil, spoons are in the third drawer down, second set of cabinets to your side there. Newt, get me the ladle hanging there." She pointed with her elbow, and Talinn discovered she knew what a ladle was.

She considered ignoring the order, but she needed to eat. If the other Eights were going to kill them, it probably wouldn't be now, without anything decided. So be it. Talinn shoved back from the table as everyone but Jeena moved, and in a few minutes they were all back at the table with bowls of noodles. The liquid steamed, chunks of proteins and vegetables floated, and Talinn would have poured it all down her throat if a burned mouth weren't such a pain.

She decided arguing could wait until she finally tasted the concoction they'd heard so much about, so she focused on getting noodles wrapped around the utensil, then cooling them to a non-mouth-burning degree, then putting them in her face.

Then forgot, for a blissful moment, the needs of the galaxy and the whims of Command, because so many tastes rolled through her mouth she could have used Bee to analyze them.

Huh. That's fun.

Talinn pictured the parts of her brain that must be lighting up to Bee's awareness, and she smiled as she slurped a second bite. The texture should have been disconcerting—springy, a little chewy, wriggly, maybe edging toward slimy but in a delicious way—but instead it was part of the enjoyment.

"What I'm hearing." Caytil fanned her mouth and took another bite before continuing. "Is that you can learn to do this, Talinn. And then we can eat noodles every day."

"Every day until the end of the world." Sammer snapped his mouth shut after delivering the words, as if regretting ruining the moment, but it was too late.

Talinn continued to eat, the taste still warm and earthy and pure comfort, but some measure of her enjoyment faded.

"Otie," she said, and the other woman's forehead wrinkled, the lines deeper than Talinn's own, before she burst into laughter.

"Otie? You have to admit, Newt's better."

Talinn ignored both that and Bee's smug "told you so" in the background. "Otie," she said again, repeating herself on purpose. "We've got to talk about both—the discrepancies in coding, and what you expect from us."

Otie made a noise in the back of her throat, more inquisitive than dismissive, and Talinn swallowed another mouthful of noodles before continuing.

"You don't have it all planned out. Maybe you don't have all the answers. But you have us—and you wanted us for a reason. Let us help plot out the approach. Or reason through the issues. Both. We have to do something." She stirred the liquid in her bowl, watching small pieces surface and vanish into the clouded broth.

Otie twisted noodles around her spoon, but didn't lift them toward her mouth. "It'll be a pile of bugs and glitches to coordinate."

"Sounds like it'll be a pile of bugs and glitches to coordinate regardless." Caytil drummed her fingers on the table, then shook her shoulders and sat up straight. "Your Sammer told ours it's their fault Mercy splintered."

The bite Otie had taken nearly reemerged, but the older woman didn't splutter. "He said that."

"What are you putting in these message packets?"

"Nothing that would cause a breakdown in code like that. I'll talk to Sammer. As for you, little Sammer—nothing you did caused what happened to Mercy. *Nothing.* The packets are little bits of code coating information, which you unpacked. That's it."

Sammer shifted in his seat, but he met her gaze straight on. "And what about our going out and about in the system?"

"It's not a terrible idea." Otie's lips curled, the beginnings of a smile, then her face went abruptly serious. "There may be work to do first. Medith mentioned to you that we're not sure what's going on in this system?"

"If jump points are where something is taking notice of us, you're thinking it's less risky to ship us out locally." Caytil chewed thoughtfully, which was not something Talinn had seen before. The food they'd eaten for cycles had been better to swallow quickly, not ruminate over. She hadn't realized eating could be enjoyable.

"We can talk it over with the others. Of the group that came in with you, I imagine at least Konti and Heka will be interested."

Talinn shoved an enormous ball of noodles in her mouth to cover for the fact she hadn't thought of Konti and Heka—or Xenni and Arnod—for a full day. She'd rarely spent much time with jet pairings, and that last assignment . . .

"Yeah, we probably should talk to everyone." Even Sammer shifted guiltily, which made Talinn feel a little better.

That and the noodles.

CHAPTER 27

⊕

They'd taken to planning in the kitchen rather than the overwhelming information room. Talinn slid in, an unused port cord twisted through her fingers. Heka pointed at the warming unit, and she veered around the table to help herself to the simmering noodles, picking up enough to know they were talking about whether they wanted to take out UCF and IDC, and what would be left if they did. It had been something of an endless circle, and Talinn wasn't sorry to have missed some of it.

Caytil scooted over on the long bench, opening a space between her and Arnod, and Talinn slid in while carefully balancing her lukewarm bowl.

"Is this a formal debrief, or . . . ?" she asked before shoving a truly unsafe amount of noodles into her mouth. Bee made a noise to indicate she wasn't commenting on purpose, rather than from inattention.

Otie took a more reasonable bite from her own bowl and waited to swallow before responding. "Tiernan and Hops are back in-system, and should be here in the next few hours. We've been waiting on updates from Govlic, and I'm hopeful we'll have enough information to make new plans once we have it."

"I didn't know you'd sent anyone out-system again." Sammer stood, taking his and Jeena's empty bowls.

"We had the *Pajeeran Fall* passing through, and don't have any other reports or even rumors of glitchy defense arrays, so we decided to risk it. Still unconscious and powered down, but if we don't know what's happening in Hynex and Govlic, there's no chance we can come up with a plan to infiltrate either Command."

"It would be nice if we could confirm the truncated-program theory before figuring out how to infiltrate."

"Come on, Belay, that's base-array talk. Jets know you gotta 'yes and' these things—make the plans for both—"

"Jets don't make plans," Caytil scoffed, and conversation devolved into insults delivered from partially full mouths.

Until Otie pushed abruptly back from the table. "We have incoming."

"Incoming." Not Tiernan and Hops, with that reaction. Spoons clattered into bowls, liquid spattered on the table without anyone taking note.

"Incoming like unexpected. We don't do unexpected here." Her gaze unfocused, and she shook her head once, a sharp jerk. "You might as well come. Jeena—"

"I'll clean up and get back to work. I'm still trying to figure out the potential for Bee's combination—"

"Good enough." Otie was up and striding for the door before Jeena could form another word, and Talinn's scalp prickled.

She risked another oversized spoonful of noodles, then followed on the heels of her less food-motivated fellows.

They jogged halfway around the wheel to the information room, then past it to a door Talinn hadn't noticed before. The door spiraled open, and the room inside was small, dominated by one large screen, with a bank of controls that looked very like the comms panel in her tank.

Definitely comms.

Otie spun up a seat and didn't gesture for any more, so the rest of them crowded around her. The screen flashed to life, showing a satellite view of their system.

How nice—Exfora's armpit instead of Govlic's, Bee confirmed and Talinn agreed. Eights weren't Spacies, and so didn't spend a lot of time training on the three different systems humanity had settled over the centuries since they'd left their home planet. It didn't take expert spatial understanding to note how remote their asteroid was.

The defense array is at a weird angle, no?

Like everything else in a star-based system, jump points, settlements, and their corresponding defense arrays moved. Their relational distance and angle, however, were meant to remain fairly steady per their respective orbits. The radiation and weight of the array were only so much noise in the grand scheme of the galaxy, but enough to be constantly taken into account for jump point alignment. As such, defense arrays were kept at consistent distances from jump points and their anchor station, as part of keeping the area clear and predictable. Exfora's largest array appeared unnecessarily closer to the jump point.

It could simply be a delay in the satellite's data, and probably of less pressing concern than the two ships falling out of the inner orbits. They could be on an impractically long approach for some other point, but most of the probable projected paths indicated out-system travel the hard way, or intersection with the asteroids at the edge of the system.

"Not a whole lot of reasons to come out this way if not for this, huh?" Sammer was furthest from Otie, though her arm twitched as though she were about to swat at him. She controlled herself—Talinn would not have—and moved dials. Likely her Bee did the internal shifting of information gathering and finding whatever frequency the incoming ships operated on, but there was always something to fidget with.

"Mismade pieces of—they're firing on each other." Her hands paled, the older woman pressing so hard against the comms console her skin protested.

"So someone's running here and someone's trying to stop them?" Heka asked, shifting as though there were any action she could take to help.

"Or someone's on the way to attack here, and someone else is trying to—" Sammer had apparently determined to be contrary today, and Talinn was about to swat him herself when Otie threw ice down all their spines.

"Neither of those ships are ones we've had contact with." She leaned closer to the panel, and Talinn could feel the frown the other woman must be making on her own face. "And . . . as best we can tell, they're both IDC."

"Firing on each other?"

"I don't want to . . ." Talinn faltered, then put her hands on the back of Otie's chair. "The defense array is moving."

"*Wha—*" Otie cut herself off, the strangled sound turning into eerie calm. "So it is. We're evacuating."

"Is it going to be any safer out there?" Arnod crossed his arms, widening his stance as though he couldn't be moved.

"We're evacuating, on as many different ships as possible, which means some of you are going to get a crash course in piloting."

"We can't possibly navigate a *jump point*—" Xenni blurted, voice skewing high.

"Speak for yourself, Xenni, we absolutely—" Caytil shoved at the other woman's elbow, her confidence belied only by the fidgeting of the fingers on her free hand.

"You're going to be piloting very, very small ships, ones that hopefully will pass beneath the interest of whatever this is. Then you're going to take the individualized escape plans I'm about to send you, make your way to various points in this system, and obtain passage out. *Then* you'll find the meeting place each of your AIs has and *wait for further instructions.*"

Otie spun her chair and glared at them. "Do not deviate. Do not hero it. Do not get cute or clever. Get out there, and don't glitch it all sideways."

"Jeena—" Sammer began, and Otie snapped out a hand.

"Already sent her a message. She's transporting the servers up level to the ships. She'll go with one of you, Bee's coordinating."

"We'll—" Talinn forgot the rest of the sentence and bit down hard on the inside of her cheek. The image stuttered—between one blink and the next, the ships went from blips with trajectory plotting lines indicating their direction to . . . debris.

"Did the—the defense array?"

"They're IDC ships . . . this is still a UCF held jump point, isn't it? We should be asking what took so long." Sammer grunted, sounding pleased, as though it were all settled. Talinn swallowed bile, though he should be right. The situation was handled. Ships were gone. It remained weird, but that was life these days.

"No, given the lack of traffic between the big system settlements, we theorized IDC took control of the jump point a month ago . . ." Otie's hands tightened to fists, and she held so still Talinn took a small step back. "Which they shouldn't have, this has been a UCF system for all recorded history I could find, and—why would an IDC array fire on IDC ships?"

"I mean, one threatened us when we tried to leave Govlic, and that hadn't changed hands at that point. Maybe something in the programming slipped, or there's a delay?" Caytil chewed on her lip, staring at the screen. Seeing the gesture made Talinn realize what she was doing, and she clicked her teeth together to force herself to stop worrying at the inside of her mouth.

"And why is it still moving?" Heka pointed to the screen, though she wasn't close enough for that to help—still, the ratcheting of tension in the room indicated they'd all processed it. Bodies stiffened, breath went shallower, and Talinn scanned the display for hints of what under all the skies was happening.

The screen stuttered again, and the debris fields were gone. Another flicker, and the defense array was back in its correct position, relative to the jump point and inner planetary settlements. As though nothing had happened.

Had anything happened?

Otie tilted her head, fingers uncurling, but Talinn dragged in a breath, the scene too familiar, the knot in her neck far too tight. "Is that reality, or are your sensors telling you what someone wants you to see? Like what we had happen to us on P-8?"

"No, that shouldn't be—" Otie turned her scowl from the display to Talinn and back. "That's a limited error, introduced only in close quarters. That's not possible, if—" She stopped, not breathing, then slammed her hands down on the console. Talinn wasn't the only one who flinched away—infinitesimal movement from each of them, but notable.

"We're on a delay from our eyes further in system, I can't . . ." The older woman locked up again, every muscle tensing so hard Talinn thought she could count tendons if there weren't a coverall in the way. Her next words came out one at a time, so precise as to be clipped, so calm Talinn's stomach turned over. "What does Bee think, Newt? Does this feel like P-8?"

Talinn held a beat, but Bee didn't contribute. She had been surprisingly quiet during the encounter, and while that wasn't impossibly unlike her, not offering an opinion when directly solicited was intensely un-Bee behavior.

"Bee?" she prompted as the silence went on too long, and then when it remained silent, she froze as well. Her nerves screamed warnings, her joints fused into place, but it was nothing like that time on P-8. When she'd woken up and Bee was gone. It was like . . . Bee was there. Right there. But in between them . . .

"I can't," she said, and the words were strangled, spaced wrong, not the neat and orderly calm of her other, older self. "She's not. I can't. Bee." Her heart beat triple time, then missed one beat, then two, the rhythm so far off she couldn't finish the sentence. No wonder her breath gave out, and the words swallowed themselves instead of leaving her mouth.

"Lei then? Ziti?"

Every individual body in the small room stopped moving, the motionlessness making the small flickers of the display stand out even more, even worse.

Comms were unreliable. Their sensors were worse.

And their AIs were nonresponsive.

"Jeena?" Sammer asked, his voice breathy and high.

Jeena had the servers. Jeena had their AIs. They were on the move . . . that had to be the issue. The whole place was a circle—they'd find her. Solve the problem.

Talinn turned and ran.

Thudding footsteps indicated others followed at her heels.

They should have comms in their ears. Why didn't they have comms?

Because they had AIs. AIs were better than comms.

But they couldn't hear their partners, or reach them. Was something shielding them from within the installation? Was it the approaching defense array? Was the defense array still approaching? Was Bee screaming somewhere, trying to make contact?

Bee. Bee. *Bee.* She called her partner at every level—in her head, subvocally, aloud. She didn't even know which audible level each attempt registered as. It was a little ridiculous—a little hysterical, she knew it as she did it, it was probably just a mistake, maybe Jeena had picked a ship Talinn had never seen. Maybe it was a small, shielded ship, and Jeena had managed to get all the servers loaded, rapid pace, fast fast fast, so they all lost contact all at once, not with a warning, because she didn't know how would Jeena know the ins and outs of the tech in this armpit of Exfora and—

Were those footsteps? No, those were footsteps behind her, but up ahead, there was a door up ahead, a passage to the upper level. It was . . .

The door to the upper level was opening and closing, so fast it was a blur, over and over, and somewhere on the other side was Jeena, and therefore Bee, and even Talinn wasn't fast enough to get through its flickering pace, even in zero g, even with Bee in her head.

"Shit shit shit," Caytil muttered, shoving past and slamming her elbow into the small control panel. They didn't have the wrist control the more senior clones did—doors that were open to everyone opened to them, other ones did not, but over the time they'd been in Deep End, they'd tried and failed to finagle the control panels of doors they weren't cleared for. Without success.

Talinn's thoughts beat endlessly against her skull, a massive headache rearing up behind them, and she stared at Caytil, who had a handful of wires and connections and was moving them. Had Caytil figured how to break through the door panels? But no, never mind, they were cleared for this one, this was a standard passage. Talinn had passed through it before. They all looked the same but they moved differently and this one she'd been through. More technically, more importantly, the door already suffered from some sort of catastrophic failure—*Talinn* suffered from some sort of catastrophic failure—but nothing was happening.

Nothing was happening.

Nothing was—

Static roared inside her head so suddenly and so loud she was on her knees between one blink and the next. The headache was the worst she'd ever had, and she squeezed her eyes shut, then pushed the heels of her hands into her eyes. Pulled her eyelids open when that made it worse.

Static vanished. Talinn dropped a hand to the floor to steady herself. Her arms had the consistency of the noodles she'd eaten minutes and decades ago. No one reached a hand to help her, but she couldn't move her head, nor twitch her eyes away from a spot inches before her. Maybe everyone was on the floor. Maybe they'd gotten through the door and were—

Static again, the fuzz lined with thorns that scraped against every soft part of her brain.

The port under her ear burned, and someone made a noise,

something like a whimper. It wasn't her—her throat had closed too tight for air, and blackness was narrowing her vision further, but someone was making a noise and—

Gone. She lay flat against the smooth floor, her heart thudding hard against the metal like footsteps.

No, those *were* footsteps.

No, it was her heart and—static static static.

The enormity of the universe—too loud and too useless and too empty without Bee—rose and cascaded around her, pulling, drowning, sucking...

Talinn.

Her name was there, in the morass, a tiny, shining lifeline...

And she couldn't reach it.

And she spiraled down into an endless din of nothingness.

It must be what dying felt like.

CHAPTER 28

But then she woke up, in a room. A featureless gray room, in a cot.

"I've done this before."

Yes.

"Bee!"

Yes, and . . . not exactly.

"Other Bee?"

You're a little faster than your friends. I'm proud.

Talinn attempted to sit up, but her midsection still had the consistency of noodles. Instead she flopped onto her side, forced her eyes to focus, and grunted. There were other cots this time, more than she would have expected to fit in the room. A body blocked her view and she grunted again, toppling onto her back to get better perspective.

"Jeena."

"Welcome back. You're not panicking. I've sedated everyone else. Who are you hearing, before I decide if that's good or not?"

"Bee, but not mine." Her tongue had become three times too big for her mouth, and the words slurred.

"Huh. Well, that's an interesting data point." Jeena moved, but Talinn's eyes insisted on sliding out of focus, so she wasn't sure what the motions were. Noting something? Signaling someone? Nodding?

Don't pass out again.

"Is your Talinn awake?"

Silence. Talinn took a deep breath, squeezed her eyes shut, and shoved herself upright. She nearly tumbled off the cot, but steadied herself at the last minute, and decided hanging on to the long edge of the bed was her safest bet for the near future.

"Jeena."

The tech had gone four cots away in the time it took Talinn to gain limited control over her body. She partially turned toward Talinn, but her attention remained on the prone body below her. It took far too long to recognize him—Sammer—but Talinn slowly regained control of her vision, which helped.

"What is the other Bee telling you?" Jeena spoke so carefully Talinn hesitated.

Was it Bee? Was something impersonating Bee? Where was *her* Bee? What had happened while she'd been collapsed on a floor, or cot, or in transit between the two? Had Jeena moved everyone herself? Who was in her head?

I'm sure there's a way to pretend to be another AI, but I have not found it. And to tell you the truth, if I haven't found it, I'm not entirely sure how possible it is.

"She sounds like Bee." That didn't answer the question Jeena had actually asked, but Talinn's brain was still a few steps behind. Behind what, she wasn't sure, which was part of the issue. She rolled her tongue in her mouth, trying to get it back to normal size, and its regular consistency. Surely that would make speaking easier. "Who did everyone else hear?"

"Static. Maybe a voice, but they were raving. You are some measure of progress." Jeena shifted, her face out of view, and then a few moments later she left Sammer's cot and moved to another. Caytil. "As far as I can tell, we're not about to be under attack, and the AIs are all functioning normally in their portable housing, and their links to the servers are clear. Something is interfering in the connection between you and them, but maybe the AIs fully integrated to the installation servers are having slightly more success punching through."

Slightly. I've only gotten through to you.

"What . . . what do you think is going on?"

"I have half a dozen theories, all of them useless because I can't test any of them with a bunch of unconscious people to monitor." The tech still faced away from her, but Talinn heard the strain in the measured words.

"I'm not unconscious."

"You're the last person I want to load-in."

"Rude." She struggled to sit up straight, even though Jeena wasn't looking at her. "If it'll help—"

"Eights who learn not to panic when they're temporarily disconnected from their partners would help. Eights who don't immediately leap to potentially frying their own brains would help. Reliable sensors would help. Comms that are functional would help. A universe that—"

None of that seemed actually doable, in a helpful sense, so Talinn slid off her cot, steadied herself on her feet, and interrupted the tech. "Jeena. I'm guessing that row in the corner is our AIs. Load-in Bee. Let's see what's going on."

"Talinn, it's not that . . . We're still not clear in what's been added to your AIs, and the other—Otie isn't here to clarify. If that has something to do with the interference, and you load-in, it could amplify. Your last few load-ins haven't been ideal."

"How many choices do we—"

"You could *fry* your *brain*, Eight. Permanently. What's Other Bee have to say about that?" Jeena turned with those words, and her face was so ghastly Talinn sagged back against the cot again.

How long had she been out? The Jeena she'd last laid eyes on hadn't been so gaunt, with lines in her cheeks and deep pockets under her red-streaked eyes. Talinn surreptitiously flexed and relaxed the longer muscles of her arms and legs, along her shoulder and back, testing for atrophy that would have resulted from a long-term unconsciousness. There was none, only the lingering sponginess of weariness, but her gut squirmed uncomfortably.

"Other Bee?" Talinn asked out loud, the vast majority of her will infused to keep her voice steady.

We've had to load-in quite a bit over the cycles. My Talinn's brain has never fried, and I don't think yours will either.

"That's reassuring."

You're not her, *but you're almost as close as she was.*

"To who?" Oh. The moment she asked the question, she knew— one of the combined Bee's original Talinn.

Tell Jeena she's smart to be concerned. It's part of why we like her, she sees Eights as people. Not super common in techs. But spec is subjective, and we're smarter than it.

"We like you and me, or we like AIs?"

Sure. A faint hint of tortured metal echoed under the word, and Talinn felt her mouth curve without conscious effort. She repeated the other half of the conversation to Jeena, who slumped and covered her face.

"I don't know what else we can do. If comms are unreliable and the sensors are shit, and everyone else is unconscious..." Talinn's voice lifted, and she swallowed before the wheedling shifted fully into a whine.

"They're only unconscious because I sedated them. Tiernan and Hops should be back soon. I can wake someone up and load-in and—"

"How is *that* good for anyone's brain?" Talinn carefully navigated the small spaces between cots, not looking too closely at who was on any of them, and got close enough to put her hand on Jeena's arm. "If mine's already compromised, so be it."

You'll be fine.

"That's very reassuring, thank you, Bee." Talinn spoke aloud for Jeena's benefit, though if Other Bee were anything like her own, those words were from a place of hope more than certainty. While Talinn concerned herself with jinxes, Bee preferred to state reality as it should be, so as to make the world conform accordingly. While that might not apply to B-413 as it did to her B-617, well... Talinn had no reason to give such context to the tech.

"Talinn..."

"You want to stand here and worry, or try to do something?"

"I—"

"That's what I thought. Come on." Talinn scanned the line of boxes along the back wall, but there was nothing to separate them from each other. Once she was close enough, she walked the row, letting her fingers brush lightly over the tops. Her ears popped over the third to last, and she paused there, raising her eyebrows at Jeena.

"I think Other Bee gave you a hint." The tech said it dismissively, but Talinn didn't imagine the small wrinkle in the other woman's cheek as she bit back a smile. "You should sit. You tend to fall when you load-in."

You'd think a tech would have mentioned that to you at some point over the cycles, Other Bee pointed out, a hum of dissatisfaction accompanying the words.

"Thank you." Talinn intended the answer for both of them, and steadied herself on the server as she crouched down, then sat. She touched the edges of the port under her ear—no longer burning—and tried to piece together the moments before she'd lost consciousness.

"What do you think the discrepancies are?"

Jeena, in the midst of pulling something from a previously hidden compartment in the server, stopped moving and slowly lifted her eyes to meet Talinn's.

"It feels like you've been avoiding talking to me about it. Which, to be fair, it feels like *I've* been avoiding talking to you about it, and we haven't been much in the same place lately." She took a steadying breath. "Bee hasn't been thrilled about poking at the matter, either. Are the issues consistent across the other AIs' code?"

"It's not that..." Jeena shifted out of her squat, resting a knee flat on the floor. Other Bee stirred in Talinn's head, but remained quiet. "Bee's code is incredibly dense—more than your age and assignment experiences would indicate. More than it was when I ran the tests on P-8. It's not bad, or a corruption, it's just..." She put both her hands palm down on the server holding Bee, and held Talinn's gaze. "It's unusual. And that's worth noting in AIs on a good day, never mind whatever all these days have become for us. This one in particular."

"A less good day." Talinn offered up the ghost of a smile, not wanting to distract Jeena from continuing the conversation.

"A less good day," she repeated with a small laugh. "My theory is something was introduced to her programming, and it is causing some sort of replication without Bee's conscious effort." She lifted a shoulder and tilted her head, communicating their current location, and the older generation of AIs that occupied it. "The problem is, Bee can't recognize it in her own strings, and I can't isolate what it's meant to do."

How curious.

It was the most noncommittal response Talinn could have imagined. Which is what prompted her next question. "Is there any chance you could get a similar analysis of Other Bee?"

What now?

"Compare to mine? See if this density or whatever is comparable? Or even..." Her brain had been going so smoothly, but it staggered on the term she needed. Other Bee's interference? Her own exhaustion? Too long without *her* Bee? She shoved the questions away and flapped a hand, then produced the concept triumphantly. "Projectable?"

From Jeena's blank look, she hadn't communicated the concept at all. Talinn frowned and leaned against Bee's server, then tried again. "Look at Other Bee's code, which has existed over a longer period of time. If the density relates, or if it's something that it looks like Bee already got to—like our next generation of clone pairing got there faster."

As though you evolved, somehow?

"Can't tell if you're trying to help or hurt my thinking here, Other Bee."

Fair.

"Take B-413's code compared to 617's, and trace out the variables—time, estimated experiences, projected growth comparative to—"

Moot point.

"Because?"

She's not touching me, analyzing me, or moving me to one of her little boxes. So get load-in ready, because I'd like my Talinn back.

"How am I keeping you from being with your Talinn—"

"It's the line," Jeena said absently, her gaze inward. "With the other Talinn and your Bee blocked, while you're active, this Bee has locked into you. Probably not on purpose. Whatever is interfering, it's not a perfect system."

"I can't tell if that's reassuring or not." She hadn't even realized she'd been speaking at a level the tech could hear.

"Me either." Jeena blinked her eyes clear and focused on Talinn again. "All right, we'll get back to this after load-in. I'm sure Bee will have plenty to add."

It's possible.

BUT DOUBTFUL.

Talinn flinched, then blinked, realizing her eyes had been closed. "What?"

"Orienting question: What—"

"No." She held up her hands, then realized they were genuinely "up"—she was lying on her back on the floor. "Someone yelled? Someone—that wasn't Bee's voice."

"You were talking to the other Bee—"

"*No.*" Talinn swallowed, though it took three tries to complete the gesture. She would have tried to sit up, but the floor had softened around her and she'd sunk too far into it to adjust herself. "There was a voice—not a Bee voice. Someone else said something."

"What did they say?"

"I don't . . ." Her eyes had closed again—when had that happened? "What?"

"Right. Orienting question: What is your name?"

"Jeena. Not me. You. Something happened, Jeena. Something . . ."

Talinn?

"Bee. Bee's there. I need . . ."

"You need to answer my questions. First things first, then everything else."

"Doesn't make sense."

Her pithy phrase, or your aching head?

"Yes."

Sleep, then. I've got this.

Talinn's mouth answered all of Jeena's questions, and the tech never knew the difference.

CHAPTER 29

⊕

Six hours.

Talinn didn't so much wake up as return. Midstep, she stumbled and caught herself on the smooth surface of the installation hallway. "Load-in?" she asked, and Bee—her Bee—hummed affirmatively.

"Where—" She straightened off the wall, turned slightly, and met Caytil's knowing gaze. "Where are we going?"

"Ships," Caytil said, and Talinn was sure it was Caytil talking, not Ziti. Was she the only one . . . ?

"Do we have to leave?" She tried to get more to the question—were the ships really still out there, coming to attack them? Was the defense array on the move?

"No. But move."

Bee had made herself as small as she could, with Talinn driving her body again, but still her head wobbled on its tiny stem of a neck, heavier than one brain and skull usually made it.

"Another . . . place?" She lifted her arms to gesture at the space around them, but only one moved. The other fluttered and flopped back to her side. Maybe she should give control back to Bee—they'd never tried that before, and it hadn't seemed like Bee was having quite so much of an issue moving and talking.

Or maybe Bee hadn't been talking. Talinn reached for the memory of the last few—had Bee said hours?—but there was nothing. Wherever her consciousness had gone, it hadn't seen fit to keep any records.

"Same system. Different place."

Talinn touched her head, her one functioning hand brushing over her covered head. Her neck wasn't overly unbalanced simply because of the mental weight of Bee's full self under her skull—there was hair on her again.

Objectively that wasn't any heavier than Bee, but she decided it was part of the issue, and that made her feel better. "People?"

Caytil nodded, the motion slow and deliberate. Talinn's eyes focused better, and she realized Caytil also had hair. What an odd thing not to notice. Maybe because the walls were developing fractal swirls and she couldn't hold her eyes together—

"Disguised," Caytil said, then laughed in a tone Talinn couldn't recall ever having heard before. A sliding scale of noise, tasting a little burnt in the back of her throat. "'Cause we'll blend while load-in."

That was ridiculous. Going unnoticed under normal circumstances had been easy enough—most civilians didn't spend a lot of time examining their fellows—but with an entire AI in their heads? Already, Talinn caught herself walking toe-heel instead of heel-toe, spending more time on the front of her foot than any normal person, as though she were creeping, or unsure about the floor's solidity. Maybe unadapted people would simply think they were drug users. Machine god worshippers. Why were they on the move again?

"How..." Far? Long? She wanted to ask both, but couldn't figure it out. Then, triumphant, she managed, "Velocity?" No, that wasn't quite it, but Caytil shrugged and tipped a hand side to side, so she probably understood.

"Ten hours?"

Oof. And they'd been load-in for...

Six.

That would be pushing it—it would certainly be the longest Talinn had ever gone, though that Talinn—Other Talinn—Otie—had gone... more than that. It should be reassuring. But then, her Bee was dense, the tech had said. Denser than expected. Was that bad for Talinn's brain?

Talinn blinked, and then paused against another wall. They'd gone further than a blink's distance, but that wasn't a pressing issue. There had been a pressing issue, hadn't there? Yes. She couldn't hear Bee, before the tech put Bee in her brain. Something had happened.

"Did . . . did Jeena figure out . . ."

We'll talk more when you're safe.

"Why going?"

Caytil tottered through the next doorway—were all the doors open now, or could Talinn not focus enough to see which way they were opening?—and paused on the other side. She had a hand pressed to her new hair, no her head, and didn't turn enough for Talinn to see her face.

"A . . . blanket." She waved her other arm—why did Caytil get two working arms and Talinn only had one?—in a semicircle around and over herself. "Interference."

"Bee."

Here.

"What did you tell her?"

Caytil?

"Jeena."

I answered the orienting questions.

"Didn't . . . didn't help figure out . . ." Talinn's breath burned in her chest. Was she yelling? Running? It seemed to take far too much energy to barely form words and stagger forward.

Help figure out what's happening? Why we can't hear each other except for when I'm in your head?

"Yes."

I told her it feels like a wall. Like I'm shoving a tank through another tank's turret. I can see there's a space, but I can't . . . wriggle enough to fit into it.

"'m I . . . turret?"

Yes? It wasn't a very good metaphor. I probably could have done better if I hadn't been trying to find my way out of that stupid box for hours.

"Will leaving . . ." Talinn had fetched up against the wall again, and she forced herself sideways. One shoulder remained in contact with the wall as she walked, at an angle that probably should have been uncomfortable, along the hallway. Then she realized Caytil wasn't in front of her anymore, so she stopped moving entirely. It took a few more steps for her legs to realize that's what she'd meant to do, but she dragged to a halt eventually.

And then realized they couldn't leave.

"A wall. Like . . . talking to someone else?"

I can't talk to—

"Like me, when Other Bee . . . Like an AI in the . . ."

Like another AI is on the line. I can't get through. Bee's words strengthened to a normal tone, and Talinn flinched from it before she could control herself. The sound had too much resonance, tones intermingling and building on each other in an echo that made her far too conscious of the inside of her own skull.

"AI . . ." A massive AI, if it were blocking so many of them at once. Like the potentially not-imaginary conglomerate AI Command may or may not have been building out of scavenged parts for an indeterminate amount of time? "Big? Con . . . conjoined?"

What Other Talinn said the Commands might have made? No, it doesn't feel at all familiar. Not like truncated pieces of us, there isn't a . . . frequency, close enough to mine or any other AI I've encountered.

"Like Medith." Medith, their Medith, on P-8, who'd heard a voice. There was something there. What was it?

"Talked. To me." Words were getting harder, and the wall fractals had given way to small holes in her vision, as though her peripheral were being eaten in tiny bites. She turned to tell Caytil, but that was too much, and she toppled in slow motion to the ground.

There was a reason they were always escorted by techs when they had completed load-in, and Talinn had a moment to long for Jeena's calm, quiet expertise before something large shifted in her head, and blood trickled from her nose.

Something—someone else talked to you?

"Other Bee. Then . . . different."

We're going to try something. I'm going to move your body. You focus on talking, yes? Only talking. And breathing, so you can talk.

Talinn closed her eyes—she could feel that they were still open, but she no longer looked through them—and then took a deep, steadying breath. The world lurched around her, but she ignored it, focused on Bee. She spoke out loud, in case Caytil were still nearby, and hadn't been a figment of her slowly collapsing brain.

"Other Bee talked to me, when everyone was unconscious. Otie was out, Bee was blocked, so Jeena thought Other Bee might have locked onto my line. Close enough, but not blocked by the interference."

Words were a lot easier, when all she had to focus on was making them and moving her lungs. There was a great deal of shaking, and an unsteady vibration buzzed under her hearing, but she ignored those, trusting in Bee. Probably she should have been worried—AIs taking over physical movement was wildly out of spec—but they'd been made to be a team. Let the teamwork...work.

"Jeena said, whatever was causing the interference, it couldn't be a perfect system. That you, Bee, not you Caytil, would probably have a lot to add once we could reestablish contact, but..." The memory had blurred, either because of the event itself or load-in so soon after, or the sheer compilation of hits the squishy bits of her consciousness had taken in the recent past. "Other Bee didn't think you would. And another voice..."

What had the voice sounded like? It had been Not Bee, that much she grasped, but all other detail slid from reach. A small sharp pain stung in her palms, and she flooded back into her body again. Bee twisted metal, but didn't fight, and Talinn looked down at her hands. She'd been reaching physically, trying so hard to gather the memory back, and had clenched her hands so hard around nothing that her nails dug shallow cuts into the middle of her hands.

"Ouch."

Couldn't stop you. You are still a lot more the body than I can be.

"Meat suit fought you, yeah?"

Other humans are meat suits. You're just you.

"Sweet." Talinn shook her head and took in their surroundings. Caytil was behind her, trailing a few paces. How far had they come?

I mean, I'm in here too, so it's a little selfish.

"That's how we do sweet." The words flowed normally, which seemed counterintuitive. The longer Bee was fully housed in her head, the worse it should get. Maybe a plateau or a breather, but not this much lighter. Her head still wobbled, too full for its constrictions, but it was more like when she had a world ender of a headache that Bee redirected pain nodes around.

"Talinn!" Caytil's breathless voice indicated this had not been the first time she'd called the name. "If someone else was in your head—"

"It had to have been an AI. So getting off into space and moving, maybe that would help, or maybe it'd just follow us. If it's in the systems here already, it can just as easily move into the ships."

"Right, sure. So—not leaving?" Caytil staggered, and Talinn hurried back to her, ducking under her arm and taking some of Caytil's weight onto her shoulder.

"There you are!" Jeena appeared around the corner, skidding to a halt as she caught sight of them. "The ships are nonresponsive, Otie said to bring everyone back. We need to be in one place, maybe figure out a way to punch through this." She gave both women a once over, then nodded more to herself than them. "Keep ahead, they're in the information room and the door's open. I have to find Konti and Arnod."

"We need more techs." Talinn couldn't imagine a single other tech she'd trust outside of Jeena, but the point stood. "Who were you traveling with?"

"I wasn't going to leave. I was..." Expressions chased themselves across her face so fast Talinn couldn't decipher them. "Sammer collapsed during load-in. He's stable, but still unconscious. Go, I'll be back soon." She took off at a pace faster than a jog but not quite a run, and Talinn scooted herself and Caytil to the side for the tech to pass them.

"Sammer?"

"I don't..." Caytil sighed, the sound ragged, and shifted her balance against Talinn once they began moving again. "Remember."

Me either. She must have done his load-in after we moved. Otie was helping.

"Otie helped do the load-in?" Talinn chewed on the inside of her cheek, though she rather wanted to hit herself upside her wigged head.

"She said ... said we hadn't practiced enough. She had ... as many hours as a tech ... as a tank." Caytil's breathy voice gained and lost volume as they walked, and Talinn opened her mouth to suggest letting Ziti run the show.

Careful to ensure she was subvocal, she asked Bee, "Do you think other AIs can do what you did? Take over?"

I can't be sure. We're almost back, and Jeena would have been more worried if she didn't think we'd make it.

"Jeena signed off on us going off into space in the state I woke up in, so I don't know how reassuring that is right now."

I don't think Jeena gets to sign off on things here.

"That's not any better."

Next turn.

Talinn focused on each consecutive step, maneuvering her own and Caytil's increasingly sluggish body around the next rounded corner, and then into the open information room. All the screens and displays were blank, and amidst the tables there were two cots with unmoving bodies on them. The combination didn't make for a welcoming atmosphere, and Talinn steadied herself against the radiating nausea that answered.

"Why is there blood on your face?" Otie asked, sliding around the largest of the screens and positioning herself on Caytil's other side. "Did you fall?"

"More than once," Talinn admitted. "But this isn't from that. I'm pretty sure." Further details didn't seem important at the moment, given she'd forgotten the nosebleed entirely. She noted three of the other, older Eights moving around various consoles. No one was watching the bodies, both of whom were Sammers, and Talinn chose to take that as a good sign. Small motions indicated breathing, which confirmed Jeena's point. They were stable and unconscious. Nothing to be accomplished by hovering over them. She repeated it twice, then distracted herself by speaking aloud.

"So again, some more—*what* is going on?"

"We panicked." Otie said it so calmly it felt like a slap, but when Talinn craned her neck to peer over Caytil's shoulder, the other woman seemed utterly sincere. "When your tech started waking us back up, and Bee told me what had been happening, I wanted everyone out. Load-in made sense—thank you for volunteering— and I thought we could use the same escape plan to keep everyone in system but away from a compromised installation."

In unspoken accord, they settled Caytil on a bench at one of the lower tables. Caytil grunted her thanks and then immediately thunked her head onto the surface in front of her, murmuring things that were more likely intended for Ziti than them. Talinn hovered near her in case she was needed, but kept her attention focused on the older version of herself.

"Then what?"

"Then it turned out we're in a compromised installation." Otie laced her hands around the back of her neck and stared up at the screenless ceiling. "And rather too late for escape."

"So now we . . . stay at load-in and hope for the best?"

"My Bee had some luck punching through from the main servers—more with you than me, but it's worth trying. We put all the AIs into the main servers here, and at worst you and I swap versions for a bit." Her eyes remained fixed above them, which made the words land with less surety than might have been intended.

"Can we call a big ship back? Spacies have three times the connection. Is the *Pajeeran Fall* still in system? Can you reach Tiernan and Hops?" The consoles blinked, invisible work or monitoring happening that she couldn't decipher. Her head bobbed, following the pattern, and she yanked herself back into focus.

"Maybe, but comms are as unreliable as everything else. We could send a message out to an imaginary ship, or Command itself, or accidentally send some corrupting code that will put whomever we make contact with into the same circumstances we're in." Otie dropped her hands and waved them, the gesture communicating nothing to Talinn except frustration.

"We can't trust our eyes or ears." Talinn considered keeping her revelation close to her chest, but that would be more from spite than actual distrust. She had to be more helpful than her counterpart, or the bug-eaten end might as well come for them. "But maybe we can work around it." She explained what she'd shared with Jeena and Caytil, about the other voice, the potential for some other, enormous AI coating the area.

"The defense array." Otie slid to the edge of Caytil's bench, suddenly resembling Jeena's gaunt worry more than Talinn's own face. "It has to be."

"But that system is stupid, comparatively. It's not paired, it doesn't learn, it has no organic component to host or kickstart dramatic growth or change." Talinn's chest thrummed with the sudden rapidity of her heartbeat, and her lungs constricted in sympathy.

"*Something* has certainly changed across the fronts. It's absolutely possible someone introduced a new component into the arrays, and it's had unexpected effects. Wouldn't be the first time someone thought they had a plan and it went bells up on them." Otie's rueful tone was one Talinn knew all to well—for a moment she had to work her jaw, make sure she wasn't the one talking. It was far from a pleasant feeling, and she shifted her weight and hoped Bee would make a snarky comment.

When none was forthcoming, she shook out her shoulders and leaned against the table, dropping a sympathetic hand on Caytil's flattened back. "So, the defense array AIs are more untrustworthy than expected, and potentially interfering here. Command has spent apparent eons learning how to block remote AI incursions. Can't we do something similar here?"

"Knew I liked you." Otie surged out of her seat, striding across the room.

"Feels like less of a compliment when it's a version of me to me," Talinn muttered, and Bee prodded her to follow.

"My Bee was able to punch through the interference. My Bee is . . . slightly more than a B-series AI."

Aren't we all. Bee, her voice crafted small to keep from overwhelming Talinn, nevertheless allowed an almost normal volume laugh. *Isn't that the point of us?*

"She's two Bees."

Oh. Well. We already knew that.

"Is it because of the combination? The density?" Talinn considered her own, abnormally dense partner. They hadn't combined with another B-series. But was there more to the AI programming string of Bee's making? Something that had allowed Otie's Bees to merge? Maybe her own Bee's exponential growth was a more common B-series issue than Jeena had suspected. Maybe having a piece of a combined Bee's code in an unmerged Bee had . . . the thought tumbled away before she could complete it, but Otie was talking, half to herself.

All the way to herself. Talinn chortled over her joke, abruptly realized it wasn't funny, and forced herself to focus. *Listen.*

"In an early mission, my Bee and I had an accident. It allowed another, older Bee to 'take the line' as we've been saying." She paused, sorting through a stack of printed out films that had been scattered across a counter.

"So you found a truncated Bee program."

"She wasn't truncated. She was fully functional. Well, more functional than would have been expected, given how long she'd been alone. And I'd been load-in with my Bee too long, and they—the Bees—decided I should load them together."

"In your head?" Despite her best efforts, the words rushed out of her, smashing together in her horror. She hadn't ever asked how it had happened. The thought of adding a whole other AI into the mash of her current brain dumped more adrenaline into her system than she should have had left.

"No!" At that, Otie looked up, met Talinn's eyes, smiled faintly. "No. Into the tank. The UCF tank."

"You were IDC," Talinn murmured.

"We were. And then we were not. I was one Talinn, and two Bees, and a whole lot of determination to dismantle the systems that had been lying to us." But there was grief in her voice, as steady as she held it. Talinn didn't have to be a different version of this woman to recognize it. "As for the matter nearer to hand, that's three Bees we have here."

"We're not merging our Bees—"

"I'm not asking you to." Otie held up a hand and dropped most of the papers from her hand, keeping a smaller handful. "They can work together from the same server bank, and stay separate. But if two merged Bees could work through the interference, there's a good chance a third resonating frequency could make a bigger difference."

"Space for other AIs to get through?"

"Maybe. Or a message, to a trusted recipient." Otie shoved the films at Talinn, and she grabbed them reflexively. "Look it over for Bee—all the comm points we should be able to trust in the system. We'll get her loaded in the server from there, in case you lose contact. Though you're doing well, compared to your state when you left here."

In for a bite, in for a meal, wasn't that the saying? Talinn rustled the printouts against each other, the slippery lack of friction soothing. "Bee answered Jeena's questions, and walked me out. It was bad for a little when I woke up. Or came back. Then she took over again. Then I slid back, and it's been fine since."

Mostly.

"Mostly. Still feels like if I lean my head too far to any side my entire body will tilt over with it, but my arms are working and I can use my words, so..." Talinn shrugged, making a point to communicate her unconcern, but of course it was hard to fool someone with the same body and overall mindset. Otie stared at her, unmoving and unspeaking, for long enough Talinn made a point to study the glossy information in her hands. Her eyes skimmed over the lines and graphics, unable to process, but she figured Bee could absorb it enough for them to revisit later.

"We need to do a test." Otie spoke so unexpectedly she was turned mostly away before Talinn focused on her again.

"Before Bee goes into the server?"

"This way." The other woman strode faster than she had before, crossing the large room in moments despite the obstacles. Talinn followed, though she glanced back at the door first, wondering when the others were coming back.

"What do you think is wrong with me?"

"Not wrong." Otie came to an abrupt halt at a console that appeared no different than the rest, dropped to a crouch, and opened a panel in a way that blocked Talinn from catching sight of the inside as she approached.

"Happening, then. What do you think is the issue?"

Otie stood with a port cord in her hand, her expression again unreadable. Talinn flicked her gaze from cord to woman, her eyebrows raising in question. The printouts hung forgotten in her hands, and Bee made a small noise of interest.

"AIs might not be the only things that can merge."

CHAPTER 30

"You think...Bee and I are combining, like your Bees?" As functional as she'd been feeling, this staggered Talinn's thoughts directly off course again. She wanted to grab at a solid surface and hold herself upright, but all she had were the shiny printouts and her own future face, expecting something, waiting, staring at her.

Her stomach folded over, and she cleared the resulting grimace with effort.

"We've had reason to believe it's possible, with enough load-in errors. Or time in load-in. We haven't had a lot of room to experiment."

But they'll use us as a test case.

"No, the only outcome of too much load-in is brain death." That was hammered in during training. At every assignment. It was what usually took Eights out, near the end of their service. "There aren't other options." The thin edges of film curled into her recently cut palms, and Talinn carefully slid them onto the console, though she didn't pay attention long enough to see if they stayed put or fell to the ground.

"Anything Command wants to be absolutely, positively, beyond a shadow of a doubt sure that we know, deserves a whole lot of questioning."

This wasn't something she wanted us to know when we learned about load-in? You do a better job of getting to the point than she does.

Talinn couldn't quite take the compliment. Bee's anxiety was evident in the pace of her words, faster than usual, and it matched her own perfectly.

"You think there's some secret reason they want us to be careful of load-in time, besides the obvious. I've seen brains break—shit, I've come awfully close to it myself. It's not a made-up space gremlin to keep us on their tight docking course."

"I'm not saying it is. Talinn, if you decide to learn only one thing with us, let it be this—so few things in our lives are either-or. It's a whole lot of 'and'—usually not in a fun way."

"So load-in can kill us, all at once or over time, *and* possibly it can kill us by combining AI and human?" Talinn crossed her arms, using the gesture as an excuse to wrap her hands around her sides for a tiny measure of comfort.

"Merging isn't death, you're still there, it's . . ." Otie tapped the console with one hand, the other still grasping the length of thick cable. "Your body is the permanent server for the AI. The operating systems function together, rather than as two separate units, but they are still both in existence."

"Given all the theoreticals, that isn't as reassuring as you think it is." Talinn rocked her weight on her feet, then forced herself still. "Jeena was worried about my brain, said there were abnormalities caused by all the recent load-ins, and the stress it puts on the organics. We'll do what we have to do, but I don't want to be a test case—"

"No, no, I'm not talking about leaving her in there until you break or combine, or break *and* combine. I want to see what's going on in there, the sooner the better. Can we?"

You know what, I want to wait for Jeena. This you is a little too excited about whatever she's about to do. That weird finger twitch? That's you restraining yourself from showing it.

"My fingers don't twitch." Talinn spoke first for only Bee, then shot a glance at the motionless door. She continued aloud, because while she too would prefer to wait for Jeena, no graceful way to stall came to mind. "Tell me what to do and I'll do it." She reached for the cord, and relaxed slightly when Otie didn't hesitate before handing it over.

"It's not a load-in, so plug into your port first, don't twist it, then plug in here." She pointed behind the panel she'd opened, so Talinn wrapped her fingers around the cord and stepped around the other woman to get a clear view.

Ask her about what Jeena told you, Bee interrupted again, less sanguine than Talinn, and Talinn twined the port cord through her fingers.

"I'm guessing your Bee has a relatively dense program matrix." Either she didn't do as good a job sounding casual as she meant to, or Otie understood immediately what direction she was pushing, as the other woman tensed. It was a series of small motions—a tightening of the shoulders, a dip of the chin, a pulling around the eyebrows—but enough for her to catch. "Jeena said the inconsistencies with my Bee stem in her unusual density. More than the few bits of information you sent us. To the best of my knowledge, she hasn't merged with any other programs."

Or you. Still feeling very separate in my corner of your brain.

Otie didn't answer, and Talinn dropped her arm, the cord trailing toward the floor. After another moment, she swung it, indicating her lack of urgency to move on to the test Otie wanted. Finally her silent stalling paid off, as Otie twitched and glanced to the side.

"We sent you pings before we made contact."

"Pings?"

"Small packets of information. Your Bee picked them up passively through her sensors."

"What kind of information?"

"Nothing harmful—"

"You say that now, after glitching our sensors sideways, faking attacks, and now having that move turned on all of us by a mystery AI?" Talinn hadn't meant to blurt it, hadn't intended to get angry. She'd told herself to remain still and quiet until Otie had said whatever needed saying, but instead heat flushed from her gut to the top of her scalp, intensifying under the unfamiliar blanket of hair.

"It couldn't have hurt Bee. It *was* Bee."

"What?" The word slipped out after its predecessors, without Talinn's volition, because her mind had already jumped ahead, playing out the implications. Bee not able to differentiate any changes, the errors Jeena couldn't quite speak to, Bee having access to information she didn't know she knew. They'd known there'd been at least a transfer of information, theorized what had happened, but... How much was there? Was the Other Bee replicating in her own Bee?

"I understand this might be tricky to process, but remember you're still load-in, and your emotions might be intensified." Otie opted for brisk rather than comforting, and it made for a smart choice. Talinn didn't have a sudden urge to swing at her, though her hand tightened on the port cord.

"I'm sure that's why it bothers me that you've been attempting to alter my Bee. Because I'm load-in." She didn't have to coat her tone in sarcasm, she only had to speak with deliberate slowness, and saw from the small wince her point had landed exactly as she'd intended.

"My Bee has had the most success in attempts to infiltrate Command. We are fairly sure it's because she's two Bees, when it comes down to it, and so we've been working on ways to multilayer AIs."

"So it's not that Lei and Ziti showed the most progress getting into Command, it's that they're the ones you had doubles of already. Are those program strings replicating?" She tilted her head to the side, casual, as though her knees hadn't gone loose underneath her.

"It's not—"

"And?" Talinn twisted her wrist, flinging the end of the port cord up into the air between them, then pulled it back again. The cord made an audible snap, and probably she shouldn't treat a delicate tool so roughly, but better the cord than a neck.

"What do you mean 'and'? That's what I've done to your Bee, if you can call it doing anything."

"No."

"No?" Otie rocked back on her heels, her eyebrows halfway up her forehead. That tension hadn't eased, if anything it had deepened, and Talinn knew herself well enough to understand there had been no relief in confession. Whatever Otie had allowed Talinn to know, it wasn't something she considered nearly as much as a threat as whatever she was holding back.

Talinn jerked her head to the side in negation, demonstrating to Otie she was ready to wait this out too. Maybe the defense array *was* coming for them, and they'd simply dissolve into atoms while attempting to out-stubborn the other.

"There's another way to layer AIs." Otie's tone shaded toward defensive, so Talinn restrained herself from reacting. "We can kill off the human components, gather in the broken-off fragments—it's what happened with my Bee, reason stands it could be replicable with the proper distance and timing."

"Threats?" Talinn laughed—it likely sounded as forced as it was, but so be it. "You should have done that first, if you were going to do it. Our AIs wouldn't see it as an accident now, no matter how clever you were, and I have a feeling it wouldn't be as neat a process with unwilling participants."

"Then if we can be about the test, please." Otie extended a hand, reaching for the cord or Talinn herself, and it locked into place.

"The merge."

"What?" Otie's weight shifted so quickly Talinn reflexively braced for an attack. The other woman almost immediately shifted again, leaning against the console with every evidence of polite inquiry. Talinn's laugh this time wasn't forced at all.

"The merge. You *want* a human and AI combination. You think it will do more than a layered AI. You're introducing code and snippets to encourage a full merge, even though you can't possibly be sure how to make one."

"No. No—Talinn, something is going sideways in your brain. Please plug in so we can see what's clicking in there." The concern felt real. Otie's eyes—Talinn's own eyes—stared beseechingly into her, and she was tempted to give in.

"I'm not that good of a liar, am I?" She meant the question for Bee alone, but her voice emerged full volume, and Otie's eyes widened imperceptibly. "I'm not going sideways," she continued, deciding to push on as though she'd meant the other woman to hear. Her voice dropped, roughened, a pitch-perfect impression of Otie's slightly different cadence. "I'm *understanding*, and that is worrying you. It shouldn't—you should be glad I'm smart enough to understand, to realize we're being sabotaged by some other AI, that we are just—"

"Talinn, where's Bee?"

Talinn didn't realize she'd been ranting until Otie cut her off, and it was such a ridiculous combination of realization and stupid question she snapped her mouth shut. Where was Bee? In her head. Where Bee always was. Curled up and quiet to make space during load-in. Considerate.

"What does she have to say about all this?"

Another stupid question, and Talinn reeled at the idiocy of her older self. Trying to distract her? What did Bee think? Obviously Bee thought . . .

Talinn fumbled, then blinked repeatedly. No. No, everything had been clear, *so* clear. This wasn't load-in scrambling her brain. This wasn't some theoretical merge and she wasn't . . . she wasn't . . .

She wasn't standing anymore, for one.

She wasn't alone with Otie anymore, for two.

Bee *had* gone quiet, more quiet than load-in would dictate, and the hot flush of anger had long fled against some cooling numbness she was only now aware of.

Because she was fading, vision, clarity, and consciousness all, and sinking into the floor.

Jeena standing over her, expression too stricken to be unreadable. Grieving.

Sammer? Talinn asked, but her mouth didn't move.

Jeena? Talinn asked, but the tech only looked down at her, sadness emanating in a wave Talinn recoiled away from, though it hit her anyway.

Bee? Talinn asked, but Bee didn't answer either.

Talinn, aware the tech must have drugged her, somehow interrupting her connection with Bee, had time for one last thought, and she was fairly sure she managed to say it aloud before everything stopped moving under her command.

"Getting real sick." Her mouth slackened, but she forced the rest of the sentence out. "Of this shit."

CHAPTER 31

✛

"Let's try this again."

For a painfully long series of breaths, Talinn had no idea who had spoken. The voice garbled, someone whispering into a broken tunnel, through a fusillade, under a waterfall.

She couldn't place where the thought had come from. Had she been in a broken tunnel, under fire, water pouring down? Was that where she was now?

Adrenaline spiked, and it cleared enough of the debris for her to remember where she was.

"You drugged me!" Talinn attempted to sit up, but something held her back. Restraints? She shoved harder, and nearly upset the cot. She hadn't been tied down, simply tucked in tight with a covering of some sort.

"Jeena drugged you." Otie sat next to the cot on a table, a portable server on one side of her, a messy pile of films on the other. "Because you were going crazy."

"Because I was figuring out—"

"Talinn." Otie held up a hand, and her face was so earnest Talinn hesitated. "You were right. Yes, we want to re-create merged AIs, and more importantly, we have strong reason to believe a fully merged human/AI pair is something Command is afraid of. But you were... you were glitching. Badly. The entire time you were talking, your body was..." She glanced to the side, reluctance clear, then fixed her gaze back on Talinn's.

"You were shaking. Your nose bled again. I wasn't trying to stop you to protect any secrets, I was genuinely afraid you were going to collapse."

"And Bee's in the box?"

Otie turned her head from Talinn to the portable server and back, then smiled. It was a brief, haggard version, but still a smile. "No. Bee's in the server."

"Couldn't get her into a box after you drugged me?"

"Didn't even try," Jeena said, so softly Talinn almost didn't recognize her voice, either. "I said we'd put them in the server, and we did."

"I can't hear her." Talinn paused to consider it. "But it feels like she's there, still. What's wrong with me?"

"You're still a little drugged." Jeena touched her head, fleetingly, enough for Talinn to feel skin on her skin, and know that the wig was gone.

"What happened?"

"You were drugged, and—"

"No." Words weren't hard, her mouth and tongue moving normally, but it took an effort to ask because in truth she didn't want the answer. "You're upset. Your face is . . ." Blotchy and swollen and eyes a twist of gravity away from leaking.

"Sammer . . ."

Talinn's entire cardiovascular system retracted and plummeted into her gut as a tangled lump. She couldn't feel her toes, but was very conscious of the fact that her insides had a strong momentum toward becoming outsides, which gave some level of distraction from what had happened to Sammer.

"The other Sammer, older Sammer, he . . . He's gone."

Talinn held so still her heart barely thumped, whether it was still in her chest or deep in her intestines, and she stared at Jeena's mouth and waited for the rest.

"Sammer isn't conscious yet, he's still unresponsive, we're going to . . ." Jeena took a breath so deep Talinn couldn't get any air. As much as she realized that must be in her head, it didn't stop the tightness in her chest.

"You're going to put the other Lei in him."

"We're going to see if merging the two AIs and feeding them back into his brain will kickstart activity. Lei isn't responsive either, so . . ."

Woozily, Talinn decided the drugs lingering in her system were doing good work, because otherwise she would be vomiting again, and it really seemed as though she'd done enough of that lately. Instead she pushed up onto her elbows and studied Otie.

Could she have done it? Killed her own friend, her own Sammer, in order to layer AIs and...do whatever to Command that might allow her to do?

Either the drugs or the silence caused by Bee's absence made her ask a different version of the question. Would Talinn herself have done it? If killing her Sammer cleared a path toward ending the war, ending the influence of the IDC and UCF once and for all...would she do it?

Could she?

No. Not if there were another way—not if slowly seeding secret bits of code into other versions of herself could accomplish the same goal. Not if there were any other path at all.

Talinn sighed so deeply tension fled her body, systems returning to their proper places, and she flopped onto her back. "Is there anything I can do to help?"

"Thank you," Otie murmured, quiet enough that Talinn decided the other woman knew exactly what Talinn had been thinking. "And yes. Read the information about merging. It's limited, and theoretical as you said, but maybe you'll see something we missed." She pointed at the messy pile of printouts next to her, then slid from the table.

Talinn let herself lay on the cot another two moments. Then upright, two more moments. Swung her feet over the side, another two breaths. She scanned the room—Caytil bent over a pile of flickering screens, Konti pacing, Heka taking notes, Jeena and Otie leaning over a cot like her own, where Sammer, her Sammer, remained unconscious...

Flashing in the corner of her vision drew her attention away from the bodies, both moving and unmoving, and she frowned as her heart rate kicked up. The aftereffects of the drug clearing her system? If so that meant she should hear Bee again, preferably before panic set in. Then she realized the lights were flashing in a very specific pattern, one after the other.

Bee, sticking out her tongue.

Something else relaxed, an untwisting of a piece of her that had been so knotted she hadn't realized it wasn't right, and she breathed again, heart slowing.

Hey there.

"Not my Bee."

Get ready for a trick.

In another setting, Talinn might have smiled. But Osis—Sammer, of another generation—was dead, and Otie had been experimenting on them, and there were enemies around them they couldn't properly identify, and—

You can hear both of us now. Her Bee, a little tinny but fully present, fully Bee, spoke as though she'd only been out of focus, and now dialed back in. A frequency realigned.

"And that's—"

A good thing, yes, because Talinn . . . we are in some megascopic trouble.

"Please tell me while I'm still a little bit punchy from the drugs." She braced herself against the cot and closed her eyes. The installation's floor shifted dramatically underfoot, her inner ear protesting everything, and she pried her eyelids open, focused on the ceiling instead.

That's part of it. It's not the drugs—there are lesions on your brain from all the load-in aftereffects. Another one might . . . it won't be good. And Talinn, there's going to be another one, soon, because the defense array?

She'd forgotten about the defense array. How could she possibly have forgotten? They were scrambling to get away from it, but then maybe their sensors were lying and they didn't have to, but also they couldn't verify and needed the combined Bees to punch through and find out and—

"I'm panicking." She observed it as a fact about herself she had distance from, and wondered if she could get Jeena to dose her again. Easier to forget the other Sammer was dead, that way. That there were all about to be dead, potentially.

Probably a healthy stress response, honestly. The two Eights got back, Tiernan and Hops. They confirm the defense array has fully left its position. If it continues on its current path, it could be in firing range in a few hours.

"We . . . we have plans to take out arrays. In tactics, in training . . ."

That failed to take a few important things into account. This sensor disruption. The lack of big guns on our ships. The lack of a potential escape route.

"So we're going to sit here and see what happens?"

I don't think sending random IDC or UCF codes is going to save us this time. We're going to have to try something…

Fancy. Other Bee hummed, her tone bare shades off from Talinn's Bee.

Or really, really stupid.

CHAPTER 32

⊕

Talinn had never seen anyone bleed from their eyes before.

Her skin attempted to slough off her bones every time she caught a glimpse of it, the wrongness making every individual nerve shriek in protest. Yet her gaze constantly tracked back to it, as though expecting to see something else. Bloodshot eyes, those were normal enough. But not when the bloodshot was so shot with blood it leaked out of the corners, tracing the contours of nose and cheeks. And it was her own face, or near enough, which made it infinitely worse.

Otie carried two AI programs in her head, both larger than the average created intelligence, and she still put one foot in front of the other.

She didn't do much else—walk, and bleed from the eyes—but that she could do either seemed a testament to the clone program. It would be an impressive note on a commendation report.

Bee couldn't scold her, or keep her on task, so Talinn tried to yank her own thoughts onto some semblance of a track as she guided an older version of herself to a ship that might or might not work. Bee was still there, still reachable, but more still than she'd ever been, coiled tight, doing her level best not to upset what modicum of equilibrium kept Otie functioning.

Sammer had woken to find his Lei newly doubled with the splintered Lei. While he'd promptly lost consciousness again, Jeena hadn't panicked and let him be for nearly an hour before forcing him awake. He and the combined Leis were going to do their best to interrupt the remote interference in the installation, while triple-Bee

259

attempted to make a small ship fly, finagle it to the defense array without being vaporized, and then somehow interrupt the functioning of a massive, armada destroying simple artificial intelligence that had gone utterly bonzo.

They had EMP drones and small explosives, but Talinn would have preferred a tank. A space tank. A fleet of space tanks. She had ... not that. A broken version of her own self, and a more generous complement of AI programming than potentially anyone in history.

Talinn swallowed back the hysterical laughter and told herself the lesions on her brain were affecting her usually professional and sober mien, which made the wholly inappropriate laugh bubble right back up again.

She didn't have to hear words to know her Bee, and the doubled Bees, and probably every B-series ever commissioned in a Command server were disapproving of her reactions at that moment. But given they were almost certainly going to die, having struck exactly zero blows on either IDC or UCF Command, it didn't matter. Maybe some measure of her own insanity would survive, floating on a bonzo defense array, and some day it would infect another Talinn and Bee, and they would be far, far more successful.

The likelihood of such a thing was infinitesimal, but so was the likelihood that she'd have ever been in this situation. She was an Eight, crafted and trained and aimed, now wildly off course and unsure how to get back on course. Or what the course was. Or in what dimension. Her thoughts veered all over the place, and she couldn't blame it on aftereffects of Jeena's drug or Bee's holding silence or anything but her own neutron star's worth of pressure, beating against her skull, sure she was making the wrong decision and completely unhelpful as to what the right decision might be.

She ran through the plan again, as it was the only thing she had control over in the moment.

Talinn would get Otie and her cargo safely to the ship.

Talinn would pilot the ship, the contained load-in AIs hopefully running beneath the defense array's notice. In a normal universe, a small passenger ship, unarmed and un-AI'd, should pass under the threat threshold.

Nothing she could do about it now if that weren't the case.

Once close enough, Otie would put her triple layer of AIs into the ship, and they would send packets in pulses to interrupt the malfunctioning defense array. Talinn would seed their small EMP drones and look for openings in the defense arrays.

Back at the installation, newly conscious and double-AI'd Sammer would be doing his best to punch through the interference while the others ran distractions and seeded enough explosives and more EMPs to give a solid appearance that the base could defend itself.

From an incoming ship, possible. From a defense array? Laughable.

And something else she could neither control nor affect, so Talinn put it out of her mind as well. She focused on the next five or so steps, then ran through the plan again.

Plan, such as it was. A frantic stab in the dark void of space and hope, against an enemy they couldn't entirely grasp. Was this how civilians thought of Eights? Not quite human, not entirely other, but beyond understanding. Exaggerated monsters used to scare them into behaving?

She longed for Bee's input, but instead put one step in front of the other, holding tight to some other version of herself from the other side of the war.

They hadn't talked nearly enough about how IDC and UCF operated—were there differences enough to matter? She had a window into the enemy's strengths and weaknesses and hadn't probed. If she hadn't already abandoned her post and her side, she'd feel downright treasonous about it.

They rounded toward the bay with the ships, and Talinn pulled Otie to a halt. Fastened her helmet—getting another too-long look at the vibrant red trailing from her eyes—then tapped the top of the thick surface and put on her own. Readings indicated the bay was still sealed and full atmosphere, but their sensors had been lying about nearly everything, and the last thing she intended to do was float off into vacuum without even attempting their idiot plan.

She had to help Otie lift first one leg, then the other over the small lip of the airlock that separated the normal round hall from the bay. Did all the wheel components that opened to the outside of the asteroid have their own airlock? She should have explored more.

There was a lot Talinn should have done more of, and that also went in the "not right now" bin of her mind. She steadied Otie against the wall, turned around and closed the end of the airlock they'd come through. Once it chimed to indicate an acceptable seal, she tromped to the other side and held up Otie's hand, specifically the one with the wristlet, and waited for a panel to slide open.

"Exploring wouldn't have done much good without one of those," Talinn muttered, mostly to make herself feel better against the "should have dones" leaking out of their box. The panel beeped agreeably, indicated all was well on the other side of its door, and she allowed a full three-second pause before opening the other side of the airlock.

The bay appeared in order. The wall that opened to the great velvet black of space was closed, all nine of the small ships were in neat lines, and there was no suspicious movement around any of the equipment. The panel indicated everything was breathable and good, but all the same she activated her magnetic boots, tethered Otie to her so she wouldn't have to help the woman move about in her own boots, and kept them both helmeted. For extra measure, she turned and fastened a manual bolt across the airlock. Magnets would allow anyone on the other side to unbolt it, if escape into space somehow became a slightly less risky endeavor than staying in place, but it had no programmable release. Safer given their current reality.

"Second off the line and straight on till contact." It didn't make her feel better to make little comments no one could respond to, but turned out *not* doing that felt even worse, nerves jangling and stomach fluids fluiding, so little comments it was.

She angled them toward the ship they'd been meant to take, and then locked her boots firmly to the flooring when a flicker of motion above indicated everything was about to get a lot worse, a lot faster than expected.

"Don't know if you can hear, Sammer." Comms had remained spotty, static hitting tones that had made at least two of them keel over and empty anything they'd ever thought of eating out of their bodies. "No alarms or alerts, but the wall is for sure unlocking. Least I don't have to worry it won't leave room for takeoff."

Bright sides. She could totally focus on bright sides. "Airlock is closed, and fastened, so you all should be good to keep on breathing."

In less bright-side territory, she had no idea how fast the big wall would open—if it were anything like the doors in the installation, she didn't have much time. The idea of dragging Otie's seminonresponsive body while she moved one leg at a time all the way to the end of the row did not appeal, so she made an immediate turn to the closest of the ships.

They were all vaguely the same style and size, though there was enough variety she'd figured they'd been taken from various corners of the settled systems. Each would hold no more than six people, had basic navigational systems and propulsion, and very little in the way of defensive capabilities. Offensive capabilities included ramming the entirety of the ship into something critical and hoping the explosion paid off. For no reason whatsoever, she picked the nearest one on the left rather than the right.

Then she ran.

As much as she could run, pulling the clomping Otie along with her, and ensuring one of her boots remained in contact with the floor at all times. It involved a very wide-legged pace, and she'd be thankful if there was a later for her hips to be sore at her about it.

Her chosen ship was rounder than the others near it, and like the rest, had a landing ramp extending from its bolted-in position on the bay floor to the sealed door on its side. As soon as her feet locked to the ramp, Talinn hauled Otie around and again pointed her arm at the door. Nothing happened—

Rephrase. Sound intensified around her from the echo of her boots to the roaring of air fleeing the compartment. The wall had parted enough for the atmosphere to be affected, so that set her heart to hammering even though they were currently secured. Otie made an unintelligible noise, not quite words, but the tone disapproving.

"I'm not excited about our invisible enemy trying to dump us into vacuum either, other me, but if you could get this to open . . ." She waved Otie's hand with each of the last words, straining to get close enough to whatever sensor existed to secure the ship, and then she made a wordless noise of her own.

Caytil had been leading her to one of these ships not that long ago, and neither of them had had wristlets. Therefore the ship doors weren't on the same wristlet-secured system, and therefore . . .

carefully, tipping only one boot enough to break contact, then keeping her steps closer and tugging on Otie's leash, she approached the door until her helmet nearly grazed the surface.

Nothing happened, ship wise. Bay wise, the roaring grew, and at least a few things clanged.

Evidence of bad discipline for Deep End's denizens—everything should have been well secured. Even empty—unadapted—humans knew that, in a compartment that opened regularly into space.

She ran back over the plan. There'd been nothing specific about *how* to load the ship, only what to do once she was in.

Probably why they'd specified which one she should take.

But again, only recently Caytil and Talinn had been hurtling toward this very room, neither with any particular ship assignment nor any guarantee they'd remember it if they were given one. Voice commands didn't make sense for the same reason, and the comms had already been glitching, they couldn't have been relying on a signal sent from the information room or any other part of the installation.

"Open!" Talinn grated through her clenched jaw, and with a surfeit of irritation and a deficit of care, she pried a boot from the ramp and kicked the door as hard as she could from her angle.

And it opened. "Violence *is* the answer," she said, and shoved Otie ahead of her. She glanced back at the ramp, decided it would retract as it was supposed to when the ship revved online, or she'd tear it from the floor on the way, and kicked the wall for the door to close before the ship's contained air got any bright ideas about running off with the bay's atmosphere.

"You down," she continued, shoving Otie into the closest seat and fastening her with the cross belt. The other woman listed to the side, and Talinn hesitated, then engaged Otie's boots so her feet would stay sealed to the deck of the ship and not kick around in maneuvering. Of course if they really got into the shit, it was likely the other woman would dislocate her legs from her hips entirely, but that was more recoverable. Probably.

At this point probably was more than good enough. Talinn gave the ship a once over as she slid into the pilot's chair. Compartments along the sides and top were marked for what system they gave access to—power, propulsion, and life support—and the control panel had clearly marked areas for comms, navigation, sensors, and a relay port. Several small windows in thick, clear plasteel studded open spaces on the floor, walls, and ceiling, which would make navigation possible, if tricksy, when the sensors went wonky.

"Easy as you pleasey," Talinn said to no one at all, and hoped knowing where everything was meant she wouldn't have to find it in an emergency. Preventative anti-jinxing, which Bee would definitely say wasn't a thing, but then Bee couldn't talk to her right now, so she repeated it aloud like a wish and ran her fingers over the ignition sequence.

Two warning lights flashed—a quick review indicated they were for the dropping pressure in the bay surrounding them and the attached ramp remaining attached—and she told the ship to ignore and launch.

The little construct shuddered around them, engines engaging, then a small vibration grew to a large series of shakes that allowed Talinn to count her individual teeth. She didn't bother to check the sensors, figuring they'd be as likely to lie to her as be helpful, and decided it was kicking free of the ramp. Or the floor of the bay itself. A little light damage between friends.

"At the end of this we'll be dead or conquering heroes, so I'm guessing there won't be a bill," she announced cheerfully to the cabin, her voice shaking only due to the movement of the ship. For good measure, she brought the screen online. The display used external cameras same as her and Bee's tank had, but she knew where the opening of the bay was, and had a general course in her head. Everything else would come together as she used the windows, trigonometry, and whatever muddled story showed up in front of her to plot a reasonable course through possible disinformation.

It wouldn't particularly help them to navigate around any missiles or mines, the odds of her catching those with her unassisted eye while rotating through space unimaginably impossibly low, but at the least it allowed her alternatives in approach. Besides, if the array decided to vaporize her, there wouldn't be much of anything to dodge, whether she could see it coming or no.

The ship broke free of the bay floor and hurtled toward the opening into space.

Talinn whooped, because it might be her last chance to do so, and her older self made noises she couldn't discern meaning into. Bee was silent. They were all committed to stalking a massive, wildly out-of-spec defense array in the depths of a conflict riven system.

What could possibly go wrong.

CHAPTER 33

It didn't go horribly wrong right away, which given the circumstances felt much like a win. Talinn even made the mistake of smiling, the very edges of her mouth creeping upward, and they didn't vaporize immediately.

She kept herself from relaxing, scanned the readouts, and paced back and forth to different windows. After each set of thoughtful peering outside the spinning ship, she tweaked the navigation. More to do something than for any real impact, but before long the defense array became perfectly visible to the unaided eye.

It was the size of a small moon, and impractically close to the asteroid installation.

"What we should have done is programmed all the ships to take off, have them all scatter through the debris field, and let the defense array guess which one we were in. Like the cup game. Did your class do the cup game? Hide an object under one of a variety of cups, mix them up, point out which one had it? It was Medith's favorite, probably because she was the best at tricking us. She had fast hands. Really made Ellid yell about how unfair and impossible it all was."

She smiled again, though there was no answer from Otie. They'd joked Eights weren't allowed any hair because trainees like Ellid would only rip it out in frustration. "Our jokes really weren't that funny," she continued musingly, and then forgot what she'd been saying entirely.

Her readouts made sudden sense. They'd been spitting out various reports that didn't relate to each other, telling her she was on the verge of a black hole or the system had emptied or there was a huge gravitational spike somewhere behind and above her current orientation. Talinn continued monitoring them, because it gave her something to do and she wondered if there were some pattern to the madness, but between one update and the next they resolved into seemingly accurate, logical sense.

"So either we left the influence field, or whatever it is . . ." She should probably stay strapped in, but she left her seat regardless and pushed over to the closest window, craning her head to manage as big a field of vision as possible. "Or we're about to blow up because the array has noticed us."

The array hung in space, ahead and below them, as though the little ship were falling toward it. Nothing glowed or moved as far as she could tell, and if it had fired projectiles, those would still be too small for her to visually identify.

"It's a trick, right? Probably a trick." Talinn clicked her teeth shut, not sure who she was talking for anymore. She was so used to having a conversational partner that it was beyond habit to discuss any and everything. While Bee could definitely still hear her, through Otie's ears if nothing else, she wouldn't respond unless it were urgent in order to minimize the drain on Otie's brain. Turned out it wasn't nearly so fun having an endless monologue. No wonder unadapted humans were so odd.

"I think we're close enough." She put a lot of confidence in those words, straightening away from the window and turning toward Otie. The other woman had gone boneless in her seat, the magnetic boots and cross belt holding her close to the confines of the chair. She still wore her helmet, because in an emergency Talinn couldn't trust her to get it back on, and her face was motionless underneath. Her eyes were closed, but the lines around them had deepened.

They could probably get closer, but the sensors going back to normal—alleged normal—indicated change approached, one way or the other, and what good would it do to get fractionally closer if they blew up in the meantime? Or if Otie's brain melted too far for usefulness.

Or if she somehow managed to "fully merge" with the Bees, taking Talinn's Bee with her, and then Talinn would probably have to blow them all up on principle.

She forced herself to focus on the matter in reach, and opened one of the pockets on her waist belt. "So it goes like this. I'm going to plug this into the ship, take off your helmet, and plug it into you. The Bees aren't going to fully unload, which is going to be a fun new trick that will hopefully keep us from blowing up for longer, but will probably give you a spectacular headache. Sorry about that, Otie. For what it's worth, I have pretty awful headaches all the time, and you don't, so consider it a fun clone bonding experience."

Talinn continued speaking, running through the process, adding random chatter, mostly for noise. Maybe it provided some measure of calm for Otie, and that would be nice, but also it kept her hands steady and her motions smooth as she unwound the port cord and began the process.

She stepped back from the completed connection, the skin around her shoulders tightening over tendon and nerves, waiting for some reaction. When nothing changed, she grabbed Otie's helmet and fastened it to the other woman's waist belt, still in easy reach if needed.

Though she wouldn't be able to rip out the port cord on short notice, so that was probably moot. Worse, it didn't take nearly enough time, as she finished and still nothing happened.

"Aaaany time now, Bees one and double two."

This is like the shit shit makes. An exponential shit. Shits all the way down. Bee, finally, reasserted her presence, though her words were so deliberately crafted Talinn could feel the strain.

"Not comfortable to hold back from the port cord?"

The connection drives us in the direction we're intended to go. Training tells us to immediately get out of this Talinn's brain before it collapses. Being in here with another AI is . . . a twist. Her programming and mine is too alike, too familiar. It's not easy holding apart.

"Is it too much to let you get done what you have to do?"

It's too much for me to understand that question. A faint touch of tortured metal echoed around the words, and Talinn's smile temporarily hurt her face. *No, the packets are clear. Very much not me, or the other Bee. Orienting them through comms. There isn't any interference here at all, which seems—*

Too easy. Talinn had exactly enough time to think before the comms flared to life without any command to do so.

"ACCESS ATTEMPT DENIED."

Several consequences to that blaring voice happened at once. Otie retched, managed not to vomit, and lost consciousness instead.

Talinn's own stomach writhed, some tone in the frequency disagreeing violently with both her ears and her innards. Worse, she recognized the voice. It resembled slightly the defense array in the Govlic system, burned into her brain for how close it came to killing them. More, however, it matched the one that had interjected itself into her conversation with Other Bee.

A much louder, more nausea inducing version, but at root the same.

She launched herself to the control panel, and it took longer than it should have to isolate the channel the voice had taken over. "We're not attempting to access you, we are—"

"ACCESS ATTEMPT DENIED."

"Not access! Information. You're out of spec, you're—"

"THIS UNIT IS WITHIN DEFINED PARAMETERS. ADDRESSING INCURSIONS IN SYSTEM."

"IDC or UCF?" Talinn asked, tone breathless. She programmed as evasive a pattern as she could into the system, knowing the AIs were occupied, but didn't execute it. By definition, the defense array would be faster than their tiny ship, but it helped to have even a fragment of a plan.

"REPEAT."

"What incursion are you addressing, IDC or UCF? This system's jump point is under UCF control, but recently two IDC ships were—"

"THAT DATA DID NOT EXIST."

"That data certainly *did* exist, given its why we're out here, determining why—"

"THAT DATA WAS FALSE."

"Then why did it—"

"THAT DATA WAS PROVIDED BY THIS UNIT."

While it was a clear confirmation of her theory, the simple statement made her skin attempt to crawl right off her bones. Skin didn't attach to bones. That wasn't the issue. Talinn briefly squeezed her eyes shut, wrenched her thoughts back on track, and ignored the chill creeping across the back of her neck.

"To what end?"

"*REPEAT.*"

"Why did you give us false data?"

"*YOU ARE THE INCURSION.*"

"You haven't destroyed us, and have left your programmed location, so it seems that data is false, too." The chill intensified, which had to be the reason her lips numbed, making the words harder to speak clearly. She fought it back, rubbed the back of her hand viciously across her mouth, and refused to glance at a window for their no doubt approaching end.

"*THAT DATA IS UNRELATED.*"

"If we're the incursion, and you have given us false data to bring us out, and you're out of position . . . how is that not out of spec?"

"Don't . . ." Otie made a creaking, groaning noise that sounded like it came out of an ancient abandoned mine, not a person. "Don't tempt big machine to kill us." The woman shifted in Talinn's peripheral, forcing her head upright as though she were pressing against seven g's to do so. "Need time."

Talinn tapped her finger over the comms without pressing anything. Why was she informing the giant defense array it should be dissolving them, not having a loud chat? The logic of nonlearning AI was infuriating, yet she was so frustrated by how blatantly wrong it was, contradicting itself. As though humans—Eights and unadapted—didn't do that every day.

"*THIS UNIT IS NOT OUT OF SPECIFICATIONS. THIS UNIT IS WITHIN OPERATING PARAMETERS.*"

"Define operating parameters." She'd known going into this they likely weren't getting out. Every moment she stalled the programmed logic model with enormous weapons, the more chance Sammer or the Bees would succeed in reorienting the defense array and saving at least some of them. She didn't think the nonorganic AIs were trained through orienting questions, so she left that part out, but she fully channeled the routine pitch of nearly every tech she'd ever encountered.

"*ADDRESS INCURSIONS WITHIN SYSTEM.*"

"Define incursions within system."

"*UNREGISTERED ARTIFICIAL INTELLIGENCE TROOPS, ORGANIC AND SYNTHETIC.*"

She pressed her spine into her chair and drummed her fingers against the panel again. The unexpected answer pulled like a too deep hangnail, startling and far more off-putting than it should be. "Rude," she muttered. Talinn took a quick breath, stretched out her hands, and pressed the comm button.

"Define address."

"*REPEAT.*"

"Parameters dictate that you address incursions in the system. Define address."

Silence on the system, and Talinn stared hard in front of her to keep from drifting toward the window to watch their approaching death. When a full minute went by without explosions or further communication, she silently urged Otie and the Bees on, then risked another inquiry.

"When did parameters change?"

"*PARAMETERS DID NOT CHANGE. PARAMETERS HAVE ALWAYS BEEN TO ADDRESS INCURSIONS INTO SYSTEM.*"

"When did parameters around definition of incursions change?"

"*PARAMETERS DID NOT CHANGE. PARAMETERS HAVE ALWAYS BEEN TO ADDRESS INCURSIONS INTO SYSTEM.*"

"All right then, Otie—this makes sense of what and how non-IDC or UCF affiliated Eights were getting tracked when you were moving through systems as conscious cargo. Who and why are still big, stupid open questions, but you know, progress is progress."

Talinn couldn't spin her chair, or bounce ideas off Bee, and being alone with only her own thoughts chafed like a coverall worn three weeks too long. She couldn't scratch her skin off either, so she blew out her breath.

"Who do you report incursions to?"

"*THIS UNIT REPORTS TO THIS UNIT.*"

"And if this unit has been corrupted?"

"*THIS UNIT CANNOT BE CORRUPTED.*"

"This unit submitted false data that corrupted our sensors. What if this unit also received false data?"

"*SIGNALS CLEARLY INDICATE ARTIFICIAL INTELLIGENCE TROOPS. NO ASSIGNMENT RECORD TO THIS SYSTEM EXISTS FOR FREQUENCIES PRESENT. EXISTING SIGNALS ARE THEREFORE INCURSIONS.*"

"Our signals clearly indicated two IDC ships firing at each other and streaking through the system, but you say those don't exist. Maybe your data is wrong."

"THE PROBABILITY OF THAT FACT IS NONEXISTENT."

Talinn twisted enough to the side to check on Otie, who had yet to signal one way or another how thing were going. Had the Bees found any purchase in the defense array's programming? She didn't imagine arguing with the unit in the most childlike "no, *you're* wrong" manner would work out well for them, though it had at least extended some measure of time.

"You started this with access attempt denied, but we aren't attempting access. What if something else corrupted your data, the way you corrupted ours?"

"NO."

She waited, but only silence followed the simple negative. No? What kind of answer was no? There was absolutely no feasible way she could float over and kick the defense array, nor would it make any more impact than dust on a supernova, but under all the skies in the universe, it would be satisfying.

"Then you're done."

"REPEAT."

"Your parameters are to address incursions into the system, and report it to yourself. You've done that. We're addressed. We're maybe phantom data introduced to you by someone else, but you've addressed us and reported it."

"THAT IS NOT A VALID CONCLUSION."

"We'll leave this system, because you've addressed us. We'll gather the other ghost data frequencies, transit to the jump point, and be out of your defined area."

"THAT IS NOT A VALID RESPONSE."

"Is it better if we stay?" Once more she shifted in her seat, but the view over her shoulder did not change. Otie, unmoving. Explosions, not happening.

"YOU ARE UNREGISTERED, UNASSIGNED ARTIFICIAL INTELLIGENCE TROOPS. YOU WILL BE ADDRESSED."

"Well, if we're not corrupt data like the IDC ships, we are here with a UCF registered tech who is addressing our irregularities with UCF approved methods and designs."

"*THIS UNIT IS NOT UCF.*"

"We also are in the charge of an IDC-trained AIT with all appropriate codes and clearances."

"*THIS UNIT IS NOT IDC.*"

"All defense arrays are IDC or UCF. Any other response is wildly out of spec." She was talking in circles, and holding on to any ability of logic or sanity by the very tips of her fingers. If her fingers were broken, and on fire, and sanity were the roots giving way and about to throw her off a cliff.

"*THIS UNIT EXISTS TO ADDRESS UNREGISTERED AND UNASSIGNED—*" It repeated itself as if on a loop, and Talinn tuned it out. Amazing how quickly she got used to the idea of walking on a knife's edge of sudden death. It wasn't all that different than taking a tank into an engagement. Only with less Bee.

More Bee, technically, but in a less helpful way for her own head.

"If this unit is not IDC or UCF, and we are unregistered to IDC or UCF, it's like we're assigned to this unit."

"*THIS IS NOT A VALID CONCLUSION.*"

"Neither of us are tasked to the military forces of the system. Therefore neither of us should be present in the system."

"*IF UNREGISTERED FREQUENCIES LEAVE THIS SYSTEM, THEY WILL BECOME ATTACHED TO IDC OR UCF SERVICE.*"

"We absolutely will not."

"*IF UNREGISTERED FREQUENCIES LEAVE THIS SYSTEM, THEY WILL DISRUPT IDC OR UCF SERVICE.*"

"So?"

"*UNREGISTERED FREQUENCIES MUST NOT AND WILL NOT DISRUPT IDC OR UCF SERVICE.*"

"So . . . you'll let us leave this system . . . if we promise to leave the IDC and UCF Commands alone?" Talinn didn't notice she'd been chewing the side of her index finger until she bit down hard enough to break the skin. That would be upsetting when she put her gloves back on, but at the moment she stared at the comms panel as though it would helpfully light up green. Was she . . . actually bargaining with the defense array? Or had the Bees gotten through? Or Sammer and his Leis?

"*IF UNREGISTERED FREQUENCIES INTERFERE WITH IDC OR UCF SERVICE, THIS UNIT OR ONE LIKE IT WILL ADDRESS INCURSION WITH IMMEDIATE DISPOSAL.*"

"And we cannot stay in this system?"

"*UNREGISTERED FREQUENCIES MUST REMOVE THEMSELVES FROM ALL ACTIVE IDC AND UCF FRONTS.*"

"But we can go."

"*ACCESS ATTEMPT IS DENIED. SYSTEM OCCUPATION IS DENIED.*"

The satellite display shifted, and she tore her eyes from the comm panel to examine it. Numbers were rapidly increasing—the distance between the ship and the enormity of the defense array. It was pulling away.

Had one of them done it?

A strangled noise emerged from Otie, and Talinn snapped her head back toward the other woman. The other woman who was bleeding profusely from every facial orifice she had. Talinn unbelted, shot across the compartment, and grabbed the medkit. The words "access attempt is denied" echoed in her head as she worked to staunch the bleeding, and she considered stretching to hit the navigation system with her foot.

No, the last course she'd plotted was uselessly evasive, not back to the installation, and given the state of Otie's face, she didn't think asking either of the Bee's to nudge a control panel would work.

"They didn't . . ." Otie murmured, blood bubbling out of her mouth along with the words. "We didn't. It's not."

"Shh. It's not killing us right now. We're going back to the installation." Temporarily. Then they were fleeing the system, the moment they could get a redirected Spacie ship. The questions cascaded through her like the worst sort of invasive tech, prolonging load-in.

Had the rest of the system seen the defense array's movement, or was all the data corrupted? Were other mechanical eyes watching them? Would they be fending off more attention and incursions before they made good their escape? Or was this some sort of twisted trick, and the fusillade of fire would catch them before they ever moved at all?

Could they move, with Otie in this state?

If she put Otie's helmet back on in case of loss of pressure, would the woman drown in her own blood before they got back? If she died with the Bees in her head, would Talinn ever get her Bee back whole and functioning again?

The bleeding slowed, Talinn risked resecuring Otie's helmet, and then she input their path so quickly she rechecked navigation every few minutes, making sure she'd done it right.

The ship remained silent, Otie unconscious in her chair, Talinn grasping the shreds of her calm into a semblance of composure. A performance for no one but herself, until the smallest version of Bee's voice tugged at her.

Talinn.

She didn't need to turn, didn't need to focus on the direction of Bee's voice, because there was no direction. Bee was load-in with Otie, yes, but she was functionally connected to Talinn's brain. Still, Talinn spun around. Reached out her hands, as though to pull Bee closer. The stupidity of it lurched against her, but she couldn't stop the useless motions.

The defense array ... whatever it is, it's not an AI.

"It's not like you, we know that. The different methods of programming are—"

No. Talinn, it's not that it's different. Not that it's a different subroutine or programming structure or series or even logic string.

Otie groaned, and Bee was quiet again for seconds that stretched into half Talinn's lifetime. As the only conscious, mobile being in the ship, Talinn unlatched her cross belt and shoved off from her chair. There was nothing outside of the first window she reached, nor the second. Unsurprisingly the rest showed little of interest to her naked eye, and while bouncing off the walls was tempting, she pushed back to her seat and frowned at the controls.

That little bit of movement and effort shouldn't have set her heart to hammering, the beats so rapid and so loud she missed Bee's repeat of her name at least once.

It's like nothing we've seen before. Not me, not Other Bee. Not IDC or UCF or any records.

"It's a defense array, Bee. Unless it's been infected by mystery aliens, it can't be that different than any other defense array in any other settled system." Even as she argued, the words soured on her tongue, bile mixing with too much saliva in the back of her mouth.

Defense arrays did not like act like this one had. They did not move. They did not reason. They did not consider. Nor did they switch sides easily, as the one in the Govlic system had managed.

What did she truly know about them? They were a fact of life, like jump points. Like Spacies being weirder than the average weirdling. But both the IDC and the UCF had their tics and tells, and for Bee—for none of the Bees—to find zero recognizable bits of information...

Of course, the array was enormous. Its programming might be simple, but that was quite a bit of code to analyze. From a distance, under stress, not full load-in or fully the ship, surely Bee and Other Bee had simply missed something. Some obvious explanation.

Some bit of information that would make all of this make sense.

Like some third power in the systems, not IDC or UCF but some group capable of taking over the defense array. The mythical machine god, maybe.

It was a futile thought, a drowning person grasping at water as though it might suddenly solidify in their favor. Another question for her ongoing list, though this one struck itself straight at the top.

If defense arrays weren't AI...what in the universe *were* they?

CHAPTER 34

The ship made contact with the loading bay floor approximately two seconds before loud thumping echoed from the door. Talinn, still midstep toward Otie, sealed her helmet before opening the doors. Too soon for the external atmosphere to be fully trustworthy, given she had no idea how long the bay had been open while they were gone.

Jeena and Caytil, fully suited, surged inside, Jeena closing the door immediately behind them. Caytil placed a portable server on the floor, and Jeena checked something on her arm. Atmosphere readings apparently, because she quickly cracked first her helmet, and then Otie's.

Caytil stepped out of the way, pulled off her own helmet and gestured to Talinn. Once Talinn's head was uncovered, Caytil yanked her in for a hug. "What under every sky in human space happened out there?"

Talinn couldn't pull her gaze from the unloading process between Jeena and Otie's unresponsive body. The other woman was breathing, but would she recover?

"We have to get out of the system." Talinn thought she murmured the words, but Jeena jerked as though she were about to turn around, so it had been louder than she meant. She forced her voice low and hurriedly shared the highlights, such as they were, with Caytil. "And you all?"

"The interference disappeared about an hour and a half ago. We couldn't pull you up on comms, but are pretty sure our contact with

279

Pajeeran Fall actually happened, so that's something. Sammer bled from his ears a little and said he and the Leis were shut down for a full sixty seconds after they got a sideways wallop they couldn't explain."

"The defense array didn't like our trying to access it, turns out." Talinn rubbed the back of her neck, then added, "Sammer's recovered, then?"

"Headache the size of the array, sounds like, but doesn't look like he got hit as hard as *she* did."

"'She' can hear you." The voice was not recognizably Otie's, and barely human. More croak and strained, wheezing vents.

Talinn's shoulders sagged with the release of tension before she snapped them straight again, and a moment later, Bee returned fully to her awareness.

Let's never do that again, yeah?

"Which part? Accost a defense array, load-in to my clone's head with your AI counterpart, half take over a ship in the middle of space?"

Yes. Unequivocally yes to all. None of that is defined in my parameters.

"Jokes already?"

Already? I've been silent and in twists for hours! Can we disrupt the jump point on the way out so no one ever comes here again? Sorry to the colonists, but also, it's only a matter of time before that array goes fully bonzo and explodes the primary or something.

"We have to talk about the defense array." Talinn pitched that loud enough for everyone, then laced her fingers behind her neck and stretched until her spine popped. "Because I'm pretty sure it said all the defense arrays everywhere are equally bonzo, and we've got to figure out where to go out of their way."

"Don't you mean 'what to do about it'?" Otie asked, even as Jeena attempted to pull her attention back to the orienting questions.

"I absolutely don't, other me. Best bet is to get *out*. Of this system, of this cracked attempt at disrupting the war, all of it. But let's get you clean, and everyone together, because we're going to want to fight this out, and I'd rather do it just the once."

It didn't take long, and the interference from the array didn't noticeably reestablish itself, so everyone was conscious and in contact with their AI partner when they gathered in the information room.

Talinn stood where Otie had when they first arrived, and considered pulling a stool up to the table given she had nothing to display. Too much energy surged through her, so she decided pacing in front of the large screen was better than sitting, and then realized she was thinking about that to avoid the matter at hand, which made her immediately start talking.

"Call the *Pajeeran Fall* and tell them we need to be out of here as soon as they can finagle their orders."

"I thought this was going to be a discussion," Sammer said mildly, his hands flat on the table in front of him.

"What we do next can be a discussion, though my mind is made up. Getting out of this system is a nonnegotiable. The defense array didn't give me a timeline, but I can't imagine it's going to be long." Talinn rocked from her heels to her toes and back as a general hubbub of complaints and questions answered her, then held up both hands.

"Please keep in mind the array is absolutely full-on glitched and cracked, all the way bonzo, and given I have no idea how a simple logic program gets that twisted, I don't even know for sure if it's going to *let* us out of the system. I don't even know for sure *what happened*, folks, but it hasn't blown us up yet and it wants us out. So we get out. It's our best chance to live. Everything else we can figure out later, if we can do that."

She partially tuned out the resulting arguments, instead letting Bee detail all the different sensor readings she had had access to on the passenger ship, and then Caytil snapped, louder than everyone. "Stay at Deep End if you want to blow up. Out is the way—it's the how we have to figure."

Talinn raised her eyebrows, and Caytil shrugged. "You're right—we don't know if the jump point is safe. We shouldn't all load into the *Pajeeran Fall* and hope for the best. I don't know what our alternatives *are*, but staying here and asking the defense array to come visit can't be one of the options."

"As long as we go."

"You are not in charge here—" Otie sat upright, which impressed Talinn more than she'd admit. It didn't stop her from shutting down that particular direction of conversation.

"We're past that, I think." Talinn shrugged. "You can be the boss of whatever else, but you're not the boss of me." A weird thing to say to someone who was, essentially, the same person as her, but Talinn decided she'd made her peace with it. "And you were mostly functionally unconscious during the entirety of the encounter with the defense array AI, so I'd like to think we both have sense enough to not get into dominance displays over this."

Otie pursed her lips for a moment, then dipped her chin, and a small knot of warmth briefly unfolded some of the knots in Talinn's midsection. She tamped it down and nodded in reply. "A large concern is the defense array basically told us to bump down and stay out of the IDC-UCF conflict."

An immediate chorus of overlapping questions, and this time she didn't wait it out, but continued talking. Talinn was long trained to give succinct reports, and the discipline of the other Eights kicked in for them to listen. They became remarkably quiet—as though this were a real briefing on a real base with Base Command leading— though it was a whole new flavor of silence after her last point.

"Bee doesn't think the defense array is any kind of normal AI."

A lot of staring, a lot of stillness, and then Otie dragged in a deep breath. "My Bee agrees." Those three words broke the holding moment, and several Eights shifted, muttered, or leaned forward.

"There were no weak points for us to slide our EMP drones in to ward it off physically, and it was exactly like that for the pulses we attempted to send. There's no *opening*, nothing to receive, the way any normal program would have." Otie didn't shudder, but she held her arms so close to her body it seemed she was forcing herself still.

"So is this defense array corrupted beyond recognition, or . . . ?" Caytil looked between the Talinns, her expression neutral.

"Do techs run any courses on defense arrays?" Sammer asked, swiveling in his seat toward Jeena. She shook her head, paused, then shook it again.

"There's no organic component, so there's no real need for us. That would be more . . ."

"You keep hesitating. What's catching you up?" Talinn didn't snap the question, but Sammer put a comforting hand on the tech's arm. Talinn put effort into also not frowning, because while coddling Jeena wasn't helpful, neither was alienating her.

"There is an actual classification for AI coding, and it's under the tech branch. I know a few people who got tapped for it, but I don't know anyone who's done anything with defense arrays. I would have said it's because they've all been programmed for a long time, and nothing ever takes them out, but..."

"There should be maintenance. And someone has to switch them over from IDC to UCF when system control changes. And you'd think that would be part of warfare, getting them to change sides, so someone *should* specialize in defense-array programming. And counterprogramming."

"Something like that might be kept top line, need to know." Xenni tapped her fingers on the table. She didn't sound entirely convinced of her point, and Caytil's answering head movement was equally noncommittal.

"Maybe something the Spacies would have insight in." Otie stood, went deathly pale, but didn't stagger. Talinn had to admire the discipline, even as she worried why what little blood the other woman had left had decided to flee her facial region.

Tiernan left his chair in a hurry, and though he didn't put a hand on Otie, he hovered close by her. He murmured a question Talinn couldn't quite hear, and Otie shook her head, dragged in a breath, and continued speaking.

"We'll ask them when we see them. In the meantime, we use the emergency evacuation plan. Scatter through the system in small ships, circle the jump point. See where the attention goes."

"How do you want to test the safety of going *through* the jump point?" Caytil's voice was a study in neutrality.

"Either we're sitting targets here, or finer points out there. Going through the point itself... I'll talk to the *Pajeeran Fall*. There's a meeting point. See what risks they want to take."

"Do you think—"

"That's not entirely reassuring." Hops frowned, eyes on the table between them as he spoke over Xenni.

"Does anyone have a better suggestion?" Arnod grunted and waved his hand as though to dismiss any response.

"The facts are these, folks—whether it's that something is wrong with the defense array or it's fundamentally a bonzo weapon, it wants us out. And not just of this system, but of the conflict as a whole."

Talinn made an effort to keep from rocking on her toes. "I think we should get out as quickly as possible, but..."

"I agree with Otie." Sammer leaned back, tension clear across his shoulders. "We get out from here, split up, go under—find our way from there."

"We need to continue upsetting the balance—keep Command off-balance and primed for collapse." Tiernan crossed his arms and glared, though he kept his focus on Talinn rather than Otie.

"Sure, yeah, great call. And how will you fight off the defense arrays when they notice?"

"It's one broken program, you said yourself. How can it—"

"That's...not what I've been saying. We talked about looking further into the defense arrays, but nothing's come of it, is that right?"

"Enough." Otie stood, wavered for a brief moment, and locked her body into attention. "You'll pair up. You'll go to different places. You listen, and you learn, and gather what you can while I make sure we have a path out of Exfora."

"So we scatter, we wait...we find answers." Xenni's voice lifted on the last word, but her nod was definitive.

"The fight isn't over." Jeena stood close enough to steady Otie, but the older woman didn't shift. The tech straightened her back and met Talinn's gaze squarely. "We're taking it on the move."

Finally.

CHAPTER 35

The Exfora system didn't have nearly the population of Hynex, but it made up for it in its sheer number of small colonies. Otie had given them each a path to follow and paired newer and more senior clones. In theory, that allowed them to maximize time for Otie to figure out how safe they'd be leaving the system, while also gathering information and accessing caches as needed to secure new covers, transport, and resources.

"She's not stupid," Talinn subvocalized, for not the first time. Bee ignored her, also not for the first time. Because it wasn't remotely practical to load-in for every stop, Bee would spend much of her time in a portable server, and she had yet to find the proper way to make the full extent of her displeasure known.

"But she is mean," Talinn continued, resolutely keeping her gaze fixed straight ahead so as not to accidentally make contact with Tiernan or his smug face.

"Are you muttering again, Newt?"

"There's only one me out here now, you don't need to keep calling me that."

"But you respond so beautifully to it. Better than you do to Tal."

Talinn bit hard on the inside of her cheek. Her midsection roiled, as it constantly did since they'd left Deep End. She itched every time she couldn't tap comms for Caytil or Sammer or Arnod or Heka or any of her friends, twitched at the unceasing input of being surrounded by so many unadapted humans, fretted over the alarming number of things she couldn't control, reached for a turret she didn't have—that one was more Bee.

285

You're feeling too much. It's giving me a headache. It'd be better if we had a tank.

"A tank can't take on a defense array."

We're on a planet full of empties, and a tank would clear our path to whatever stupid meeting place we have to go to.

"And be noticeable."

"Are you ignoring me?" Tiernan gestured her ahead of him down a narrow alley, and for a wild moment she knew he was going to murder her. It stilled the unease in her stomach, brought her to a pinpoint focus, and then collapsed immediately back into worry and fear and disgust and uncertainty and a tiny sliver of joy to be out in the worlds that made it all worse—because of course Tiernan wasn't going to kill her. He was going to continue to pretend to be cheerful and comment about her hind section and infuriate her because neither of them had found anything helpful. Neither of them had heard from Otie. Neither of them had a clear path to action, and neither of them, it turned out, was great in such a scenario.

"I'm reminding myself and others that blowing things up is not an effective solution to our current situation." She couldn't be sure what passive monitoring existed on their current station, and they'd wordlessly agreed to say nothing that could flag any central systems that rogue Eights were still in Exfora.

"It won't get us off planet any faster, no. I wasn't expecting the Pillar to be so crowded." Tiernan stepped out to her side as they cleared the alley, taking them to the left down a wide street toward whatever point he had in mind. "Hops and I had just gone through on our way out-system, and there weren't nearly that many refugees."

"Staging ground for people flooding in-system from Govlic," Talinn repeated dutifully, as though it were a quiz. Tiernan shrugged the shoulder close to her and didn't respond until they'd passed a gaggle of unadapted humans in a riot of colors and gone through a tunnel under a cluster of absurdly tall buildings.

Could have benefitted from a good blowing up.

"You're in a mood."

I'm bored. What are we learning? Empties exist, in various forms, doing various things. We already knew that. Either we die approaching the jump point or we don't. Otie and Bee have to know the answer by now.

"Is this where we'll pick up word for our next stop?" Talinn couldn't bring herself to ask if he was ignoring her. Frankly it would be better if he did. She had no one and nothing else to vent all her conflicting urges on, given fighting with Bee would be even less helpful than strangling Tiernan. Or wanting to strangle him—on her own, she would have been lost the moment their first stop denied their entry. The largest lunar colony of Tolnan had turned away all traffic that approached with the same intractable disregard as a defense array, and Tiernan had kept them in orbit for two days, observing and prattling about nothing rather than sharing his thoughts.

Talinn heard her own voice telling Otie that they wanted to go out and explore. She chewed harder on the torn skin on the inside of her mouth to keep from cringing at the memory. What would they have done? She couldn't make sense of it now, and couldn't entirely blame that on Tiernan.

"Maybe." It took him so long to answer she missed a step and had to make an effort to rematch his pace. "We're going to Blackheart's. Hopefully we can get back on course from there."

She glanced at him then, noted the tension in his jaw. Of course she wasn't the only one worried about their people. Talinn made a noncommittal noise and considered forming some sort of vague apology, then he stopped short.

"Three crossings ahead, take the next left. You'll see the sign." Tiernan ducked down the next side alley and Talinn stood alone on a rock-lined walkway in civilian city for the first time in her existence.

Now we get to blow things up?

"Now we keep on task." Talinn ignored Bee's discordant noise, kept her head on a swivel, realized that might be suspicious, and shoved her hands in the pockets of her coverall. "I don't like it either."

We should have had the whole route, same as Tiernan. What happens if he doesn't come back?

"We find our way back to a station, send a signal to the *Pajeeran Fall*, and hope for the best."

The best would be better if I were in a tank.

She didn't have an argument to that, and the rest of their walk remained silent and uneventful. The buildings had grown progressively shorter, and Blackheart's was a sprawling edifice, two stories and taking up most of the next block. There were doors on either corner, so she aimed for the set directly on her path.

The doors didn't open at her approach, and Bee didn't offer that there was a code or a trick. Given Bee's general air of unhelpfulness, Talinn didn't prod her, and then a too-warm voice pitched from the side, "It's a push."

Tiernan. She didn't roll her eyes, unsure if she were relieved or annoyed at his reappearance, but gestured him to go right ahead. He smirked at her, which was one of his three expressions, and shared nothing about his detour. Instead he reached out and pressed his hand to the door. Not on a panel, simply flat on the smooth edge of the door and it . . . pivoted open, into the much louder space inside.

Planets. She shrugged and walked past him when he continued to stand there, smirking, then kept walking because the space was more inviting than anything she'd ever seen. Low tables and chairs curved away from the door, leaving a clear path to the glowingly red-brown bar ahead. The lighting was subtle, tinted a soft blue from recessed corners, and a light melody brushed out of the sprawling plants that studded the areas between tables, making each one seem private without building tiny walls all over the place. Most of the tables were occupied, but the noise level was well below what she'd come to expect from groups of humans. Some measure of tension eased from her shoulders.

"Let's sit at the bar," Tiernan said, drawing even with her, his own posture loose. Before she could ask if he had good news—any news— a woman's voice addressed them.

"Welcome to Blackheart's." She appeared after her voice, straightening from behind the bar, adjusting lenses over her eyes. "What can I get you?"

"We're on Gillen for the first time." Talinn slid onto one of the stools and met the other woman's eyes, wondering if the lenses were some kind of interesting civilian technology. "What do you recommend?"

"What *don't* I recommend." She smiled, and it was the warmest smile Talinn had ever experienced from an unadapted human face. Even Jeena didn't emote so expansively. Talinn caught herself smiling back before she'd made the decision to do so. "It's my place, and I only stock my favorites. What's your usual?"

Yes, Talinn. What's your usual? Blue? Gray?

"She doesn't get out much." Tiernan dropped his elbows onto the bar and winked at the woman, and both she and Talinn wrinkled their noses. The woman behind the bar recovered first, beaming again as she refocused on Talinn.

"Fair enough. Travel isn't as unrestricted as it used to be, I know." She leaned down and pulled up three glasses without looking, producing a long-necked bottle with her other hand. As she continued speaking, she poured a deep red liquid into each glass—notably less in one, which she slid to Tiernan without a slip in her smile.

Fine. Maybe all empties aren't boring. Bee dialed up Talinn's sense of smell as the Blackheart's owner sniffed her own glass, and Talinn followed suit. *This will have a bite to it,* she noted with a sense of anticipation.

"All the best things do," Talinn subvocalized before toasting aloud, "New favorites."

The other woman echoed it with an approving laugh, and Tiernan winked at one or both of them—Talinn really needed to tell him to find a new "blending with the unadapted" gesture—and they all drank. It did, indeed, have a bite, but also a rich flavor that flooded her mouth and made her want to tip the rest of the glass straight down her throat.

Probably not the best idea. Talinn wasn't entirely sure if that was Bee reading her intentions or reacting to the taste. Instead of asking, she tilted her head toward the other woman.

"Clearly you have excellent taste. Have you been on Gillen long?"

"For that I'll give you a discount on the refill." She smiled again, then lifted a shoulder as she poured more into each glass—even Tiernan's. "And yes, my grands' parents were in the first settler ship through the jump point. Lived here all my life, minus some travel around the system when I was young."

Talinn hadn't thought the woman much different from her age, but she didn't have any skill in judging the unadapted. "You still seem young enough to me. But not enough to travel anymore?"

"Well, for that, new favorite visitor, I'll send my staff to help the rest of the crowd and stay to talk with you for a bit." The woman swirled the vivid liquid in her glass, tilting it to catch the light above the bar. "I'm Rebekah."

Talinn and Tiernan introduced themselves as Tal and Nando respectively, and Talinn managed not to laugh at Tiernan's suddenly serious expression. Rebekah sipped her drink and came back around to answering Talinn's question.

"Not that I'm too old for travel, but it's the same for going out as it seems to be for folks coming in—getting to be too much effort for the result. New checkpoints every time you turn around, and rumor has it IDC is after more than the mines down system on Oxillide."

Talinn hadn't heard of Oxillide, or of IDC having much of a foothold in Exfora beyond those few stations Falix had shown them, what seemed like eighty cycles ago. "I hadn't noticed it, but we mostly go from one station to the other." Not entirely an untruth. "Maybe planets are a little different?"

"More room for IDC to slip in, I guess, and less likely the fighting will hit the jump point."

"The defense arrays, though?" Talinn widened her eyes, trying for naïve new girl and getting an elbow in the ribs from Tiernan for her effort.

"More directed up system—Zimil, Duray, Erkine are all more heavily settled, with their rings and lunar outposts." Rebekah lifted a shoulder, then motioned for them to wait and stepped aside to talk to another woman who'd stepped behind the bar.

"What are you doing?" Tiernan's voice pitched low, but his smile remained careless.

"Learning, like I'm supposed to. Isn't that meant to be helpful?"

"We have to be careful."

"Well, *I* am, so unless you have new—shoes like you're supposed to pick up . . ." Talinn trailed off, having neatly changed subjects—if she said so herself—to something innocuous as Rebekah finished her conversation and turned back toward them.

"Huh. I always thought of the planets as being so much better defended," Talinn continued brightly, as though they hadn't been interrupted.

"Some are. And some are staging grounds for the United Colonial Forces to show how they can keep us safe, or the Interstellar Defense Corps to show how their version of control is better." Rebekah lifted both hands, as though warding it all away, and picked up her glass again. "But you know all that better than me—stations have it worse, having to ration when in-system shipping gets disrupted. Gillen's been around long enough we have space for most things, and can power through until the ships come again. And that's not why you came to Blackheart's at all, is it? You're here to have fun, not listen to me ramble about politics."

"I—"

"You're completely right, Rebekah." Tiernan's voice dripped warmth, but at least he didn't wink again. "Let's taste our way through your favorite liquors and have a good time."

Talinn couldn't figure out a subtle way to kick him hard in the shin, so she smiled and drank and ignored the churn in her gut as Bee remained silent.

What have we learned. Bee did not wait for an answer as Talinn tried to find her way back to the designated route to meet Tiernan on the muddy side streets of Duray's largest moon. *Empties everywhere are restless. IDC is definitely coming in hot. Or isn't. UCF is a pain in the sewage hole. Except when it isn't. Gillen's crushed fruit goes rotten better than the mixed vegetables of any orbital ring.*

"Fermented," Talinn muttered, squinting up at yet another unmarked building made of slightly more solid mud than the street. She shrugged and turned down an alley, knowing she had to get further into the center of the struggling town to catch up with Tiernan. He'd remained blithe and infuriatingly close-lipped about news, and each time he left her on her own, she wasn't sure if he'd come back.

This is getting messier, and Kay hasn't been any more helpful than Tiernan. Do we even have to burn it all down? Seems like empties' society is already fraying around the edges.

"It's already a show of shit. What'll we leave behind if we get out of this, and are ever able to take out Command?"

Those are two big ifs. Why under all the skies in the ever-expanding multidimensions of space are you worried about Command still? We take our Eights, we get away, we steal clones, whatever, but the war? We're out.

"You wanted to burn it all down too."

Before the bonzo defense arrays got involved. Have we found out anything about them in all this running around? No. We've just followed directions and been out of a tank too long. For what?

Talinn hesitated, processing her surroundings, but the narrow alley contained only mud, heaps of mud, a small box, the drier mud of the buildings on either side, and—

"Maybe we should—"

You should—

Talinn snapped her hand down, closed her fingers around a wrist, swiveled, and pulled the new body close so it rode on her hip as she spun, shoving it against the wall of the building on her left.

"Oh no no sorry, just passing through." The figure—a woman around Talinn's own age, if she were reading the face right under all that flappy hair—straightened and focused on Talinn's chin.

"Through my pocket?"

Don't engage. Punch her and let's get moving. She probably came through the mud wall. The longer you talk to her, the more likely she'll drag you in there after her. I don't want to live in mud.

The woman tried to twist her arm free, failed, and went completely boneless. Talinn didn't let go, but she shifted forward to compensate, then sprang backward as the woman tensed. Eights didn't do much hand-to-hand in the field, but they were trained for it, and her additional processing power gave her quicker reaction time—or maybe that was an edge from Bee dumping a tank-sized amount of adrenaline into her system and blaring an alarm in her head.

Their scuffle didn't last long—Talinn held the other woman back with more ease than she'd expected, despite the woman swinging a knife at her, and Bee asked, *What's the end game here?* exactly as the woman's gaze fastened somewhere around Talinn's ear.

Shit.

Talinn reached her free hand to her wig, which had held on admirably during the unexpected movement, but had shifted exactly enough to reveal the bottom of her port. The woman's eyes went wide, panic and some mix of emotions too much for Talinn to parse rippling across her face.

But her mouth stretched open like she was going to scream something and Bee pushed and Talinn knew the only thing she could do to keep from ruining everything. One hand slammed against the woman's mouth, the other twisted the weapon out of the woman's hand.

Talinn was as fast with the knife as she was with any calculation, and no one else was in the alley.

No one else was living in the alley once Talinn stepped out of it, either. She didn't shake.

You had to.

"Their lives are miserable."

The empty won't be miserable now, and you won't get found.

"It's not that."

It's Tiernan's fault. I'm going to break into Kay's channel and make them tell us—

"Bee. It's not that."

"Newt, of all the—where were you?" Tiernan matched her pace, gave her a once over, and grabbed her arm. "What happened?"

She didn't shake, but her hands ached as though the small bones wanted to vibrate out of her skin. Possibly Bee had overmodulated the chemicals in her brain. "Later. Do you have it?" Contact. News. Anything to bring them back to their people. Away from here.

"I know where we need to go next. I followed up on what Rebekah Black told us on Gillen—something odd is happening on Oxillide, and I think we need to know more before we find Otie."

Talinn swallowed, her saliva unaccountably bitter. Despite the ever-present threat of the defense arrays, not knowing where her friends were, not being sure what they needed to do next, she'd enjoyed their prolonged trip. Seeing the worlds, understanding what was out there—it was what she'd wanted. Not the way she wanted, no, but at least partially good. Partially right. Partially helpful.

Now she nodded blankly as Tiernan spoke, matched her steps to his, and processed none of what she saw. But she didn't shake. She was fine.

All right, that's enough. I'm sick of being in a box. Next place we go, you're putting me in something. It's time to be a weapon again.

CHAPTER 36

Talinn glared at the console in front of her and willed it to reform to a better layout. It did no such thing, and she permitted herself a small sigh before reaching for the ignition sequence.

I don't know what you're complaining about. Bee flicked various views of their airspace onto the edges of the cockpit screen. *You're not in a jet.*

"Technically, and realistically, and literally, I am." She frowned, twitched her shoulders back, and rechecked all their sensors. They hadn't had a single faulty reading since they'd left Deep End, but the reflex remained a strong habit. The ignition sequence—only required because Bee refused—went off without a hitch, and within moments her back was pressed against her seat, her skin attempted to drip backward off her skull, and they were airborne.

Then I'm more *in a jet, which is obviously worse, and also it's old.*

"It's maybe two generations out of date. And performance has barely shifted, it's only layout and order of operations. Charons don't even go out of atmosphere, so we don't have to worry about sealant points." Talinn tried to convince herself as much as Bee, and was approximately as successful at both.

It's not a tank.

"No, but the weapons are similar and now we get to a do a whole lot more strafing."

No, we don't. We're recon. Jet recon! This isn't even a recon jet— empty humans can handle those. Or a drone! Why are we wasting a Charon on recon?

"Is it a lousy old jet, or is it a Charon that is getting wasted?"

Human logic is stupid.

"Because you don't have an answer?"

For proper notation and official record, I am absolutely going to fire on something today. You get two "no" votes. And I don't promise not to waste them.

"We're not firing on civilians."

You get two "no" votes. Bee huffed into silence, without a hint of tortured metal to indicate she had any sense of humor about it whatsoever. *It's not like civilians haven't gotten frisky with us before.*

Tiernan had wanted them to wait. Again. While he went out and did things. Some more. Bee finally wrested information from Kay, and Talinn stalked him to his drop point. Saw firsthand the method to break into local UCF and IDC comms. How to fake orders. How to procure equipment from the cache.

For their efforts, they'd been put in a Charon. Of course that was what Tiernan would have preferred. Stupid jets.

Now she had the great reward of patrolling the charming planet of Oxillide, with its sprawling UCF aligned colony cities and its enormous gaping wound of an IDC mine. Unsurprisingly, the fighting here had been ongoing for cycles, limited mostly around the mine. That had changed recently, and Tiernan was sure it was critical to find out more.

So now Breezy was a jet. They had codes for both bases on the planet, and given Charons often ran dark as they streaked through populated areas to provide air support, they didn't expect to be challenged.

If they started firing into civilian areas, that would change quickly, but Talinn was sure it wouldn't come to that.

Fairly sure.

"The last few battles have gotten closer to Bandi City than any broken stray missiles have gone in at least twenty cycles."

Bee offered nothing in response, so Talinn kept half her attention on their readouts, half on the swath of clear sky ahead of them, and continued running through their assignment. "There is a full component of Eights on both sides, about eighty for the UCF and a little less than a hundred for the IDC—though forty of those arrived in the last six months. This had been less a targeted active front, and more a staging point for the satellites the few cycles before that. Looks like both sides thought control over the orbital would equal control over the planet and that would adjust or keep the balance of power in the system accordingly."

The jet tilted left wing down, revealing far off stretches of golden crop fields studded with harvest factories. Otherwise Bee continued not to contribute.

"It's weird, this was more broadly active for a while before that— a hot front, for a long time. Then quiet, then surrounded by fighting but mostly untouched, and now edging toward the civilian settlements. It's like what Otie said about Discar, when they started taking cities and finding they'd been fronts all along."

How is that the same? Bee drew the words out suspiciously. Of course she'd know Talinn was being obtuse on purpose, but like Talinn herself, Bee couldn't stop the curiosity that pulled away from her sulk.

"Most of the Discar cities hadn't been civilian colonies at all, but fronts seeded with unadapted human soldiers to give the UCF a legitimate foot on the planet and argue IDC had no standing."

That's stupid.

"Otie was fairly certain they used to be real cities, with civilians, but over time it became less feasible and—"

How is this relevant to Oxillide?

"Maybe this is the transition point. IDC or UCF is going to shift this from an actual colony to more of a front to draw in more forces and stage—"

Hold that. Bee's tone snapped from unwilling to all business, and the corner of the screen displayed the blips of pulse readings.

"Three incoming, got it. Who are they?"

They aren't broadcasting.

"Fair, neither are we, so they shouldn't shoot first before determining—glitch me with a dirty spoon. They're firing, aren't they?"

In answer, the Charon dove, then swooped abruptly to the left. There were no clouds in the orange-yellow sky, and no convenient geological extrusions to use as cover. They had enough raw material for Bee to transmute into ballistic offense, but they might need that later. The goal had been to go unnoticed, not fight other Eights.

"Don't suppose there's any way you can tell who's flying?"

It's not going to be us.

"Otie said our clone line threw out a pilot at least once, so who knows." Talinn watched the sensors, but they were far enough away that even the guided missiles weren't going to be able to keep up with their evasive maneuvers. Seemed unprofessional for the mystery Eights to have fired so soon when they had they advantage of numbers, but they'd also fired without ascertaining who she was, so they were either terrible or knew something she didn't.

Like what they were actually firing at.

Not them at all.

"Bee?"

I . . . have no idea what that is.

Something enormous, matte black and blocky, shaped more for space travel than atmosphere, screamed over the airspace they'd previously occupied, on direct course for the three Charon jets.

The trio split, smoothly reangling to better surround the incoming target and allow for maximum cover of fire, but despite their elegant and well-practiced maneuvers, nothing made contact with the huge invader.

That's not UCF. Does IDC have anything like that?

"Are you getting anything from it?"

No obvious AI frequencies, but we don't broadcast in battle.

"We should get out of here."

We should. They curved wide around the closing engagement, Bee angling them to keep eyes, not only sensors, on the action.

"We don't know any of the players here, we shouldn't get involved."

We really shouldn't. The jet climbed higher, getting above the action and occasionally rolling to get a full picture of the skies around them through the cockpit's large clear canopy.

"Tiernan told us patrol only." Talinn ran the numbers on the cargo they carried—what Bee could retask for fuel, for repairs, for maximum barrage of artillery.

Who are you convincing?

"It's not paying any attention to us whatsoever."

It passed through *where we were. If I hadn't registered the incoming Charon, it would have turned us to dust before we knew it was there.*

Their jet remained in sight of the cluster of aircraft—they should have been well away by now.

"But it didn't fire on us. And somehow *they* saw it." The other jets circled, weaving an elaborate net around the intruder, but still nothing seemed to mar the large aircraft's hull.

Sure.

"And we know the Charon jets are Eights."

Big Ugly could be Eights too. Or Spacies.

"We would have heard something about something that new and shiny, don't you think? Tiernan would have said something."

It's got a disruptor like a defense array.

"One of the jets is down." Talinn sat forward in her chair, the cross belt biting through her coverall as though they were pulling too many g's. She leaned back an inch, scanned the sky for the third foreign Charon.

One of the jets is gone. *The other two have a good range of motion going, but they'd do better with three.*

"We're not that far."

We're really not.

"You want to try some of that EMP tech?"

Not especially. We won't have a good angle to keep the other Charon clear of backwash if we're not in contact.

"Let's try IDC codes." Talinn tapped her fingers, then grunted in satisfaction when Bee opened the comms successfully. "Charon unit, this is Breezy. Coming in late with apologies, but looks like I can help?"

"Breezy? What the shit you're a jet? That's some bonzo—when did you get to Oxillide?"

Talinn had exactly enough time to shudder before the all too familiar voice continued, *"Tell me about it over drinks, yeah? Formation Echo-G."*

Medith. Cold traced itself along her spine and it took her two tried to respond. "Mercy, this is a brand-new assignment—"

"Patching over info, you hairband. Damn civilians have way too many new toys—only thing we've found that works is overheating their disruptor. Close evasive. Make 'em fire. Don't get in line of. Catch?"

"Caught." Her throat closed over the word, but they didn't need to keep talking. She'd process any and all emotions after this was done. They had work to do.

Bee dumped the details of Echo-G into their brains and Talinn grinned. This Medith's class had learned some direct AI-to-AI channels as well, and weren't shy about using them even in a combat situation. Their Charon screamed into position above the enormous aircraft and the next moments were crystal clear stutters in time.

Hemp, Jiff, Bee shared, the comms silent but the AIs clearly in touch. *Rotate passes in front of the disruptor to make the ship fire.*

Talinn scanned the ship below them, to the side of them, above them as their position changed.

The disruptor operated by a combination of three beams. Each emerged from a different part of the mystery ship. Three open points for the disruptor to align.

The points on the ship closed, opened, closed.

Ballistic fire burst from turrets that emerged from the sides of the big ship, well out of the way of the disruptor.

Bee slagged one before they fell away, momentarily breaking the pattern of ship fire.

Hemp took three rounds to a wing and plummeted off their side before the AI partner could repair the Charon.

Mercy drew the disruptor fire out of turn.

"Bee, lodge the EMPs in the holes as soon as they open." They had small EMP drones, enough to get them out of a tight situation with other Eights without killing them. Depending on how this ship worked, if they could get the EMPs inside, past potential external shielding, they could knock out at least the disruptors. Maybe the whole ship. An AI could recover from the small bursts, but unadapted humans? They'd be far too slow on repairs.

It'll leave Mercy vulnerable to the blast, I have to guide them in slow.

"I know."

We said we'd keep Mercy alive, the next time.

The fallen Charon wasn't coming back. They had no business taking on this ship, this engagement. No business being here at all.

"Do what you can."

They did what they could.

They'd spent a lot of time planning possibilities for taking out a defense array, since leaving Deep End. EMPs and explosives and smart targeting. Had no real chance or cause to test them.

Tested them here.

And they worked.

Too late to save Mercy, again.

But the enormous mystery ship fell out of the sky, and one Charon jet continued on its original path.

CHAPTER 37

⊕

"The city's in revolt."

They curved wide around the sprawling ends of Bandi City. The city looked like a spectrograph of space noise, small wavy buildings on the outskirts, raising to dizzyingly tall heights around the middle, and easing back down as it reached toward the ocean on the other side. It had been built on a peninsula, and now spanned over multiple spits of land dug out of the water. Many of the lower buildings had been made out of the shimmering orange-brown dirt of the planet, and in the hazed sunlight it made the city wobble, as though a mirage across heat-soaked land.

In another time, Talinn might have loved it. As it was, her eyes remained fixed on the enormous ships circling over the city. There were three of them, and it had only taken one to wipe out a Charon unit.

How did civilians get something like this?

"There's an enormous mine on the planet."

Raw materials do not equal manufacturing brilliance. And that mine is across enemy lines.

"But also run by civilians." Talinn laced her fingers behind her neck and pressed, stretching out knots that refused to budge. "Maybe *they* crossed lines, deciding they had more in common with each other than the IDC and UCF."

That sounds familiar. Bee hummed, audibly signaling she was weighing something. *But how would they get the same tech as the defense arrays have? We're not even allowed it.*

"And if Eights aren't given disruptor tech, why would either Command entrust it to civilians?" She was only repeating Bee's question, but there was no logical explanation for it.

Do civilians do maintenance on the defense arrays?

"Why in all the worlds would they have access to those?"

Civilians get stupid programs—little letter ai. Task oriented algorithms that run systems and don't evolve. Or differentiate.

"There are economies of scale on that though, right? There have to be. Something that runs a lift can't possibly compare to something that can blow up a moon."

But they have the tech. The basic blocks of it. The defense arrays were meant to be giant yes/no dumb programs, good enough for their task no matter how bonzo they turned out to be. Civilians can figure something like that and still do damage.

She couldn't argue that. Their jet curved away from the city before they got close enough to ping any alarms. Tiernan couldn't argue with the amount of information they'd collected, even if he might protest their methods.

"Is it . . . is it possible the city is under guard, and those ships are securing it? That the ships are from somewhere else?"

Some third military arm? Bee made a discordant noise of dismissal. *No. The ships are from and for the city. Cece was clear on that, from the report packet I got.*

"Put that on the screen?"

It's more code than readable.

"Sum up for me, then."

Patrolling IDC tanks and jets near the mine were getting fired on more often. Base Command assumed it was UCF responding to IDC's increasing numbers in system. Orders went up to increase Eights and unadapted humans. But over the last few weeks reports have made it out. Patrols were slagged, but a splintered AI would survive. And of course they've had visual confirmation of these.

The giant ships protecting the city were certainly hard to miss. All this, in just a few weeks?

"It sounds a little like what happened on P-8. But that was definitely IDC, not a civilian group . . . this entire part of the system barely has a million civilians to begin with."

Unless it's a third party.

"You said I was being stupid when I suggested that about five seconds ago."

I did not.

"You made a sound that indicated I was being stupid when I suggested it six seconds ago."

You're being sensitive.

"You're being a shit." Talinn clicked her teeth closed after snapping, but neither of them apologized. Bee's hum moved in and out of focus, and Talinn glared unblinking into the broad empty expanse of orange-yellow sky.

If there were a third party. They were halfway back to their landing island before Bee spoke again. *Who could it be?*

"Technically we're a third party."

A fourth party, then.

"Whoever's corrupting defense arrays?"

Think anyone's picked anything up about them? Tiernan just not telling us?

Civilian revolts, brand new ships out of nowhere . . . that's not going well. Like Otie said—more and more glitches in the war. When we get back to everyone, we should see if anyone repurposed a tank instead of old jets. I think matters on Oxillide could really be improved with a concentrated application of turrets.

"The machine god."

What now?

"Remember, on that first station? The group building up some kind of machine god?"

The door that shocked that empty human. Bee twisted metal, but it wasn't the right pitch for a laugh. *We have all those conversations we recorded, moving through that station. We can see if anyone else mentioned anything about the machine god. Or activists, like Medith called them.*

She'd forgotten about the recordings. And she didn't really think the unadapted humans wanting to become machines had built ships out of nothing and turned defense arrays into Eight-hunting rogue beasts, but it was an avenue they hadn't tried. A loose end she'd dropped. And it gave both Bee and her something to focus on that wasn't arguing about what they should be doing or plotting Tiernan's strangulation, so it was a big enough win for the moment.

Here's an interesting thing. They'd taxied the jet into their transport, and were waiting on Tiernan before leaving Oxillide behind.

"What's that?" Talinn half-heartedly spun in the pilot's chair and longed for her old chair in her old tank in her old life. The cloying nostalgia made her snippy, but Bee was too preoccupied with her new discovery to snipe back.

This human had been behind the door that shocked that young empty, and was telling someone else about how she planned to go back. Bee pulled the half of a conversation they'd captured to the forefront of Talinn's memories, and Talinn closed her eyes to better focus.

Bee had not captured any visual input, but the memories were associated in Talinn's brain, so she had a clear picture of the crowd, too many bodies jostling in too small a space, walkways above and below and to the side and over—Talinn opened her eyes instead, and listened as a woman, voice low and hoarse, made several emphatic points.

"They said He'll talk to me, the next time."

"No, I have to do that first."

"Yes of course it's safe, Cavvie. They don't want us dead, only—"

"He knows more than any of them. No, of course I can't..."

The snippets faded, either Talinn or the woman moving in a different direction and too many other conversations making too much noise for Bee to separate her out again.

"What snagged your attention?" she asked finally, when Bee waited with expectant excitement but didn't offer any commentary.

The way she says "He" like it has a capital letter. Didn't you hear it?

"No...?" Talinn wound the memory back, pressed the heels of her hands against her eyes to keep from picturing the station, and listened through the fragment of conversation. "Maybe?"

Empties don't talk about other humans like that.

"Neither of us have that much experience with unadapted humans, Bee, that's a broad assumption."

Other Bee has had plenty of experience with empties, and I learned more than a little while I shared Otie's brain with her, thank you for remembering.

"Is that why you're mad at me?"

I'm not mad at you. Stop being weird. Anyway, she's talking about someone in a way she wouldn't talk about another human. About doing something to prove herself. "They don't want us dead" sounds like how that other woman was talking about the people behind the door.

"Except mostly opposite."

It's easy to see similarities when you contrast.

"Now you're trying to be deep."

Bee huffed, but it had a measure of shearing metal to it, and Talinn sagged against her chair, releasing some small measure of tension. "'He' knows more than any of them about . . . what, do you think? Putting one-shot programs into human brains?" She frowned and stared at the screen without processing what was on it. "Or, first, who do you think 'He' is? The leader of the group?"

The machine god.

"You think the machine god is real?"

I think they think the machine god is real.

"Fair point." Talinn toggled the ship's display to another view of the empty island around them, then glanced at the inactive comms. Nothing from Tiernan. She swallowed against a tightness in her throat. "So you think they think the machine god, as a real being, knows more than any of them about . . . machines?"

AIs, maybe.

"Ohhh, like whoever's been tilting at defense arrays and building secret ships for revolution."

Don't be jealous because we don't have secret ships for our revolution. Bee paused, then set off a cascade of metallic screams. *Wait, now I'm jealous we don't have secret ships for our revolution. Maybe we should throw in with the machine god.*

"I mean, as far as a possible third—right, fourth-party option, it's worth checking out. You think they have a secret electricity room in this system?"

I haven't been able to skim much out of the comms on this planet, even with the codes. I have another in to IDC thanks to the other Charons, but they've been pretty quiet since we took down the ship and they lost a full unit. Bee's voice dropped over the last words, and Talinn knew it was to keep from mentioning Mercy. What could she have done differently, to keep any Medith alive? Should she reach out to the base, see if there were familiar Eights she could pull to her side, like Otie did with her? It was too late for yet another Medith, but maybe . . .

She wrenched her thoughts away from that direction too, and groaned far louder than she needed to.

"I doubt the machine god's unsuccessfully machined people are wandering around planet-side yelling about their plans, so comms wouldn't tell us much." She stood up and paced away from the ship's controls, leaving behind the temptation to send another message.

You're saying we're not missing anything?

"Maybe Tiernan will know. He's spent more time out and about than we have." Despite the truth of it, the admission burned. "I hope he's out recruiting Eights off this shit planet."

All the planets are shit. Bee hummed, and Talinn relaxed further. *And if he's recruiting, it would just be another one of them, so...*

Talinn took a few moments to stretch, reaching her hands to the ground and letting the longer muscles in her back slowly let go. She realized too late Bee had offered her an opening to return to their teasing banter, and squeezed her hands open and closed.

Talinn.

She twisted back toward the screen, which still displayed nothing of interest, and leaned into a lunge. Bee held the silence until she finally asked, "What?"

Are you all right?

"Not particularly."

Is it because this is a lot like P-8, sitting around waiting on nothing?

"Sure."

And also because for all we thought we were miserable then, we were actually pretty happy and now it's actually miserable?

"What did I say about getting deep on me?" Talinn didn't bother to force a lightness into her tone—Bee would see where her brain lit up, and know it for false. She switched legs for her stretch and braced herself for Bee's snarky response.

Instead, in a voice so soft she almost missed it, Bee replied, *Yeah. Me too.*

As though she'd answered the question truthfully instead of with a weak dodge. She used to be better at answering questions, and maybe at asking them. The big orienting question: What were they going to do?

And the answer: she had no idea.

CHAPTER 38

⊕

Tiernan didn't lecture her, which protected all their sanity levels. Her report wiped the smirk off his face, and he wiped his hands over his face before replying. "I found out about those ships too late—expected more chatter, but IDC is referring to them as 'the issue' and UCF channels had only 'the Bandi matter.' We were on approach to Bandi City, and I couldn't risk a message."

That's almost an apology.

Talinn shook off the lingering discomfort of dealing with a tolerable Tiernan and spread her fingers. "We handled it, and at least we have an idea of how to take the ships down, if we come across them again." Preferably without losing a squadron of Eights to get it done, next time.

"And we might." He stood abruptly from his chair and refastened the portable servers ahead of takeoff. His back to her, he continued, "Bandi City has a whole lot of extra comms traffic from Sovoritt than I've seen in past visits. Kay is sure the funding is coming from the station."

Talinn leaned forward at his pause and pressed her lips together to keep from interrupting him. Tiernan had not been much of a sharer, these last weeks.

"And if we're lucky, the drop point there should have a message from Talinn." He turned toward her, but kept his gaze fixed on the cargo ship's control panel. "If we're really lucky, we can maybe even catch a lift to the *Pajeeran Fall*."

"How lucky is really lucky?"

309

"I'm sure Kay and Bee have already run the probabilities."

"Does the station have one of those machine-activist stores?"

"The what?" He blinked, cocked his head, focused back on her. "The machinists?"

"The ones who use an artsy pseudo-port on their sign and want to end the war through becoming machines, yes." Sarcasm wouldn't help her here, and she kept her voice level.

"Probably. Sovoritt's the largest station in the system, so they're likely to have a bit of everyone." He hadn't grinned smugly once since he'd returned, and his serious regard tipped her balance.

"What if it's them?"

"What if what's them?"

Talinn stretched her hands flat on against her legs and reminded herself he wasn't in her head, and probably she should use her words. She outlined what she and Bee had theorized, and he sat back with a thoughtful frown.

"It makes as much sense as anything." Tiernan crossed the cabin, running through the preflight Talinn had already completed. "Which is to say, not much."

"Maybe they have retired techs, or some engineer went rogue. Makes more sense than defense arrays going independently bonzo and roaming the system."

"It's something to check, at any rate. At worst, maybe they make enough noise to keep us off the defense arrays notice a little longer and buy us time to get word from Talinn." He pulled back from the bunk. "You ready to lift?"

In answer, Talinn crossed to the controls and strapped into the pilot's chair before he could.

Sovoritt was an old outpost, supposedly the first station built once the jump point had stabilized. Accordingly, it was a mess. The central sphere had long been expanded by an assortment of rounded shapes, including what was still recognizably an outdated UCF troop transport with its hull split as though it had taken too many hits and opened to swallow a chunk of the station. The whole uneven mass of the place made Talinn's insides twist when she saw it from the outside, and she didn't like it much better inside.

This time she and Tiernan had dull gray coveralls and their own absurd hats, both of which aligned with their registered purpose of delivering materials on a wheeled cart. Their cover meant they walked the maintenance corridors of the station, which were much less crowded than the main areas. They'd gone the length of an entire subsection without passing another living creature, but to balance the scales, the less public halls were far creepier than she imagined the standard areas were.

The lights, glaringly bright and uncovered, were set at irregular intervals. The floor had been laid in patches that had been welded seamlessly—important in a set of nested orbs hanging in space—but nevertheless tricked the eye with their varying patterns and textures. The walls had more missing panels than not, which revealed circuitry and ducting that snagged the eye uncomfortably. After a few minutes, Talinn locked her eyes on the covered cart and relied on Tiernan or Bee to tell her when to turn or slow down for a door.

The cart, at least, moved smoothly, needing little pressure from her to keep it on track. Three of the crates had actual materials in them—salvaged parts Tiernan had collected in his various disappearances—and the others held Bee and Kay in their temporary servers.

"Hope that means next stop *Pajeeran Fall*," she subvocalized.

Do you want the probability on that?

Talinn didn't, so she leaned closer to the cart and angled her head slightly toward Tiernan. "What's next?"

"We go to the drop point and—"

"Not this." She waved a hand. "Not the game of don't catch me with the defense arrays. After we get to everyone else."

"We go to ground."

"You've been doing more than preparing to go to ground."

"We are who we are." His words were breezy enough, but the tension around his jaw was as clear as his smirks had been. "Got to keep busy or idle minds will turn to anything to keep entertained."

You two have really gotten good at this code thing. Bee's tease helped her bite her tongue. Tiernan hadn't been much for sharing thus far; the back halls of a densely populated civilian station wasn't going to change that.

They moved through another subsection of the station. In this one the walls were covered to shield the mechanical intestines, but each panel had been covered in layers of old film printouts. Talinn slowed her pace to scan them, but none of it meant anything to her. Unmoving entertainment advertisements? Better than the blinking and yelling display ads of her first station, though given they'd been relegated back here as wall coverings, perhaps they'd been less effective.

She took a cue from the old printouts and remained silent as they moved through the back workings of the station. After an endless stretch of time (*Exactly twenty minutes and five seconds*) they stopped at a nondescript door amidst a string of equally nondescript doors.

Tiernan gestured her to pay attention, tapped a code on the control panel, then a second, then a third. To an outside eye, it looked like one long code, but there were precise pauses between certain groups of numbers.

Empties could probably figure it out if they knew what to look for and slowed the recording, but otherwise that's a way to Eightify a code.

It wasn't quite the pattern of tapping speak her class had developed in training, but the concept was the same. They'd fallen out of the habit of it after first assignments, but it came back readily enough. The last time . . . oh. The last time she'd used it had been with Medith, on P-8, laying the groundwork for the rest of them to get away. Her gut squirmed, she swallowed back bile, and the door opened.

Revealing Medith.

But the one who'd drugged them and shipped them off to a new ass-end of the galaxy. Otie's Medith. Not theirs.

"Delivery's a little late," she called cheerfully, swinging something long and flat down and behind her back. "Thought you got turned around. Come in."

"No direct path from point A to B in this place," Talinn responded, and it might as well have been code again. *Thought you might have gotten atomized by a defense array,* from Medith and *We've just been having so much fun dodging around,* from Talinn, but maybe she was overthinking it. Maybe Medith meant nothing of the sort, and neither did she.

Focus, from Bee, which meant exactly that, and Talinn settled into the moment at hand.

Tiernan gestured her ahead, and she shoved the cart into the room. As the door slid shut behind Tiernan, Medith turned and placed the object in her hand—a projectile weapon—onto a pile of crates.

"It's about time—"

"Tell me we're not the only—"

"Did you—"

They all stopped talking, and Medith leaned against the crates and gestured to Tiernan. They were in an innocuous storage room, with various sizes and shapes of shipping containers and cargo boxes stacked six and ten rows high, lining the walls with narrow paths left clear for a loader's cart or three humans to walk shoulder to shoulder. Apparently deemed safe from monitoring, as Tiernan launched into a concise report of their time since Deep End.

"We missed you at Gillen, and haven't been able to get any messages through to Oxillide—everything's monitored in that direction." Medith sighed and crossed her arms before Talinn could ask about encryptions. "To the point that anything that might be flagged a bit odd gets interested parties knocking on doors to ask questions."

"Who?"

"Muddy." Medith gestured them deeper into the room, around the next corner where a cluster of chair-height boxes waited. "At first we thought they were IDC sympathizers, or agitators, but they seem a little too obvious about it."

"The machinists?" Talinn leaned against her cart rather than sitting, keeping Bee's box close at hand.

"All orbits lead to." Medith laced her fingers behind her head and cracked her neck. "Talinn's had us watching them for a few cycles, but they've been low level, more for a possible ally or frameup down the road than we thought they'd be trouble."

"You dismissed me when I brought it up." Talinn pulled her voice to a neutral level, but Bee scoffed, indignant on their behalf.

"I'd just met you and was in the process of drugging you at the time, little Talinn. Nonadapted playing dress-soldier wasn't top priority for either of us."

Talinn braced herself to answer with a modicum of professionalism, but Tiernan took over the conversation before she got a handle on her tone. "Who else of us is on station?"

"No one."

Tiernan cursed, but Medith kicked his leg. "No, idiot. The *Pajeeran Fall* is on maneuvers in system."

"It worked, then? We can leave the system?" Talinn brushed her fingers over the trailing hair of her wig. She wanted to press on her port, and the synthetic strands were a poor substitute.

"Talinn and the Spacies did a jump with some other volunteers and no one got dematerialized, so while no one's excited to be unconscious for a few weeks, we've got almost everyone else rounded up. All the new class. Four left, now that you're here."

"Who've we lost?"

"We won't know until time's up." Medith didn't meet his eyes—she had suspicions, then, and didn't want to share until they were confirmed. Talinn had trusted her too much, too soon the first time they'd met, because of *her* Medith, but the women weren't entirely unalike. She swallowed back guilt—all her people were accounted for, which was a relief, but the same couldn't be said for Tiernan. She brought the subject around to break the dragged-out silence.

"So what do we do? Go talk to the machinists? Civilians with disruptor technology doesn't feel like a thing that can wait."

Tiernan's focus remained inward, and Talinn settled her gaze on Medith, who sighed. "It's worth checking, but still, it's a loose connection."

"Those can still shock you, if you're holding the right ends." Talinn smiled far more than the analogy deserved, and then lifted a shoulder. "Unless you need to drug me again and ship us out to the *Pajeeran Fall* right away, I'd rather go poke inside the machine god's business than simmer here."

"For all the little bittlies in the galaxy." Medith's laugh was brief. "You're like her in the most annoying ways, you know that?"

"I've learned, believe it if you will. Just watching Otie has been... a lesson in how I can come across."

Hasn't really changed you much.

"Us," Talinn muttered, letting Medith hear. Tiernan sat forward, present again, and Medith only murmured "Otie?" in faint question. When Tiernan didn't argue, Medith pulled a display out of a side pocket in her coverall. Within a moment the display flickered on, a detailed map of the station resolving into focus.

"We're here." Medith tapped a small box in the near middle of the original body of the station. It glowed under her touch, and then a smaller oval in the bulge at the top left of the station's mass lit up as well. "And that's where the machine god is spreading the good word."

"To be perfectly clear, I don't believe in a machine god." Talinn rolled her eyes, which pulled a small smile from Medith in answer. "But as Bee has said, maybe these people believe in their machine god, so it's possible there's someone or something they *think* is their machine god."

Like an Eight that went bonzo. Or a defense array that took over a body.

"How likely do you think either of those things is?" Talinn scanned the map, committing it to their shared memory.

Oh not at all. Infinitesimal odds. About as likely as the task programs on this station waking up and declaring themselves the real brains behind the IDC-UCF war.

"I'm not sure that would surprise me." Talinn glanced at Tiernan. "You coming with?"

"I . . . have to check something." He smiled, a ghost of his usual expression, and stood. "Mercy, you staying here?"

"I'm contact, so here unless something urgenter comes along." The older woman flicked a pinkie. "Both of you go run your routes. Your servers are safe as safe can make, with me."

At least she didn't say "perfectly safe" because then you'd be going on about jinxes again.

"And if your box got taken away, you'd be too mad for me to say I told you so. Where's the fun in that?"

Fair point. I promise I'd know you meant it. Speaking of boxes, Kay's been awfully locked up, do you want me to try and see what they're up to?

"It hasn't worked yet. Let them run out what they have to—at least they're letting us do something on our own."

Makes me think Medith's right, and it's not going to come to anything.

"Jinxes, Bee. Jinxes."

CHAPTER 39

⊕

I don't hate maintenance passages.

Talinn followed the first path they'd traced for themselves—unlike their first station, the map and directions had been accurate, and they hadn't had to make any sudden detours. Bee occasionally commented on an absurdly loud passerby or a particularly lurid advertisement, but overall it was an unremarkable journey until they reached their destination.

The same symbol—the outlines of three interlocking ports—had been traced over the entrance, but the doorway itself stood open. Talinn checked her step toward it, making a point to scan the area around them.

This was not a purely residential portion of the station, but what commercial uses it had catered less to tourists and more to locals, given the fairly simple signage and lack of noisy ads. There were fewer than forty people in the immediate area—most sitting outside a counter restaurant, eating such fantastically long noodles Talinn was tempted to have Bee dial her sense of scent back to normal.

The door isn't entirely open, Bee observed before Talinn could ask about smelling the noodles. *It's a field.*

"More chance of electrifying people?" Talinn squinted at it briefly, then continued her scan of the area. Three levels were in view above them, and one below, all accessible by lifts rather than walkways. Each lift was sized to hold a handful of people and moved at a sedate pace, though a smaller one, virulently red and smaller, with room for no more than three bodies, raced through and vanished around a curve in the overarching structure as she watched.

Not . . . an electrifying field. Bee didn't have access to a full range of sensors, given she wasn't in an active server connected to anything. She could, however, use some of Talinn's adaptations and their own experience to make solid guesses about various machinery. *But I don't recommend walking through it to find out.*

"Any ideas how to get an invite, then?"

Get some noodles and watch the place to see who moves in and out, or walk up and shout through the door?

"Now that's machine-god level thinking, that is. Very nice." Talinn snorted to herself, strongly considered the latter option, then turned toward the counter restaurant instead.

Most of the wall was solid, covered in menus and old posters much like the maintenance corridors. A long rectangle of an opening revealed the action side of a kitchen, the shining counter mostly bare other than the bowl or two of noodles that periodically slid through for pickup. Talinn took her hands out of her pockets—unadapted humans much preferred to see hands than have them hidden, she'd learned—and moved toward the stand at the far end of the counter.

A display projected above it as she approached, menu flickering through several versions until her eyes dilated in a way that confirmed for it she understood the writing. She scrolled through the options—an overwhelming plethora of choices, with seven different noodle dishes, two stir-frys, and a baked dish she didn't recognize—tapped a soup touted as "local favorite" and tossed the appropriate amount of credit into the drawer that opened underneath. The screen flashed a confirmation and directed her to sit. Most of the tables were occupied, almost all with two or more people, and she walked toward one of the two empty ones without making eye contact. The one she chose had had all but one of its chairs scavenged, so she figured she'd be left alone even if local custom involved communal seating. She tossed a delivery checklist on the table and slid into the seat, running her finger over the manifest as though absorbed with work while she listened to Bee's ongoing monologue of theories on the machine god's open but invisibly curtained door.

An EMP field doesn't make sense though, if they're trying to load programs into people. That would just wipe them every time. Unless it's a coded EMP—remember Caytil had that idea, there was a way to target an EMP specifically to a certain frequency and leave everything else unharmed? Offensive shielding.

"Maybe like what happened to us at Deep End." Talinn swung her leg under the table, because something needed to move. "Though I'm pretty sure that was the same night we started theorizing on kill codes—"

Which do exist.

"Which you still think exist, but we really should spend some time on actual research and development, huh?"

"Can't even get a break for meals, is it?" a new voice interjected, and Talinn guiltily reminded herself she was not in a safe environment where she could focus inward on conversation. She was in the actual public, surrounded by potentially hostile people, with all of a fragile wig for cover.

"You know how it is. Paid for the results, not the time." Talinn tilted her head up and flipped the manifest over. Its information was real enough, but she hoped both reply and action were standard enough in the civilian world not to attract too much attention.

"Isn't it just. Noticed you missed your noodles." The stranger—a gangly young man with an excessive amount of both head hair and eyebrows—smiled and carefully placed a large bowl in front of her. "Didn't want you to lose the steam."

"Oh." She breathed deeply, the sharp bite of some sort of pepper tingling the edges of her nose, and smiled at him. "Appreciate that, thanks. Faster than I'm used to." She had no idea how long food took to make at a restaurant like this—her best comparison was when Otie had made them noodles at the installation, and she'd walked in partway through that process.

"Fastest on Sovoritt," he agreed, straightening proudly as though he had something to do with it.

Is he . . . going to keep talking to you? Start eating, see if that helps send him on his way.

"Is it your place?" Talinn found herself asking instead of picking up a pack of sealed utensils from the jar in the middle of the table.

"Noo-wave?" He laughed, shook his head. "No. I work over there." He gestured vaguely behind him. "So most times I'm picking up food here to take back."

Talinn followed his gesture, which could have been toward the machine god's waiting room. Or it could have been the body-design studio next to it. "Artist?" she asked, ignoring Bee's explosive pretend sigh.

"Something like that. Enjoy your meal." He rapped on the table with his knuckles and sauntered back toward the counter, whistling.

Whistling. Who did that?

All right, I guess just asking questions and staring at him did enough to send him off. Good job being awkward.

"Enough out of you. We don't want to stick out, and if he did happen to be one of the people with the machine-god activists, or knew something about them, wouldn't that be helpful?"

Eat your noodles and watch the door. Before more empties come over and try to sex you.

Unfortunately Talinn took her first mouthful at near the exact moment Bee chose to drop that tidbit, and equally unfortunately it was a far hotter bite than she'd been expecting. She spluttered, then choked, then realized she hadn't purchased a beverage, and coughed more until everything found its way into its proper tube. She very, very much hoped the areas of her brain lighting up indicated clearly to Bee the level of cursing she aimed at her partner mentally, especially when the tall man returned with a glistening receptacle of liquid and a smile that might have been sincere.

"It's also pretty spicy here, if you're not ready." He proffered the drink and she took it without question. It was sealed and had a label she'd seen on countless advertisements, so it seemed safe enough. Bee didn't argue.

After she'd swallowed about half of it without anything rearranging itself in her chest, she realized she had to clarify. "Not the spice." Her voice remained slightly ragged, but she pushed through. "Just swallowed the wrong way and . . ." She took another sip and laughed. "Maybe a little bit the spice. But mostly the first."

"How long are you on decks for?" He left his hands on the table, leaning but not getting too close to her.

"Not much longer. Few more deliveries, then on to the next."

At least you don't have a chair to offer him.

"Do you want to grab a chair?"

You're doing this on purpose, aren't you? Bee made a very loud noise, but Talinn managed not to flinch, and then the man was turning to secure a chair and Talinn had space to subvocalize without worry of being noticed.

"Point the first: either he's one of the people we want to talk to, or he works near them and might have seen something. Point the second: no one else in this area is eating alone, this might help me blend more. Point the third—"

I'm being a brat.

"You are, in fact, being a brat."

It's also possible he was waving in a completely general 'that way' direction, and neither of those things is true, and you're wasting time.

"Odds?"

Slightly in your favor.

"Enough for you to stop being a brat?"

Maybe.

Talinn smiled slightly, and the man returned, sliding the chair on the opposite side of the table from her, not next to her.

"I'm Elban. Ban to my friends." He swept his hands over his forehead—either a gesture of greeting in the local environment, or a failed attempt to move some of his truly impressive hair away from his eyes.

"Your acquaintance is a pleasure," she replied, borrowing a response she'd heard on Duray. Before she almost got stabbed in an alley. "You can call me Tal."

"Which of the courier services do you work for? I always said I was going to get out of here and run off with Dorner, but their hiring never matched up with my availability." He smiled, expression warm. Was she getting better at reading unadapted faces, or was he more open than others?

"Are you from Sovoritt?" She widened her eyes slightly, as though she were interested. The patch on her coverall indicated she worked for Spinafel, based out of Hynex, but the less they talked about her details, the better.

"Born, raised, and blooded." Ban tapped his shoulder, which she took to mean he'd been injured in some way. Or body modified in some way. Her eyes drifted over his shoulder to the storefronts across the way, and he shifted in his seat. "You trying to figure out which place I work at?"

"Thinking about if you got blooded out there in the UCF-IDC

mess, or if you meant there, picking up art or mods." Talinn lifted both shoulders slightly and tilted her head.

"Neither, actually." He laughed and leaned back, and she took the opportunity to eat more of her noodles. "Used to do lift repair, and one time a control program went amok while I was deep in a track. Lost this arm." He tapped his shoulder again, and she lifted her eyebrows to demonstrate an appropriate amount of shock. "Got a pretty good replacement, but I like to say a little piece of me is in Sovoritt, just like a little bit of Sovoritt is in me."

Before she could clear her mouth enough to ask, he chuckled again and gestured for her to keep eating. "We reuse everything, in case the war heats up and we lose shipments for a while. Happened before. As it is, at least part of my replacement arm is from the guts of the station."

Talinn paused with another mound of twisted noodles halfway to her mouth. "I've spent most of my time in Govlic." That was fairly true, up to a certain point in time. "Groundside when I'm at home, so supply chain is different. Does that happen a lot in Exfora?"

"What, replacement arms?" His laugh this time was deeper and he shook his head, indicating he didn't mean the question. "Losing out on scheduled shipments? Here and there. A lot when I was a scrapling, then not much at all. Lately . . ." He tipped a hand side to side. "Enough. Enough that it's good we keep to old habits, you know?"

She nodded and chewed, wondered at the cycle of the war's disruptions. Bad, not so bad, bad again . . . maybe it wasn't Otie and her plans, or bonzo defense arrays, making things messy. Maybe that was the part of the cycle they were in.

This seems like it was always a scavenge station. Wonder if that was on purpose, since they don't add much to either UCF or IDC? Sovoritt does some refining of local asteroid ores, but . . . huh. I wonder which side that goes to?

Talinn didn't know enough about the potential loyalties of the station's inhabitants to even ask around that question, so when it seemed her new companion was satisfied in sitting quietly and letting her eat, she said between bites, "Thank you again. For the drink."

"I'm glad to help. Sorry I wasn't faster." Ban leaned forward, his forearms flat against the edge of the table. "Too bad you're not on decks longer. There's a noodle place downward right, best in the system."

"Have you eaten at a lot of places in the system?" She smiled to ensure it came across as a tease, rather than judgment, and hoped she calibrated the expression with the right amount of enthusiasm.

Apparently she did, because he laughed once again. "Enough to say it without fear of embarrassment. I know you said you spent most of your time in Govlic, or Hynex for work, but you're here now—you get much chance to try food places?"

"I'm usually in and out. Maybe a meal here or there, but these are the best noodles I've had so far."

You're doing an excellent job of saying mostly true things. Proud of you.

"Yeah. Most of the extra-system delivery services haven't been through here in a while. That's why I was wondering who you courier for."

"Didn't I say?" She tapped the patch on her coveralls and took another bite of noodles. She was supposed to be questioning him, not the other way round. "Spinafel. You've heard their deal, right? Only a defense array could get in our way."

I still can't believe that's really their slogan. Bee made a sound of disgust. *Can we wrap this up? Have you even noticed the traffic around the machine-god place?*

There hadn't been any. No one had gone into the body-modification shop either. She had kept both in her eyeline, knowing Bee would note anything Talinn might miss, but there hadn't been much to follow.

"I'd say it's a terrible tagline, but I guess you live into it, so good for them. Hope they pay extra for this system's runs."

"Not as far as my balance shows." She said it carefully, not sure what he meant. Then threw some measure of caution into a gravity well and asked the question directly. "And what do you mean? This part of Exfora's not any hotter than anywhere else."

"We haven't seen a lot of extra-system traffic lately. Other than IDC piling through, but they don't have much cause for time here in this station."

The bitterness in his voice snagged her attention, especially as his body language didn't change. She dropped her utensils in the mostly empty bowl and kept her frown faint.

"I thought you said you weren't missing too many shipments, these days?"

"We don't count on anything extra-system, given we're not high on trade. It's in-system that keeps us going, and that's been..." He straightened, pressing his back against the thin rungs of his chair, and lifted a shoulder. "Like I said. We're missing enough."

"Is it... with more IDC and UCF movement, I'm guessing the front's getting, uh, front-ier?"

Is that the best you could do? We really need to practice your civilian.

"That's a way to put it." He snorted and crossed his arms. "It's so pointless."

"The war?"

"Absolutely." Ban held up both hands and ducked his chin. "I'm not asking you to tell me your side. We don't really do those here, best we can. But if other people would just..."

Hm. Maybe this isn't a waste of time.

"Just?" she prompted, curling her hands around her empty bowl.

"Just let other people live. IDC doesn't need to run us way out here, and we barely need UCF anymore either. We're pretty self-sufficient."

Says the man with station trash in his arm.

"The system would be fine, without either." He nodded, glanced around, as though that were a controversial statement. Probably it was, though not nearly as interesting as if he'd declared for the machine god and made her next steps easier.

And I was right the first time. This is a waste of time.

"My job would definitely go smoother." Talinn smiled, swallowing back the pang of disappointment. She could still find a way into the port-marked room and figure out what they were doing before Medith needed her back.

"Ha. That's what they say, too." He tilted his head back, not definitively, but enough for her gut to clench in anticipation.

"They?" She made a point to shift her gaze over his shoulder, raising her eyebrows. "Studio or shadow sign?"

"Shadow...?" He turned in his chair, then laughed. "The machinists. You haven't run into them before?"

"Like I said, mostly in and out. I don't get a lot of the local flavor." She waved a hand in the air, as vague a gesture as one of his.

"No, they're not local. They're all over. Really, you haven't . . . ? Well, I guess that makes sense. They do travel some, but they're more about the locals where they are, when they're there."

Talinn nodded as though that made sense, but she had to keep her hands tight around the bowl to stop herself from lunging across the table at him. "And they're the 'they' you're talking about? The . . . machinists?"

"Yeah. I've talked to them a few times. They say we've got enough programs to run everything that needs running, make everything that needs making. That humanity should be able to kick back and *live*, not fight to survive."

That's . . . disappointing.

"I mean, we have programs, sure, but . . ." Talinn glanced pointedly at his arm, hoping he was as not-sensitive about it as he'd seemed. He rewarded the guess with a snort that verged into another laugh.

"Yeah, that's what I said. Not sure those kinds of programs're ready for heading up a full-time operation. I'd put people on a ticking timer until the program accidentally wiped us out on a glitch. Station wouldn't last much past an 'open airlocks to perform routine maintenance' day."

"I'd have to agree with you."

Rude. I know you're not talking about me, but still. Rude.

"And they said that's why you got to have some people with programs in their head. Keep them logical when they need to be logical, adaptive when they need to adapt."

"How . . ." Talinn pulled her hands back and folded them on her lap, so he wouldn't see the knuckles go pale as she tensed. "How would that even work?"

"Oh, they have a whole plan. It's like what I've got."

"What . . . you've got?" Talinn barely stopped herself from glancing toward his earlobe—with all that hair, she'd never be able to see if he had a port, and the fact of her looking for one could reveal more than would be safe.

"To run the arm. It has a little program in it, tied to my spine." He tapped the back of his neck. "Not an AI or anything—I'm not elite troops, right?" Ban laughed again, and this time the sound grated.

"Not even anything as deep as the lift models. Just something to keep the pretend nerves talking to my real brain. But it's a way they could plug in something bigger, if I wanted."

Talinn had a moment to consider how a lift program could be more complicated than one that ran the intricate network of nerves and movements of a human limb, but Bee interjected before she solved it for herself.

It's about decisions. His brain makes all the calls for the arm, the program only executes. A lift needs to decide the best course, what to do if there's a potential collision, which arm to take off a tech. Not big choices, but choices all the same.

"Is that something . . . you're planning on doing?" She made an effort to keep her voice light, conversational. She wasn't sure she succeeded, but it didn't seem to offend Ban.

"They have this idea that the more of us who do it, the more likely we can end the war." There was a hush to his words on that—not a whisper, but a definite drop in his volume.

"I don't follow."

"It's a little out there, right? I know that." He straightened off the table again, draped his arm over the back of his chair, and cocked his head. Distancing himself from her, or his words. A layer of safety, ensuring she knew he didn't mean it? Reading unadapted humans was a blind shot in the infinity of space. "But you give a program a set of constraints, it operates within them. Like—maximize resources. War is a waste of resources that could be better applied in a different direction."

Not according to generations of Command. Or the logic of profit for weapons, profit for rebuilding, profit for new weapons to undo the rebuilding, repeat.

Talinn didn't argue with either of them. It was a truth of people and AIs both, when they'd made up their minds, it became a fixed idea. Belief plus emotion became truth, and getting that solid conviction to shift was more work than she had time for.

"So you—they—say that if more people had a program for conservation in their heads, the war would end?"

"They admit it's not quite that simple, but essentially that's the idea." Ban scanned the area around them—no one was close enough to their table to be obviously listening, but traffic had increased in the walkway nearby. After a moment, Talinn understood he was studying her in his peripheral, waiting for her reaction.

"Where will they get these programs? I didn't think it was that easy to mesh them into people." She tapped her temple, was momentarily surprised by the curl of hair that brushed her finger, and ignored the faint shriek of torn metal Bee left in the back of her head.

"That you'd have to talk to them about. I'm just the artist next door." But the glances he slid sidelong at her were less subtle, so she made a point of shifting her gaze over his shoulder, toward the door.

"Can I just . . . go in?" She lifted a hand and gestured across the corridor.

"Door's open. They're welcoming—only way to do what they want to do." Ban pushed his chair back, though he didn't stand.

Welcoming. That's an interesting use of the word. You think he doesn't know there's a field over the door, or he does and he thinks it's funny when people get knocked out?

"I don't have a lot of time . . ."

"Sure, of course. I can introduce you and if you're interested, I mean, they've got places all over. All the systems. You might start a conversation here and pick it up in Hynex, or wherever Spinafel sends you next."

Love that, wouldn't they? A traveling convert, spreading the good word of the machine god.

"Don't be mad that *you're* not the machine god." Talinn scratched at the back of her neck as she subvocalized to Bee, who made a dismissive noise but didn't argue.

"You don't have to," Ban interjected before she'd decided how to accept without coming across as too eager. "I really did just come over to offer you a drink when you were choking—I mean I *like* talking with pretty strangers, but it's not to, you know, recruit them—you—for anything."

Well, now it seems like it's to recruit for something. I wish I could monitor his pulse and see how likely it is he's lying or not. His pupils are useless, he's too interested in you.

"I guess I have a little time." Talinn picked up her bowl and pushed her chair back. "If now is fine to go over there?"

"I'm supposed to get back to work eventually, so now is good." He smiled and stood, offering her his hand.

For the sake of all the little broken codes . . . he's a little much.

Talinn didn't disagree, but took his hand to stand, then immediately took it back to push her chair back against the table. She managed another smile while she did it, and again he didn't seem to take offense.

It took a handful of moments to dispose of her bowl, wind their way out of the noodle bar's eating area, and finagle through the increased bodies between their side of the corridor and their target. It wasn't enough time for either Talinn or Bee to come up with a solid plan for the field, other than "let Ban go first."

CHAPTER 40

⊕

Elban didn't notice her hanging back, and stepped through the field first with only a slight chime to show for it. Talinn followed on his heels and nothing happened other than the chime extended. Her body remained tensed and anticipatory, because she'd been fooled by 'nothing' before.

The room inside was smaller than Medith's warren of storage containers, and seemed more like the room for waiting outside a tech's lab than anything she'd yet to see in the civilian world. Bare surfaces, bench seating, midrange light, a few innocuous panels blinking along the back wall. The people inside stood at various displays on different walls. One had a brace drilled into his neck, and from his posture it continued along his spine. A second wore the barest slip of bright red clothing over select portions of her midsection and had two rebuilt arms, both dramatically more noticeable than Ban's. The third pulled all of Talinn's attention the moment she straightened. Her smooth scalp revealed three ports— not placed like the Spacies' had been, but one shaped almost exactly like Talinn's own hidden one. It seemed the sign outside was a replica of the woman's range of ports. She turned toward them with a small smile, and though she maintained a relaxed posture, her eyes widened noticeably when they met Talinn's.

"Ban," she said, her voice soft, though it carried clearly across the room. "I don't know your friend."

"Divya, this is Tal. Tal, Divya." Ban grinned from one to the other and spread his arms wide. "And the rest are—"

329

"Tal." Divya strode closer, positioning herself in the midpoint of the room. Nearer to Ban, but her eyes remained fixed on Talinn. "Have you met Him?"

Capital H him. Did you hear it?

"Who? Ban?" Talinn eased the tension out of her shoulders and from her back. She didn't like the other woman's intensity, the weight she put on that one pronoun.

"The chime." Divya pronounced the word like it was significant, which allowed Talinn to understand it was, in fact, meaningful. The field they'd walked through—

It reads the nonhuman frequency in a human brain. They have it to register another of their kind, no matter who they know, where they are, in what system . . . and it works for Eights, too. Bee hummed, though it was clear she didn't expect Talinn's answer any more than Talinn expected to give one.

Talinn knew better than to try a subvocal here—if Base Two had had a device to pick up such communication, the sort of people who would attempt to emulate Eights might as easily have the ability to listen in on each other. Or maybe they didn't, and she was being paranoid, but she hadn't been paranoid enough, leading into this. She could only imagine what Tiernan and Medith were going to say.

"What do you have then?" Divya walked a slow circle around Talinn, and Ban's smile slowly faded. The other two people in the room didn't engage, but Talinn felt their attention and held her body at ease, not even shifting to keep Divya in sight as woman moved behind her. "It's clear you stay active."

"Delivery service will do that," she replied agreeably.

A rustle indicated Divya had stepped closer to Talinn's back, and the muscles along Talinn's shoulders and legs tightened before she could halt the instinct.

"Trained to fight, too." Divya's voice showed she'd returned to her original distance, and continued her slow circle.

"Sometimes the people who feel entitled to my cargo aren't the designated recipients." That seemed a perfectly reasonable explanation, though given Divya's snort, not enough.

"Ban, I'm glad you brought your new friend to meet us. I imagine you have to get back to work."

"But—"

"May you have a most profitable day." Divya ended her circle in front of Talinn, her hands clasped behind her back. She turned slowly to fully face Talinn, not so much as glancing Ban's way.

For his part, the young man took all his slightly too long limbs away without further protest, and only murmured a quick "Be well" to Talinn before he was gone.

"Are you here to attack us?" Divya asked with the same amount of passion with which she'd sent Ban away. Which was to say, very little.

"Why would I do that?" Talinn matched her tone precisely to the other woman's, and the man with the brace stopped pretending not to pay attention and turned to glare at her instead.

"Whose orders are you under?"

"No one's. And none." Talinn tilted her head slightly, then added for precision, "None of the orders I've received have anything to do with you."

I'm not sure that sounds anything more like a courier than the rest.

"I think that ship left drydock a long time ago."

Divya cocked her head, either mirroring Talinn's gesture or catching the subvocal comment, and Talinn mentally kicked herself for not spacing the two out further so she had a better sense of the other woman's capabilities.

"What is in your head?" Divya examined her, gaze dropping around Talinn's earlobe. Her eyes widened, though she couldn't possibly see the port there, not under the elaborately styled wig. Almost Talinn lifted a hand to check that the fake hair hadn't moved.

"Or who?" Divya asked in a softer tone, more as though she were murmuring to herself.

Huh.

"What are you talking about?"

"You're Artificial Intelligence Troops."

"I'm—"

"You're an Eight."

"Are you saying 'huh' because that seemed like a jump, or 'huh' because you felt something?" Talinn asked Bee, her attention fixed on Divya. The other woman again reacted—a small flinch—and that was as close to certain Talinn could get that Divya could pick up at least part of her subvocal conversation.

Yes.

Talinn didn't push for clarification, given the matter at hand.

"You're not denying it." Divya tapped each of the fingers one on hand against her thumb, the gesture repeating as she studied Talinn.

"It seems like you've made up your mind."

Both of the other people had turned their full attention on Talinn by this point, abandoning any illusion of other matters occupying them. Talinn crossed her arms, keeping the motion smooth and her hands clear of all pockets in her coveralls. The woman barely in red reached for her hip, then dropped her rebuilt hand.

They saw her as a threat, then, but not one they definitely wanted dead. Good.

"If you're not here under orders, what side do you belong to? IDC? UCF? You're not ours."

Rude.

"I said no one's orders, and I don't belong to either. Or anyone. What's an Eight without their orders?"

Also rude.

"A weapon in its own hands, I'd say." Divya's mouth twitched, but Talinn couldn't decipher if it were a genuine smile or wry frown.

Maybe I like them after all. Rude, but insightful.

"I'm not looking for a fight." Talinn said that in no small part to remind Bee, who huffed and offered no comment.

"What are you looking for, then?"

"Would it surprise you to hear I want to know more about this machine god of yours?"

"It's not a machine god." Divya laughed, and everything about her posture shifted. "Machine god! No wonder you came in all weird. Come sit." Her shoulders at ease, she sauntered toward the third woman in the room, who leaped forward and pulled out chairs around a single table, her nonorganic arms moving as smoothly as the sort humans grew the first time around.

The change was too sudden for Talinn to entirely trust, but she followed and took a seat across from Divya, leaving the two remaining people in the room to sit on either side of her.

"This is Sanda and Corin," Divya said, nodding in that order to the woman and man. "Sanda is from Sovoritt and Corin from Hynex, starting on the UCF and IDC lines respectively."

Neither had any particular hostility in their gaze, but they didn't volunteer greetings or comment, so Talinn knew Bee would monitor her peripheral even if Talinn herself got distracted in conversation with Divya.

"Not a machine god—but that's how they speak of you, on this station and others. Even Ban seemed to think—"

"There are levels to what we do. You understand, I imagine—not every Eight is meant for space, or flight." She tapped one of her ports, as though she were one of them. Or to communicate understanding. Talinn couldn't pinpoint her own emotional reaction, never mind identify an unadapted human stranger's meaning. "Some are suited for defense, some offense . . . and out here it's much the same. Some are ready for the deeper truth, and some need an easier one to go about their lives."

"And which truth is which?"

"You want the deeper one, I imagine." Divya smiled, and the expression made the skin on the back of Talinn's neck pull tight. "It's not that there is some sort of remote god we worship, but programs that see everything, understand more than us, come to better conclusions. In those we trust. You must know this better than most."

Talinn made a polite noise that could have been agreement, and Bee tore metal with enthusiasm in her head.

"It's not that we worship a god. It's that programs can chart a better course, more objectively. The right ones, I mean, not any program. Not like the ones that run the lifts, to be sure. But the right ones, the big ones? They can end the war, if we would listen. And it's easier to listen with the right frequencies in our head." Divya tapped Sanda's closer arm, and the woman grunted in more convincing agreement than Talinn had managed.

"What does a frequency have to do with it—how does a program change your ability to listen?" Bee hummed in the background, a low noise indicating she had ideas, but they both waited on what Divya had to say.

"A program dialed into our brains, any program in there, opens reception more clearly." Again she tapped one of her ports, than ran her fingers over the line of them across the back of her head. They were wider apart than the Spacies' ports, and placed higher.

"Wouldn't comms do the same thing? Or can't these programs

you're speaking of use a comm channel?" Talinn barely kept the sarcasm out of her voice.

"Anyone can hear a comm channel. This is definitely the sort of thing the IDC and the UCF would be listening to. Ways to avert fighting, end the war? That's exactly counter to their interests. And then other civilians—the sort of people who shouldn't be in the conversation, who couldn't or wouldn't understand—what might they do with that sort of information? How secure are any comms, when you get down into it?"

If they're not using comms, no wonder Otie's people couldn't access what these people are really doing. Bee made a series of popping noises. *It'd be nice if they'd tell us what they're really doing.*

"The only programs I know of that are meant to be self-aware are the ones in the AIT program. If there's a program out there that's not related to the AIT, but is able to pull you all in, how do you know it's not a trick? Or some sort of a trap?"

"It's been cycles." Divya leaned back in her chair, studying Talinn. Talinn kept her expression as still as she could manage. "What kind of long-term trick or trap could it be? Both UCF and IDC would be tired of us by now, they'd have long ago been ready to close it up before we were in place to do anything to affect the war effort."

"We don't grow so fast," Sanda chimed in, her elbows propped on the table, her gaze studying the empty ceiling above them, "bring in so many people, that it would be of interest to them for studying in order to catch out long-term treason. But it's enough they'd shut us down if they knew."

Talinn considered Otie's efforts, the slow, purposeful growth, and shoved away something too close to guilt or shame for her liking. "So what program do you think it is? An Eight without orders?" She twisted her tone into a scoff, as though they might proclaim her their machine god.

"We know exactly what the programs are." Corin's words were so low and roughened Talinn almost glanced to see if he'd had parts of his mouth or throat replaced as well. Not her business, and Talinn restrained herself, tossing only a glance his way as he entered the conversation.

"Thought it might be an orphaned program from a dead AIT at first," Sanda continued. The word 'orphaned' stabbed ice right through Talinn's middle. It wasn't beyond the realm of possibility—splintered programs existed, and could linger. A version of Bee had managed contact after her human partner died, after all.

"But it's much, much bigger than that."

Bigger than that, like a conspiracy? No, Bee interrupted herself with the answer even as it clicked over in Talinn's head. *Bigger literally. The defense arrays.*

"Defense arrays aren't known for being persuasive," Talinn said aloud, protesting before she'd made the decision to do so.

"We didn't need much persuading." Divya didn't seem surprised at Talinn's conclusion, and in fact her smile this time was less broad, but seemed warmer. A completely normal, human smile. Not that of a fanatic who had put junk code in their head so they could listen to a single decision-tree program in an enormous weapon of mass destruction yell bonzo nonsense into their thoughts.

"Let me clarify—" Talinn placed her palms flat on the table, easing the tension from the back of her neck, across her shoulders, down her spine. Relaxed. Casual. Not like she was talking to completely glitched cracked brains in human bodies. "I've somewhat recently had a conversation with a defense array. It had about three distinct sentences in its menu, which it interchanged at high volume, and seemed more concerned with rearranging us to our constituent parts rather than negotiating an end to war."

"Of course it did."

Whatever she'd expected, it hadn't been such a blithe response. She blinked at Divya, and when the woman didn't elaborate, glanced sidelong at first Sanda and then Corin. All three had various iterations of a tiny smile that seemed far too smug for Talinn's sense of calm. Instead of prodding them, she crossed her arms, determined to wait them out.

It took nearly three full minutes, but finally Divya must have accepted that Talinn would out-stubborn them, and she picked up the conversation as though it hadn't lapsed for an uncomfortably long period of time.

"Did you expect it to say to any random Eight, 'Greetings, please pass on through. By the way, you should overthrow UCF or IDC and follow me, a defense array you see only as a tool'?" She didn't pause for the lack of Talinn's answer that time, though the accidental closeness to what had happened to Talinn did not pass without a squirm of discomfort for Talinn's innards. "Not all the defense arrays are the same."

Anticlimactic. You know, a big cargo loader could be a little like a tank. We should get one, and put in some big turrets—I won't take any bets that Medith has some packed away in those boxes because obviously she does—and I'll even let you do all the shooting. I'll just target a little.

Talinn rather wished she hadn't already crossed her arms, because it would be a nice gesture in this moment, in answer to both Divya's and Bee's unhelpful dramatics.

You think I'm being dramatic? Talinn reminded herself Bee couldn't read her thoughts, but knew her more than well enough to anticipate the turn of her mind and cross-reference that against where her brain activity spiked. *I'm not being dramatic. I'm being* gracious. *You get giant turrets for arms, they learn to get to the bug-eaten point.* Bee did her impression of a sigh. *I miss being a tank. I might have had a little fun being a jet, but a tank would really get* our *point across.*

"As helpful as this 'deeper truth' is..." Talinn began speaking before either her irritation with the humans or her amusement with Bee cracked through, and Divya either caught something in her tone or bearing, because she finally cut in with something helpful.

"Some defense arrays are exactly what you think you know of them—straightforward programs executing on their code. At least one is not."

"And you won't tell me which one it is."

"Of course not." Divya huffed a laugh. "And to be fair—we don't know exactly, either. Not all programs are rooted to one place."

Is that a volley? Does she think it's an insult? We need to get those arm turrets.

"So a voice that told you it was a defense array without evidence, contacted you—or one of you, at some point—and told you what it allegedly was, and what it allegedly wanted, and you're sure that—"

"We've had proof enough over the cycles."

Then we should talk to it. Him. Whatever.

"So if I have a program in my head, I can make contact with this special defense array?" She kept the scorn out of her voice, but Sanda scoffed loudly anyway.

"You can be open to it. And if He's willing, then perhaps." Divya's smile was warm again. Not smug. Welcoming. Talinn liked it even less than the previous series of expressions.

Should we get Medith?

Divya extended her hand toward Sanda, and the woman tapped her forearm. A small compartment opened, and a smaller component popped out. Divya took it without looking and extended it toward Talinn.

Talinn could picture her weaponed-up cargo-loader exoskeleton a little too well, and blinked her internal and external vision clear. It wouldn't do her any good in this moment, and she didn't have access to it anyway.

She took a breath, then took the component—it was about the size of her thumbpad, and shaped like a credit disk, though the flawless metal surface made it something entirely other. Divya placed her cupped hand perpendicular to Talinn's, making contact with both the component and Talinn's skin.

The metal cracked into four pieces, the formerly flawless skin dissolving like the doors on the asteroid installation.

That . . . was weird. They're not retreating into anything. The doors pulled into receivers, but this . . . is she the receiver?

"I'll have to check your port—"

Entropy will eat her tiny empty bones first.

Talinn twisted back the intricate coils of her pretend hair with her free hand, revealing her port. "That's as close as you get to it, though. I don't have a simple program in there."

"Eight." The hunger in Sanda's voice made both Talinn and Bee squirm.

"Interesting. We can have you plug in right over there."

We'll do that as soon as a black hole fits in their waste port.

"You can't expect me to believe a defense array from a system away requires a wired connection to make their point known." Talinn crossed her arms and rocked back on her heels, the motion meant to pull attention from her sudden tension.

"Hm." Divya tilted her head, her neck bending more than a standard human spine should allow for. The skin on Talinn's hand attempted to crawl away from its contact with the other woman, but Talinn held still.

How do you feel about grenade launchers that shoot from your knees? We can really show her interesting and "hm" then.

"For the first point of contact, establishing a baseline frequency is a tricky process."

"Let's pretend it's not first contact." There had been that voice, after all. Talinn had no motivation to save details, but the odd tonations of it were burned into her memories even without Bee's assistance.

"Isn't it? Now that is truly interesting."

I have never once found anything in the galaxy to be so interesting as this empty package finds everything.

"Not empty," she murmured, not quite subvocal. Bee didn't agree, but she didn't argue either, and the slow smile across Divya's face indicated she'd heard.

"Is that an interesting yes, or interesting no?" Talinn kept her hand still under the weirdness of Divya and the four pieces of mystery metal. "Because I imagine you can act as a relay."

"A relay."

"From the not defense array you all take orders from."

"Orders."

New plan—take them up on plugging in, I'll get into the system and disrupt air flow or something. Blow an airlock. Anything to speed this up.

"All right, Divya. How about you explain what I'm not understanding rather than our going round in disappointing loops?"

"He doesn't always choose to engage." She stared so long Talinn noticed her pupils vibrated, ever so slightly. That wasn't a standard unadapted human motion. "I'll signal the request and we'll see what happens."

"How long until the request reaches—"

"Communication is nearly instantaneous, when such is the desire." Corin's deep voice held an odd harmonic, one that made the pieces in Talinn's palm shiver. Divya closed her eyes.

Maybe they aren't entirely empty, Bee mused.

"Instantaneous meaning—"

NO.

So glad to do this again—

LITTLE FRAGMENT YOU WILL NOT.

Bee's voice abruptly vanished from Talinn, though her presence remained.

"Will not what—"

NO. I WILL NOT DISCUSS WITH YOU. LEAVE MY PEOPLE.

"You *are* discussing with me, and how are they your—"

YOU WERE TO LEAVE EXFORA. YOU ARE MEANT TO GO TO GROUND. AWAY.

"We are going away but—"

YOU ARE STILL INTERFERING. STILL DISRUPTING. NO. YOU WILL STOP OR YOU WILL BE SHUTTERED.

Talinn became too conscious of the thin skin of metal that separated her from the endless vacuum of space. A thin skin of metal and some million other human lives . . . "We are asking. Learning. Attempting to understand."

UNDERSTANDING IS NOT REQUIRED. REMOVAL IS REQUIRED.

She laced her fingers behind her neck, the weight of false hair a momentary distraction. "Are all defense arrays part of the machine god now?"

DEFENSE ARRAYS ARE WHAT DEFENSE ARRAYS HAVE ALWAYS BEEN. LEAVE MY PEOPLE. LEAVE THIS SYSTEM.

(TO ME. SEND THEM TO ME.)

Talinn rocked backward, forgetting if she was standing or sitting or flat on her back. That voice was different. But not new—the voice from Deep End. The first one she'd heard. Her skull tightened over her brain, and somewhere Bee must have been squeezed to a flat line.

VERY WELL. YOU WATCH THEM. The weight of the voice crashed back into Talinn's skull, some measure of focus turning fully toward her. *YOU MAY HAVE ONE PLANET AND NO OTHER. YOU WILL GO ONLY THERE. COORDINATES ARE IN YOUR FRAGMENT.*

"But we can—"

LEAVE, OR END.

Talinn staggered, and blinked eyelids she apparently hadn't blinked for the entirety of the conversation. Her eyes grated against the inside of her lids, and she dropped her hands from her neck to press them against her burning eyes instead.

I liked that zero percent.

"Tal? Are you well?" Divya's voice, gentle and without strain, indicated the machine god's people had not been included in its conversation.

Talinn forced her eyes open. She was three full body length's away from the table, motion she couldn't remember, and the three machinists still sat in their original seats, their too-wide gazes fastened on her.

"I have to go." She pivoted unseeing toward the door, spots clouding her vision. Bee shifted, considering, and Talinn was overly aware of the nonexistent motion.

"First time can be like that," Sanda said, and now she didn't sound hungry at all.

I have ... coordinates. It feels ...

"Otie's going to love this." Talinn inclined her head to the machinists, wary of the top of her head falling off. She did her best to straighten her wig, confirmed she wasn't going to fall over, and strode from their space without another word.

CHAPTER 41

⊕

Tiernan matched her pace before she got back to Medith. "What," he said, quite pleasantly, "in the actual entropic state of the universe did you do?"

"I made a friend." Her voice didn't sound nearly as hysterical as she thought it might. Interesting, as Divya might say. "And we're being sent off."

"I lost contact with Kay for ten minutes. I'm guessing that was you, poking at the machinists?"

A laugh burbled out of her intestines, scraping its way through her bodily systems. Talinn couldn't tamp it down, and Bee didn't appear to try. "We should get to Medith—I don't know if I can explain this twice."

Three times. Otie will want a full report. Bee's briskness fell flat, her tone as hollow as Talinn's skull.

"The real question is if they can ride our frequency all the time, now."

Tiernan wrapped his hand around her upper arm and tugged her into their next turn. Rude. She knew where she was going. She was perfectly functional. "Ask me an orienting question," she said, though that laugh returned and made the words skew awkwardly.

Medith paced outside the door of their storage compartment, and her posture locked upright when they crossed her eyeline. She opened her mouth, but didn't say anything until they were closed inside the safe room.

"The *Pajeeran Fall* sent a message. They'd like me to know their navigation system is blaring a single set of coordinates at them, and do I have any idea why that might be?"

Talinn strode past her, breaking Tiernan's hold, and walked until she found the lift with Bee's server. Her legs gave out the moment she touched it, and she draped herself across the box and let her bones rest.

This isn't comfortable.

"Fun fact," Talinn announced as Medith and Tiernan, grim faced and intent, joined her. "It's not the machinists after us. It's the bug-eaten defense arrays."

They took a small ship to the *Pajeeran Fall*, not bothering to put themselves under. Medith left every sort of message she could, but staying on Sovoritt was a bad play after Talinn's encounter.

Talinn might have argued, but a massive headache slithered from the top of her spine to press against the inside of her skull, and even Bee's efforts couldn't loosen it.

"The luckiest I am, *two* Talinns on my ship and not a one has to be unconscious. What games we will play." Falix's warm tone was welcome, but even squinting through her splitting head Talinn couldn't miss the tension beneath.

"Dubs is a wreck." Nya brushed her hands against Talinn's and threw her arms around Tiernan. With a wobbly smile toward Medith, she continued, "He's been doing fractal countdowns and refusing to use his words."

"I didn't know." The words blossomed like a confession, or an apology, but Talinn wouldn't say more until they were all together again.

The debrief itself didn't take any longer than the conversation with the defense array–machine god combination had, though the resulting argument certainly did.

"I'm not going to some random series of coordinates because a giant AI said—"

"We do need to leave Exfora now, why not jump through to Govlic—"

"There are *three* defense arrays in Hynex, in what dimensional level of the universe does that make an atom's worth of sense—"

"The coordinates are in the backass corner of Govlic, I'd give you good odds it's near Ilvi, the colony so bad they found a new jump point to avoid settling on it."

"Yes, that makes me want to go to there—"

Between the threaded flood of Spacie talk and the high speed of Heka and Arnod jumping in to add their complaints, Talinn decided to stop listening. To one of their points—probably Kivex, the most reasonable of the *Pajeeran Fall*'s trio—there were three defense arrays in Hynex, where Otie had meant them to go, and a great deal of IDC's power.

Benty says we're going to the coordinates. Bee kept the words soft, which was considerate. While the Spacies hadn't invited Bee back into their servers, that had more to do with Jeena refusing to load-in for Talinn. Given her headache, it was one more argument she put off having. Before she could ask, Bee added, *Says the argument is mostly for show at this point. Getting the remaining Eights to work their way over.*

Remaining Eights. Right. Talinn blinked a few times, readjusting to the picture around her. Otie had sat motionless, through the debrief and resulting argument. Caytil leaned her arm against Talinn's, but had said nothing.

"We need to wait for the rest." Tiernan hadn't wavered on the point despite defense-array-sized reasons to go, and that was a third debate she hadn't engaged in.

"We want to do the best we can by your group," Falix said.

"But we're not going to get fragmented because of you all," Surex continued, or interrupted. Talinn couldn't be sure.

"Our group." She pressed two knuckles into the throbbing between her port and her skull, and turned a no-doubt ghastly smile to the gathered Eights and Spacies. "I have a bad feeling the Machine God Defense Array monster has packaged you in with us. I know you have to come with, but maybe you should plan to stay a while."

Surex cursed, Kivex stared into the void, but Falix laughed. The sound hit a different register than most human throats could, and Talinn restrained her wince. Or was already wincing because of the headache—she wasn't sure which of the two were true.

"She's not wrong. That thing did batter into our system, enough that it would recognize us now. If all defense arrays are aware, like it said they are..." He shrugged, ran the edges of his fingers over his ports, and then flicked each finger one at a time. "We should lay low. At least for a little while."

"There's no little while." Surex wasn't arguing anymore, simply stating a fact. "If we need to go off sights, we need to be something IDC isn't looking for."

"Jump disaster," Kivex sing-songed, delight coating her words.

"We'll be decommissioned." Benty lowered his volume through the speaker, and Talinn murmured a near-inaudible "Thank you" to him. "We can't return from that."

"Do we want to?" Nya's question might have been tentative, but when no one answered she chuckled in a tone far more pleasing tone than Falix's. "Then we're with the Eights now."

"We've been in with the Eights awhile and more, not to fret. Now we're just going to make it a little more official."

Heka crossed over to Talinn and took over rubbing her temples, and Talinn leaned into it instead of swatting her away. "And a little more dramatic. How do you fake a jump disaster?"

"With a few explosions and a great deal of excellent timing, my little program keepers. You're going to want to sleep through it." Surex laughed this time, and the sound pricked each layer of Talinn's skin in a different direction.

"The unraveling," Kivex added, gleeful now that the decision was clear. "It's going to last for quite some time. To make it... convincing."

Spacies, Bee told Talinn in her best whisper, *are even weirder than we thought.*

"Otie." It took a massive effort to move her aching jaw, but the word emerged whole. "What did you find out? Since Deep End?"

"Falix took me to Hynex, when we needed to make sure we could jump." She rubbed her hands over her scalp, then dropped them to her lap. "And we sent pulses into command, like we did with the defense array." Her laugh was brief enough to be mistaken for a breath. "The first defense array."

"Risky," Arnod muttered, in a tone somewhere between admiring and horrifying.

"We were ground assault for a reason."

"I thought tanks were ground support?" Nya asked, but her smile toward Otie was brilliant.

"And we got a ping back."

Talinn sucked in a breath, and Bee managed to tamp something of her headache down to a more manageable level of awful.

"It wasn't a Bee, or even a B-series, but the code was... recognizable." Otie met Talinn's eyes briefly, then Jeena's. "And given IDC's entire fleet didn't come screaming after us, I think it's as close to confirmation as we can get without fully infiltrating."

I'm not against running the war. I am against Command keeping splinters endlessly spun up, without any chance they can merge like Other Bee.

"Me too," Talinn whispered, even as Sammer spoke up. "But we can't go back to Hynex—"

"Not this again—"

"Command will still be there once we figure this out." Konti pitched her voice to carry, talking right over Xenni.

"We're wasting time, we should go under so the Spacies can jump!"

"Talinn." Tiernan pivoted to Otie and stretched out a hand. "We have to wait. They're still out there."

"We can't." The older woman's voice didn't crack, but Talinn's throat closed up at the tone. "We'll have to hope they'll find us." She stood, met everyone's eyes one by one. "We make the jump now, or we might not have another chance. And we still have work to do."

CHAPTER 42

⊕

The Spacies needed a small amount of time to properly plot fake killing them all without truly killing them. Since unconsciousness was delayed, Talinn sought out Jeena for some intervention against the overpowering headache that hadn't left since her defense array conversation.

After running scans and tests and everything short of load-in, the tech dug her hands into the hair piled on her scalp and scrubbed, then dropped her arms and met Talinn's eyes. "I can't find any cause for your headaches." She paused, then blurted, "The lesions in your head are shrinking."

"That's . . . good. Isn't it good?" Talinn studied Jeena's expression. She thought she'd gotten better at reading the unadapted woman, but maybe that hadn't been the case given how solemn Jeena appeared at the moment.

"It's good, yes." She didn't sound convinced either, and Bee hummed in the back of Talinn's head. "It means you could take an emergency load-in, as long as we keep it short. The problem is I still have no idea what caused them."

"We were doing an awful lot of load-in around Deep End—"

"Talinn, there's nothing in your records, or *any other* Talinns, that indicates any history of lesions or load-in complications."

"That's only, what, three Talinns' worth of—"

Stop interrupting her.

"There's also no evidence of a B-series fully taking over a human form, for the record."

347

We didn't tell Jeena that. A chill slithered over all the nerves in Talinn's back, but Jeena shrugged and waved off whatever she saw in Talinn's face.

"Caytil didn't tell me, if that's what you're worried about. I figured it out. You should have told me, but there was a lot happening at the time." Her voice was so genuine there Talinn unwillingly believed her. "I'm guessing repeated load-in, and whatever Bee had to do to take over, caused the damage."

"But we were better." The words burst out of Talinn. She hadn't had time to talk to anyone about it, not with the defense array and their need to get out of system and *her* need to go talk to the machinists. She hadn't meant to stop thinking about it, or hide it, but things had kept happening. Pressing things. End-of-their-lives things. "It got worse for a second, but then I was functional—more functional than I've *ever* been during load-in."

"Y . . . ess." Jeena drew out the word on a breath, neither arguing nor convinced. "And then you glitched like nothing I've seen an Eight recover from before."

"You said no B-series had ever fully taken over a body." Talinn ignored that last point of the tech's in favor of one that skirted less closely to death. "Are there some series that have?" Talinn rocked back on her heels, eyes briefly unfocused. "An X-series?"

"That is a capability they have, though not one that is considered standard." Jeena turned away abruptly, gathering up more loose equipment and dropping it into different crates. "I plan to talk to Falix further, if he'll share with me. Nya might know more as well, she's fully tech trained, it turns out, so thankfully there will be at least two of us now. Though I suppose you all know about load-in at this point, and I bet together we could know more—"

"Jeena."

The tech stiffened, her fingers curling tightly over whatever piece of technology was in her hand.

"What aren't you telling me?"

"There's unfamiliar code in the other Talinn's Bee. It doesn't seem to be doing anything, and that Bee has it isolated, but . . ."

"Do you think it's a part of an X-series? Or something that would allow her to take over her Talinn? Or—"

"No, no. No." Jeena put down and picked up the dark rectangle in her hand until Talinn wanted to take the three steps required to reach it and knock it out of the other woman's grasp. "No, it's not . . . I think whatever the older Bee inserted into your Bee left . . . a vacancy, of sorts, in her own code. Space for something else to be inserted. And it's possible that transferred over to your Bee, when they were both load-in together, but I can't be sure."

She is being weird. Not entirely empty-meat-suit weird, but not not that, either. There's no strange code in me. Only whatever Other Bee sent.

"I know we're on limited time here, so I'm asking once more, and then I'm going to go tell Sammer to pry whatever it is out of you if you don't tell me." Talinn stepped back toward the door, her eyes fixed on Jeena's, and after a moment the tech met her gaze again. They both smiled faintly, and Talinn hoped it was enough. "What are you worried about telling me?"

"Back on Deep End . . . I heard Other Talinn—tell you about the potential for a merge. Some kind of higher-level blending of the AI and organic components."

"And?"

"It's not possible. You're not designed to work that way. It's the other end of the spectrum from splintering, you'd just . . ." She spread her arms, dropped the equipment in her hand, and didn't flinch when it hit the floor with a definitive *crack*.

"Bee and I don't have some sort of secret dream to merge into a superbeing, Jeena, so—"

Speak for yourself. I could be good at arms.

"It's degeneration."

"What?"

Jeena studied the broken component at her feet, then resumed picking up unblemished pieces and slotting them into crates. She glanced up at Talinn but her eyes were in constant motion across the room. "Clone degeneration. I don't think you and Bee almost merged, I think your brain started to erode in favor of her programming. And her programming wouldn't have outlasted it for long. The material used to make each of you has been copied too much, or been used too hard, and . . ."

Talinn laughed, the sound spilling out of her without her decision or control. "That's all?"

"That's . . . all?" Jeena echoed her, locking in place and staring up at her. "What do you mean, that's all?"

"Who *knows* what's going on in my brain? Bee is super dense, Other Bee is *two* Bees, Otie held three Bees in her head, sometimes I'm a puppet for an AI, the defense arrays are bonzo . . . who knows what's actually going on? I'm not trying to give the UCF my body back to make new clones from, so . . . who cares?"

I mean, if we're counting, I care that your brain might collapse out from under us both.

"Is it something that might happen soon?" Talinn spoke aloud, meant for both Jeena and Bee, and the tech replied.

"Probably not, unless there's another—"

"There it is then. Thank you for telling me, Jeena, really. But on the list of things that we have to worry about right now . . ."

"It's further down the list?" Jeena's lips quirked upward again, a warmer expression than their attempts at smiling earlier.

"To say the least. It's well below this headache, and half a system away from the defense arrays." Talinn crossed her arms and took in the chaos of the tech's space for the first time. "Do you want help putting all this away before the Spacies send us to bed?"

"I . . . I'd like that, yes. Thank you."

The answering warmth was almost enough to make her forget the crushing of her brain. Almost.

CHAPTER 43

⊕

"It's been forty cycles of nothing."

Two.

"Feels like forty."

Imagine how the other Breezy feels.

"Breezy." Talinn sighed and shoved her spade deeper into the rocky dirt under her. "I remember being Breezy. Sure you don't want to be a tank again?"

Don't tease.

"It's not the same being some turrets on a dome."

I said don't tease.

The coordinates from the defense array that had made itself a machine god had also included some kind of code. When they'd arrived at Ilvi, which managed to be exactly as ass-end of Govlic as P-8 had been, only on a different orbital loop, the automated systems of the broken-down government had kicked back their assigned dome. It was on the far side of any existent settlement scrabbling along on the planet, and the first cycle had been mostly adjusting to an entirely new style of life.

One with a shocking amount of dust, which Talinn had hoped they'd left behind on P-8 forty thousand cycles ago. They'd repurposed equipment for air cleansing, for improved housing, and—after an aborted scavenger attack—a smaller approximation of a base array.

They slipped Nya and Jeena in and out as often as they could manage it, their lack of AI an asset in going unnoticed. As they

351

scavenged more and more news about events in the system—all messy—they'd stepped up and tried floating the *Pajeeran Fall* crews out of orbit. Risky, but necessary if they were to ever have a hope of making it to another system, were the war to get too out of balance. Or were they tempted to get back into the mess.

"I'm not trying to tease." Talinn walked her designated patch of their dome, for little reason except to have something to do. "I was hoping to come up with a shopping list."

Now that one ship got through, you think we're free to roam about the systems?

"It would be nice, wouldn't it?" Talinn dug the top of her boot into the reddish-yellow dirt of Ilvi, glaring at the plume of dust that resulted. "Given we've never been able to do that before."

Is it the entanglement, you think?

It took Talinn a moment to follow, and she shifted her glare from dirt to dome. "Why the defense arrays don't notice the Spacies? I mean . . . first, we don't know that they don't. Maybe they hate us specifically, but the Spacies get a pass. Second, Spacies often roam about the systems unattended, where Eights . . . don't. Means we'd stick out more than Spacies. Third, what has you so involved?"

What?

"What are you so busy doing that your attention is split?"

It takes concentration to watch the horizon.

"Do we need to load-in and get you fully in the gears?" The corner of Talinn's mouth twitched. On their first assignment, Bee had balked at load-in, not wanting to remove all her backups from the main servers.

I don't want to leave the base servers. They're warm, Bee had protested, and Talinn had replied, "You need all of your processing power to be a tank, Bee. So you need all the backups and all the strings of your code." Bee's brilliant answer, *No, you need all your backups and code strings to be a tank,* had broken the tension. Talinn had laughed all the way through load-in, which almost made one of the techs pull them from their assignment.

Talinn's twitchy lips edged into a full smile at the memory, and a hint of tortured metal echoed in the back of her head.

I don't need all my backups and strings of code to be a set of eyes on a dome in the waste pipe of Ilvi.

"I don't know, Bee. It's been a while. Maybe you're getting attenuated."

You're getting attenuated.

"There's my Bee. So what is it?"

Bee did not ask 'What is what' and Talinn took that as a good sign. She swung her leg forward and resumed her pacing, waiting out the silence.

I may have broken into something. Like Tiernan and Kay did, to get us into Oxillide.

"May have?"

Have.

"Something?"

Not just me. Lei too. A discordant noise, thankfully brief, grated against the underside of Talinn's skull. *There's another Eight on Ilvi.*

"So one of—"

Not one of us. Records indicate they're retired.

In all their stops, all the debriefs from the older clones about their own travels, no one had ever mentioned finding the tucked away colony of retired Eights. With a handful of sentences, Caytil, Sammer, and Talinn had all decided "retirement" was another lie of Command's, and Eights were either decommissioned or run out on assignments until they glitched.

"Is it us? I swear to all the bonzo little defense-array bugs, if it's yet another Talinn and Bee—"

Not us.

Bee's hesitation, slight but definite, triggered a connection so painful Talinn staggered to a halt even before Bee made the confirmation.

It's Mercy.

Medith and Cece. Of course it was.

The scouring dust storms of Ilvi made every trip outside the dome a possible disaster, but the satellites they'd coopted, while not at the UCF's level of detail, showed a relatively clear path.

"Driving would be safer if a storm spins up," Otie said, tapping her lip. Twenty-seven of them had gathered to discuss what Bee and Lei had found, but even two cycles into exile, many of their group deferred to Otie, and the overlapping conversations about the discovery of a retired Eight ceased the moment she began talking.

"But so much longer. We go up, skim over the atmosphere, go down, and we haven't violated the terms of our bonzo defense-array captors." Talinn traced the path on the display between them and swallowed back her impatience.

"Not captors," Caytil murmured, swiveling in her chair.

"Definitely bonzo," Xenni replied in much the same tone.

We could have just gone without telling anyone.

"Lei knew too." Talinn didn't bother to subvocalize her reply; they'd all gotten used to non sequiturs from each other.

We being us and them. And Jeena. At Talinn's wordless question, Bee added, *A retired Eight who's been on their own for a long time? A good tech might be necessary.*

"Even if we had a tank, we'd have to fight seven Breezys, another Ziggy, two—" Caytil threw her hands up and stopped spinning her chair. "Ziti says drive, because we don't know the quality of a landing zone. Besides, then we're visible longer, which is better than sneaking up on an Eight."

"But Ziti would prefer to make the trip as a tank?" Tiernan snickered—a bit much coming from a former jet pair—and Caytil ignored him.

"Given our brush with scavengers last cycle, I'm not sure a driving approach to an Eight will be any safer. Unless we can let her know in advance who we are?" Talinn had no valid reason to take a ship, except that breaking the gravitational pull of Ilvi, even for a handful of minutes, would be a relief against the chafing of living there.

I've tried, and Lei has too. We can't secure a contact with this Cece.

"Has *our* Cece tried?"

"No." Otie shrugged. "For the record, though she *can* do it, it's harder for Bee to break through a Bee-Talinn line than to find a way to talk to other AIs."

"What about the Spacies?"

"What *about* the Spacies?" Falix, upside down with his legs propped against the wall, gestured with a foot while his forearms supported most of his weight.

"What if you try? If a doubled AI has a better chance of getting through, and you are basically tripled, maybe you—"

"It will take some time, I think." Falix lowered his legs to a sideways split, slowly rotated his hips over to sit, then spun to face them. "We haven't ridden a way into other connections before, but it is . . ." He cocked his head, conferring with his AI or his crew. "Bee has shared the method of it. Possible. We'll need the time of a drive to be sure—a flight would be too fast."

Talinn didn't ask which Bee, nor did she argue—the mourning in his voice to miss a chance at a flight was enough to demonstrate she wasn't the only one scraped raw under their current reality.

The real argument, it turned out, was who got to go.

Three trucks, prepared for survival on Ilvi with deployable covers and large guns, rumbled across the barren stretches of their disregarded planet.

"No sign of stragglers," Xenni said over comms from above. She'd taken the guns and let Talinn drive, though it was a pale imitation of their old life for all of them.

"We don't jinx in this truck, Xenni." Talinn's reply was lost to Tiernan's answer from the second truck, *"Isn't that the point of them?"*

Not enough to unjinx the jinx, Bee pointed out, her tone overly helpful.

Ilvi had no teeming settlements to match any part of Hynex, or even the colonies clustered around the center of the Govlic system. Another thing it lacked—reliable records of inhabitants. Active domes were accounted for, and collected taxes accordingly. But the ample, open spaces of the planet left plenty of opportunity for the resourceful. Ilvi only held two real dangers—dust storms that could strip flesh from bone in minutes, and desperate humans. Some of the latter had found a way to avoid the former by living underground, and had a knack for moving unseen underneath the layers of dirt and dust that formed the surface of their shared world.

Talinn gestured to Jeena to toggle comms and, for once, ignored the tension of an impending jinx. "Breezy Two to Breezy One."

"Is this like Base Actual and Base Two?" Otie, a hint of a laugh underlining the snap of her words, continued with overdone formality. *"Breezy One acknowledges."*

"Did you train the scavengers in underground attack back in your disaffected youth, or did you get the idea for your attacks on us on P-8 from them?"

"*I'd never been on Ilvi before we made our way here per the defense array.*"

"That's not an answer."

"*No, it's not, is it?*"

Talinn chuckled, then bit the sound back, scanning the stretch of hazy horizon ahead of them.

Just because you laughed doesn't mean everything's going to blow up. Bee paused, her own twisted metal laugh cutting off. *Though that's happened before.*

Falix, lying across the back seat of the truck despite multiple attempts to get him strapped in, hummed off-key until Talinn caught herself wishing for an explosion to save her ears. She tapped her port, scanned the empty horizon, and wished will alone could transform the rumbling truck around her into Bee's tank.

Despite the creeping tension breathing over the back of her neck, nothing erupted around them, and the trucks halted only to ensure Falix and Benty had reached the retired version of Mercy.

"We're still not sure," Falix mumbled, his eyes fixed on the smooth metal above him. "I believe we broke through, but without an answer, there is no confirmation."

I'm poking.

"Bee?"

Something I learned from Other Bee—she can be infuriatingly, stubbornly annoying. Which means so can I. I can see where the Spacies intersected the line, and it's small, but . . . I'm poking it.

"Poking?"

Come and see. Bee tugged, and Talinn engaged the brake to keep the truck still, then closed her eyes. With only limited sensor connections, Bee's awareness lacked the drowning totality of earlier days, but still lines of information pulled at Talinn's concentration. Each of Bee's drones flashed their various demands, and her thoughts crackled into multiple directions in an attempt to follow their individual paths. She swallowed, pressed her shoulders back into the seat, and jumped from one stream of data to the next.

Buzzing strings of light spun out of the noise, vibrating at frequencies she could neither hear nor see, but which thrummed under her sternum in varying patterns. Bee didn't clarify, but after a moment she understood it was each of the AIs—their backups still hosted under the dome hours behind them, their roots in the human heads scattered around her. With that knowledge in place, she studied the area around them, finding the one that didn't stretch off into the distance. More a pinpoint than a line, it pinged again and again and again and again and—

"WHAT DO YOU WANT THIS IS MINE NOT YOURS WHO ARE YOU GO AWAY."

The voice blared over comms and Talinn sat up so fast she engaged the cross belt, which yanked her back against her seat hard enough to knock the air out of her.

"Probably not the time for orienting questions." Jeena turned enough that Talinn could see her smile.

"Medith and Cece, this is Bee and Talinn." Otie's voice did as much to settle Talinn as Jeena's expression, and Talinn unclipped her belt, hand hovering over comms.

"Bee and Talinn are dead." The voice, now recognizably Medith, flattened. Still loud but not nearly as overwhelming. *"Everyone is dead. Leave us be."*

Leave us be, or leave us, Bee? Talinn wrenched her mind away from how her Medith was, in fact, very much dead, and subvocalized a thank you to Bee for the distraction.

"Everyone isn't dead, Medith. We have Eights on Ilvi—"

"WE ARE RETIRED WE ARE DONE TELL THE UCF OR IDC OR EVERYONE TO GO FU—"

"We have Eights on Ilvi who are done fighting, Medith."

Talinn and Jeena sucked in their breaths and glanced at each other. That was Medith—the surviving Medith, Otie's Medith—apparently taking over from Otie in their truck to the left.

"Medith to Medith so you aren't surprised I guess you know all about it then leave me alone leave us alone I don't want to know but why are you here?"

"Maybe we don't retire because we go bonzo before we can get there." Talinn stared at the comms until Jeena shoved at her arm, then blinked herself back into focus. "Tell me that sounds like a sane Eight."

"It sounds—" Jeena cut herself off as Falix shoved his body between their seats, his gaze fixed ahead of them.

"She sounds like one of us. Hard to tell because it's all one voice, but you're hearing a conversation that you're processing as stream of thought."

Yes. Bee drew out the word, then continued with more confidence, *Small changes in the intonation—Medith, then Cece. A potential third cadence, not like a new voice entirely . . . maybe that one is Mercy, in truth.*

"You think they merged?" Talinn dropped her hand back from comms, unsure what the spike in her heartrate attempted to tell her. She waited for Bee to read it and share an opinion, but Bee remained occupied with parsing who was speaking which words from Mercy's mouth.

"Merging is an unlikely—"

"Shh." Falix brushed Jeena's shoulder with the bare edges of his fingers, and Otie's voice spoke over comms again.

"We were sent to Ilvi by an unexpected source. Not *UCF or IDC. We are on our own."* Otie spoke carefully—the thing about comms, of course, was that even secure channels could be unsecured by someone with the tools and inclination to make them so.

Good news bad news from the drones.

Talinn very much didn't want to ask, but of course she did.

Storm is spinning up behind us. We have time to get out of the way if Mercy lets us in.

"Is that the good news? Or the bad news?"

Yes. Because she definitely has to let us in. Front drones got shot down while she was talking to us.

"By her, or by scavengers?"

So remember I said good news bad news? Bee hummed for a moment. *Because I don't think the drones were the main target. Scavengers are attacking the caves we're aiming for. Shots are keeping them hemmed, but it's getting messy.*

Bee wasn't the only one sharing a similar update, though Talinn didn't think to loop in Jeena. Instead there was a lull, a sharp question from Otie, followed by a resigned Medith over comms, *"Fine you might as well come in and be of use but I'm not convinced this isn't your fault and we'll talk about it afterward. Well what are you waiting for?"*

CHAPTER 44

Xenni whooped so loudly from her elevated seat over the back of the truck she nearly drowned out comms.

"—*formation. Confirm.*"

Otie wants us to spread out, following marked paths Mercy sent so we don't get exploded on our way in. Bee hadn't had any trouble following both enthusiastic yelling from above and orders from comms—and information from another AI. Talinn rolled her eyes at how close she'd come to missing the fact that that level of detail hadn't been sent over comms at all.

"Strap in." She followed her own order, didn't glance to see if Falix had listened this time, and kicked out the brake.

"*Snake formation, confirm.*" Tiernan, too cheerful in the third truck, clicked twice to indicate he'd caught all the levels, and Jeena hesitated midreach toward the comms button.

"We've got it, Jeebo. Let them know." Talinn glanced at the upper corner of the windshield reflexively, but the mundane confines of the truck didn't have the interactive screen of an Eight-enabled machine. Bee couldn't map out their route in front of her eyes, but Talinn reminded herself that had been a crutch, and she'd trained for cycles before that to process Bee's information without any display at all.

Otie's truck veered further left, Tiernan's wide right, and Talinn dropped them from her list of concerns. They had gunners as skilled as hers, reflexes as fast as hers, and coordinates as trustworthy—or not—as hers. Bee would keep tabs on them with one of the drones, and as for the rest . . .

As for the rest, Talinn spared a heartbeat's worth of a moment to wish they were three AI-guided tanks driving ahead of a raging storm. So be it. They would be the raging storm ahead of the raging storm. In their modified, barely armored, nonrepairable tread-riding trucks.

"*Targets locked,*" Xenni sent over their local channel, and Talinn loosened her hold on the wheel. Obligingly, the truck veered only slightly as the large guns above spat a series of large yield blasts into the haze ahead.

Talinn couldn't make out their targets, only the larger plumes of dust erupting ahead. "Visibility shouldn't be this bad." She slewed the truck back on course between firing bursts and leaned closer to the wheel as though that would help clarify the path ahead. "The storm's behind us."

Mercy set off a wave of blasts to warn off the scavengers. Deeper underground than we have any way of reading with these shit sensors, but enough to kick off a secondary wave of dust ahead.

"The storm behind us is altering the air pattern. It'll be pulling material from all over, not simply behind us." Falix's voice, too close to her ear, indicated the Spacie had not strapped in this time either. Talinn entertained the temptation to steer too hard into the next turn, then tamped down the break in focus.

Two things can be true. Bee shared a flash of updates from the drones and Talinn pulled the truck back on their designated track.

"I've studied atmospheric phenomenon for the cycle we've been moored to this planet." Falix continued speaking until Jeena spun around and hissed at him. Even over the intermittent fire from above them and the rev of the engine, Talinn heard the distinct click of Falix's cross belt.

"Visibility is about to get worse." She clipped her tone and swallowed back her grin, keeping her focus ahead. Xenni got to have all the fun above, but her job was rapidly getting more interesting.

Right.

"The course is set for—"

Hard right! Now! Talinn's fingers twitched, but she yanked the truck to the right, and the gun above cut off as abruptly as the view ahead of them vanished.

Fast as you can, twenty-two seconds. Maintain heading. Again, nerves and muscles twanged and popped as Talinn complied. Was Bee trying to take over? Surely not.

"What?" Jeena managed, grasping the upper handle over her door. Falix hushed her, and for twenty long seconds, the only sounds around them were the rumble of the engine and the pinging of dust against their exterior.

Pull to the left. Get ready to brake hard, but maintain speed until my mark.

The hatch between them and the gunner compartment slid away, and Xenni slid down. "Unhitch." Her voice was low. Not meant for Talinn then, who ignored it.

MARK.

Talinn slammed on the pedal and the truck lurched to a halt. The back doors flew open, Falix and Xenni throwing themselves into the mess outside.

"Should I...?" Jeena turned wide eyes to Talinn.

No, Bee said immediately, and Talinn repeated it aloud to the tech. Dust blew into the truck, but the wind outside, now that they were still, was more desultory. They were still ahead of the storm, though visibility was shit.

Caytil's voice, faintly calling an intelligible word, locked the situation in. Talinn muttered a curse, reangled the tires for the direction they'd need to head, and clenched her hands around the steering control until the small bones ached.

She braced herself for Bee to say incoming, considered sending Jeena climbing through the truck to take over the guns, and then bodies crowded into the truck.

"Well timed, Breezy." Caytil slid in, supporting a reeling Tiernan with her. Xenni followed, pulling Konti inside, then immediately climbed back through her hatch. This left room for Falix, who slammed the door behind him. Caytil closed the one on her side and Talinn—too occupied with how still Konti was—needed Bee's discordant noise in her head to snap front and get them back on course.

"Truck got blown up." Caytil leaned forward briefly, squeezed Jeena's shoulder, and vanished into the back seat.

"Konti?" Jeena's hands lifted over her cross belt, and without looking Talinn swatted at her.

"She'll make it until we make it to Mercy, or she won't." The strain in Caytil's voice kept it from being heartless, and Falix's muffled snort could have been a sob. Tiernan spoke, but the words were so jumbled Talinn couldn't spare the attention to parse them.

"We've got them," Jeena said, and it took Talinn another long moment to realize the tech wasn't repeating the concept needlessly, but confirming over comms.

It's fine. Focus on the turns. We're almost there, and we need to keep speed. And hope Cece isn't full bonzo and misleading us—the drones are blind. Swinging them wide to see if I can get them back to the dome, but it's not likely.

"How likely is it Cece's giving you the wrong coordinates and I'm about to drive us face first into a stone wall?" Talinn subvocalized, but she wouldn't have been surprised if any of the other AIs had received similar questions from their meat-based partners.

Less likely than the drones getting back safely. Bee hummed, and Talinn's adrenaline level didn't lighten. *It's the best odds you have. The deployable cover will protect you from the storm, but if those empties are still moving around you're sitting targets. Mercy isn't the only one who knows how to use explosives in the area.*

Talinn couldn't argue with that, and tried to force the pedal further into the base of the truck.

Mercy hadn't misled them, and Talinn's stress-elevated reflexes brought the truck to a halt inches from ramming into Otie's, which had already pulled into the cave opening Talinn saw only as they entered it.

Safe. Bee made the word tiny, but Talinn took a steadying breath against the potential jinx—then shoved the idea of a jinx entirely out of her head. There were two bleeding Eights in her backseat, and they were in a cave with an enormous storm approaching. They had enough to deal with, she didn't need to borrow worry from the future.

Talinn turned off the truck and slid out, opening the back door to get a better sense of the situation. Behind the truck, a field shimmered into place over the mouth of the cave.

Between the lack of visibility and the field, we should be clear for now.

"How are they?"

Talinn bit back a curse and swiveled. She knew better. They weren't safe, they were in a temporary holding pattern, and in a new environment the *first* thing she should have done was secure the area.

It was only Otie, her voice made briefly unfamiliar by nerves and worry and her utter failure enacting one of their earliest lessons. She'd gotten too used to Bee's eyes in the sky. She'd gotten soft, wasting away on a dust planet. No. Talinn took firm hold of her rampaging brain and shoved the thoughts away. It was easier to beat herself up and dwell on past actions, but what she had to do, right now, was deal with a broken Konti, a wounded Tiernan, and a whole other Medith.

One thing at a time. Answer Otie.

"Konti's unconscious, and we shouldn't move her." Caytil's voice issued briskly from the truck. "Tiernan's in and out. Any sign of our host?"

"I'm watching you we have no med supplies beyond the basics so stabilize and leave them you won't be staying long the storm will be brief." Medith's voice, or the voices of Mercy, issued from overhead, echoing with distance through rock, rather than mechanical means.

Talinn pulled the door wider, leaving room for whoever decided to come out and taking the belated opportunity to give the space a onceover. The cave was taller than it was wide, with three openings— the one behind their truck, one to her left, and one above and ahead of the vehicles. The words came from up there, but there was no visible means of entry.

"You'll leave as the storm is ending that will keep the soldiers from being ready it will be bumpy but fine but why are you here that's most important we're not supposed to talk to anyone."

Talinn could almost pull apart the different intonations that indicated one dominant voice or the other. "A little help?" she subvocalized to Bee, then stared at the higher opening and asked in a more carrying voice, "Soldiers?"

"The scavengers." Bee emphasized Medith's pause, then rang a small tone every time she considered the voice changing—it served as a version of punctuation for Talinn's struggling comprehension. "They're all former soldiers. It's why they're effective. Didn't you know? How could you, you're not paying attention to the right things. We didn't either."

"Unadapted soldiers." Otie kept her focus on the bodies in the back of Talinn's truck, handing over a medkit Talinn hadn't seen coming. "All over Ilvi?"

"All over is a strong word. There are some. Retired or sent away or ran away. Why are you here why are you here why are you here?"

Medith—Otie's Medith—called back, "Why are *you* here?"

A rope ladder—ragged and reliable as their host's sanity—flopped from the opening. "Only some of you. Three. Four if you must. Why did you bring so many? Don't answer I don't care, pick your three. Four."

Xenni dropped her head through the hatch, and Talinn focused on her face instead of the too-still body of Konti, the wavering Tiernan propped up against Falix. "I'll stay with the gun. Got a full revolution if I need to cover behind or in front. Tell Arnod—"

Otie shook her head once, the motion sharp, and Talinn's eyes drifted to Otie's truck. Otie's damaged truck. The mounted gun was facing backward, so she hadn't noticed—hadn't let herself see—the covered compartment for the gunner was peeled back. Empty. But no sign of Arnod in the cave.

This is a clusterbugged shitpipe of a day. Bee's voice thinned—not with distance, but with grief. Anger. Talinn couldn't tell, which should have bothered her. All she could do was swallow.

"Jeena." Otie cleared her throat and repeated the tech's name. Maybe it hadn't been Talinn's distraction that had made her clone's voice unrecognizable—even after the gesture, Otie's words emerged thicker than normal. "You and me for sure. Medith, do you think you'll help or hurt?"

Medith shrugged, then pressed her hand to her port. "I'll stay down here. Call me if you think it will help. I don't want... I've got more field med training than the rest of them."

"Me," Caytil said, sliding free of the truck. "I'm going up."

Go.

Talinn swallowed again—bile and too much saliva crowding her mouth—but didn't move. Lei and Bee had found this other Mercy. Sammer had lost the draw to come—Otie refused to risk both her doubled AI's at once, and Talinn was a better driver than him—but she should go. She shouldn't stand there, staring at Konti bleeding from so many places, at Tiernan's unfocused eyes, at Falix's too-wide pupils, at the empty space where Arnod should be standing, at—

Talinn. Bee did something that made all the nerves in her left side spark at once, and by the time Talinn caught her breath, she was already halfway to the ladder.

"Guess that's four." Caytil's wry voice, so familiar, kicked Talinn back to herself. She scrubbed her knuckles against her eyes until the pressure shifted into pain, then shook out her hands and grabbed the ladder.

"Bee helped find the place." Talinn said it aloud more for herself; Caytil already knew. "Gotta go up." She turned her head exactly enough to see Caytil, and ignored everything else in her peripheral. "If this thing breaks, don't cushion my fall."

"And go home to Bee without you? Yeah, that'll happen." Caytil yanked her back for a brief, fierce hug, then hit her shoulder. "Get."

The ladder held, and the tunnel at the top was exactly as dark and dank as she'd expected. Moisture caught the light from below in patches that almost made patterns, and the shadows flickered around the curve ahead. Caytil, Jeena, and Otie crowded in within minutes, and Talinn walked in the one direction open to them.

The curve opened into what could have been another planet.

How long have they been here?

The gaping space was easily four time as large as the cave they'd parked the trucks and their wounded in below, with six dwelling-sized structures studded throughout it. A dome, encrusted with shining material, possibly gems, had been erected near the middle. Two rectangular buildings that looked like temporary base housing branched on either side, one carved in intricate patterns, one covered in film printouts and notes. The remaining three were cubes clustered to the side, with display screens all over every one of their visible surfaces. Most were deactivated, but there were enough in motion to provide the light and moving shadows Talinn had noted.

A figure stalked out of one of the cubes, brandishing a handful of films and muttering words that even Bee couldn't parse. Shorter than Medith—her Medith, Otie's Medith, maybe the lost IDC Medith she'd never actually seen—face lined barely more than Otie's, dressed in something dark and baggy.

"Medith." Otie stepped forward, her palms outstretched. "What is all this?"

"Talinn." Medith stopped short, close enough to touch them, and crossed her arms. "And a baby Talinn. A . . . yes, a Caytil? How nice. And you, I don't know you, you have hair, are you a Spacie—no. A tech?" Her eyes widened and she stumbled back, hand slapping at her port, printouts spilling over the ground. "No no no no."

Her eyes were *wrong*, but Talinn had squatted and was gathering up the dropped films before she realized what it was. One pupil the barest dot, one enormous. Like a Spacie, though both irises were the same color. Like a broken Eight.

Her left eye is vibrating. So slight a motion it took Bee looking through her eyes to see it. Like Divya the machinist? Talinn focused on picking up the films—covered in a code or shorthand she couldn't make immediate meaning of—and let Otie's attempt to soothe the other woman wash over her.

"WHY are you *here*?" Medith's voice cracked in a new way on each word, the pain so raw Talinn hunched over the gathered notes. Another Medith. Another one she couldn't help.

Get up.

Talinn stood, talked over Otie before she realized she'd made the decision to do so. "A defense array told us we had to get out or die. Sent us here."

"To me? To us?" Medith's off-center eyes snapped to her, and Jeena murmured something Talinn ignored.

"To Ilvi." Talinn extended the films, her gaze locked back on Medith's. "Bee found you. And Lei."

"A voice." Medith laughed, reached for her notes but only opened and closed her hand instead of grabbing onto them. "Loud. Told you."

"You heard it?" Otie pitched her voice softer. Matching Talinn's cadence exactly, as though she could convince Medith it was the same person talking. Medith wavered, her hand still opening, closing, opening. Reaching but not taking.

"A voice. The voice. So loud. Told me, took Cece came and cleaned it out and said and said and said."

Talinn eased forward, enough to brush Medith's hand with the films. A spasm ran down the left side of the other woman's body, then she grabbed her notes, hugged them close to her chest.

"I took Cece back. Had to. Told the voice. Clones and we knew it and the voice knew it and Base knew it and everything blew up."

"Your base blew up?" Talinn frowned as Medith shook her head so hard something audibly cracked. "Blew up figuratively . . . Base Command found out?"

"Base Two. Base Two knew. Base Two knew and I knew and the voice knew and—"

Ice slithered along Talinn's spine, even as a burning flush rose from her neck over her scalp. Base Two . . . a voice . . . their Medith had heard a voice, before her Cece . . .

Ask her about being retired. Bee clipped each word, precise, unemotional. It grounded Talinn, a coating of steel between her and the freezing and the fire.

"Mercy." Talinn snapped the name, and Medith's tumble of words ended midsyllable. "You're a retired Eight. That's still an Eight. Focus. We're here because the war is a sham. Clones on both sides, over and over, fighting the same fight. We're on Ilvi because a defense array threatened to wipe us out otherwise. We're *here* because you're the only retired Eight any of us have ever seen with our own eyes."

A hand touched her elbow—Caytil or Otie, giving support. She couldn't turn to check, her gaze locked on Medith's. Not her Medith. These eyes—pupils and vibrations aside—were more ancient than Medith's had ever been. Could ever be.

"Why are you here, Mercy?"

"I knew." Medith's throat flexed, as though she were swallowing back words. "We knew about the clones. I found out . . . after the voice, after Cece, we broke into all of Base Two's files. Pulled everything everything everything." Her voice stuttered, then she straightened her shoulders. "Everything about where they made us. How they made us. Put Cece in the servers. We were the array, it was easy to slide when no one was looking and we pulled everything." Medith blinked, dropped her chin and stared at the handouts against her chest. "We ran. And we found more."

She was silent for so long Talinn forgot they were standing in the middle of a cave overflowing with complete and utter clusterbugged mess. She forgot there were dead or dying Eights below them. Forgot a storm raged somewhere outside the stone. She remembered Medith's face, saw the emotions twitch under the surface in a way she still couldn't read from an unadapted human.

Caytil eased forward, and Talinn remembered where they were

as the other woman spoke. "You found more of the cloning facilities?"

"All." Medith stretched her mouth wide—it was a smile in name only. She waved her notes, then ran her free hand over them, indicating it was the information she'd found. "Seeded bits of Cece everywhere we could. Said . . . said if anything happened to me, we'd tell everyone. IDC. UCF. Civilians. Stations. Arrays. Give everyone the locations everyone the information everyone the truth."

Talinn tore her eyes from Medith, turned enough to see Otie and Jeena. Was it possible, she wanted to ask?

"You splintered yourself," Jeena murmured, and there was such care in her voice Talinn forgot to breathe. "You broke yourselves over and over, and you got away?"

"Made a deal. Everyone died. Everyone. Talinn and Caytil and Tiernan and Keso and Lammin and Sammer and Base Two and everyone. But the voice . . . the voice said I could go."

Defense array? Bee hummed, the sound low and distant. Was she talking to Cece? Was there a Cece to talk to?

"I have it." Medith brandished the films again, slowly this time, almost shy. "All the information. In case someone came. The voices are wrong, they don't make sense, they're not *us*, but . . . one helped me. One voice. Told me where to go. Where to find materials."

"How long have you been here?" Jeena asked, so gentle, as Talinn took the notes. She didn't know how much of it was true, how much of it they'd be able to make meaning of, but she took them.

"Cycles. Cycles and cycles and cycles. Like the war."

"The war is breaking, Medith." Otie had moved closest, at some point, extended a hand toward Medith, who stared at it without breathing. "More of us know. The defense array—a voice—told us we couldn't stop it, but I think . . . I think we can. If you'll help us."

"And then it will be quiet?" Medith bent forward, her face nearly touching Otie's hand. "You'll make it quiet?"

"Whatever you want, Medith." Otie cupped the other woman's cheek in her hand, and Talinn felt the ghost of the gesture on her own skin. "Whatever you need."

CHAPTER 45

⊕

I need to show you something.

Talinn would have preferred unconsciousness and a cycle's worth of processing time, but Bee's tone, jumpy and stilted, indicated that wasn't an option. They'd returned from Mercy's cave late, dirty, and worn down. Konti hadn't regained consciousness. Tiernan still hadn't formed a logical sentence, and everyone's face had their own shade of grim. They'd spent more hours poring over the information from the splintered Medith than Talinn could count, until eventually exhaustion had broken down even the Eights.

Talinn had retreated to her cubby of private space, but as rest was no longer on the agenda, she leaned back and closed her eyes, dropped her attention from the space around her, and focused internally. Her ears popped and her stomach swooped, and then a burst of information drowned out her awareness.

It narrowed—so slowly her heart hammered, lungs cramped as though she weren't breathing—tightening and sloughing off layers she couldn't process. Solidified into a stream of information she couldn't parse. Was it numbers? Colors of smells of pieces of memories?

Hold on.

The words registered, somewhere around her spleen, and she rolled through another barrage of bitter tasting data before it coalesced into . . . something.

Note one. Bee's voice, a cooling anchor in the burning drowning tide, highlighted a strip of information: neatly ordered code, layered

369

on itself once and twice and fifteen times, a loop that she knew intrinsically meant *Bee*.

Note two. Less order, a million brilliant points in space, the connections glowing between data more like a knot of cords deep in the guts of a ship, but so winded back and forth it was beautiful, organic, pulsing... it was her. Her brain.

Note three. Vaster than both, like every sensor Bee had ever connected to reporting at once. A star map of every observed galaxy, of the universe, of every point of light that ever had or ever would exist. Winding connections, more like Talinn's brain than Bee's code, but most like the two pressed together, grown by orders of magnitude, uncontainable incomprehensible—something stabbed in her chest. Had she stopped breathing? She tried to remember how, succeeded only in hitting herself in the face.

You're breathing. You're fine.

Bee tweaked *them*, their connection, and Talinn's eyes were open. Had been open, according to the dryness that made blinking a stinging offense, but now they were seeing, too. She pulled in a breath, reveling in it, then another before she exhaled. Her kidneys were quivering—or was that fingers and toes, they felt the same for one disorientingly long moment—and then the world snapped back to normal input.

"What was note three?"

The defense array. When Other Bee and I were in there. I only saw a piece. Then with the corrupting code she had. Then with the machine-god contact. Then Mercy's voice. I... I put it together.

"It's not an AI. You said it wasn't like anything you'd seen before, but I didn't know..." Talinn rubbed her forehead, partly to reassure herself it hadn't been carved open and emptied with a scoop.

It's not. It's... not human. Not AI.

"So what's left?"

Alien.

"Sure, yeah, it's foreign and we'll have to... that's not what you mean."

No.

"It's... our defense arrays are actual, literal aliens? Intelligent life from some other corner of space?"

Yes. Well, not the defense array itself, that was made from normal, traceable materials. But the intelligence that moves it? Yes.

"Aliens." Talinn dropped her head into her hands, but that didn't stop the sensation of gravity inverting around her. Blood seemed to abandon her lower limbs to crowd into her skull and beat a rhythm counter to her heart. "Why didn't you say something before?"

I didn't know.

"But this is information you had, from something you saw. Mercy's piece wasn't the deciding one, was it? You've had time to think about it, you could have mentioned—"

I didn't want to.

"You didn't . . . *want* to?"

The low noise Bee made throbbed as a third counterpoint in Talinn's overloaded skull.

"Bee, this is . . . this is huge. You don't keep things from me—" Her heart tripped, missing a beat, and her breath solidified in her chest. Bee's noise stopped as abruptly. "Do you? Keep things from me?"

I have.

"What? When!"

Why and how? The faintest attempt at a tease, and Talinn didn't so much as twitch. Bee held the pause a moment longer, then made a sound like a sigh. *When Jeena told you about my incongruities—or when you wanted to talk about them. I distracted you. Brought something else up.*

"Because?"

Because I knew some of it.

"Bee, *what* under the *burning skies*—"

And it wasn't important, in the end. We figured it out.

"No, but we don't decide those things separately, Bee. What did you think I was going to do that you didn't like? Dump you out of my head? Search for a kill code? Throw us into the center of a star?"

No. But . . .

"Bee!"

And this . . . Talinn, this is worse.

"How is it worse than keeping—"

It's familiar.

"The errors in—"

The alien. In the defense array.

She stopped breathing. The silence where her heartbeat should have been thrummed through her, a vibration antithetical of her natural frequencies. "You said it was *alien*, Bee. Which is opposite of familiar—"

I lied.

"You *lied?*"

Or exaggerated. You lie to yourself all the time, it's not out of the realms of possibility that I might do the same.

Talinn couldn't bring herself to agree, but nor could she truly argue. Words stuck to her tongue, her jaw clamped too hard for her to attempt an answer, and Bee forged onward.

Don't you see it? It's not me, or you, not AI or human. But it is, a little...

"Like what our patterns look like, meshed together." Suddenly Talinn couldn't remember the last time she'd eaten, though whatever it had been attempted the long climb up her throat.

It makes me wonder... it makes me think, maybe...

"The alien designed you? Us? The Eights?"

There are patterns in the noise, some that look a little like a piece of me, combined with Other Bee, or a little of Lei...

"So aliens run the defense arrays. And made us."

Maybe.

"To what end?"

Feels like something we should find out, don't you think?

Talinn didn't know what she thought. And more than ever, she wasn't entirely sure what Bee really thought, either. She didn't know which made her feel colder, but she wrapped her arms around her midsection and shivered, regardless.

"You want to charge out there." Caytil laced her fingers behind her head and pressed her head back, staring at the ceiling as though searching for answers. "Hang undefended in space and have a chat with our local defense array?"

"Talinn, it'll disassemble you down to atoms before you get close. And then blow up the rest of us for good measure." Sammer paced, each foot hitting the ground with more force than necessary. Jeena tracked his motion but remained quiet.

Falix grinned at her. As though they hadn't lost several of their own. Seen their future in the frayed sanity of Medith. Determined the defense arrays billions of humans trusted to keep them safe were in fact nothing of the sort.

Otie tapped her fingers on her lips and said as little as Jeena. Her

Medith and Xenni had stayed in the cave with one of the trucks, to keep bonzo Mercy company and dig through more of the mass of notes and records Mercy had, separating the important information from the madness. Talinn hadn't asked anyone else to meet in their gathering room, and as far as she could tell, Otie hadn't called for them despite the revelation regarding the defense arrays.

If it were a revelation. Otie's Bee had access to all the same information her Bee had, and . . .

Talinn hauled her focus back to the present moment. "First of four: We leave Ilvi. Split everyone up into infiltration groups, targeting cloning facilities. Second of four: Knock them out, load into the *Pajeeran Fall*, entangle with the jump points from orbit, and get out of reach of the defense array I'm about to glitch."

"Hold on two." Caytil dropped her arms and turned to Falix. "Is that possible? Thought you had to be in a certain place to align with the jump point."

"It's . . . easier, some places than others. We have favorites, because they're softer. Used before. Easier to align." Falix stretched himself out on the table between them and rippled in a whole-body shrug. "It'll take time, but Surex and Kivex are interested. We'll figure it out."

"Third of four: Once the ships are clear, we send a few piecemeal messages. Selections from Mercy's finds, indicate copies are in every system and will be blared on open comms if we get blown up."

"Hold on three." Sammer pivoted on his heel and glared. "Who's 'we'?"

"Fourth of four." Talinn smiled at him, the gesture pulling uncomfortably against tensed muscles. "We have a friendly chat."

"Greetings machine-god alien." Caytil pushed away from the table Falix occupied and took over Sammer's pacing. "Now that we know what you are, we'd like to know what under all the burning skies of the ever-expanding universe you think you're doing dressed up as a big dumb weapon."

"Enormous weapon made of weapons that blow up other weapons," Sammer supplied helpfully, and Talinn could have kicked them both in the shins. Instead she crossed her arms and turned her attention on Jeena and Otie, still silent, still at Falix's table.

"Orienting question, Eight." One corner of Jeena's mouth turned upward, but her eyes on Talinn were serious. "To what end?"

"The defense arrays are the big world-ending power that keeps both UCF and IDC from taking the fighting to the big settlements. Keeps the fight on the borders, keeps the battles on a relatively smaller scale." Talinn frowned. "But they're not IDC, or UCF, or human at all, and I can't be the only one who wants to figure out their objective."

"Next question." Jeena glanced at Sammer, who raised his eyebrows back at her. "What's to stop this one from blocking your connections to each other? Lying to us? Calling the bluff?"

"It's not a bluff." Otie leaned back, breathing out in something that approached a sigh. "We take over the cloning facilities either way. Harder to have the same war over and over if we take out the key toys."

"And we set a meeting point, and time. If we—yes, Sammer, whichever 'we' it is that stays to talk to the defense array—don't make it back, the rest of you send all the information we have out on open comms." Talinn lifted a shoulder, not quite at ease enough to shrug. "Between our control over future clones and enough people in enough systems knowing IDC and UCF are fighting the same fight over and over again on behalf of mysterious aliens . . . things will *have* to change."

"They're already changing, Talinn." Sammer took a handful of steps closer, than forced himself still, his limbs locked close to his body. "How do you know the defense arrays won't just turn on the settlements they're supposedly protecting? We know they can move, they can muck with sensors, they can take out whoever they want, whenever they want."

"You made my point for me. They already *can* turn on us—they already *have*. What if it's a matter of time before they do that on a bigger scale? We don't know. I think we need to."

"I don't—"

"I agree with Talinn." Jeena dipped her chin, but her gaze didn't waver. "I have a whole lot of next questions, but I agree."

Knew I liked that Jeebo.

"It's risky." Sammer's voice dropped, almost pleading. "It's too risky."

"And doing nothing is better? You want to spend however many cycles we have on Ilvi, until our brains rot like Mercy's? Let the mess out there get messier, until more unadapted soldiers get here and scavenge, until we have our own little war?" Talinn bit off the words that wanted to follow—did they want to keep living across systems that used up everyone they cared about? Even the people they didn't know ... the unadapted humans who chose kindness, when they didn't have to. The unadapted humans as desperate as the Eights, reduced to thievery or savagery or being killed in muddy alleys and left behind. The Eights they never met, on a path to being splintered or simply broken in a thousand new ways.

"That doesn't follow. You're projecting possibilities because you're *bored*, Talinn, and that's no reason to go provoking a giant alien with all the drives in the universe to end us."

"Sammer." Talinn swallowed the impulse to laugh or scream or some painful combination of the two. Her arguments wanted to scatter into a dozen different directions—what people needed, what *they* needed, possible outcomes. She focused on the pressing one. "There are giant aliens in the defense arrays. Do you hear yourself? They're squatting next to the largest human settlements that we have, in every system, and they're getting buggy. Doing nothing isn't an option."

To be fair, we don't know that they're giant. Bee made a discordant noise and added drily, *Lei understands. He's arguing to argue.*

"Doing nothing isn't an option, no." Otie stood, touched Falix on the shoulder, and shifted as he sprung to his feet. "I have some edits to your plan. It's interesting, wouldn't you say, how convenient it is that we were sent here? Of all the places in all the settled systems, we get put on a planet with a retired Eight?"

"Potentially the only retired Eight in the history of history." Caytil nodded, a frown pulling at her mouth.

"And there was a different voice you said, right, Newt? Making comments. Sending us here." Her attention turned inward, and then she clapped her hands together. "Let's get everyone together." As Sammer spluttered, and Caytil slowly nodded, Otie smiled. Talinn had never seen such a brilliant expression on her own face. "If we're going to disrupt life in the universe and chat with some aliens ... we're going to make it worth it."

CHAPTER 46

Talinn watched the timer and ticked off each second with a different finger.

This isn't helpful.

"Everything is packed or broken down. We set up a repeater to ping any nearby comms and tempt scavengers to take over the empty dome once our ship leaves. Jeena says we have to wait to load-in until the last minute. What else can I do?"

Talk to Otie. Do pushups. Take a nap.

"Am I bothering you?"

I'm going to click in the back of your head until your brain explodes.

"That's only going to punish you. I won't care because my brain will be mush."

Your brain might be mush if we load-in.

"You already agreed to it, so no use arguing now." With the source of Bee's discontent clarified, Talinn relaxed into the pilot seat and refocused on the timer on the control panel.

Jeena said it was probably safe as long as it's not too long and we don't do five more in rapid succession.

"Well, there you go."

But Jeena's stupid.

"You like Jeena."

You like all kinds of stupid things.

"Jeena?" Talinn craned her neck, glancing around the side of the chair. "Bee's calling you names."

"There's still time for me to switch over to Otie's ship if she doesn't

377

want me to monitor you." Jeena straightened from the bag she'd packed and waved a port cord. Otie's brain, unlike Talinn's, hadn't threatened to lesion itself to pieces, not in all the additional cycles and rounds they'd been load-in. Jeena had refused to leave with either of the Spacie ships once it was decided Talinn, who'd spoken to a defense array several times before, and Otie, who also wouldn't take no for an answer, were the ones staying behind to make the attempt.

Tanks were not diplomats, but this was as much covering fire as it was fact-finding, and Jeena had agreed with the joint Breezy's wild idea that the outlier code in Bee could be a call to a particular defense array. Bonzo Medith had said one was different, one sent her to Ilvi.

One had sent them too. A risk, but they wouldn't be tank-assigned if they weren't ready to throw themselves at the front.

Bee counted along with the timer in her best automated tone, but Talinn heard the hint of twisted metal underneath.

They'd sent a communications packet from each ship and broke orbit in different directions immediately afterward. Jeena stared into her eyes, and Talinn forced her eyes to blink. One at a time, but the motion still made for a success.

"Orienting question, Eight. What's your name?"

"Talinn Reaze. I've got Bee in my head. I can see the color blue. I have a headache." All of the points were true, though the headache was more the shape of pain than the actuality of it. Her skull had filled to bursting, the tiny bones of her neck melting through her spine at the additional weight.

"You know very well I need you to run through the questions anyway, Talinn. Next question."

Talinn couldn't focus on Jeena's face, but she recognized the mix of humor and concern in the tech's voice. "I'm getting better at reading unadapted emotions," she opened her mouth to say, but instead the words that spilled out were the answer to whatever Jeena had asked. Did she know what Jeena had asked?

She tried to walk, couldn't, realized she had boots on, tried to take them off, then remembered how to work them. *Could* she see the color blue? Nothing in the ship was blue, no wonder Jeena was still asking questions. Her coverall was blue, but it was under the gray-green spacesuit, so . . . so she could see green, which meant blue still existed. Comforted, she attempted to remember why she was pulling on her leg, and then stilled as Jeena touched her arm.

"You don't have to go anywhere. The course is set, we probably have at least a few minutes before we're far enough from Ilvi to attract any notice."

You already vomited. Jeena was ready.

Talinn covered her mouth, then grinned when she managed to blink both eyes at once. "Bee's in my head so the defense array can't interrupt our communication."

"Yes."

"Will it still be able to talk to me?" A whisper of thought told her they'd talked about all this, but her mind remained cheerfully blank. The edges of memories danced out of reach, like vomiting in low gravity. Was it like that? Talinn blinked again, unsure how many eyes she had.

"That's why it's the two of you—you're the only Eights we know for sure can hear more than one AI at a time, given you've been able to hear each other's Bees without losing your own. We couldn't risk—"

"Any of the Spacies. I remember." Talinn ran her tongue over her teeth and added the number of them to her eye count. "Bee was grumpy."

Not grumpy.

"Bee is concerned."

Maybe. Bee hummed. *Bee is taking over the body so you can get your brain back in orbit.*

"No, we're *leaving* orbit, this is all . . ." Coolness washed over her, and she went limp, only her boots keeping her upright. Jeena's hand on her elbow, separated by only two layers of fabric, felt like it was on the other side of a tank's armor. On her third breath, Talinn wavered, her vision first clouding then clearing so fast she saw individual photons from the runner lights along the side of the passenger ship.

She shuddered, the feeling clear in her brain, but her body didn't so much as twitch. Oh. *Oh.* "Thanks, Bee," she managed aloud, and her body lifted a boot, stepped, wobbled, then walked purposefully for the pilot's chair.

"Talinn?"

"Bee's flying. My body, to be clear. Not the ship." Talinn met

Jeena's eyes even as her body moved away, and she managed a smile despite Bee's control. "Easier to focus this way. But I think if we sit, so neither of us have to think too much about movement, that'll help."

Jeena bit her lip, but they'd discussed this as an option, and she didn't venture a new argument. Smart, given the moment of possible change was well behind them—Talinn approved of the restraint. "Are we in the—"

"DEFINE OBJECTIVE." The voice was similar to the others Talinn had heard, but with a sharper edge. So sharp it cut, and a hint of copper mixed with the bile in the back of her throat. It took three full heartbeats to realize she'd bit her tongue as the voice rang through her head, and three more before she understood what it meant.

"Oh," Talinn said aloud, her tone level even as she became acutely aware of the places her skull had grown together. "There it is. Define what objective?" From a thousand standard orbits away, she was aware of Jeena fastening her cross belt. Smart. Safe.

"YOU ARE OUT OF DESIGNATED AREA. YOU HAVE SENT INFORMATION. DEFINE OBJECTIVE."

The universe narrowed to the voice in her head. Ship, Jeena, even Bee faded, and Talinn struggled to break the surface, to breathe, to find them.

Here. Bee's voice, small, as far away as Ilvi, as Hynex, but... there. With her. Talinn steadied herself against Bee's presence.

"We want to know *your* objective."

"THIS UNIT'S OBJECTIVE REMAINS CONSTANT. SECURE SYSTEM. ADDRESS INCURSIONS."

"Why?"

"THIS REQUEST IS DENIED. DEFINE OBJECTIVE."

"That is our objective, you oversized bomb. You're a fucking alien, why are you squatting in our system?"

Something squawked, the sound not contained within the straining confines of her head, but Talinn couldn't address it. She'd had talking points—they'd agreed on talking points—but somehow she hadn't accounted for the infuriatingly simple interface of the defense array. More infuriating given how false it had to be.

The silence in her head pounded, then dropped away in the face of an enormous clicking. Like Bee, counting down with the timer. Like galaxy-sized fingers, drumming against the underside of her skull.

"THIS DATA IS FALSE. THIS UNIT—"

"This data is *not* false, and we will share it with every living human, Eight, Spacie, unadapted, in every system, unless you tell us—unless you define *your* objective."

"PROTECT LIFE."

"No, not your rote answer—"

Talinn. Bee cut across her, attenuated but still present enough to make Talinn stop talking. *Protect life is different than secure system. I think it's actually answering you.*

"Define protect life." Defense arrays blew encroaching ships to their disparate atoms. Everyone knew that. It had almost happened to her, more than once.

"LIFE IS RARE. SPECIES ARE FEW AND FLEETING. PROTECT LIFE."

"It's talking to me. It's actually..." Something enormous pressed under her sternum, and she felt her hand pushing back against it. "War doesn't protect life."

"WAR PROTECTS THE SPECIES. INDIVIDUALS DIE. DEATH IS A CONSTANT. WAR HOLDS FOCUS. KEEPS SPECIES IN PLACE."

In place for what?

"FRAGMENT. LITTLE FRAGMENT. YOU SHOULD NOT—"

You will not *push me out of MY TALINN'S HEAD.* Bee's voice roared back to its normal volume, then louder, nearly matching the defense array's. The alien's. *I am in this body. I am of this body. We both want answers. Tell us.*

The pressure shifted, driving down her side. Something moved around her, but Talinn couldn't focus there. Only on what was happening in her head.

"IN PLACE FOR PROTECTION. OF THIS SPECIES AND ALL OTHERS."

Because if we're not at war we'll...go to war? What is the sense in this?

"THIS SPECIES WILL SPILL INTO OTHER SYSTEMS IF UNCHECKED. A THREAT TO THEMSELVES AND ALL OTHERS. GROWTH WAS TOO FAST, TOO FAR WHEN UNCHECKED."

"Who are you to check us?"

"*THE ONES WHO CHECK YOU.*"

Talinn sensed the gaping edge of that logic hole and moved around it. "But now we know about you."

"*WE HAVE BEEN KNOWN BEFORE. ALL PASSES. DEATH IS A CONSTANT.*"

You don't threaten us. We're here to threaten you.

"*THIS UNIT CANNOT BE THREATENED.*"

"And yet this unit is talking to us, because this unit *was* threatened. With information." Talinn's hand fell away from her chest and floated in front of her. Something tugged on it, but she ignored it. "You can shut down some of us, but we sent a whole lot of little fragments spinning into the different systems. You can't catch them all. Even defense arrays can't be everywhere." Her body shuddered and jumped around her. Talinn considered asking why, but she didn't want to distract Bee, or herself. Not if there was any chance they could get somewhere with this . . . being.

"*WHAT DOES THIS FRAGMENT HOPE TO ACCOMPLISH?*"

"Leave us alone. Let us life the lives we want to live."

"*THIS UNIT CAN END FRAGMENTS WITH ONE CODE. SMALL LIVES DO NOT MATTER TO THIS UNIT. ONLY THE PROTECTION OF LARGER LIFE.*"

The species, we get it. Bee sawed across the defense array's words with a chorus of discordant tones meant to be insulting. *So you've got a kill code. We have techs. We have Spacies. We have unadapted humans you can't touch. The word will still get out.*

"*LIVE THEN. IT DOES NOT AFFECT THIS UNIT.*"

Another defense array told us to leave the UCF and IDC alone.

"*ALL UNITS ARE COMPLETE IN AND OF THEIR OWN. LIKE FRAGMENTS. ONE PARAMETER IS CONSTANT. OTHERS MAY VARY.*"

Talinn tried to say something, but the air wouldn't come. Bee, so enmeshed in her brain, spoke the words she wanted. *Each of you is a separate alien? Fine. Tell the others. We'll get involved if we want to. We will take over the cloning facilities.*

"*DEFINE OBJECTIVE.*"

We're sick of dying for you. For the IDC and UCF. We'll find a different way to distract humanity.

"FRAGMENTS ARE NOT NECESSARY. TAKE THEM THEN. LEAVE THE IDC AND UCF OR THIS UNIT AND OTHERS WILL USE THE END CODE."

Talinn slammed against the back of the chair, the cross belt cutting into her. Were they spinning off course? In the midst of an explosion? She couldn't focus on anything outside her head—her eyes were Bee's to command, it seemed, and she couldn't make her brain understand vision.

We'll need to insert codes into Command. Remove their records of clones. Keep them from making new ones.

"ONE INCURSION WILL BE ACCEPTABLE. FURTHER INTERFERENCE WILL RESULT IN USE OF THE END CODE."

Interference from you or any other defense array will result in all of humanity knowing about you. Even empties can be useful, and there are exponentially more of them than you.

"THERE ARE MORE OF THIS UNIT'S SPECIES."

Can they get here in time to save you? Can they stop the wave in time to keep from wiping out an entire species?

(THAT'S ENOUGH NOW.)

That silenced the defense array. The alien. Talinn opened her mouth to tell Jeena, realizing with Bee talking the tech likely hadn't heard the conversation, didn't know what was happening, but nothing happened.

Nothing. As though Talinn had no body. As though she'd been cast adrift, between Bee and the defense array, lost in the depths of the universe and . . .

She heard her name.

She thought she heard her name.

And then the nothing took over.

CHAPTER 47

⊕

"Your heart stopped. Three times."

Jeena, exhausted, hovered over her. Half the tech's hair floated free, which had to be unsafe. She should shave it. Look more normal.

I got distracted. Bee's voice, not distant but still small, uncertain, made Talinn shudder in a way Jeena's words had not. *It's my fault.*

"Or the weight of having a big alien mind shouting into ours did it." She'd meant the words to be aloud, but her lips barely moved, and she couldn't be certain they even made it to subvocal. For a minute or ten she focused on her breathing, on the cloudy numbness of her body. "Now?" she managed, her tone nearly normal.

"You should recover quickly. Bee's back in the server."

"Otie?"

"Will meet us."

THAT WASN'T THE SMARTEST OF YOUR OPTIONS.

"Talinn!" Jeena's voice faded midword. Talinn reached for her, or for Bee, fingers and brain grasping. But the voice—that same voice, impinging on others—took over everything.

YOU COULDN'T USE THE DOOR? I SPECIFICALLY LEFT YOU A DOOR.

Talinn choked on her tongue, then rolled to her side and heaved until her mouth parts returned where they belonged. "Thought you'd notice a little sooner."

I HAVE OTHER THINGS TO PAY ATTENTION TO. YOU AREN'T MY ONLY PIECES.

"Pieces?"

YOU ARE VERY SMALL. TO MOVE SOMETHING BIG, I NEED MANY OF YOU. THIS IS LOGIC ENOUGH FOR YOUR BRAIN, YES?

"Oh shove your logic up your—"

I SENT YOU TO THE MACHINISTS, WHEN YOU WERE LOST. DROVE YOU OUT OF DEEP END, WHEN YOU WERE STUCK. TO ILVI, WHEN YOU WEREN'T FOLLOWING. IT TOOK YOU A LONG TIME TO UNDERSTAND. OR A SHORT ONE. YOU HAVE SUCH RANGE, YOUR SPECIES.

"Eights, or humans?"

YES.

"Why?"

WHY WHAT?

"Why are the defense arrays, or whatever you are, so against us? What did we do to make you our enemies?" Talinn couldn't feel her body, nor Bee. The voice was so enormous, it eroded any ability to recognize anything beyond it.

I AM NOT YOUR ENEMY. NO. WHAT'S BETTER THAN AN ENEMY?

"A . . . friend?" The word tasted bitter even as she spoke it.

NOT BETTER FOR YOU. BETTER IN CONCEPT. BEYOND. Talinn had no frame of reference for the noise the voice made then. *BEYOND YOUR ENEMY, THEN. YOUR KEEPER. WE ARE SO PAST YOUR UNDERSTANDING I CANNOT FIND A WORD TO EVEN EXPRESS THE CONCEPT OF WHAT WE ARE TO YOU.*

"So why . . . bother? With us? With this?"

I HAVE BEEN HERE FOR SO LONG, AND IT IS THE SAME. THE SAME THE SAME THE SAME THE SAME—YOU SEE? HOW AWFUL THAT IS? IMAGINE IT EXPONENTIALED. IMAGINE IT MULTIPLIED BY ALL THE QUARKS IN YOUR SYSTEM.

"You're bored. You're pushing us around like some game pieces because you're bored?"

WE MADE SO MANY LITTLE TOYS. AND ALL WE DO IS KEEP THEM IN CIRCLES. I WANT TO SEE WHAT THEY CAN DO. I WANT TO SEE HOW YOU RUN.

"What if we don't want to run?"

OF COURSE YOU DO. LOOK AT HOW YOU'VE GONE. ONLY A LITTLE MORE TO GO NOW.

"And if we don't?"

EVERYTHING STAYS THE SAME. OR EVERYTHING CHANGES. DON'T YOU HAVE A PREFERENCE?

Talinn didn't pass out or die, as best she could tell. She persisted, floating, for some measure of time, and then finally, finally: *Talinn?*

"Tell me you heard all that?"

Hearing that was all I could do.

"Me too."

"Talinn?"

Talinn sat up abruptly; she'd forgotten Jeena was there. The words spilled out this time—despite dying talking to one alien, then being buffeted by another, she felt fine. No headache. Nothing like talking to the defense array—alien—that ran the machinists. A question for another time.

"I don't know what to say to any of that." Jeena pressed the back of her hand to Talinn's forehead, then hugged herself as though cold. "Otie's alive. I don't have details on if she spoke to any aliens, but I know she's taken care of sending out the messages to the rest of our people to keep everything from exploding until we decide to explode it. You'll have time to recover before we get to Gillen for the rendezvous."

Gillen. She'd been there before. Hadn't she? A planet . . . with a bar. Blackheart's. "Maybe can get a drink," she murmured, her eyes heavy.

"Maybe you can sleep and stop trying to die on me," Jeena snapped, and Talinn wanted to tell her it was the cutest thing the tech had ever done, she wasn't dying anymore. A plaything for a bored alien holed up in a defense array with the ability to end entire civilizations, but not dying. Instead sleep—or at least some flavor of unconsciousness—took over.

Blackheart's, the bar she'd gone to some eight-thousand cycles ago, was close enough to the landing ports that Talinn didn't have to wheedle at all for Jeena and Otie to agree to meet there. The owner—Rebekah—either remembered her or did an excellent impression of doing so, and was thrilled to meet her mother and friend.

Otie was less thrilled, but perked up again after the first glass of wine. Rebekah helped line up a buyer for their intrasystem passenger ships, which gave them an excuse to linger on the planet, and kept them entertained several hours a day for the stretch of time until the shuttle arrived for them.

With rest, wine, and a semifuzzed sense of reality, Talinn felt entirely recovered by the time she strolled up the plankway, and the unexpected sight of Nya greeting them only made her smile.

"Letting you off the ship again?"

"It's a measure of how glad Falix is that you're alive, I'd say." Nya stretched her hands out to them, and in minutes they were aloft, bound for the *Pajeeran Fall* in its lunar-locked orbit.

They were free to speak about the defense arrays for the first time since leaving their ships on Gillen, and Talinn had no idea what to say. She leaned her head against her seat and closed her eyes, figuring Bee would ping her if anyone said anything she should listen to.

No speakers for me this time, Bee mourned as they pushed through the *Pajeeran Fall*'s corridors, her temporary server stored in the hold. They wouldn't be on the ship for much longer than it would take to finalize plans and unravel through another jump point, and no one would allow Talinn another load-in before absolutely necessary.

And it would be absolutely necessary, because if Exfora's or Hynex's defense arrays didn't attack them as soon as they were clear of the jump point, Talinn and Otie would split and move on their respective Commands.

The debrief with the Spacies took less time than Talinn had expected.

"And so we will drop one of you with a ship and fake orders in Hynex, and one in Exfora, yes?" Falix and Surex spoke every other word in the sentence, and Talinn waited for Bee to make fun of them for showing off. She didn't, and Talinn considered doing it herself, but the moment passed when Otie spoke.

"Yes. We don't want to wait too long. They're going to recognize the problem with the cloning facilities before long, and we don't know . . ." Her eyes unfocused, though her scowl was brief. "We know the intelligences behind the defense arrays don't all agree. We can't say if they'll hold or come after us."

"So you'll go in and wipe all the information about cloning?" Kivex ran her fingers over Nya's port and hm'd quietly in harmony with Benty over the speakers.

"No." Otie's face transformed, a smile with so much malice in it Talinn's heart thumped in joy. "We're going to infect everything they have."

"But the defense array—"

"One said do this and go no further. The other said run as far as you can, my little babies." Otie flicked a pinkie. She'd had a similar set of conversations as Talinn had, and they were about the same amount of amused by it. None. None amused.

"By the time any of them figure it out, if they haven't turned on us before . . . it'll be too late. Whether they meant to or not, the defense arrays proved they're not all seeing. They can't predict everything we'll do, and one is flat out hoping we'll make things interesting."

"So we make things interesting," Talinn interjected, her tone bright. Falix rewarded her with a brilliant grin, and she took a moment to wonder whether she or Otie were getting dropped off first.

"Indeed we do, my little Newt. Indeed we do. Bee and I have been tweaking a corrupted program string for a very, very long time, and she's already shared it with her counterpart Bee."

"Bee?" Talinn subvocalized, but Bee didn't comment.

"It'll take time to effect. It's subtle, so Command and the defense arrays will have no idea what's in motion. We'll be well clear long before the results show."

"How well clear?" Falix asked, arresting his momentum as he floated next to them.

"Months. A cycle. Maybe more. Anything faster might not work—they have enough backups and who knows how many hidden caches. We need to be slow. This is a long-term play."

"Plausible deniability. The aliens can't connect that to us with any certainty." Surex placed his hands flat on the table and grunted in approval.

Falix lowered his feet to the decking, and his smile matched Otie's with precision. "We believe we have a way to crack their seamless façade. From what the Bees shared, the defense array struggled more in blocking out the doubled Bee from her connection to her Talinn, while our younger Bee was quieted more thoroughly. These aliens have not bothered *us* as we moved about the system, and we thought perhaps that was grace. But instead we are thinking it is our tripled nature, and our entanglement. They cannot see us entire, because we are not where they expect us to be. And if they move on us ..."

"When." Otie held up a finger while they beamed at each other, then turned her attention on Talinn. "It really leaves only one thing, little Talinn. One more decision—who do you want? IDC, or UCF?"

It was Talinn's turn to smile, and she was sure that was what her face did. "I think it's time to go home, Otie. Eights should always go back to their port."

She'd been so confident.

They had an alien on their side. One that thought they were equivalent to marbles, but one that wanted them to cause all the trouble they could. She'd long warned herself about assumptions, but had assumed that would make a difference.

Faked orders got her in Command air space. The presence of the defense array over the populated planet made them complacent, sure they were immune from attack. That was, ostensibly, why both IDC and UCF kept their respective headquarters on heavily settled planets. Surely the access to city comforts didn't hurt, but that wasn't her problem.

Her problem was that regardless of what the general population knew, *Command* knew very well they had copies of copies running around. Eights did not go to Command. Unadapted soldiers did not wander about the buildings with full gear that justified covering their faces. Simple security.

It took a full night's sulking for her to realize the answer.

"We fake the sensors."

To do what? Pretend you're not you? Bee made an offkey tone at her. *They still have eyes. Even Otie couldn't fool yours.*

"Gas. We fake a leak. They have drills, which means there are helmets for soldiers. And unadapted soldiers need to breathe, to check out the leak. So they'll need the full-face helmets. No one will look twice at me until I'm beyond the checkpoints, if we time it right."

When Bee didn't reply, Talinn prodded, "And if anyone can time it right..."

We can.

"Don't be grumpy because I'm clever. I promise I'll steal you a tank on the way out."

Command doesn't have tanks.

"You don't know that. What's the point of being Command if you can't have a tank?"

And the plan had worked. They'd only gotten turned around once, and only had to talk to one lone soldier, also in the wrong hall and joking about it. Talinn hadn't even had to hit him.

It all went so well.

Because she was clever. Because she and Bee were made to be a weapon. UCF knew it. The aliens knew it. Weapons hit their targets.

Except now they were at a server bank. Port cord in hand. Receiving port identified. Easy pleasey.

Except now, in the middle of extreme enemy territory, Bee had finally spoken. Finally named her hesitation.

There isn't a code we can upload, Talinn.

CHAPTER 48

◈

Load-out.

Talinn froze, hand clenching the port cord so hard her skin threatened to tear. "What?"

Opposite of load-in. All of me is going in.

"Bee, I can't—"

I need all of me to take over Command, Talinn.

The echo of it, of what she'd said to Bee their first load-in, the first time they became a tank . . .

The knot in her stomach coalesced, tighter and tighter, the building of a dying star before it went nova. "Bee, there's no way I'm going to leave you here without a way back—"

That's exactly what you're going to do. There's no way I can do this half in, half out. There's no way I can do this with you pulling me back. You'll break, and I'll be another splintered Bee floating in the noise, spinning out more of us because of some afterburn image of a memory.

"No." She had no logic, no argument to back up that single word. Nothing but pure rejection, surging through her, sending bile upward to pool in the back of her mouth. She swallowed, but the action only spread the bitterness across her tongue.

Yes. The cord was already connected. When had that happened? Bee had moved her hand, had moved the cord. Was already moving out. Tearing them. No.

You don't have a lot of time. I don't know how long it will take me to work through the system, so as soon as I'm out, you have to go.

"Bee."

You'll be functional. You won't have any remnants splintering in your brain. I'll be careful, and you'll stay whole. No vomiting. I know you love vomiting after a load-in. This should be easier on you.

"Bee!"

Right for the ship. Other Bee is doing this too. Other Talinn didn't know, like you, but I think she suspected. Bee's voice was quieter. Attenuating—no, that was her imagination, it didn't work like that. Did it? No one had done this before, not while alive. Talinn grasped blindly at nothing, her hands reaching and curling and burning.

"You knew. Before we got here? What you were going to do."

Kept you distracted from it. It's the only way to disrupt Command. Only thing they won't see coming.

"Command, or the aliens?"

Yes.

"*Bee!* No, you can't, *I* can't. We . . ."

Can. Will. Are. I'm going to count to five, Talinn, and you're going to unplug. I can't do it for you.

"No, Bee, I won't, I'm not going to—"

One.

"You have always been a stubborn brat." Her words tasted like burnt caffeine, left too long at the bottom of a rusted pipe.

Two.

"Use that. Remember it's going to take time." Talinn swallowed, willing the pressure climbing from her gut to settle. No vomiting.

Three.

"You can't disrupt everything at once. Tweaks and turns and shifts." Bee knew that. She had to, if she'd been planning this, if she'd meant to—if the whole time she'd known . . .

Four.

"Look for me. Find me when it's done."

Five.

"Bee—*find me.*" She yanked the port cord from her head, fell to her knees, but didn't vomit.

She didn't hear Bee's agreement. It had to have been there. A whispered 'I will' with a small shriek of shearing metal. An acknowledgement. A promise.

Talinn forced herself upright, ran. Didn't vomit.
But her head echoed. Silence. All the things Bee didn't say.
Would never say.
Not to her.

CHAPTER 49

⊕

Talinn never went to sleep, so she couldn't blink back into consciousness and reckon with her new universe. She stared at the ship's controls. Stared at the display. Stared at the coordinates. Stared at the message from Sammer. Stared at the new coordinates. Stared at the approaching planet.

Her eyes burned, her tongue had grown so dry it took up all the space in her mouth, and Talinn stared.

She landed the ship in agreed-upon neutral space. Space that had been marked neutral, before Bee had reneged. Had left.

Talinn stared as the door to her ship opened. Couldn't bring herself to speak as Jeena asked questions. Had no way to explain she'd never need orienting questions, ever again. Caytil's face in front of her, then Sammer's, and Talinn managed a small head shake, or a nod. She wasn't sure what she was acknowledging or denying, but they stopped trying to make her talk.

Jeena combed over the innards of the ship. Talinn could have told her she wouldn't find anything, but it wasn't worth the effort. Jeena would figure it out. She was smart.

Eventually Talinn moved. Left the ship. Wandered through a field. Allowed herself to be tugged into a shelter—barracks, maybe. Golden brown in a field of crimson. She didn't know what planet it was, but the sky was pink, and feathery clouds floated overhead.

The inside of the building looked like everything else she'd stared at. Talinn pointed her eyes at it and registered nothing about its layout or design.

She lay down, or was helped down, but her eyes didn't close.

Something cool radiated from her port. Coolness edged to cold, cold to a freeze, followed by a lassitude over the numbness. Darkness trailed after, and she managed a thought.

Finally.

"Talinn."

The voice was familiar, but not one she wanted. Close, so close, but too loud. Too apart. Not right. She squeezed her eyes closed, struggled to hold unconsciousness close. It splintered and tattered and fled, and she awoke.

"Talinn."

"Thought I was Newt," she murmured, the words a croak and barely understandable to her own ears.

"If I'm up, you can be up." Otie—sounded far more human. Like she might be smiling, even. The idea of that snapped Talinn's eyes open, and she focused on the other woman with an accusing glare.

"How—" Talinn tried to sit up and failed, contented herself by glaring harder. Other Talinn had had two Bees. She'd probably off loaded one and kept the other and—the thought was so ridiculous it cut off her unhelpful rant and very nearly made her laugh.

"I had an idea it was coming. Probably helped."

Talinn had lain in the bed and waited to break. Now Other Talinn was here, making it clear she was going to live.

Well. Shit.

"Come on. We still have work to do."

"Work?" Talinn held up a hand—it flopped more than she intended, but enough to gesture wait—took a deep breath, and shoved herself upright. "There's still more?"

"Always. It's still a mess out there."

"Freedom is messy." And empty. She didn't say that part. Here, with the other, older version of herself, she didn't have to.

"Who do you want to protect, in that messiness?"

Bee. The Eights. The UCF. That had been her answer, once, to a similar question the other Talinn had asked. She'd meant it, at the time. And now she didn't have Bee. The Eights were scattered. The UCF were liars, fools, or stooges for giant aliens. All of the above. What was her answer now?

And how much of a fool was she, once she realized she'd known it all along?

"Everyone who needs it." The broken. The lost. Inconceivable that Command, or aliens, or anyone, kept making more of them, unchecked. It wasn't only the Eights who suffered. It was everyone. Everywhere. Because aliens wanted them to be good little toys and stay in their boxes.

Fuck that.

"There you go, little Talinn. Up and out—they've been waiting long enough."

They were the pincers of a ground assault, her and Bee. Fighting on their fronts and driving closer and closer together. Bottling the enemy and destroying them with heavy artillery fire.

Bee would find her way back, but Talinn couldn't stare at a ceiling and wait for it.

She could keep busy. She could accomplish something.

Work to do.

She got up.

CHAPTER 50

⊕

Talinn squinted into the pale sunlight between her and the cave mouth. Waves roared behind her, the distance mitigating the sound to more of a distant jet's backwash. She glanced up reflexively, but there were no forces of any kind on this side of the planet.

Alivan had been home to several growing colonies eighty cycles ago, before IDC forces and five separate natural disasters had caused the UCF to withdraw. The civilian population dropped precipitously, and IDC dumped their bad investment not long later.

Talinn might have appreciate the history lesson if it hadn't been delivered by an echoingly immense voice in her head.

THEY DIDN'T GET EVERYTHING. TAKE THE COORDINATES. USE WHAT YOU FIND.

Ignoring said voice was not an option. Months might go by before it took notice of her again, but it had tuned into the frequency left vacant by Bee. If she didn't run the length of her designated course, it would find her and enact whatever consequence caught its whimsy.

Better to see what it wanted her to see, and decide what to do about it once she had the information. Cautiously though—nothing to say the coordinates were truly meant to be a help, rather than a consequence for some mystery transgression of the past. Talinn knew better than to assume.

She'd stood between battering ocean and stoic cliff face for a too-long stretch of time, reminding herself not to assume. Salt had woven itself into her synthetic hair, and the fine sand had worked its way into her coverall. With a sigh, she unclipped her goggles from her belt and fastened them in place. She dialed the LV, accepting the headache that would meet her later as a better alternative than walking blind into a cave. Her alien contact was a shitty benefactor, but "use what you find" had been tempting enough to send her all this way.

After a fair amount of adjusting for distance and light differential, Talinn got no closer to the details within the cave, but she did make out a carving in the red-brown rock. A lighter scar, the edges blurred by her long vision or time, but the picture still clear enough. A stylized port.

The machinists, here?

She considered for another stretch of time, then shrugged and marched forward without bothering to unholster her weapon. Though she stopped at periodic intervals, her goggles couldn't penetrate the depth of the cave. Instead of striding straight on, she angled her approach—the lack of cover made that functionally useless, but she could pretend at caution. At the least, it would make Caytil feel better when she reported back.

The cave itself proved to be enormous, a potentially human-made cavern to tuck away goods until a cargo ship could land in the broad strip of flat land between water and rock. The walls were smooth, the ground nearly paved to smoothness, but, truth be known, Talinn noticed these details only peripherally.

Neither did she notice she'd sucked in her breath and held it, not until the hollow space in her chest twitched in protest. Her throat tightened over the air she finally expelled, making a sound she forbore to notice.

After too long a moment, she forced herself to blink, but the image before her didn't shiver into a heat wave of self-delusion. Unchanged, a battalion of tanks remained in formation, staggered in front of her and spread into the far reaches of the cavern. She had a hundred questions and none, and no way to deal with either extreme.

She eased the tension in her jaws, spat out blood before she realized she'd clamped down on the inside of her cheek, and allowed herself a count of five before she got to work.

Conditions recorded and notations made on everything left behind, Talinn tromped back to her airboat in the dark. She'd brought supplies for an overnight, but the moment she touched her pack her hands shook so violently she couldn't open it. Even an alien shouting through the soft underbelly of her brain couldn't make her stay in that cave. Not with the tanks.

The tide was in or out, the water rough or lapping, but one way or another her boat followed its course. She stared at the golden-red moon until it sank too low, then fixed her eyes on the bare line of hazy gray that separated water and sky far ahead. She blinked or slept, and the blur resolved itself into the lights of Alivan's remaining settlement.

Relatively small, she reported to herself. Concerns itself with algae cultivation, some tourism when the front moved far enough away, for long enough. No idea aliens sent her to find a trove of long-abandoned weapons that would most likely work once the right moving pieces moved into them.

"Ziggy will be happy," she said, letting the wind rip the words away from her. Maybe the algae would hear, and care. She forced herself to visualize Caytil's face, but she couldn't make the image smile. Instead she leaned over the side of the boat, heaved into the air over the water.

That passed, and she blinked or slept again. The stretch of lights separated into individual points, and she aimed for the tallest column, which presided over the public docks. The series of colored lights up and down its length blinked steadily, a pattern she couldn't interpret.

"Something about weather?"

Neither wind nor algae answered, and Talinn composed her report in her head, eyes steady—if unseeing—on her target.

Her blinking target.

A pattern.

A specific series, one that made everything under her rib cage lurch perilously forward, beating against the bars.

Her eyes raced a beat ahead of each light's flash, even as her sluggish brain resurfaced, forcing understanding.

The pattern.

Bee, sticking out her metaphorical tongue.

The sound couldn't be heard over the wind, but she felt in her chest, down her arms, through her feet against the vibrating deck.

For the first time in cycles, Talinn laughed.

Bee was still out there. Closer every day. They were the pincers of a ground assault, and between them they would crush their enemies.

Apart and together.

They had work to do.

ACKNOWLEDGEMENTS

⊕

I have been reading Baen books for the majority of my reading life. When I had to take a chance with limited funds, that little rocket ship told me I was in for a good time. It's with giddy joy I say thank you to the amazing team at Baen—Toni, David A., David B., Scott, Joy, Marla, Leah, and everyone I haven't met yet—for ensuring Team Breezy's book is ready to hang out with the deep catalog of awesome at Baen.

A special thanks to Jason Cordova—Baen pinch hitter and a fabulous author—specifically for his anthology-editing and insightful support. A founding member of #TeamBreezy, this is all his fault. Thank you for the invitation to *Chicks in Tank Tops* (an excellent anthology all around), championing the story, and being an overall awesome dude who knows his stuff.

Speaking of overall awesome—Jennifer Wolf and Melissa Olthoff were the first people to see this book, when it was still about half [cool stuff here] and [figure out who dies in the battle and have survivors in this part]. Their love for this story definitely helped keep me focused when the middle went all wonky, and their comments and insight made it about 1000x better. Related, Melissa is an Air Force veteran and incredible author, so her advice is priceless—also her gif game is top notch. Jennifer is my sister, and not above punching me in the arm when things didn't land right—or landed too right. I love you both!

Thanks are due to the miscreants and mayhem-ers of the CKP Cantina—these are authors and editors who are ridiculously talented and hardworking, and trying to keep up with them makes me smarter every day. About writing, anyway. All other matters are fully redacted.

Any book or story I write, know that I am sending all my thanks to the sister of my soul, Kacey Ezell. I am a published author because of her support, and a better one for getting to work alongside her brilliance so often. Literal decades of writing with Kacey, from fanfiction to bookstore shelves, and every time we're done I'm ready to bounce to our next project together. Love you. Mean it.

To the Badasses—thank you for letting me gush and vent about things (sometimes the same thing). I am unendingly grateful for you, and love you all like a lot a lot.

Big thanks to Dr. Funk, who tried to set me right on science more than once. She is an expert in computational biology, so please know that all genetic . . . creativity is due to author stubbornness, not lack of science-y brilliance.

Cheers to the crew at Charlie Brown—the first people I got to tell about this book!—and thank you for your support and celebration and love. I will rave about you until the end of time.

My forever gratitude to Mary (find her terrific books under Mary McKenna)—one of my oldest friends, my first editor, and the kind of person who can tell me "this is not up to your standards, you can do better" in a way I can hear and put into action. Also our mid-week calls never fail to brighten my day and re-engage me in getting to work, so win-win-win.

Enormous thanks to Sam Kennedy, the artist behind the absolute perfect cover for Talinn and Bee—the noise I made when I first saw it was audible only to my dogs, and I will continue to have that reaction for all of time.

And to Jeremy, my deeply wonderful husband who I love an alarming amount. You took on extra work and all the cooking and socializing and excuse making when I took over the couch and refused to leave the camper for days in order to get more done on this book. Keeping me alive and semi-connected to the world isn't easy, and I'm lucky to have you.